RAYMOND L. NIBLOCK

The Last Independence Day

Secession

BISHOP'S TRUST
publishing

This book was professionally typeset on Reedsy.
Find out more at reedsy.com

For the late Colonel Gwen Robbins of New Mexico Military Institute. You were an exceptional mentor and confidant who taught us to be brave.

The only thing necessary for the triumph of evil is for good men to do nothing.

ROBERT MAYNARD HUTCHINS (1899-1977)

Contents

Preface

During the summer of 2022, I considered the outcome of the forecasted "Red Wave" for the midterm elections. I asked myself what it would look like if the Right succeeded. If MAGA-inspired criminals attacked the Capitol on January 6th, how far could they go if their extremist ideas become policy?

We must reject and combat extremism if we value a democratic and free society. The Right deserves special criticism for its willingness to cry about liberty when they do so at the expense of those they dislike. The Left offers its own brand of repugnant extremism. The warring points of view paralyze the Middle. In the vacuum, an exhausted Middle allows extreme ideologies to flourish unchecked and often unchallenged at the ballot box.

A striking example is the recent political rhetoric advocating a "national divorce." Many believe, "Oh, that's crazy. It could never happen here." In our disbelief, we write off the crazy talk while proponents of the drivel continue getting elected. Once in office, they use the very protections our law offers to disassemble the institutions they are sworn to protect. One need not look beyond what became of the Weimar Republic as a contemporary example of what happens when extremism goes unchecked.

Will there be a tipping point, and how will it come about? How long will we tolerate the cruel rhetoric until it inspires violence that threatens our way of life? How long before we say, "Enough?" How many more books need to be banned before the police burn them in the street or arrest our librarians? What will become of the memory of Rosa Parks, Jim Crow, Slavery, Martin Luther King, Stonewall, or the Holocaust? How long will it be before we forget the history we have ignored?

This novel is a cautionary tale about the risks of complacency, charting one man's journey from apathy to action. As the storyteller, I will leave it to others to speculate on this story's scenarios. However, one doesn't need to look too far into the future to recognize current events and their potential consequences. To evolve into a more mature democracy, our society must curb extremism from both sides of the spectrum. Left or Right, we must work toward that which is reasonable. It sometimes requires compromise, and that in and of itself is something worth fighting for.

Acknowledgement

I am grateful for Jesse, my husband. He is my number one cheerleader and champion. In addition to him, I am thankful for my beta readers and advisors. My niece, Amanda, gave me the first round of feedback, helping me see the bigger picture. Marcus, a long-time friend of mine and avid consumer of books, was there to remind me that every sentence must fight for its life. I must also credit Ray Braun, who proofread my manuscript and offered invaluable advice in addition to catching my many errors. And last, my dear friend Gina Cothern, a colleague from my complex litigation days. She was as compassionate as uncompromising in her effort to help me tell this story better.

1

Red Wave

On November 9, 2022, a siren woke 56-year-old Jonathan Christian Freeman from a fitful sleep before his 6:00 a.m. alarm on a foggy morning. He looked east at the gathering morning light behind the wooded crest of Mount Sequoyah through the tall bedroom windows. The inevitable sunrise would soon burn off the fog and fill the bedroom with light.

Jon reached for his phone on the nightstand, eager to check the election results. Beside it lay a half-read copy of *Moby Dick*, a book he was diving into for the third time. Drawn to its core theme, Jon saw parallels between Captain Ahab's relentless pursuit of the white whale and past patterns in his life. Melville's novel reminded him that leading a balanced life is better than indulging in obsessions.

MAGA[1] Republicans had swept through the state legislatures and governorships of 34 states and both houses of Congress.[2] The Right promised to remake the United States into a Christian nation, and they had a good start with 27 states achieving supermajorities in their state houses. The Republicans could steamroll the Democrats in those 27 states, and nothing could prevent it. It was a devastating defeat for the Democrats, who could not staunch the inevitable tide of legislation that would attack minority groups and compromise civil liberties.

Jon pondered the election results as he swung his legs onto the floor to collect himself. Sure, the Right was hell-bent on outlawing his marriage. Right-wing politicians promised to criminalize all abortions. Some vowed to prohibit same-sex relationships, jail drag queens for public performances, and forbid interracial marriage. Others on the Right campaigned to add the Bible as a source of law and establish evangelical-style Christianity as a state religion. Despite the right-wing political rhetoric and campaign promises, Jon didn't believe the Right would achieve its agenda. Surely, the right-wing agenda could not succeed in the United States.

Social media buzzed that the folks who stood to lose the most didn't vote. Racial minorities, LGBTQ, women, and young people. Especially young people. It amused Jon that the woke ones who held up signs and raised hell were too high or hung over from the night before to cast a vote on election day. Or worse, if they made it to the polls, they wasted their vote on a useless third-party candidate.

Setting aside his concerns, he wanted to linger a little longer beside his husband, Martin, but a day ahead remained in a busy law practice. Clients to meet, work to be done.

Carpe. Fucking. Diem. Election or not, I must face the morning. Take the body. The mind will follow—no time to cry over spilled milk.

* * *

Jon was intellectual, active, and fit. He led a busy but simple life focused on his husband, family, friends, and law practice. Being white, educated, and well-off fed a subtle apathy, inspiring his belief that "everything would be alright." Being married to a man living in the South didn't affect him because he could "pass." After all, he navigated "don't ask, don't tell" while serving in the Army during the '80s and early '90s. No one ever suspected. He excelled at the art of getting along and blending in. It was his stock-in-trade.

Jon loathed the MAGA Movement despite being too busy to do much about it. Those asshat MAGAs represented a dangerous extension of the rightward political swing inspired a long time ago by Pat Buchanan's "Culture War" speech during the 1992 presidential election. The epic insincerity of Buchanan's speech that year represented a gigantic festering boil on the ass of the Grand Old Party, and Jon would have no part of it. How Republicans could carry on about individual liberty for themselves while seeking to deprive others of theirs proved unforgivable.

Buchanan's speech angered Jon so much that he wrote a letter to his friend and confidant, Jennifer Romero. Jon had come to know "J," as he called her, through her two sons, who were cadets with Jon during his high school years at a military school in Roswell, New Mexico. After high school, Jon attended college at the University of New Mexico, and during that time, J had become a central figure in his life. The two spent many evenings together at her home in Tesuque, solving the world's problems late into the desert night over bottles of wine.

"Mark my words, J," he wrote, "these 'Christians' will be the death of our country. They will take over one day, and the rule of law will end when they do. They will round up everyone they hate and kill or put them behind bars like the Nazis did to the Jews."

Time and age dampened Jon's passions. Profound disagreements with the Left balanced his disdain for the Right, but his short fuse for "wokism" was legendary among his friends. To Jon, self-styled "woke" progressives indulged an arrogance that saw no limits. He lumped the lot of them into a category of people willing to roast an infant on a spit rather than indulge a different point of view. "Those woke assholes are as useless as tits on a fish," he would say during debates with his friends and associates.

Politics and the nation's state concerned a younger Jon, but his day-to-day life had taken precedence as the years marched on since his 1992 letter to J. As with many people, double-talking politicians and broken promises nurtured an insidious belief that his vote stopped counting long ago, even though he never missed an opportunity to cast one.

* * *

These days, Jon had his routines. Like every other weekday morning, he neatly combed his light brown hair and left the house well-dressed in his chinos, brown oxfords, and a button-down shirt topped by a waxed canvas jacket. He descended the stairs from his quaint bungalow and proceeded down the hill toward busy College Avenue. From there, he walked another block to pick up a coffee from Baba's, a local coffee roastery.

Jon approached Baba's along the cracked sidewalk. He saw Stan, one of the proprietors, wrestling a box from the back of his 1986 Subaru Brat. Stan was a charming aging hippie of 62 years who peddled a plethora of liberal conspiracy theories. This morning, Stan appeared especially frazzled, and he stopped to rail about the midterms as Jon walked up.

"Those fuckers pulled it off," Stan proclaimed. "Can you fuckin' believe it?"

"I can," Jon said. "The people who mattered didn't vote."

Stan huffed and disappeared through the back door with his box.

Okay, do I sit down inside or take it to go? To go! I don't have time for this today. Everyone will want to talk about the election. No, this has to be in and out.

Coffee in hand, Jon made for the door.

Mission accomplished.

Stan hollered at Jon just before the door closed behind him on the way out, "Hey, Freeman, what did the dung beetle say to the bartender?"

Jon turned to look back at Stan for the punchline.

"Is that stool taken?" Stan said, with a look of satisfaction.

Jon bowed with a flourish, grinning, "See you tomorrow morning. We'll nail those fuckers, you'll see. This isn't over yet."

It was a cliché to say something like that. A platitude to extricate him from a conversation about the election he didn't want to have. It wasn't that Jon didn't care about what happened. He was just too focused on his routinized life.

No time to give a damn, not today.

The warmth of the coffee comforted Jon. He strolled up the hill into the morning. He passed the food trucks and continued to his office three blocks away along the avenue.

He walked past the old KFC, now a run-down den of culinary atrocities masquerading as a Chinese food place. He laughed to himself about how many times he ate there against his better judgment. Aside from some of his complaints about the questionable Chinese food, he couldn't help but think about the luxury of living a village life a few blocks from work. He enjoyed his simple and, by all appearances, mundane day-to-day life. Every day was the same. Up at 6 a.m., stroll to the coffee hut and then to the office. He relished his husband, family, work, dogs, and the simple life he carved out for himself. He treasured his sense of belonging. To him, his pleasant life was a hard-won prize after a raucous youth.

Jon arrived at the law firm where he practiced with his brother. The Brothers Freeman, as they were sometimes called, inherited the practice from their father. The late Bear Freeman was a legendary trial lawyer who established the firm in 1961 after Bear's wife reminded him that he had a family to support instead of squeaking by on the meager salary of a Red Cross worker.

Bear's wife, Ruth Freeman, helped him start the firm, and she remained a fixture there where she was known as the "Colonel." At the age of 90 years, though not a lawyer and not a colonel, she would have excelled in either role. She was a force of nature, a touchstone against which everything was measured, and the unquestioned matriarch of the family.

"Jesus, what the hell happened yesterday?" Jon exclaimed as he walked into his older brother's first-floor office.

Shaking his head while keeping his eyes on his computer screen, Ira, Jon's 65-year-old brother, said, "People didn't get off their butts to vote, so the rednecks got to vote against their interests without any opposition. It won't affect us, though. It isn't good for some people, but we'll be fine. They may try to pass some legal reforms, but the courts will keep a lid on the social stuff," his brother suggested.

"I don't know," Jon said, "Those cocksuckers campaigned on coming after my marriage and going after anyone who isn't white, straight, or Christian. Still, it is hard to imagine any of that stuff coming true. Not here!"

Looking up from his computer, Ira said, "Nah, that can't happen. The courts won't let it, and people will figure out how stupid these knuckleheads are."

5

"Oh well. I guess we'll see. I gotta get to it," Jon said. "I have a ton of desk work to get done today."

Jon left toward the stairwell leading up to his comfortable office on the second floor of the 19th-century prairie-style mansion the brothers converted into a law office. Every room in the old house was wood from floor to ceiling - Brazilian Cherry floors and hardwood paneled walls.

So much for the election.

Jon sat down at his leather top desk to check his email and review his punch list for the day. He then picked up the phone to make his calls, but he kept getting interrupted by texts and phone calls from his friends about the election. Finally, he gave in to the onslaught and called his friend, Tiny.

"Tiny, would you call the crew? Let's meet up after work. I suppose we'll have to talk about the election."

"Hell yeah, Boss," Tiny replied enthusiastically. "4:30, Dickson Street Pub as usual?"

"Yes, sir!" Jon responded. "See you then, my friend."

* * *

Jon found himself at the Dickson Street Pub with some of his buddies and associates later that afternoon. He arrived first, then in lumbered Tiny, who was anything but. At 5'9" and three biscuits, the super-loyal Tiny, with his bad at-home dye job, couldn't shake his rural Arkansas River Valley upbringing. What a study in contrasts, that one. Tiny was an insurance adjuster in his fifties but remained a country boy who faithfully regurgitated right-wing talking points while covertly sleeping with a guy the crew knew only as "Non-Existent Rick." Go figure.

Right behind Tiny followed Alex, a dandy of a lawyer who preferred to go by "Alexander." Alexander was a new addition to the group in his mid-thirties. He was tall and thin and always dressed well. His quick wit and a quicker tongue complimented his perfect teeth and good looks.

Big Head also joined in. He was an awkward herpetologist with a Ph.D. and thick glasses.

The bunch assembled with the addition of Mary Lynn, Tiny's sidekick, who would get shit-faced at their gatherings without saying so much as a "hello" until it came time to order dinner. Like Tiny, food never failed to capture Mary Lynn's attention. She had never missed a meal, and it showed. One was wise to keep his hands away from her plate when she was eating.

Jon had been cavorting with this band of misfits since his thirties. He enjoyed their inevitable antics and nonsense even though he had long ago traded his shot glasses for AA chips. AA's grit, ruggedness, and honesty were an excellent trade-off from the hangovers and the near brushes with the law of his earlier life.

Everyone settled on a stool in the low-ceiling bar, and Tiny started holding forth.

"What about the election, y'all? The snowflakes just got double fucked!" Tiny said with a chuckle, trying to get a reaction.

Jon chimed in. "What about our governor? I'm sure she is happy, even if she is a cross between Manbearpig and a linebacker."

"Fuck her," Tiny agreed. "I bet she has a bigger dick than her husband, poor S.O.B., having to wake up to that every morning!"

Tiny turned to Alexander and said, "I bet you'd like it if she had a cock, wouldn't you!"

"I'm married, remember?" Alexander deadpanned.

"Oh, come on, mother fucker," Tiny declared, "that ring don't plug no holes!"

Everybody laughed.

All the while, Mary Lynn sat with a silent grin after knocking back her second shot.

So driven and successful, Alexander was perched on his stool, drink in hand, then set it down on the table.

Oh shit, here it comes.

Alexander announced with more flair than usual, "I think we are going to be fucked once power transfers after the new year. They are coming after the gays! My dear husband, Pretty? He couldn't pass as straight if he had to."

"Oh, come on, you got nothing to fear from them people," Tiny said. "They simply want 'Billary' Clinton and the woke crowd to leave them alone. That's all there is to it. They're tired of being told who to sell wedding cakes to and shit like that."

Even though Jon was the one who called for the meetup, he wasn't ready for a considerable political debate. He hoped the gathering would lighten his mood, but he sensed Alexander was about ready to throw down with Tiny. Those two could turn any friendly debate into a blood sport and still walk away as friends.

Jesus, what the fuck difference will any of this make? We are going to be worked up over nothing. There is no fucking way the public will stand for that crazy right-wing crap.

"Come on, Freeman, say something!" Tiny jabbed.

"Y'all, none of that shit the Right wants will happen. They are going to attack abortion like they always do. We know they are going after drag queens, but the courts will stop all that stuff eventually. I don't see how, in this country, any of that crap they campaigned on will ever become law. Until it does, I have bigger stuff to worry about - I'm so fuckin' busy at work, plus I have to go back out to the ranch to check on things there. Then there's the Matachines Dances next month at the Jemez Pueblo. I can't miss it."

Tiny had momentarily forgotten Jon was the trustee of a vast cattle ranch in Northern New Mexico, a concern that periodically required his presence.

Tiny laughed at Jon, "Okay, number one, Cowboy, don't you have a ranch foreman? It isn't as if you will be pullin' calves or cuttin' nuts with the boys this fall. And number two, what is a Mata-what-the-fuck-dance?"

Alexander interjected, "Yeah, what's up with the ranch, Amigo? You rarely talk about it and still haven't invited me like you promised last year!"

Jon replied, "Shit, man, I'm sorry. I've been caught up. Covid, all of it. But yeah, let's plan something. I'll fly us out. Your husband is welcome to come along, too. We will put his lazy ass on a horse!"

Alexander laughed and said, "I'll go, but Pretty? No fucking way. He's too prissy! I love him to death, but seeing a dirt road or breathing too much mountain air might give him a heart attack. Take me, though. He'll gladly have the house to himself for a few days."

Jon smiled, turned to Tiny, and added, "The Matachines Dance is a festival at the Jemez Pueblo. The tribal governor invited me, and since most of the ranch hands are from the pueblo, I need to appear and play local politics. I'd invite you, but you wouldn't enjoy it much. They'd likely put an apple in your mouth and stick a carrot up your ass before throwing you in the village barbecue pit!"

Tiny smirked, leaned to his right, and farted.

"Dude, you need to check yourself," Alexander snarked.

Jon pondered the truth about the ranch in the passing moments between the conversation and Tiny's remarkable flatulence. It had been over a decade since he had taken up his "trusteeship," as he called it. The ranch was worth far more to him than a cattle operation or its other endeavors. It was the place of his childhood dreams. His one-day forever home, but his loyalty to his family, the practice, and the Colonel was paramount.

My life is here. Maybe one day I can leave and make the ranch home. I don't have to decide this now but I must get out there.

"And NO, Tiny," Jon said as he returned to the present with a raised eyebrow, "I won't be pullin' calves or cuttin' nuts. I'll be shaking hands and looking over the books!"

Jon had a thousand reasons for hanging up the law practice in favor of relocating to the ranch, but he wasn't willing to leave his mother, much less give up the deep sense of belonging that tied him to his life in Fayetteville. He didn't relish uprooting his husband, leaving his law firm, or moving west while his mother, the Colonel, still lived.

After more cavorting, shots, and political banter, it was time to head down to a local steak joint or walk up the hill to Highland House for dinner with Martin. Jon had enough of politics and didn't want to think about it anymore, so he excused himself.

"Night, y'all," Jon announced. "I'm heading home."

His friends were a hugging crowd. Tiny was first in line for his. After exchanging hugs, Jon walked to the long bar filled with college-aged kids and neon lights to pay the tab. The jukebox played the last track in his lineup: *Sinnerman*. He flagged the bartender and paid everyone's bill without saying a word. He walked out to the darkened street and turned his collar to the cold.

* * *

Jon opened the creaky side door and walked inside the dimly lit hall. Highland House was the only home he had ever loved. His two dogs, a thoughtful Labradoodle and an over-exuberant Aussiedoodle, hurried across the rustic wood floors to greet him with tails wagging. The house was a mix of traditional and modern. Opposite the state-of-the-art kitchen was a glass door leading to an outside deck surrounded by oak trees. Martin, Jon's 32-year-old husband, sat outside on the darkened deck. All Jon could see was the glow of Martin's smartphone reflected on his face.

Martin was a sporty and attractive man, 25 years Jon's junior. He was a variety "streamer" on social media with a live show and nearly 250,000 subscribers. The two got along famously despite being at distinct stages in life and having different interests. Their relationship was a mystery to some of their friends, who wondered how the two could be so compatible despite a significant age difference. But it worked.

Jon cracked open the kitchen door, "Hey, babe. I'm home. I have to check something on the computer, and then I'll come out. Need anything?"

Martin raised his head, waved, and returned to his phone. He was preparing to put on a late-night video stream for his fans. The whole "video streaming" thing was foreign to Jon, who could still remember having a TV set with three channels, but Martin's YouTube show had become wildly successful and lucrative.

Jon steeped a cup of Earl Grey Tea and took his cup and saucer to his study to check his calendar. He considered flying out to the ranch for the rest of the week. If his calendar and the weather would accommodate, it would be an opportune time to visit the ranch and catch up with Foreman Sam.

Jon had a private pilot's license, and flying his plane to New Mexico would be refreshing. He gazed at his tablet and selected his home airport, where he kept a Cessna 182 in a hangar. Optimal weather for departure—clear skies and cool temperatures overnight and into the morning. Pulling up one of the weather maps for the region covering Oklahoma, Texas, and New Mexico revealed a blue "H" poised right over the center of New Mexico and another one centered over eastern Colorado.

Good flying weather.

He finished his tea, rose from the desk, and walked outside to pull up a chair beside Martin, who was still absorbed in his videos, surrounded by the cooling darkness.

"Hey, you got a second?" Jon asked.

"Yeah, what's up, babe?" Martin said as he paused a video he was watching on his smartphone.

"I'm going to fly to New Mexico tomorrow morning and stay through the weekend. I have some ranch business I need to take care of," Jon said. "I'll come back on Sunday or the Monday following, weather permitting. You want to come with?"

"I'd love to, babe, but I can't," Martin replied. "I have a long video stream tonight and one Saturday, and I expect a big crowd for each."

"So," Jon pressed, "you don't mind if I go without you and take the dogs with me?"

"No worries, sweetheart. Go for it. I know you haven't been out there in a long time. It will be good for ya."

Jon got up, hugged Martin's neck, and walked out of the darkness into the kitchen glow to complete preparations for tomorrow's departure for the Valle Grande Land and Cattle Company nestled in the Jemez Mountains of Northern New Mexico. It would be a relief to return to the mountains he loved.

2

Valle Grande

4:45 a.m. came early the following day. With a microwaved breakfast burrito in hand, he was out the door with the dogs by 5:15 a.m. for the half-hour drive to the airport.

Jon relished early morning flights in the cooler air. As a fuel truck left the hangar, Jon pulled his Range Rover up to park beside his plane. The dogs knew this routine and got a little rowdy in the back.

"Settle down, you two. We'll be headin' out soon enough."

He hopped out of his SUV, walked over to the hangar door switch, and hit the button to close it. While performing his preflight, he let the dogs out so they could run inside the hangar to sniff around. He soon completed his preflight and opened the hangar door.

"Dogs!"

He motioned them to a patch of grass outside. They came running, "Let's hurry up!"

After the dogs did their business, he picked them up one at a time and lifted them into the plane's back seat, where they sat dutifully upright. He pulled the aircraft out of the hanger, powered up the avionics, and started the engine as the sun rose. After making his radio calls, his Cessna 182 lifted off Runway 18 at 6:39 a.m., bound for the Valle Grande Ranch 600 miles west as the crow files.

The flight at 8,500 feet continued across Oklahoma in smooth, cloudless air. The ride got slightly bumpy over the Texas Panhandle as he climbed the plane to 10,500 feet because of the rising western terrain of the Caprock Escarpment. His last waypoint was Redondo Peak, which stood at 11,258 feet. Upon crossing the southern rim of the caldera with the ranch beneath him, he descended toward a 3,000-foot grass runway in a narrow valley parallel to a ranch road.

"Valle Grande Traffic, Skylane 7276V. Inbound for landing, full stop, five miles south of the airfield at 12,500 and descending. Request weather."

Sam Hernandez, the ranch foreman, was monitoring the radio and answered. "Welcome home, Jefe. Winds are 230 at 5 knots."

"Roger," Jon replied.

Jon loved the hell out of the approach to the Valle Grande because it felt like "real" flying into the narrow valley where the airstrip lay between peaks and ridges. On his final approach, his speed was just right as he crossed the runway threshold, cutting the power to glide the plane gently onto the grass runway. The sink was steady. As the runway grew in his vision, he lifted his eyes to the horizon to begin his flare.

Gently. Patience. Patience. Pitch up a little more—pre-stall indication.

The stall horn blared. Touch down. He taxied toward a hangar positioned midfield next to the forest's edge. A smiling young ranch hand approached as Jon opened the cabin door and volunteered, "I'll take care of the plane, Señor Freeman!"

"Hey, thanks," Jon smiled. "Do you mind grabbing my bags while I deal with the dogs?"

"No problem, Jefe!" said the eager young cowboy.

Jon pushed the passenger seat forward, and the dogs leaped out of the plane. They bolted together at full speed toward an adjacent meadow. Just then, a Silver Dodge Ram 2500 4x4 with the Valle Grande logo on the doors rolled up with a trail of dust drifting toward the tree line behind it. Foreman Sam climbed out of the cab. He was a thin, spry, brown-skinned man in his sixties with closely cropped salt and pepper hair underneath his black Stetson.

"It's good to have you back, my friend. What took you so long?" asked

Sam.

"Too much work and not enough help at the firm," Jon replied, extending his hand to shake Sam's.

"If you have time, I can fill you in over supper," Jon said.

"Sounds good," Sam replied. "I told Lorraine not to expect me for supper so that I could join you. I figured we have a lot to discuss."

Sam continued, "Let's get your things. Everything is in order, just the way you left it. We also have a new cook and houseboy. Mind you, everyone at HQ wants you to drop by."

"Yeah, of course," Jon said. "Drop me at the house, and then I'll roll over to HQ."

Jon yelled toward the dogs, "Hey, dogs! Let's go!"

The inseparable pair came bounding through the tall grass where they had been investigating piles left by local elk that shared the valley. Jon opened the back door of the crew cab, and the dogs leaped up right next to where Jon's flight bag sat on the passenger side.

Sam drove Jon and the dogs up to the pea-gravel circle drive in front of Jon's home, which he called La Hacienda. The driveway, lined with sage, rosemary, and lavender, framed the entrance to the massive territorial-style stucco home designed as a large rectangle with an enclosed courtyard in the center. Inside were vaulted ceilings with latillas, corbels, and massive vigas harvested from local ponderosa pines.

Jon hopped out with the dogs.

"I won't be long, Sam. I'll meet you at headquarters in a few minutes."

After a call to Martin to tell him he was safely on the ground, Jon dropped his things and grabbed the Range Rover keys to drive to the headquarters of the Valle Grande Land and Cattle Company.

* * *

The Valle Grande Land and Cattle Company Ranch headquarters occupied the original homestead where his lifelong friend Cullen Dunigan grew up. Jon had spent many a summer with Cullen during their youth at the ranch.

Jon adored the Old Adobe, as he called it, making it a perfect place for the ranch headquarters when he decided to build his own home.

The ranch occupied the heart of a vast caldera left over by a supervolcano, forming the Jemez Volcanic Field, encircled by mountains. This Northern New Mexico caldera spanned nearly fourteen miles across and was host to natural hot springs, fumaroles, natural gas seeps, and volcanic domes, with Redondo Peak as its crowning feature. The ranch covered 100,000 acres, encompassing creeks, rivers, and broad grass-covered valleys known as "valles" by the locals. The largest among them, the Valle Grande, stretched endlessly along the caldera's south rim.

The Valle Grande had a long history as a working ranch dating back to 1876 when a wealthy family from Mexico operated it—known then as the Baca Unit. The caldera and its surroundings supplied the Bacas with a fine living until subsequent generations squandered their fortunes by infighting and family dramas. Consequently, they lost ownership of their beloved valles to John Dunigan, an Irish immigrant who purchased the ranch in 1963 to save the withering Baca Line from bankruptcy.

Three years later, in 1966, Dunigan's wife died in childbirth, giving the widower a son named Cullen. Born the same year as Jon, they met in 1981 as cadets at military school. During their shared military school years between 1981 and 1986, Jon and Cullen were inseparable. Some people whispered the two boys might have been more than friends.

After graduating and several years afterward, the two remained devoted to regular visits. Over time, visits were less frequent as Jon went on to study law while Cullen took control of the ranch from his aging father. Then, in the spring of 2005, Cullen called Jon out of the blue to ask for help with a divorce. Cullen's wife, Griselda Jaramillo, had turned nasty. She was abusive, bitter, and contemptuous.

What should have been a simple divorce became a titanic battle when Griselda claimed the Valle Grande belonged to her because of alleged ancestral ties. Thanks to John Dunigan's estate planning and a prenuptial agreement, Griselda did not have a winning argument even though she proved a ruthless adversary.

Despite years passing between Cullen and Jon, Jon came to his friend's aid. The only cure for Cullen's misery was divorcing that hateful woman. Jon never liked Griselda, and the feeling was mutual. Griselda had no use for Jon. Her jealousy of Jon's closeness with her husband was undeniable.

Thankfully, after a long, hot summer in 2007, Griselda's claim died unceremoniously in the New Mexico Supreme Court. The court sent marshals to eject her the day the opinion came down, and she was never to be seen or heard from again.

After the divorce, Jon resumed spending time at the ranch to rekindle his friendship with Cullen. With his renewed presence at the Valle Grande, Cullen ensured Jon learned all the ranch operations, from the stable boys' jobs to the foreman's duties. Gradually, relief appeared on Cullen's face as the days marched away from Griselda, but the divorce took its toll on Cullen. He had once been a vigorous and athletic man for the better part of his life, preferring to work with his hands rather than spend his time in the ranch office looking at books and numbers. Cullen liked working side-by-side with the cowboys, or "Los Caballeros," as he called them. But as can happen with horrendous stress, he eventually succumbed to aggressive cancer, diagnosed not long after the divorce ended. Cullen kept his diagnosis secret from Jon until his gaunt frame couldn't hide it any longer.

* * *

In the Fall of 2010, when the aspen trees were quaking, Jon was at Cullen's bedside, accompanied by the scent of death. Jon remembered clearly their mutual friend, a somber Van William "Will" Thomas, walking into the Old Adobe, much to Jon's surprise. Will was a tower of a man with a bald head and imposing presence. Jon had no idea Cullen had hired Will to be his lawyer, especially because Cullen's trust in lawyers was as scant as the list of them was long. Still, Cullen and Will were also close friends because of their military school bond. The three men shared an indelible brotherhood.

It was a relentless night when Cullen died.

"Jon," rasped Cullen, "We need to talk, the three of us. Here, you two help

16

me up."

Jon and Will reached over to lift Cullen and prop some pillows behind him so he could sit straight up in his bed covered by Navajo blankets. Will handed a leather portfolio to Cullen full of legal documents that looked nearly 100 pages thick.

"Jon, I don't know if this will be a blessing or a curse for you," Cullen began, "but I'm giving you the Valle Grande along with all its assets and mine. There is only one condition. It is yours, forever, so long as you continue the employment of every ranch hand who desires to stay working here and you continue to operate the ranch for at least thirty years from this day forward. Can you do that for me, brother? I can't let our people go back to the pueblo without jobs. Listen to me. They all love you, and they will follow you. I'm also appointing Will to be the lawyer for my estate. My death is very fucking nigh, and the least I can do is not trouble you to deal with my estate. He will do a fine job. Other than you, Jon, there is no lawyer I trust more. You run the ranch and leave the lawyering up to Will? Okay? Then, you can come to kick my ass one day after you cash your chips, assuming we reach the same destination."

A silence settled in the room but for the crackle of the piñon burning in the fireplace.

Jon looked into Cullen's sunken eyes.

"I'm speechless, and I am unworthy."

"My brother, no one is worthy of this place other than the men and women working it daily and the native people whose birthright it is. Besides them, and perhaps me, no one loves this place more than you. So, please take it. I want to know while I am still breathing that this place will be in good hands."

"I don't know shit about ranching," Jon protested, "I mean, I can ride a horse with the best of them, but fuck, that's about it!"

"You know more than you think you do," Cullen counseled. "Why do you think I asked you to come out here more frequently after my divorce? I was sick, man, and I knew you would be the only one who could continue this place. Plus, I know you. You covet your memories here and are truly

17

at home in these mountains. Allow me this pleasure, please. And you have Sam, Waha, and Jennifer, too. These people are your New Mexico family. They always have been since our military school days."

Indeed, these people were like family, including Alfonso Waha, even though he was a mystery. Waha was a wise and ageless Jemez Pueblo shaman who had been on the ranch at least since the Baca Family owned it. No one knew how many moons Waha had racked up.

Will, well-known for his directness, interrupted.

"Let's do this while we have time, shall we?"

Jon cast a raised eyebrow toward Will.

"Never one for mincing words, that one," whispered a depleted Cullen.

"He's right, Jon," Will said plainly. "Let's quit mucking around. Go and retrieve the witnesses. Let's get this done."

Cullen might have been in a horrendously weakened state, withered, grey, and with a strained voice, but there was no doubt that Cullen meant what he said, and Jon knew it.

"You win, my friend," Jon conceded. "I will do as you ask. I'm not sure how I will do it, but I will do it."

Cullen's eyes locked with Jon's, "You will find a way. You always do. Your real life is here, and it always has been. You will understand one day even if you do not believe it now."

Cullen could not have spoken more fateful words. Jon was torn between the world of his birth, Arkansas, and the world of his rebirth, the Valle Grande, where his soul soared.

"All right, Jon, out with you," Will commanded, now in full lawyer mode with the witnesses in tow.

Sam Hernandez, Waha, and Jennifer assembled in a semi-circle at the foot of Cullen's bed. Jon exchanged a conciliatory glance with Cullen, then pulled the thick pinewood door behind him.

The candle wax dripped and dripped into the night. The only company for Jon in those moments was a giant Hopi Eagle Dancer positioned across from him in a niche and the ever-present scent of piñon.

With the witnesses present, Will began ceremoniously.

"Cullen Dunigan, is this your last will?"

"Yes, it is," Cullen voiced.

"Did you, yourself, ask me to draft it?" Will asked.

"Yes, I did."

"And when was that Cullen?" Will continued.

Cullen replied, "I drove to your office in Albuquerque in 2007, the day after the divorce from that hateful woman I improvidently married. And I asked you in your office to do this work for me."

Cullen was fading.

"Can you continue?"

"Yes, please, get on with it," Cullen gasped.

"Is it your wish outlined in this, your last will and testament, to give over everything you own, both real property, tangible personal property, and intangible personal property, to Jonathan Christian Freeman that a trust or some other document hasn't already given?"

"Yes, and I asked you to draft a trust along with that will of mine," uttered Cullen.

Without relenting, Will continued the ritual.

"And in that trust, upon your signature this day, you intend that every single possession of yours, including this ranch and everything on it or under it, go to Jonathan Christian Freeman?"

"Yes. That is my wish," Cullen nodded.

"And Cullen, do you know these people assembled here at the foot of your bed?" Will asked.

"Yes. The people here are my chosen family," Cullen replied.

Continuing the ceremony, Will produced the documents.

"Very well," Will said. "I need you to initial every page at the bottom right-hand corner."

"Yes, Yes," Cullen uttered as he scrawled his initials.

Will then withdrew the trust agreement from a portfolio.

"Jesus. Do I have to initial every one of those pages?" Cullen asked.

"I'm afraid so, but why don't you sign the last page first." Will allowed.

"Jesus," Cullen complained.

Reaching the end of the initialing, "Fuck, finally. Bring him in," Cullen demanded.

"Come," Waha's old, wrinkled lips whispered as he approached Jon to lead him back into the room.

When Jon reentered the room, Cullen spoke.

"Fuck all this legal stuff. Here, Waha, bring that bowl, and Jon, you come around over here."

Waha picked up a worn-looking clay pot bearing ancient Jemez designs. It had to be at least one hundred years old, maybe older, and full of dirt and dried sage flowers.

"Help me," Cullen asked as Waha handed the pot to him. The bowl was heavy.

Waha helped Cullen hold the bowl up at his chest, and Cullen said, "Okay, Jon, come here and take this pot from me, please."

Jon approached and reached out with both hands and grasped the clay pot full of sage and earth. Before releasing his grasp, Cullen said clearly, rallying one last time: "Jonathan Christian Freeman, you have been my closest friend and brother for many years. Take this dirt and sage and make good with it. As of now, dead or living still, this ranch and all I have is yours."

Waha held the pot to ensure Jon didn't drop it as Cullen released his grasp and collapsed back against his pillows. Standing opposite Jon, Jennifer started some piñon coals in a well-used hand-scraped bowl and sprinkled a mixture of sage and piñon needles on top of the burning coals. With the thick smoke rising, she wafted the smoke over Cullen with a fan of eagle feathers. Jon held on to the pot for a few more moments until the singing started.

The thick incense must have been a comfort as Cullen Dunigan closed his eyes for the last time. Waha began drumming while singing a death lullaby in his native tongue, Towa.[3] When it came, Waha's singing drowned out Cullen's death rattle. Jon's closest friend was dead, and the Valle Grande was his.

20

* * *

Suddenly, as if waking up from a dream, Jon found himself standing in the great room of the Old Adobe. Sam stood before him.

"Where were you, Jefe? Come on. We have some things to discuss, so let me catch you up," Sam invited.

"Sorry, Sam. I was remembering Cullen." Jon said.

Sam Hernandez had been the ranch foreman since 1995. He was responsible for all ranch operations. He had gathered capable ranch hands, Los Caballeros, and developed an intensely loyal staff. The ranch operated like a big family but was profitable and efficient. After Jon took the reins, the Valle Grande Land and Cattle Company increased to a net worth of nearly half a billion dollars from its cattle operation and other endeavors, including gas and oil wells, geothermal energy operations, and mineral extraction. There were also ranch units in different locations. Jon acquired large tracts of land near Cabezon, New Mexico, and a recent acquisition of some 25,000 acres of grazing land adjacent to the Cimarron Valley up on the Llano Estacado.

While there was plenty to talk about, Sam was keen to orient Jon to the more pressing matters, such as upcoming talks with Los Alamos about geothermal energy, the movement of some livestock to the new properties, and the development of the meat processing business on the llano. Sam had another message for Jon: spend more time at the ranch.

3

Buckshot Brandy

Early the morning after the election on November 9th, Governor Suzy Brandy Landers walked downstairs to meet her State Police Protection Officer at the Governor's Mansion in Little Rock. At 34 years old and the father of two charming girls, one six and the other eight, Lieutenant James "Jimmy" Earl Pettigrew presented an imposing 6'2" 250-pound frame in the foyer dressed in civilian clothes. The governor didn't call him "Haystack" for nothing.

Not to be outdone, the Arkansas governor dressed out at about the same weight as Haystack, only not as tall. She donned her signature red-leather cowboy boots and wrangler jeans pulled up a little high around her waist, capped off with a black long-sleeved jersey stretched to the limit over her Double-Ds and imposing gut. The governor cinched her ensemble with a western-style leather belt and an oversized silver rodeo buckle. The shiny buckle depicted an elephant holding a shotgun. The governor pulled her long, straight brown hair back through the loop in her matching red ball cap. She was ready to kick some ass, high off her party's election victory.

"You ready to go, Haystack?" she yelled into the foyer.

"Yes, ma'am!" Lieutenant Pettigrew replied.

"Alrighty then, let's get it!" she said.

Jesus, that outfit leaves nothing to the imagination, Lieutenant Pettigrew mused as the vision of his governor descended the stairs. He did not particularly like her, but it was not his job to like her. He was a professional.

The governor made up for what she lacked in the looks department with a ruthless cunning that inspired many in far-right circles. It was her unapologetic support for far-right policies that evangelicals and nationalists admired. People both loved her and feared her.

The midterm election decimated the Arkansas Democratic Party while Buckshot and her Arkansas Republicans celebrated a landslide. Republicans were eager to get to the governing business beginning on the second Monday of January 2023, when they would all be sworn in. Republicans planned to overhaul the state and had the votes to do it. Democrats fretted and furrowed their brows.

To prepare for the new legislative session, the governor was on a mission to attend a meeting in Big Sky, Montana, to unify like-minded governors, politicians, evangelicals, business leaders, and "movement" believers. She kept her travel plans secret. A super-early morning departure would help evade the press. Her mission was to get red-state governors like herself to enter an agreement called the "Red State Compact."

The Red State Compact began as an idea among the governors from the original 11 Confederate states in 2016. After MAGA took hold, the sentiment spread to other red-state governors who wanted to join the effort.[4] By the time midterms rolled around in 2022, the idea had grown long roots, and there were 27 states with Republican supermajorities that would be represented at the meeting in Big Sky.

The Red State Compact sought to force real change by constitutional amendment or force. To amend the constitution, the compact states required seven more sympathetic states to join the cause and call for a "convention of states" under Article V of the United States Constitution.[5] If they could get enough states on board, they could use the convention to either emasculate the federal government or push for secession. Either way, a war of words or blood was imminent.

* * *

Lieutenant Pettigrew drove her across the low Little Rock swamps to the private air terminal at Adams Field to an awaiting Dassault Falcon 2000. Two hours later, the governor and Lieutenant Pettigrew landed in West Yellowstone, Montana, where they transferred to a helicopter that delivered them to the Yellowstone Club in Big Sky.

She stared out the window as her helicopter landed on a pad near the lodge. A handful of guards dressed in black fatigues and armed with automatic weapons met her there. Even her driver, who said nothing to her or Lieutenant Pettigrew, was dressed in the same black uniform.

She dismounted from her passenger-side rear seat and spied the Governor of Texas. His security detail was wheeling him up a ramp next to the front entrance of the lodge.

"Hey Bill, damn good to see you," she called out. "You got yourself a new chair. Looks official!"

"Yo, Biggin'," the Texas governor acknowledged over his shoulder, "See you inside."

It was a big day for Buckshot. She was the keynote speaker where the attending governors would formally create the Red State Compact and coordinate a massive legislative agenda each state would pass. As she walked up the stairs to the main lobby with its soaring glass windows and log beams, she could not help but think how strange a marriage it was of angry, under-educated, poor white trash to ultra-wealthy patrons. The powerful, who had nothing in common with the poor dullards they counted on for votes, had convinced them to vote against their interests so people like her could exercise power.

Unfuckin' believable. Only in America!

The secretive group funding the meeting and the "Big Sky Initiative" had only one interest: perpetuating the already developing oligarchy in the United States. They needed an authoritarian government or a weakened federal government to secure it. Over decades, the tiny group of financiers, billionaires, and industrialists orchestrated and inspired vengeance against the "liberal agenda." It was a vengeance they would need to take over.

If those rich folks want to give us their money or pay to fly us around on their jets to stir up these rednecks, that's fine with me, so long as they stay out of my way and pay the fuckin' bill.

It was 10 a.m. local time. Buckshot stood in an opulent conference hall to meet, greet, see, and be seen before her talk. She moseyed among the tables, observing name tags and making small talk with the folks milling around before the meeting came to order.

There rolled in Governor Bill with his new wheels. Ironically, he had the distinction of single-handedly erasing every meaningful benefit Texas offered disabled persons during his tenure as governor.

That mean-spirited son-of-a-bitch gets stuff done!

And there was Reverend Jim Bob Dealer, who preached about a country returned to being a "Christian Nation" based on the "Old Testament" Word of God. Hallelujah. She caught a glimpse of another "reverend" who believed that all the "gays" should be rounded up and either put in camps or killed if they didn't reject their homosexuality, take a spouse of the opposite sex, and pump out some kids.

Oh shit, she laid eyes on Marjorie Boeber, the leader of "White Christians for Jesus," with emphasis on the "white" part. Her group was a well-armed and well-funded militia outside Rapid City, South Dakota. Their motto was "Praise the Lord, and pass the ammo."

Buckshot approached the dais and stood at the podium in the giant hall.

"Y'all, hey, howdy. Y'all settle down. Let's get to the business of getting our country back on track. We're only about 200 years behind schedule. Come on, now! We will return our country to the way the Founders imagined it. The states will have their God-given power and sovereignty returned, and Christianity will flourish again. We will remake this country where the right to keep and bear arms is sacrosanct. We will go back to a county led by white, Christian, God-fearing men and women who are rewarded for their hard work. We will end freeloader handouts and put money back in the taxpayer's pockets. And by God, we will get our noses out of other countries' business. America first, Goddammit! Once and for all, we will be done with woke, liberal, snowflake, baby-killing perverts who want to control our thoughts and lives."

Few were surprised by her use of the vernacular. Her foul mouth was legendary.

"May I be plain, folks?" she continued from the podium. "We must put an end to woke ideology. We end it by unifying this movement, something the Left will never be able to do. After all, they can't agree on anything. Listen up. We will leave this place with a plan to put us on the right road, pun intended, once and for all. But to do this, we must unite under one purpose and one flag. So let me outline our key legislative goals."

She noted nods of approval as she scanned the room while a large white screen lowered behind her. Armed guards shut the doors leading into the ballroom and locked them.

On the screen behind her, a slide appeared entitled "Slaying the Liberals' Sacred Cows" in large, bold black letters that showed a photograph featuring a matador and a bull bleeding from the neck.

"He might be a Mexican," she laughed, "but he damn sure got that right! Show me the beef!"

Laughter spread among the crowd.

Pressing on, "Look, we gotta go at them hard and fast and slice the throats of every liberal sacred cow just like that Mexican Matador fella. If we move fast enough, they won't see it happening until it is too late. Next slide!"

The following slide was titled "Top Ten Legislative Goals." Beneath the title, ten bullet points read:

- Criminalize abortion and contraception with bounty laws.
- Criminalize same-sex and interracial sex with bounty laws.
- Criminalize "immoral" propaganda and communication (Tender, Grindr, PornHub, etc.).
- Nullify same-sex and interracial marriages.
- Enact "Free Exercise" laws.
- Create state morality tribunals with an interstate enforcement agency.
- Limit public office and professional licensure to the morally suitable (No immigrants, gays, non-Christians, or racial minorities).
- End publicly funded medical care and entitlements - Social Security,

Medicaid, Medicare, and Veterans Administration.
- End the Environmental Protection Agency.
- Establish the Independent Legislature Doctrine as the law of the land.

"That's quite an agenda," she pronounced, "and let me remind you of what a legendary opportunity we have to reshape our nation."

She strutted across the stage and stepped down to the floor in spitting range of the first row. With a toothy smile, gesturing with open arms, she declared, "Not only did the 27 states represented here achieve Republican supermajorities, but the United States House and Senate belong to us again. Let's not fuck this up, boys and girls. We will break the liberal grasp on this nation."

The room erupted into a spontaneous cacophony of cheers, clapping, and whoops as everyone rose to their feet.

"When I finish this little dog and pony show, we'll break into the assigned working groups for each item on the list. You'll see, especially you governors, that each working group comprises top thought leaders, lawyers, and political thinkers from around the United States who share our views. Look around you. What a crew we have assembled here today! We also have propagandists, marketers, religious leaders, and political strategists to help us implement our plans."

Her voice raising, she professed, "I believe, no, I know, I know that by the end of our time together, each of us will be able to go home to our respective states with a complete legislative package and a strategy to implement it while daring the federal government to stop us."

The list presented the essential White Christian Nationalist goals. For everyone else, it represented a means to an end. In truth, the "list" would busy the masses while politicians and their enablers enriched themselves. It was not a moral proposition. It was business. If it meant the destruction of due process and minority rights for any number of people or even the establishment of a *de facto* state religion, so be it. The people at the top would be immune from all of it anyway.

The morning session ended at 11:00 a.m. Buckshot decided to stroll around the grounds and onto the vacant golf course that offered an uninterrupted view of Lone Peak and the surrounding mountains. She asked her friend, Bill, to join her.

"Hey Bill, you feel like letting me wheel you around while we chat?" she asked.

"Sure thing, Buckshot, as long as we leave our minders behind," agreed the Governor of Texas.

"Haystack," Buckshot called, "why don't you and Bill's minder grab a coffee or somethin'? Bill and I are gonna have a chat."

"Yes, Ma'am," Lieutenant Pettigrew replied.

Jesus, that woman.

While Buckshot wheeled the Governor of Texas around the pathways on the golf course, Bill inquired, "You think we can pull this off, Buckshot?" He asked. "It will be a shit show no matter what."

"Yeah, Bill, we can. It could lead us to a civil war, but I'm sick to fucking death of those goddamn people in Washington telling the rest of us how to live. Most of the voters in my state agree with me. I'll hand it to those rednecks. They get out and vote! But the blacks, Mexicans, the "woke," Gen-Z, and middle-class? They are too fucking lazy. If they turned out, we'd not be having this conversation. The fact is that they don't vote, and it is because they don't give a fuck that we'll win this fight."

"I hope you're right," Bill said. "Texas is still red, but Austin's liberals have made progress mobilizing despite remaining weak and disorganized. I hope some crazy mother fuckers in that crowd of liberals don't grab their balls and start shooting one day. Shit, my protection chief briefs me once a week on threats, but there hasn't been an attempt that I know of yet. One of these days, they might be smart enough to figure that the Second Amendment applies to them, too."

"Well, Bill, admit it, you're not all that lovable. I mean, you could be less of a dick."

Bill laughed, saying, "That's why the Reds love me so much!"

"It is my red boots, foul mouth, and big tits my people love," Buckshot returned. "Goddamn, I never thought that growing up as a preacher's daughter would be useful in a million years, but Papa taught me to excel when I take the Lord's name in vain!"

The Governor of Florida, a short, hard-boiled man named Hector DeSoto, watched Governor Bill and Buckshot strolling onto the golf course together. He approached one of his colleagues, the Governor of South Carolina, a handsome man in his 40s with whom he had established a rapport at previous National Governors Association meetings.

"Hey Jackson," Hector said, approaching his friend, "who the hell died and put that bitch in charge? Isn't she a bit much?"

Jackson Rutherford was as brilliant as he was good-looking. With his South Carolina political machine, he had carved out a place for himself among the New Right as a rising star. Some had pegged him to run for president one day.

"That woman right there," Jackson said while gesturing toward Buckshot as she pushed Governor Bill along the rolling course, "is a force to be reckoned with, my friend. I have never met someone more dedicated to the cause than Buckshot. Hey, you know how she got that nickname, right?"

"I heard something about her shooting a rapist," DeSoto responded, "but that's about it."

"Then you didn't hear the half of it. After shooting the guy with a double-barreled shotgun full of double-aught buckshot, she scalped the bastard with a kitchen knife while he was still alive. The rumor is that she framed the scalp. She's got more guts than most men I know, and she isn't afraid to go to any length to get her agendas passed. In the last legislative session in Arkansas, she ran over a legislator with her golf cart because he didn't vote on a bill he promised to support. Broke his arm and then called him a pussy!

But there are darker things. Whispers. I know she has a cabal of white-nationalist supporters who do her bidding in the shadows. I know this because she told me I should contact her if I ever needed help with a difficult politician. I don't think she'd hesitate to have someone killed if it suited her."

Hector continued looking through the tall lobby windows at Governor

Bill and Buckshot in the distance.

"I just can't see it. I mean that mouth on her. Jesus."

"She has a mouth, no doubt. But people follow her. Fanatically. Something about her unflinching resolve grabs people. I'll be honest, Hector, it grabbed me. Her utter lack of fear grabbed me," Rutherford said.

"Well, I'll give her one thing," Hector said. "That woman is super smart, even if she doesn't always let on that she is. It is obvious she has all this worked out."

"It's her secret weapon," Rutherford said. "She can make people think she is right down in the middle of the shit with them, even when she is the smartest person in the room. Her ratings among Republicans are through the roof because of that."

The meeting at the Yellowstone Club continued through the week and into the weekend. Until that Sunday, there were no leaks to the public or the press about what was happening, but the press had picked up that the governors of several states had been absent, and they were closing in. Speculation was rampant, and some people were scared about the future.

4

Ranch Business

Curtis Chee was an efficient, tall, and polite Navajo that Sam recently hired. He came from the Mud Clan, one of the original Navajo clans. He was born in the Checkerboard area of the reservation but later moved to Kayenta, where his grandparents herded sheep.[6] After graduating, he left and asked for a job at the ranch. Sam hired him, but he wasn't sure Chee would fit in with the other staff and ranch hands, mainly from the Jemez Pueblo, because of the history of hostility between the Navajo and Pueblo tribes. Nevertheless, Sam started Chee in the horse barn, and Chee learned the ropes quickly until it became evident that Chee was far too intelligent and articulate for that job, so when the former valet at the main house quit, Sam knew Curtis Chee would be a perfect fit.

One of the traditions at the Valle Grande was that the "main house," or La Hacienda in this case, always had a valet. A relic of a bygone era, the valet was responsible for all primary house operations and coordinating any activities for its guests. One of the jobs included waking the house every morning at 6:00 a.m. In furtherance of another strange tradition, anyone staying at the main home was treated to a morning cup of black tea with cream and sugar. As unfamiliar as it was to Jon initially, he continued the tradition when he took over. It was just how things were at Valle Grande, and he had no intention of upsetting how things ran from day to day.

So, promptly at 6:00 a.m. on this day, like every other, Curtis Chee knocked on the door to the master suite.

"Hosteen Freeman, good morning. I have your tea."[7]

Jon rolled over on his back as he lay on the far edge of the king-sized bed covered with a Navajo blanket, "Yeah, good morning, Curtis. Come on in."

The master suite took up an entire wing of La Hacienda at the end of a long hallway. Inside afforded an expansive view across the caldera toward Pajarito Peak and Cerro Grande that stood guard over the Valle Grande. The tall, dark mountains cast long shadows across the valley in the mornings until the sun crested their summits. Beyond was Los Alamos, the birthplace of the atomic bomb. Mist often hovered above the grasslands early in the predawn light. At sunset, the mountains often glowed orange, reflecting the last light of the day.

Chee silently traversed the room to set Jon's tea on the nightstand, and then he walked to a switch that opened the drapes covering the bay window. After he pushed the button, the drapes parted, allowing grey light to displace the darkness.

"Mr. Freeman."

"Call me Jon."

"Sorry, Hosteen Freeman. I mean, Jon. Breakfast will be ready shortly."

"Thanks. Let Chef know I'll be right down."

After breakfast, Jon asked for Chee.

"What can I do for you, Hosteen?" Chee asked.

"Jon."

"Jon. Right. Sorry, sir."

"Would you call Foreman Sam and tell him I'd like to meet him at HQ around eight," Jon asked. "I'd be there earlier, but I have some things I need to take care of first upstairs."

"No problem," Chee said. "Anything else you need at the moment?"

"No, thank you."

Then, turning to Chef Wiles, who was putting things away in the kitchen, "And Chef, thanks for breakfast. May I call you with lunch plans around ten?" Jon inquired.

"Sure, Boss," Chef said.

"I will know by then what, who, and how many. I want to gather everyone over here for lunch if we can. You up for that?"

"You got it, Boss," Chef said.

"Thanks, Chef," and Jon was off, walking back down the hall toward the master suite where there was a wall opposite the bay window with a built-in bookshelf full of leather-bound fiction novels, including all the works of Louis Lamour, Zane Grey, Tony Hillerman, among others. It was no secret that Jon loved Westerns. On the edge of the bookshelf, Jon pulled out a novel by Louis Lamour, *Education of a Wandering Man*, and pushed a button underneath it.

Click.

The bookshelf swung about an inch, allowing Jon to pull a recessed handle to open the hidden door that exposed a staircase. He went up.

The top of the stairs opened to a room of similar dimensions to the bedroom below. A leather-top Hemingway Desk was next to a large window. Opposite the desk were two red velvet sofas separated by a rectangular-shaped copper Moroccan coffee table his friend J gave him as a gift when he graduated from law school.

He sat down on one of the velvets with a coffee and called Martin, who surprisingly picked up.

"Hey babe, you picked up! Good morning," Jon said excitedly.

"Hey Jon, it's early there. Everything okay?" Martin asked.

"It's the ranch, remember? Everyone is up early," Jon said.

"So, what's up?"

Jon took a half-breath and held it for a moment.

"Babe, I need to stay out here a little longer, maybe up to a week or two. I need some time here. Is that okay? Matachines is right around the corner. I might as well make the most of my time out here. If you want to come out, I'll get someone from the air club to fly you out here."

"Yeah, babe, that's cool," Martin allowed. "I had a feeling you'd need to stay longer than just a few days. For now, I think I'll stay home. Tell me, though, how are the puppies? Are they having the time of their lives out there?"

"Oh God, yes," Jon replied. "They have been chasing cows, running amok, and keeping the staff busy. Our new valet, Curtis, is great with them. They might like him more than they do me at this point."

"Well, don't let them get carried off by a bear or something! I worry," Martin said. "That place is fucking wild, and the dogs are city girls."

"No worries, we keep an eye on them. They'll be fine, promise," Jon said as he realized he had no idea where they were.

The next call was to his brother, Ira.

"Morning," Jon began. "Sorry to call so early, but I wanted to tell you that I need to stick around the ranch for at least another week or two."

"No problemo," Ira said, "enjoy. We'll keep a lid on things here. Anything I need to know about, or is everything covered?"

"Yep, everything is covered." Jon expressed, thankful to have time at the ranch to focus on things.

"Alrighty, I gotta go visit with the foreman," Jon said. "Come check this place out sometime, you'd love it, and the steaks are the best in the world!"

Maybe one day I'll come clean about this place, but not today.

The Valle Grande was Jon's sanctuary and his greatest secret.

Jon's perception of himself as an equal family member was clouded during his younger years. With an underlying fear of being exposed, he naively grappled with his identity. As was the case for numerous gay men of his generation, he often felt like an imposter, perpetually observing the family's dynamics from the outside. It wasn't until he served in the U.S. Army and embarked on a legal career after his father's passing that he realized his worth.

Taking on his rightful place within the family and the firm, Jon found validation by remaining steadfast with the latter. Sticking with the firm was a testament to his sense of loyalty and belonging.

Yet, it was undeniable that Jon also held the position of authority as the head of a separate family at the Valle Grande. The Valle Grande Land and Cattle Company bore deep-rooted traditions and a rich history that fell under Jon's capable leadership.

The next call was to Brother Carl, a University of New Mexico college buddy who lived in Corrales, on the west side of the Rio Grande from Albuquerque. He got Carl's voicemail.

"Hey man, hope I didn't wake you, and if I did, get a cup of coffee," Jon said over voice mail. "Listen, I'm at the Valle Grande. I flew in yesterday. Come up this weekend if you're not too busy starting shit. Let me know if you want to stay a while, and I'll set you up in one of the guest suites at La Hacienda."

The last call he made was to his friend, Jennifer Romero. She was as devoted a friend as a relentless critic, often holding up a mirror so Jon could see the flaws in his character. She was also a student of the "Old Indian Ways," as she called them, having found herself a teacher in Alfonso Waha.

Voice mail. J did not like talking on phones.

"Hey J, I flew in last night," Jon said, leaving a message. "I'm going to see if Chef can whip up something for us for supper tonight if you'd like to have dinner together, just the two of us at La Hacienda. I have to meet Sam at HQ here shortly, so maybe I'll see you there."

One last thing he did was log into the ranch's books to check the account where he had ranch distributions placed. He rarely took money from the ranch, and because he didn't take money often, his capital account had accrued a value of nearly 70 million dollars.

God knows how much capital I have. How I manage not to live like a pimp with all this cash is a goddamned miracle. Jesus.

Jon finished his finance review and walked down the stairs. It was 7:55 a.m. when he rolled down the driveway for the half-mile drive over to HQ along the perimeter road.

* * *

Jon walked across the 100-year-old Spanish tile floor into the Old Adobe foyer, and Sam came around the corner to meet him.

"I heard you pull up. Come on back," Sam smiled as he extended his hand

35

to shake Jon's.

Jon followed Sam into the great room, where it had remained the same as when the Dunigan Family lived there with its tall ceilings and smell of piñon. They sat down to talk, and Sam began, "Your timing is pretty good, Jefe. We have some things we couldn't do over the phone or on Zoom."

Sitting across from each other in the living room, Sam reported the livestock headcounts, the condition of various pastures and paddocks, and that they would move some of the cattle to the Cimarron Property on the llano.[8] There were headcounts for the other livestock, including sheep, and the status of the growing elk heard that they planned to monetize. But the biggest news Sam shared was that they were well ahead of schedule on a planned expansion of the geothermal operation.

"Jon, you know the deal with Los Alamos County and the National Lab has exceeded our expectations, but we must overcome some legal and political issues to export the surplus onto the grid."

"Yeah, I recall you mentioning that in our Zoom calls. What's up with it?"

"PNM is reluctant to take our surplus. Plus, they want to know our total output, but the National Laboratory wants to keep the power it consumes a secret."

"And you believe a face-to-face with Los Alamos will help," Jon said.

"Yes, that is true," Sam replied, "but we need to press the Public Service Company of New Mexico. They insist on knowing total output, which could compromise the Lab's secrecy."

Jon looked through some reports Sam had handed him for a moment, then looked back at Sam.

"Seems political, Sam. Why don't we visit the Lab people and then go to PNM? Let's get the lay of the land so we will know how to proceed."

"We might need you to call your friend, Mr. Thomas," Sam suggested. "Didn't he work for PNM long ago before he became a lawyer?"

"Will?" Jon replied. "Yeah, he did, right out of school. I'm not sure if that ended well for either side, but I'll find out. He can help us decipher PNM's reasoning behind the demand for total power output. I don't see what that has to do with anything since the loop is closed between us, the Lab, and

Los Alamos County. They only need to know how much we'd put onto the wholesale grid. But anyway, Will could help us."

Will Thomas possessed high standards but tended to overdo it when it came to burning bridges. Nonetheless, his expertise was indispensable for exporting surplus energy from the geothermal site. With a bit of luck, PNM might have forgotten the shared history.

The project greatly benefited Los Alamos County and the National Laboratory by significantly reducing energy costs while generating tremendous wealth for Valle Grande, mainly if it could export surplus energy.

"Shit, I forgot to call Chef Wiles," Jon said suddenly. It was nearly 11:30 a.m.

"Give me a second, will you?" Jon asked as he reached for his cell to phone Chef Wiles.

"Hey Boss," Chef answered, "I got you covered. I figured you'd be into it, so I pulled something together for all of you if you wish to come down. I have room for 12. I prepared a whole mess of green chili stew."

"Thanks, Chef," Jon said with relief. "I'll round up who I can, and we'll see you down there shortly."

Jon terminated the call.

"Chef has some green chili stew for us. Shall we?" Jon asked. "You, me, and room for ten more. Let's have the staff come down. What do you say?"

"Good idea, Jefe," Sam responded. "Head down to the house, and I'll gather the rest. See you there in ten."

* * *

The scent of green chili stew greeted Jon when he entered La Hacienda. Behind him followed Sam, the head cowboy, the in-house lawyer, the chief accountant, the hedge trader, a secretary, Alfonso Waha, and Jennifer Romero.

Jon turned around to greet everyone and hugged Jennifer.

Jon beckoned Chef Wiles, "Hey, Chef, take a load off and fetch Chee. We'll need some help with all this food you made."

After the crew devoured the stew and piles of sopapillas, Jon invited everyone to the great room for a sit-down and conversation. The mood was festive, with everyone trying to catch up with Jon simultaneously. Waha and Jennifer were characteristically quiet.

The grand room, with its unfinished plaster walls, reflected shades of beige, terracotta, pink, and burnt orange, depending on the sun's angle. The 20-foot ceilings and tall windows looked out to the ponderosa forest on one side and the central courtyard on the other with its fountain and stands of rosemary, lavender, and thyme.

While Jon's guests chatted, he turned on the TV above the fireplace to check the news. Jennifer shot him a glance, indicating it was a bad habit. Just before he took the hint and turned off the TV, a "breaking news" report flashed across the screen, stating that "Red State Governors missing since the election."

More bullshit, Jon thought, and just as he reached for the remote to turn it off, Jennifer's hand rested upon his.

"Wait, this might be important," Jennifer cautioned.

The newscaster came on.

"The governors of several red states have not been seen since the midterm elections on Tuesday, but we learned they are meeting at a Montana resort. Our sources tell us they are there to form an interstate agreement to challenge the federal government and possibly lead to a constitutional convention or secession. We will update you with more news as it comes in."

Near one o'clock, Sam stood up to get the crowd's attention. "All right, everybody, we gotta get back to the office."

Then, turning to Jon, Sam allowed, "We'll catch up Monday. Take the weekend and relax. If you'd like to work some, we'll get that mare you like saddled up. Some fence lines need mending along one of the northern pastures. Come Monday, let's discuss going to Los Alamos and maybe down to Albuquerque on the geothermal deal."

The staff got up, each thanking Jon for having them over for lunch as they filed out.

38

What could those governors be up to? Interstate agreement? A constitutional convention or secession? How could they pull any of that off, Jon wondered as he went to the kitchen for a cup of coffee.

5

Two Worlds

Jennifer Romero was a stately woman. At 5'10" and 76 years old, she kept her long, straight, graying hair tied back with a simple silver brooch. She exuded poise, strength of mind, character, and dignity. Since they met when Jon was a teenager, J always stood tall and crisp.

Late into Friday evening, Jennifer thoughtfully swirled a glass of red wine while Jon sipped his club soda against the flicker of firelight in the great room.

"Jon, the news from today troubles me. You predicted the evangelicals would eventually take over when you wrote me that letter in 1992, and now it looks like the Right is making moves. You seemed committed to fighting the Right back then but stayed out of the fray. Why? You are far too capable a leader to remain silent. Your talent begs that you stand up and fight against what you predicted over 30 years ago, but you have ignored your calling to meaningful service in political office. You opted for the easy way and grew fat, lazy, and complacent. I love you, but someone must lay this truth on you."

"I'm not fat, goddammit!" Jon protested.

Jennifer smirked.

"I think you are!"

"No way," Jon returned. "Well, okay, I need to shed 20, all right, but fat, no goddammit, no!"

"You're dodging the issue, Jon!"

Indeed, Jon wasn't "fat," but at 185 pounds on his 5'11" frame, he found himself approximately 20 pounds away from optimal health. Throughout his life, he maintained a slender physique, weighing around 160 pounds. However, his blissful, stable, and predictable life with Martin had contributed to those extra pounds. Having spent a decade together, Jon found immense contentment in their relationship's security. He was reluctant to take any action that might jeopardize his pleasant existence. Nevertheless, he couldn't ignore that his complacency had become an unflattering habit, especially when compared to the potential he could embody in the eyes of his friend, Jennifer.

"I know on some level I have disappointed you by my choices, but J, those right-wingers aren't going to change anything," he argued. "It'll blow over. It always does. This happens every election. The fringes raise hell, talk a bunch of shit, get on their social media, and beat their chests. They are a bunch of mouth-breathing bullies. All their tough talk about abortion, ending gay marriage, and taking away people's rights and religious freedom is a crock of shit. There is no way people will cave to their crazy ideas."

"You're still dodging the issue, Jon!"

Jon lifted his hands as if to say, "I give up!"

"Look, J," he continued, "it's just more of the same, and as far as politics or activism, that's not me. Maybe it once could have been? I don't know. I made my choice to honor my father's legacy and continue what he started with the firm. That activist shit is for kids, not middle-aged men. I have a law firm and intend to remain there while my mother is alive. I have a duty to my family!"

Jennifer interrupted.

"You can still make a difference," she said, "and let's be honest, money isn't the issue, at least not since you inherited Valle Grande."

"It's not about the money, J," Jon protested. "If I left it to do god-knows-what, run for office, or even hang it up and come here full time, I think it would kill my mother. And after getting beyond years of childhood resentment, I want to enjoy the time she has left. I like my place there, and

41

I want to savor it. If I didn't, I would have said 'to hell with it' and moved out here long ago."

Jennifer leaned forward in her seat, pressing.

"Little Brother, I note that you said you 'like' your place there, but I didn't hear you say you 'love' your place there. I think you've settled. To me, it's plain as day. Look, no one stands up to you! You are not used to being challenged, are you? So, you have to hear this from somebody. Man up and stop living your life for someone else—especially your mom. The Colonel has lived her life, and if she knew what you were to this place, I swear she'd think you'd be casting your pearls before swine for not coming out here and making this place your own. You do not know your mother!"

"Perhaps. I must admit," Jon reflected, "she has always lived her way. But a sense of duty also drove her, something she instilled in me."

"That may be true, Jon, but recall that it was your dad's firm before all this. You were there to practice with him. Then, after you had done so long enough, you planned to move back to New Mexico. When he passed away, you stayed. Now, you remain there because of your mother, or does Martin figure into it also?"

"You're right about one thing. When Bear died, I was paralyzed. Though I dreamed of it, I couldn't harbor the thought of moving back out here. New Mexico, all of this, was my dream from the time I first came to the state for military school. The deserts and mountains captured my imagination, and they still do."

"What about Martin," J asked. "He's lovely, but you stay there for him, right? I know he doesn't love this place like you do, but you stay there because you are afraid to be alone. You don't want to rock the boat. I have news for you, my dear little brother. Martin is much stronger than you give him credit for. You have always been afraid to step into the middle of your dream and embrace it, and here it is, right under your nose. If he knew the truth of what this place is to you or knew your capability as I do, I am convinced he'd be on your team 100%. I mean, have you discussed any of this with him?"

Jon sat blankly, eyes cast down before returning to meet J's gaze.

"I can't say I have ever discussed these things with him. It never seemed relevant, and my head was in a different place when he came into my life."

"Well, Little Brother, we don't call these 'your mountains' for nothing. This is the heartbeat of your soul, these mountains, and this place. You shouldn't forsake it and keep Martin in the dark about what this place is to you, either. But I must confess something. I deeply fear that once you decide to seize your true power, you may have to sacrifice even this place to do what needs to be done."

Shaking his head, Jon replied, "That won't happen. Leaving Arkansas to return here will be hard enough. I didn't ask for this. Cullen, fucking Cullen. I miss him, J, but sometimes I resent him for laying this place at my feet. And yet, I know this land has always been my destiny. I have just been saying, 'tomorrow,' all this time. But you know, I first stepped foot on it when I was 16. Even then, I knew this place was special, but something else always came first. Now you're telling me that as I'm on the cusp of seizing this place, I risk losing it to what, take on the Right? Politics? Seriously."

Jennifer took a slow sip of her wine and carefully set the glass on the coffee table.

"Jon, we're wiser when we are young because when we're young, we don't have as much to lose. Our ideas are more pure. Everything lies ahead. "Possibility" is just beyond the horizon. You're no exception. You were wiser when you were in your twenties than you are now! Look at you. Expectations still restrain you from tapping your true potential despite what you know and your access to vast resources. My friend, you cannot let this go. There is too much at stake. The governor of your state looks to be in charge, and you are in a unique position to do something about it. You may be used to working in the shadows or behind the scenes with your connections, but you're going to have a step up to front and center this go around."

Jon looked away over toward the courtyard and then back to Jennifer.

"J, I have to turn in. Can we pick up on this in the morning? Take the guest suite. Let's continue this tomorrow or the next day. You have me cornered!"

Jennifer rose and looked kindly at Jon, "Good night, Love. You know I'm right. By the way, Waha will be gunning for you tomorrow, so be ready!"

"Fuck. Waha. He will be busting my balls!" Jon laughed.

"Good night, Little Brother," Jennifer said as Jon stood up.

Jon excused himself, but instead of going to bed, he walked up the stairs to his hideaway, where he left the lights off, and laid himself down on one of the velvet sofas to think through things in the moonlight pouring through the bay window.

* * *

Saturday morning came in the blink of an eye, but Jon had beaten Chee to the punch, rising before 6 a.m. The house was dark except for a glow from the kitchen as he walked down the hall to brew himself a cup of coffee. There sat Alfonso Waha at the breakfast table.

"Better bring a jacket, gloves, and a hat. We're going for a ride," Waha said quietly.

Jon replied, "Coffee?"

"No time. Daylight burns," said Waha.

The two quietly rode out into the early morning dark, Waha leading the way. He was silent, and Jon knew better than to break it with small talk. The two followed the tree line of ponderosa, where it met the tall grass of the Valle Grande. They came upon a horse trail that followed a creek into a pine forest and climbed up through aspen groves and low scrub. Only hooves against the rocky trail broke the silence while color began painting the early morning sky.

Maybell, Jon's mount, was familiar. She was a capable quarter-horse of bay coat, black mane, and a star on her forehead. Only the most experienced Caballeros rode her when Jon wasn't on the ranch, but she was his when in residence. She was such a capable mare that Jon could let his mind wander as they meandered up the mountainside.

The two proceeded up the switchbacks leading to the summit of Redondo Peak. When they reached it, Waha hopped down from his horse. He was agile underneath his brown skin and faded jeans. He smiled at Jon through the lines of his swarthy face as he unfolded two thick wool blankets on the rocky ground. The summit was the tallest perch in the southwest quadrant of Valles Caldera, the highest peak in the Jemez Mountains, and a holy place for the Jemez People. Even though he legally owned it, Jon didn't dare go up to Redondo uninvited. It was sacred ground.

"Come, sit," Waha said. "You are standing in the Father of the Northern Mountains, a sacred place to my people. It is where the life-giving waters flow, providing energy and sustaining us. This location holds one of our most revered shrines, which connects us and Walatowa through the Underworld Trail. It is our ancestral home, and we share it with you today."

Jon was motionless, hanging on every word.

"You understand my people, and my people understand you," Waha said. "We recognize you did not seek ownership of these lands when your friend passed away. We believe you accept that you are a caretaker entrusted with preserving this sacred place. We express our gratitude for your respect towards our traditions and for the efforts you have made to protect the land."

Waha continued.

"There is no way to make you a member of our tribe, so you will always be an outsider. However, we will forever regard you as a friend. And as a friend, I brought you here so that you could witness how everything we hold dear rests in your hands. We hope you will embrace your connection with this land. You are a welcome foreigner among us, and the land beckons you to safeguard it. Yet, there might be more than just the land that requires your protection."

"Thank you for your words, Waha," Jon shyly said.

"Do not thank me. I know this is a burden. We, the people of my tribe and the Dunigan Family, should thank you. Because of you, the stewardship of this sacred place continues. But now you should listen and listen well. You are about to be tested, and many people will seek answers. There will be many demands on you. You will be asked to make tough choices that place you between two worlds. Use this time wisely in our holy place and

45

on these lands to think and ask the Great Spirit for direction. Now, let us sit here a while."

Waha withdrew a dear antler pipe from a pouch, packed the bowl with some tobacco, lit it, and passed it to Jon. The two sat silently for about an hour, smoking the pipe in the alpine air.

Thoughts swirled.

Tested, how?

Jon knew better than to ask Waha, who would only answer him with more riddles.

What worlds? Why choose when I have the best of both, he thought naively, focused on the only worlds he thought this was about, the Valle Grande and his life back in Arkansas. But Waha's analogy was too simple. Was he pointing Jon toward something more profound, and if so, what could it possibly be?

Not long after lunchtime, they descended the mountain, riding through the aspen groves until Jon peeled off and loped through a meadow toward the Old Adobe to see if Sam was around.

"You looking for Sam?" asked one of the clerks who was from accounting when Jon walked in.

Jon nodded.

"He's down at the stables," the clerk said, "I'll buzz him for you if you like."

"Yeah, do that," Jon asked. "Tell him I'm going to meet him down there."

"Yes, sir," the clerk replied. "Right away."

Jon left, trotted toward the stables, and found Sam standing in a round pen adjacent to the horse barn, watching one of the Caballeros working a colt on a lead. Jon dismounted, and one of the stable boys came out and took the reins.

"Sam," Jon began before Sam cut Jon off.

"Waha got to you, didn't he, Jefe?"

"Indeed, he did," Jon said.

"I should have seen that coming," Sam said, adding, "Hey, you want me to drop you at the house?"

"Nah, the walk will do me good," Jon said.

Two worlds. Two worlds.

He reflected on Jennifer's comments from the night before.

Waha and J have been talking.

Jon recognized J's observation that he took the path of least resistance. He lived a simpler life in Arkansas out of loyalty to his family and the law firm. Still, he wondered whether he could have significantly impacted politics and public service. Despite this, he found fulfillment in managing the ranch and benefiting both the people who worked there and the tribe.

But, maybe it is time to make some changes, he thought.

Maybe it's time to talk to Martin about returning to the ranch permanently, but that would mean leaving Arkansas for life in Valle Grande. Jon may have forsaken his true potential because he refused to roll up his sleeves and get his hands dirty. He asked himself all these questions, but he didn't want to confront any of them. Instead, he relied on his habit of approaching life with a "suit up and show up" attitude to the day-to-day and the ordinary, with no expectations. His routine made for a comfortable life, but was he leading a life of "quiet desperation," as Henry David Thoreau wrote in *Civil Disobedience*? He idolized Thoreau, the hero of his literature and philosophy classes in high school and college, but had he put aside his true talent and potential in favor of ease and comfort?

"The mass of men lead lives of quiet desperation," wrote Thoreau, and the answer to Jon's many questions was bubbling up, and he didn't like it.

* * *

Jon was exhausted when Chee opened the drapes on Sunday at 6:00 a.m. sharp, as he did every other day of the week.

Jon thought he'd slow down this morning by riding to the geothermal site to check it out and get some fresh air.

"Curtis," he called from the breakfast table.

"Yes, sir?"

"I'd like you to saddle up two horses and bring them up here. You and I are going for a ride. We'll take the dogs, too. I've got some things to take

47

care of while you sort all that out."

Jon walked back to his suite and up the stairs to his Hemingway. He made notes to remind him of things that needed tending in the upcoming week, like meeting with Sam at Los Alamos, PNM, and possibly seeing Governor Toya of the Jemez Pueblo. After he finished his lists, he went to the kitchen for another cup of coffee and walked into the great room to wait for Chee and the horses.

"I brought the horses," Chee said as he entered the great room.

"Good deal. I want to ride over to the geothermal complex and Hidden Spring."

The two rode toward the rising sun along the Caldera Perimeter Road, with the dogs following behind. From their vantage point, they could observe New Mexico State Highway 4, which runs along the southern edge of the Valle Grande, where tourists parked and aimed their cameras across the expanse for the postcard view.

Jon led the two of them into the tree line away from the road but kept it in sight as they picked their way through the stand of 100-foot-tall ponderosa. It was quieter off the caliche over the soft layer of pine needles that released their scent with each step.

After about half an hour, Chee asked, "Is the spring near the geothermal site?"

"Yep," Jon said. "I want to check out the geothermal plant, and then I'll show you Hidden Spring before we head back."

The road wound northward, with the morning sun warming their shoulders. They followed a farm road that circled a lava dome and then into a narrow valley. Steep hillsides channeled them into a field of steaming fumaroles, mud pots, and the pungent scent of sulfur.

"Whatever you do over here," Jon warned, "don't ride off the road and into that field. That crust is brittle. We've lost a few trespassers here who were more curious than intelligent if you know what I mean." And as he said that, he looked for the dogs on their heels, following the horses in a single file line.

Today, we might find out how smart or dumb these dogs are, Jon thought wryly.

Martin would kill him in his sleep if something happened to those precious dogs. Thankfully, they proved more intelligent than the trespassers who had been cooked to death on previous occasions. Perhaps the dogs knew nothing good could come from the steaming earth.

They followed the farm road about a quarter mile past the geothermal field and around another rocky outcrop that revealed the geothermal plant. It was a complex of three large industrial metal buildings and some smaller outbuildings spread across five acres linked by metal tubes and pipes that came up from below the surface, then routed into one building, and then to the larger building, and then past it to another one where the pipes disappeared into the hillside.

Jon pulled Maybell up alongside Curtis, and the two sat their horses, appraising the complex.

"So, the building on the far left, the larger one with the gray metal siding, that is where hot water is piped up from beneath the surface, and then you see the pipes leading out of that building to the middle one next to it on the right, the bigger one, see that?"

"Yes, sir," Chee said.

Jon continued the brief lesson.

"That building is where the generator is. Then, the last one on the right is where the cooling towers are for the steam to recondense, and once it is cooled, we inject the reclaimed water back into the earth. We siphon off some of it to provide the ranch unlimited hot water."

"And you plan to provide the pueblos with free energy from the surplus?"

"I hope so. These lands used to belong to the Jemez People. It would be great if we could free them of energy costs or dramatically reduce them." Jon said.

They departed and rode toward a discrete trailhead. Following a narrow path up the hill in single file, the two reached a natural formation that overlooked a broad valley to the west, and in the middle of it was a pool with steam rising from the surface.

"Here we are," Jon said to Chee, "this is Hidden Spring."

Perched on the western flank of the lava dome about 200 feet above the valley floor was a shelf surrounded by a mix of ponderosa, scrub, and aspen. Jon was glad Chee wasn't much of a talker, so he could use the time to think and take in the view. Plus, it is never a good idea to roam around the ranch alone. After all, many things can hurt or kill you. And according to Waha, some things in these hills don't respond to bullets.

Getting away from the ranch operation was a luxury, even for a morning to think about all that Waha had said before returning to La Hacienda with a pair of tired dogs. Jon noticed a bright yellow 1957 Bel Air Post in the driveway as they neared the house.

Son of a bitch, he arrived!

6

Big Sky Revelations

After dismounting Maybell, Jon headed straight for the front door to find his college mate, Brother Carl, sipping a glass of 16-Year Laphroaig in the kitchen. Jon and Carl were fraternity brothers at the University of New Mexico who shared numerous adventures and misadventures throughout the region, contributing to Jon's fondness for the American Southwest.

Carl looked up from the breakfast table as Jon walked in, "You haven't seen the news yet, I take it," Carl said with a grave tone.

"No, I've been riding all morning. What's up?" Jon inquired.

Carl huffed.

"Oh, for fuck's sake, you won't believe it. I had to take a break from it. Here, come on. I'll show you," Carl said. "You'd better get ready, my brother. They are coming for us!"

The two went into a little recessed den adjoining the great room, where they sat together and turned on a TV. When the TV came to life, TNN featured a flashing red "breaking news" banner beneath the anchor on the screen.

"We are about to show you a snapshot taken from the cellphone of a person present at a conference of red state governors who have been missing since election night. Now we know what they have been up to. For the safety of the person who took the photo, we shall not identify them," the anchor said. Then, a photograph of a slide titled "Top Ten Legislative Goals" appeared on the screen.

"They have been running this story about a list of policy goals all morning over and over. Look at it! Let that sink in, my brother," Carl declared. "It's time to go to war! No, it is time to take those cocksuckers out once and for all."

"What the fuck, Carl? No way they can get away with any of that shit on that list," Jon exclaimed. "Not a chance. It's all bullshit. People will not let that happen."

"Dude," Carl replied, "just keep watching because you haven't heard anything yet. That is just the beginning. Since this aired, some crazy fucker took a shot at the president earlier today, and around the same time, someone else took a shot at the House Speaker. It's on, bro. It's on. You'd better be glad you have this ranch because there ain't going to be a goddamn thing left of Arkansas once this catches fire. Just listen because the news people believe that your governor from Arkansas is leading this thing."

"Seriously, some right-wing nutters tried to assassinate the president and the Speaker of the House? I can believe that," Jon said, "but that plan, dude, there's no fucking way people will let that happen."

Carl was on a roll.

"Jon, pull your head out of your ass," he said. "Wake the fuck up! You can't fuck this off. They are discussing passing laws that will round up people like you and like me and kill or put us in camps. And God help you if you're black, a single pregnant woman, or don't fit their right-wing idea of a Christian. You're safe, Jon, because you are here and not in Arkansas, but when you go back there, you won't be safe, and neither will Martin. Your family, his family, they will not be safe."

"It just seems impossible," Jon argued, "because half that shit would require amending the Constitution, and we all know how difficult that is. But I do have some friends down in Little Rock. I have a full day with the foreman tomorrow, but after that, I'll start calling around to see what I can find out about all this. One guy I can call is the attorney general. We used to hang out during law school. But seriously, dude, I don't see how this could be more than red meat for the masses to get everyone fired up after midterms, don't you think?"

"Jon," Carl persisted, "it is too fucking late. In your state and the others, come the first of the year, you will have Republican majorities in all branches of government that could enact these laws."

"My brother," Jon said calmly, "why don't you stay here for a few days? Get settled in. I'm going to get some lunch and make a couple of calls. I'll catch up with you for supper."

Carl looked intently at Jon, "Don't fuck this off, goddammit! I know how you are, my brother. You see the best in people, and I know you covet your life back in Arkansas, but you will have some decisions to make. Don't forget where your true home and family are. We are here! It is this ranch! It is us!"

"Yeah, I know, man. I know I need to bite the bullet and return and stay here. I know it, and this may be the time to do it."

"You have been saying you'd be staying in New Mexico since we were in college," Carl countered. "Fuck, you should have never left, but I get why you did. I don't get why you didn't pick up your shit and return here after your dad died in 1999 or when Cullen gave this place to you after that. That, I never could understand."

"Dude, I just couldn't leave my family after Dad died. I was paralyzed. If you'll recall, I had a place selected in Taos and a pretty lucrative practice situation set up. But when he died, I couldn't leave my mom."

The two remained glued to the TV for a bit longer, with all the news channels saying similar things about how the "list," as it was being referred to, was an unprecedented attempt to undo decades of progress in civil liberties and would usher in an authoritarian state. News anchors were apoplectic except for Fox, but in an ongoing panel discussion, even Fox pundits suggested the list was a bridge too far.

"Fox anchor Richard Flanders said, "So far, we haven't been able to get anyone to comment on the list, but that photo places the Governor of Arkansas at that presentation. So, the slide in question, put that up back up please," and the list reappeared once more.

"Let's take these one at a time, shall we? And we'll start with you, Jeanne Conway," directed the anchor.

"Thanks, Richard," Jeanne replied. "These items look like a White Christian Nationalist wish list, but it is just that, a wish list, and I can't imagine even red state governors getting this plan passed. I mean, I can see the Right passing anti-abortion and contraception laws, and I can even see states invalidating gay marriage but criminalizing interracial marriage and gay sex. What about this business of 'immoral' propaganda? What, they are going after porn sites and social media? The last time I checked, there was still a First Amendment."

Another panelist, Robert McClarren, a far-right radio host and political commentator, cut in.

"Come on, Jeanne, don't be naive. Think about the last one, the Independent Legislature Doctrine. If it becomes the law of the land, it's game over, and we will own the Libs. If the Supreme Court signs off on it, the rest of those things could become a reality because there will not be the votes to stop it. The Libs would be gerrymandered into oblivion, so we will finally be able to stop the Left's attempts to win elections through fraud."

"Bob, the public has put that whole made-up presidential election scandal behind it," retorted Commentator Jayson Whippet. "Not a chance!"

"The point you are missing, Jayson," countered McClarren, "is that it won't matter what people think if the last item becomes law. Like it or not, the Left will be silenced, and I couldn't think of a better thing to happen for our country."

Jeanne Conway piped in, "Let's assume that item gets past the Supreme Court. What is the logical, perhaps absurd, conclusion if all this comes to pass? Supermajorities will what, end Medicaid or Medicare? Open tribunals to police social media? Round up immigrants, gays, or trans persons? All of you are insane if any of that stuff will ever translate into policy. Even this Supreme Court would overturn that agenda on Constitutional grounds."

Bob McClarren added, "For once, I might be forced to agree with Miss Conway. If you look at the logical conclusion of how the entire 'list' plays out, perhaps the Right doesn't get everything at the beginning, but if they get number ten, all bets are off. The rest looks like political theater to stir up the base."

Jon looked over at Carl.

"Flip it to NBC. Let's see what they're saying."

Talking heads on NBC were unhinged, and the anchor was on a roll.

"Would you look at that?" Jon said. "Those guys at NBC are madder than a pack of wild dogs on a three-legged cat!"

"Mark my words," the anchor said, "these things may not become law next year or the year after, but they show you what your neighbor thinks. Already, there is a Republican majority in both houses of Congress, and the red states represent over half of the U.S., where people are of the mind to lock you up if you use a condom, put you in jail if you are gay, or arrest you if you married someone of a different race. And think of the proposed Free Exercise Law, allowing everyone to exercise their religious beliefs freely. What does that mean? If you get a divorce on Monday, do your right-wing friends stone you on Tuesday? There is no telling where this can go. No friends, wait and see, wait and see what happens to your country in the days to come."

After that, the anchor said, "We have new information, and we will switch over to our affiliate in Big Sky, Montana, where press members are assembled outside the gate of the Yellowstone Club. Go ahead, Mikayla. What do you have for use?"

"Hello, my name is Mikayla Covington. I am here with about two dozen reporters at the gates of the Yellowstone Club in Big Sky, Montana. We have been waiting for someone to come out and make a statement."

A camera panned across the front gate featuring six masked men in black fatigues carrying automatic weapons.

"As you can see," the reporter continued, "security is visible, but we hope to gain enough attention that someone will come out and talk to us."

And as she said that, a black SUV rolled slowly toward the gate and came to a stop. Governor Suzy Brandy Landers emerged from the SUV in the same outfit she wore in the leaked photo of the list. She strode up to the gate, and one of the guards opened it for her.

The Arkansas governor faced the gaggle with Lieutenant Pettigrew in civilian clothes on one side and masked men on the other.

"Hi, y'all. Well, I'll be honest with you right off the bat. None of us here wanted anyone to see that slide everyone is so upset about. Look, there's a reason why people have closed-door meetings! Now that the cat's out of the bag, I can say those are political talking points and nothin' more. We just won the midterm elections in over half the country and were hoping to get together without the fake news media getting in the way. Like, who's voting for us, why they are voting for us, and what kind of policies might sound good to the voting public."

There was a clamor as nearly every reporter tried to jump in with a question.

"Y'all, y'all, all of you, Jesus! Give me a break. I won't answer questions about what is meant to be a private conference. Come on, now! You all are worried about the Right getting together. How would the Left feel if we crashed one of your parties? Seriously! Look, you all have nothing to fear here. We are politicians, and we are doing what politicians do. We got together, talked, and exchanged ideas. This meeting has been nothing more than brainstorming. Do you think we will try to round up a bunch of pregnant women or arrest people for being black? We are the party of the big tent, come on! Go home, relax, and tell your networks that none of the stuff you read was supposed to be for public consumption. It is nothing more than a group of folks getting together to exchange ideas. After all, it is a free country!"

She abruptly turned around, saying to her handlers, "C'mon, boys, let's get the fuck outta here."She briskly walked behind the gate to drive away from their microphones, jabbing the air for another quote that wouldn't come.

* * *

While Jon and Carl watched the TV with mouths agape, Buckshot Brandy and her escort pulled up behind the main lodge next to a row of dumpsters that smelled of rotten food. Buckshot stepped out and approached a skinny college-age kid dressed in a waiter's uniform of black pants and a white club shirt. His hands were zip-tied together. The lad was bruised black and blue.

Buckshot started in on him, "You proud of yourself, son? You thought you could leak that photo and not get caught, didn't you?"

He vomited. Buckshot's frown turned ugly when the sweet smell of his puke hit her nostrils.

"Shoot his woke sorry ass," Buckshot ordered, and one of the black-clad guards withdrew his sidearm from his tactical leg holster, screwed on a silencer, and squeezed off a round into the left side of the young man's head. The barely audible snapping sound of the bullet met with a gust of wind as the boy's head vanished for a second in a cloud of red and grey as he spun around, splattering the dumpster with what remained of his brain mixed with strands of his long blond hair.

"Well, boys, it's just another afternoon in Big Sky," she said, "and be sure to seize his phone and see what other stuff he sent. Then clean that piece of shit up and get rid of the body. He probably was a pole-smoking faggot. Good riddance. He ain't woke no more."

Buckshot walked around with her entourage to a side door to rejoin the conference. As she entered the lodge, she ran into her friend, Governor Jackson Rutherford. He pulled her aside in the hallway for a word.

"Hey, Buckshot, let me help you."

"What?"

He pulled out a handkerchief.

"You've got something stuck in your hair."

"Well, aren't you a gentleman," she exclaimed.

"I might come across as one, but in this case, it's self-serving. I'd like to see you elected to lead our compact, but we can't have you go up for a speech with a piece of that kid's brain stuck in your hair," he whispered.

"You saw that?" she asked.

"I did. I heard some commotion, so I came to investigate. That boy had it coming," he said. "Listen, I'm all for you, but some of these people in our group don't have the strength of your convictions. Let's not give them any reason to doubt you, alright?"

"Tell you what, Jackson, you'll go places, my friend," she said, patting him on the back. "Stick with me, and let's see what we can get done."

* * *

While the two guards unceremoniously tossed the young man's body like a sack of potatoes into the dumpster 1,000 miles north of the Valle Grande, Jennifer Romero and Alfonso Waha appeared at La Hacienda.

"Oh shit," Carl said, looking toward Jon. "It's on now, mother fucker!"

"No doubt," Jon said. He knew why they were there.

Jon, Carl, Jennifer, and Waha assembled in the great room. Jennifer and Waha sat beside one another on one sofa opposite Carl and Jon.

"What are you going to do, Mijo," Jennifer asked. "Do you believe me now?"

"I do," Jon replied. "But I'm having a hard time wrapping my head around all this. God damn them."

Waha was silent, appraising Jon's reactions.

Later that evening, when Jon was getting ready for bed, he reflected on a quote he had read from *Moby Dick*.

"For there is no folly of the beast of the earth which is not infinitely outdone by the madness of men." I think Ishmael was right about that. Those fuckin' Christians are some of the worst human beings imaginable. Madness!

Jon was determined to discover what was happening and whether the revelations that leaked out of the Big Sky Conference were real or just more conspiracy. But there wasn't much he could get done from the ranch because a good bit of his investigation would be face-to-face back in Arkansas when he could get back there, which would take some time. For now, the ranch had its demands.

7

The Arkansas General Assembly

J on remained at the Valle Grande for several more weeks, except
for a few short visits to Arkansas. Martin flew out to join him for
Thanksgiving. The two remained at the ranch until they took the
Cessna and flew home on December 20th, a Monday.

When they arrived at Highland House, Jon went to his study to call the
Colonel to let her know he was home. He had missed her ever-polite
cantankerousness.

"I'm glad you're back home, son. Ready to get back to work after your
adventures?" the Colonel asked patronizingly.

"Oh, always," he replied. "It is incredible what you can get done with the
internet."

Then came the Colonel's predictable jab. "Yes, but there is nothing like
being in the office, wouldn't you say?"

"Oh, naturally," Jon replied, refusing to take the bait.

Jon knew the Colonel and his brother were unhappy that he had been
gone from the office for nearly two months, and there would be a reckoning
about it. He had never been away from the firm for a long time, and some
of his work had to be contracted out to other lawyers. Questions that might
force Jon's hand to come clean about the ranch and his true relationship to
it would be asked.

After encountering the Colonel, Jon called his friend, Winston "Win"

Purcell, the Arkansas attorney general. They were law school classmates who often played Skee-Ball at Maxine's Tap Room accompanied by cheap beer and popcorn.

"Attorney General's Office," an officious Shanice Walker answered.

"Hello, my name is Jonathan Christian Freeman, a lawyer from Fayetteville. I am an old friend of General Purcell's. Is he available to take my call?"

"Hold on, sir," she said, and after a short wait, the attorney general was on the line.

"Jon Freeman? Good lord, to what do I owe the pleasure?" asked the attorney general.

"Win. Thank you for taking my call," Jon said. "Can I get some time on your calendar to come down and visit you over lunch in the next few days? I have some things I'd like to ask that are off the record."

"Oh hell, sure, my friend," the attorney general replied. "They don't allow me to set my appointments anymore because I fuck 'em up almost every time, so hold a sec, will ya?"

There was a pause, and Jon heard Win through the phone, "Shanice, what do I have going on the rest of the week?"

He came back on.

"Hang on, partner. Let's see what we have," Win said—more waiting.

A few moments passed, and Win was back.

"Okay, Jon, I've got tomorrow afternoon completely free. Want to meet for lunch at Doe's? What do you say?"

"Yeah, that's great," Jon answered. "Thank you so much. I like to ask you some questions about some political stuff, but I'm not gonna lobby you!"

Win chuckled.

"Well, now, a lunch without being lobbied. I guess I'll be buying then! That would be a first. See you tomorrow."

* * *

Jon flew his Cessna to Little Rock the following morning and parked the plane at the Adams Field Fixed Base Operator, or FBO.[9] A courtesy car was available, so he drove to downtown Little Rock and parked near Doe's Eat Place, a local steak house in a 100-year-old rundown brick and stucco building. It was an unassuming eyesore with its chipped stucco exterior that belied the quality of its steaks. The inside was rustic, featuring crowded four-top tables covered with gingham tablecloths served by surly college-aged girls wearing tight jeans and tee shirts. 1970s-era classic rock played loudly in the bustling restaurant.

Jon entered through the commercial glass door, dressed in olive gabardine trousers, brown leather oxfords, and a light blue shirt topped by his trademark waxed canvas jacket. He stood inside the door next to a round table with tickets and an adding machine. An overweight, balding man sat at the table. He did not look up from his numbers.

"Jon, Jon, over here!"

Jon caught sight of Win sitting at the only two-top table shoved in a corner by the ice machine.

"What brings you down here?" Win asked when Jon approached.

As Jon removed his jacket and draped it over his chair, he replied, "I might as well cut to it. I am worried about what will happen after the legislature convenes in January, what with the governor's red-state 'agenda' that we learned about from that meeting in Big Sky, if that was even a thing."

Win leaned forward in his chair, "Oh shit, my friend. It's real."

"The governor isn't fucking around," he continued. "Who knows if she will get everything she wants on that list, which no one has seen since that video leaked. When she returned from that thing in Montana, our Freedom of Information department was overwhelmed with requests for my opinions. Thankfully, and genuinely fucking thankfully, the law does not require me to issue an opinion on something that doesn't exist or hasn't happened legislatively or judicially. But I can tell you this. People are scared. They aren't just scared of the governor, either. They are scared of her supporters."

Jesus, Jon pondered, looking blankly toward the front door.

"Win, you know, I don't believe shit like that could go down in this country.

It always blows over, every time." Jon explained.

"This isn't blowing over, Jon," Win replied. "I have always been a Republican, but I believed all that super right-wing crap was just to get votes. No one took it seriously until Trumpism took over the party. Maybe it was always like that, and the veil has been lifted. But let me tell you, there are some rabid motherfuckers taking office come the new year, and with a supermajority in both legislative chambers, they will be able to do what they want."

"What are you going to do?" Jon asked.

"Honestly, I don't fuckin' know. I mean, while the governor can't legally fire me, I'm sure she'll find a way to get rid of me when she figures out I don't support her agenda. Until then, I'll hang on as long as I can."

After working through their ribeyes, a waitress took away their plates, leaving the two men sipping iced tea. Jon wore a bewildered expression.

Win interrupted Jon's thoughts, "You know, Jon, do you have a plan in case the shit hits the fan?"

"What do you mean, plan?" Jon asked with an eyebrow raised.

Win leaned forward in the rickety wooden chair that squeaked as he shifted his weight and rested his elbows on the table's edge. "Jon, you need to consider getting out of Arkansas if these crazy fuckers accomplish even one-half of what they are after. It won't be safe for you, your husband, or your family. I mean, that list. It may not be policy now, but the governor will stop at nothing to fulfill everything on her agenda. She believes she has a mandate, and the evangelicals preach it at every church service throughout the state. Things could get bad fast, and the courts will be too slow to stop it. Shit, most of the state judges are in her hip pocket. I don't even know that I'll be able to remain in office, especially if the governor asks me to defend some of the laws that could come down the pike."

"Win. I've had my head stuck in the sand about all this for a long time. It is hard to imagine that our court system at the state or federal level will allow this to transpire."

"But Jon, think about what has already happened. Just take the abortion issue as one example. The Supreme Court abandoned 50 years of precedent with the stroke of a pen. Now, abortion is a 'state' issue, and look at what so many states did the minute that decision came down with triggering laws.[10] Recall when the governor said she would consider deploying the National Guard at our borders to detain single women traveling alone long enough to determine if they are pregnant to stop them from going out of state for an abortion? She'll be able to do it now. Think about what that would look like if put into practice. And that is only the beginning!"

"Jesus," Jon muttered. "I remember her speech where she said that, but I never for a moment believed she meant it!"

"Yep, she means it. That woman is a piece of work," Win said. "And the gays? She is coming after the gays, so be prepared!"

"It's just so hard to believe," Jon persisted. "I thought society was finally going to put all that old-school homophobia behind it."

"I had hoped so," Win said, "but evidently not, and it looks like the conditions are there to enable the states to dial back LGBTQ rights by using the protection of public health and safety as the argument to sustain it constitutionally. Just watch for it. Civil rights are going to be a thing of the past."

"Jesus Christ," Jon sighed again.

"Hey, remember studying the *Korematsu* decision in law school?"[11] Win asked.

"I remember it, yeah, about the internment of Japanese people during the Second World War," Jon said.

"You watch, the government will begin to use the same rationale in that opinion to justify all sorts of horrid things, including arresting and detaining people simply because of their orientation or if they claim an identity that is any different than their gender at birth. Instead of using war as a reason, you'll see states declaring LGBTQ people enemies of the state, people who threaten order, public health, and safety."

"I have to admit one thing, Win," Jon said. "Our current US Supreme Court is certainly capable of looking the other way as states begin to ignore the 14th Amendment, and it will do so using that bullshit doctrine of Constitutional Originalism. It's a load of crap!"[12]

Jon checked his watch.

"Hey, Win, I appreciate the time, but I need to return to the airport before it gets too late. Do you mind if we stay in touch about this situation?"

"Let's do that," Win said. "But don't call my office. Use my cell. And don't text my office phone. I wouldn't put it past the governor to monitor my communications. She's ruthless."

Win penned out his cell on a napkin and handed it to Jon. The two shook hands as they parted ways on the street, and Jon headed toward his courtesy car for the drive back to Adams Field, wondering why any politician would put up with this governor's bullshit.

I might fuck all this radical stuff off, hang up the law practice, and move to the ranch for good. But do I want to run away? Or should I fight this? Fuck. Gotta think about this later—time to fly.

The next day and the day after that came and went, as did monotonous news cycles of relative political quiet leading up to the Christmas Holiday and into the New Year. But while most people were recovering from the holiday season, Buckshot Brandy and her political cohorts were busy putting their Big Sky agenda into action through a coordinated frenzy of legislation. The magnitude of the numerous acts she intended to ram through the state assembly would overwhelm the opposition, and there would be no way to stop it.

* * *

On a bitter-cold Friday afternoon in early January 2023, Buckshot sat in the plush drawing room of the Governor's Mansion accompanied by Billy Bob Cadell, the Arkansas Speaker of the House, and Isaac Pennington, the president *pro tempore* of the Arkansas Senate. A half-empty six-pack of Budweiser sat on the coffee table between them.

Buckshot announced beer in hand, "The legislature will begin its general session at noon on Monday. We've got a lot of legislation to pass before the courts get in the way. Are you boys ready?"

"We are," Billy Bob said in a matter-of-fact tone. "We have our bills, and the Senate has its bills. Isn't that right, Isaac?"

The president *pro tempore* of the Senate sat at the table with a grin, slurped his beer, and said, "Yep. The Senate legislation is ready with sponsors lined up, and no one has leaked anything."

"Governor, what about the attorney general? Is he in the loop?" inquired Billy Bob.

She laughed.

"That nosy son of a bitch? Fuck no, that fuckin' lawyer is wise that something is going on, but I've been keeping him under-informed," she said with air quotes.

"Easy on the lawyer bit, Governor," Billy Bob smirked.

"You know what I mean, Billy Bob. I can't trust him, and I can't fire him. He's the only AG we have unless I can get rid of him somehow. Goddamn RHINO. He is a gigantic pussy."

Isaac Pennington, who usually listened more than spoke, spoke up.

"The Senate has the gay, Bible, and state religion bills, even though we're not calling them that. Heaven forbid we hurt anyone's feelings. Billy Bob, you have the abortion bill, the interstate compact bill, the morality bill, and the Medicaid bill. Right?"

"Yep," Billy Bob said, "I have them."

"Can you boys pull this off?" Buckshot asked.

"Oh yes, ma'am, we can," Billy Bob answered. "Isaac and I have this sorted. We'll have to send all these measures to committees, but we'll grease it up like a slick pig beforehand. The committee members know something is coming and that you expect fast action. I've kept the details to myself, but these guys know enough for their imaginations to run wild since that story leaked from your Montana trip. We won't have any Boy Scouts. It'll get done. Don't you worry."

* * *

At 11:59 a.m. on Monday, January 9th, 2023, all 100 Arkansas House of Representatives members were seated at their desks in the Capitol Building in Little Rock. The Speaker stood at the imposing Presider's Chair behind the rostrum. The Great Seal of the State of Arkansas loomed above. At the same time, the 35 Senators were assembled in their chamber at the opposite end of the Capitol Building. Then, as if choreographed, the legislative dance began one minute later at noon as the presiding officers of both chambers called the 94th General Assembly for the State of Arkansas to order.

Modeled after the US Capitol, the Arkansas Capitol Building boasts ten-foot bronze doors that reveal a rotunda adorned in 24-karat gold leaf. On any given day, the marble floors echo the hurried footsteps of legislators, lobbyists, and staffers. However, this day was a spectacle. Like a beehive disturbed at dusk, the chambers emptied at 5 p.m., spilling all 135 representatives and senators into the hallways in an unprecedented tumult after one of the most historic legislative sessions in the state's history.

Elation coursed through the Republicans while the dumbfounded Democrats sought shelter from the metaphorical falling sky. Among them was Hal Ledger, a respected liberal Senator from Fayetteville. As the esteemed figurehead of the Arkansas Democratic Party, Ledger led a tight-knit assembly of what was left of the Arkansas Democrats. Senator Ledger was old and wise, and he had consistently earned the respect of his peers across party lines. However, this session of the General Assembly introduced a slate of novice legislators. This fresh-faced group dismissed tradition, procedures, seniority, and decorum. If you didn't play for their team, you were invisible. The degradation of political norms disgusted the Senator, leading him to the grim conclusion that Arkansas was straying from its better self, especially in light of the legislation introduced in the first session.

"Hal, we need to do something," one of his exasperated Democratic colleagues said while they stood in the rotunda.

"I understand your concerns," Ledger replied. "But the Republicans have a supermajority. They can suspend the rules, and we can't stop them. They will pass bills without debate. I suggest we contact the media and the public to fight them that way. If there ever were an example of the tyranny of the majority, this would be it. Talking to the other side will be a waste of time."

* * *

Jon was monitoring the TV news on Monday as revelations about what was happening in Little Rock blew up his phone. The Arkansas General Assembly had declared war on civil rights. Toward the end of the day, Jon called everyone in the firm to his office to watch the news.

UNBC's Chip Wellon had the most concise coverage that afternoon.

"Today, in what appeared to be a coordinated effort among the leaders of both houses of the Arkansas General Assembly, Republican leaders introduced draconian bills in an unprecedented attack against civil rights not seen since before the Civil War. There's a list of what was introduced in both houses. Let me start with the Senate. There are so many. I'll read them off one by one," Chip reported.

"Arkansas Senate Bills 1-6 target same-sex couples, making their relationships illegal and punishable. SB 1 criminalizes and invalidates same-sex marriages and partnerships, while SB 2 criminalizes anyone who assists in same-sex marriage or partnership. SB 3 resurrects the old sodomy laws and criminalizes same-sex relations and displays of affection. SB 4 awards $5,000 to anyone who identifies prohibited same-sex behavior and proves it in court, and SB 5 adopts the Bible as the supplemental law of Arkansas. Finally, SB 6 designates Christianity as the main religion in Arkansas and establishes a commission to determine authentic Christian denominations."

"Jesus Christ, this is worse than I imagined," Jon said out loud while Chip Wellon continued his broadcast.

"Now, on with the House Bills," Wellon continued. "HB 1 outlaws all abortions, even if performed in another state. It also makes seeking an abortion a capital offense for the woman under certain circumstances. Anyone involved will be subject to the law. HB 2 creates an interstate compact and law enforcement agency that grants broad powers to a new paramilitary police force. The bill will permit member states to police their borders, cross state lines to make arrests, and other alarming measures. HB 3 establishes a commission empowered to pass regulations based on moral considerations, such as suspending professional licenses if someone falls short of its standards. HB 4 eliminates Medicaid in Arkansas. Lastly, HB 5 asserts the legislature is the only competent government body to determine voting regulations, standards, and districts. We learned that it makes election certification an entirely legislative function and replaces all non-partisan county election commissions with gubernatorial appointees instead."

Jon stood up just as the talking heads started to discuss the items Chip had just read on TV. He was angry. The room was silent as the staff, even his brother, Ira, continued watching the newscast in disbelief.

"I'm going home, y'all," Jon stated. "I got no words."

Jon left his office, hoping a short drive down south along the old 71 highway with its curves and hills would clear his head. He called Martin to let him know he would be late.

"You okay, babe?" Martin asked when Jon called.

"I'm okay, yeah," Jon said, "but you should turn on the TV. There is some crazy shit going down. It's terrifying. The legislators in Little Rock have lost it. I need to think it through, but we may need to consider Plan B because Arkansas may not be safe if they pass half the shit I just heard on the news."

Jon was resolved to sleep and wake up with a new perspective when he got home. He was sick of feeling paralyzed and weary of hearing himself complain. He was angry about what was happening to his state and his country, and the evidence was clear from the newscast earlier that day and yesterday's chat with the attorney general that neither he nor Martin would be safe if they remained in Arkansas.

I have some decisions to make soon because the shit is about to hit the fan.

8

The New Law

P
er the governor's wishes, and with a supermajority in both houses, the Arkansas General Assembly quickly passed the Republican-sponsored bills. The bills were returned with a "do pass" recommendation in record time, preventing debate. Governor Suzy Brandy Landers was ready to sign the first set of bills into law within ten days of the 94th General Assembly's opening session.

The governor chose the Governor's Reception Room on the second floor of the Capitol to sign what could become known as the "New Law." The governor planned to sign the first group of bills on live television at the head of an elegant conference table. The stately room was adorned with craftsman-style quarter-sawn oak paneling and carved stone heads of the state's early Native Americans, explorers, and settlers. The room exuded officialdom. The opposite end of the room was cordoned off for reporters and photographers assembled to document the governor's historic signing of the most stringent measures ever imposed on the state's citizens.

The time was 1:00 p.m. on Wednesday, January 18, 2023, and Governor Landers was beaming. The conference room was filled with proud politicians, the leaders of both legislative chambers, and some executive branch members. She also noticed that Attorney General Purcell was absent and whispered to Lieutenant Pettigrew, "Haystack, I need you to call the AG and tell that piece of shit to get his ass over here."

"Yes, ma'am," Lieutenant Pettigrew dutifully replied, and he briskly walked outside, withdrawing his cell phone from his back pocket to make the call.

While they awaited the AG, the governor got up, circulated through the room, and shook hands with dignitaries. Thirty minutes later, Lieutenant Pettigrew reappeared with a sullen-looking General Purcell in tow.

"Glad you could make it, Win! I need you on the team. Everybody, take your places."

The governor's entourage moved aside as she called on the Speaker of the House and Senate president *pro tempore* to assemble behind her chair along with the secretary of state, lieutenant governor, and attorney general.

"Roll it," she said, and red lights on the cameras opposite her lit up.

"Fellow Arkansans," she began, her tone laced with solemnity. "I stand before you today to sign into law ten legislative masterpieces borne out of the 94th Arkansas General Assembly called the New Law. The New Law marks a historic pivot as we return to our foundational Christian principles. We are charting a course to pull Arkansas and this nation from the mire of moral decay, weakness, and discord towards a future where truth and justice are again our guiding stars. We are trailblazers in this endeavor. I am aware that controversy may shadow these measures. Yet, I implore you to remember our shared legacy of resilience. We've endured the Civil War, weathered the Depression, and overcome droughts, recession, inflation, the Spanish Flu, and Covid-19. Each challenge has only bolstered our unity and resolve."

"Embracing this legislation may be demanding for some, but remember that the right path is often hard. Rest assured, not all of these bills will come into effect instantly. But let me tell you, this is a monumental stride toward our shared dreams because we must end the cultural divide that has riven our state and nation. I assure you, these bills, and others in the pipeline, will restore our alignment and unify us under our God, our flag, and our country. So, without further ado, let us march forth on this journey of renewal."

On cue, a page walked in through the door with a stack of ten red leather portfolios, each bearing the state seal. She placed them on a side table that was next to Governor Landers. There was a golden fountain pen nestled in each portfolio. The page, an attractive blond of about 20 years, wore a red dress that matched the folders and the governor's boots. The page handed Governor Landers the first portfolio. She opened it, withdrew the pen, and continued her remarks just before she affixed her signature.

"Arkansas passed SB 1, the Marriage Restoration Act, which aims to invalidate all same-sex marriages and domestic partnerships retroactively. The bill requires same-sex couples to apply for a court order to dissolve their marriages within 90 days, and it becomes a felony offense to remain married afterward.

She signed the document with bright red ink. After she signed it, she called out, "Reverend Lawrence, get your hiney over here!"

Pastor Lawrence Lee Huckabee's distinguishing middle-aged feature was a grill of oversized fluorescent-white chiclet teeth bared in a grin so wide you could count his teeth from across the room. Wearing his best ultra-black Giorgio Armani double-breasted suit and matching purple suede shoes, he hugged the governor and smiled for the cameras as she handed him the pen she used to destroy the marriages of thousands of gay and lesbian Arkansans.

"God bless you, Governor. God bless you," gushed the pastor.

"It wouldn't have happened without your help, prayer, and guidance, Cousin," oozed the governor.

Pastor Lawrence and his chiclets withdrew toward the wall behind her. Next were the rest of the anti-LGBTQ bills.

"The next three bills will ensure Arkansas will not be burdened with the scourge of homosexuality," she said. "SB 2 criminalizes same-sex marriage and anyone assisting in obtaining one, whether performed in or out of the state. SB 3 makes any same-sex activities illegal, which includes public displays of affection. SB 4 allows any person to sue and collect $5,000 from an individual if they prove illegal same-sex behavior. The bill also allows an individual to sue anyone facilitating illegal homosexual activities. These bills address the serious threat to Arkansans' public health and safety, so they have emergency clauses and take effect immediately."

She smiled as she handed out the golden pens, one to another pastor, one to an Arkansas State Senator, and another to an Arkansas House Member.

"Next in the lineup is SB 5, my personal favorite. Let me explain why. SB 5 adopts the Holy Bible as supplemental law. Among the Right, we often discuss our nation's foundation in fundamental Judeo-Christian values because our core values are rooted in the Bible. Arkansas is now proudly taking action to uphold these principles. I am confident that other states will follow our lead, and I'm honored that we are the first state to implement this. The Good Book has earned its name for a reason, and because he taught me those reasons, I will present this pen as a token of my pride to my father, a pastor and former governor of this state. This bill will go into effect on Easter Sunday this year, which seems fitting, don't ya think?"

The red ink flowed as Michael Shelton Cotton approached for his golden pen.

"God bless you, Daughter!" He blurted out as he reached down for a hug. "What a day this is! I am so gosh darned proud of you!"

"Love you, Papa!" the governor proclaimed with a toothy grin.

* * *

While watching the spectacle, Martin called Jon's cell just as Governor Landers hugged her dad. Jon picked up as he stepped back into the office from his noon-day walk.

"Hey, babe, have you seen the news?" Martin asked.

"Hi, no, I haven't. My walk went a little long today. I went all the way up Mount Sequoyah and around. What's up?" Jon asked.

"Oh Jesus," Martin said, his voice shaking. "You need to turn on the TV. The governor is signing a bunch of bills into law, including one that makes our marriage illegal and a bunch of other wicked shit. It's terrible. The state is forcing us to divorce! Hang up, run to your office, and turn on the TV. Call me later, okay?"

"Hang on, babe," Jon said calmly, "no one will force us apart. Ever! I love you, okay? I'm gonna run up and turn the TV on. I'll call later."

* * *

When Jon turned on the set in his office, Buckshot was into her second batch of bills.

"Okay, everyone, on to the House bills," the governor continued.

"HB 1 signifies an unparalleled landmark in the journey for the right to life. A law for the ages, it encapsulates a principle as old as the scriptures themselves: the sanctity of life from conception. The bill prohibits abortion, the act of terminating a pregnancy by any means, or facilitating access to such procedures in any way. The penalties for an abortion may include capital punishment for those sinful baby killers. This bill also acts to safeguard life by outlawing any forms of contraception. The Good Book commands us to go forth and multiply, and we must fulfill that mission. Possession of contraceptive devices or medicines or facilitating access to such is now a crime."

The red ink streamed again. She handed the pen off to firebrand right-to-life advocate Cynthia Keller.

"HB 2," she announced with a flair. "This bill joins us in an interstate compact with other member states to cooperate in law enforcement efforts and investigate and prosecute across state lines. It is called the "Red State Compact," and it will streamline extradition procedures. We are the first to implement it, but other states in the compact will join soon. This new law will help us prevent women from obtaining illegal abortions. If there was ever an emergency, this is it. We will stop the baby killin' and arrest those people wherever we can find 'em!"

She signed and handed the golden pen to the Arkansas Director of Public Safety.

"HB 3," she continued, "will establish a commission and tribunal to regulate and adjudicate moral wrongs and crimes. The commission will have various regulatory powers, and the tribunal will possess judicial and enforcement powers. For example, the commission will specify standards of moral fitness and other qualifications for persons seeking state badges, licenses, or public office, among others. So, gentlemen, keep your drawers pulled up, and ladies, watch what you do with those panties! This bill won't take effect until Monday, May 1. Law Day."

More red ink. She handed the golden pen off to Tom Hardy Blasingame, a balding, short, and chubby right-wing representative from Conway who would become the tribunal's first chief judge. His pasty white face wore a self-righteous smile. For a long time, he was one of the loudest voices advocating these measures in the days before anyone listened. Finally, his day had arrived.

"HB 4. Part of being a Christian nation is self-sufficiency," the governor said. "That means that we are ending government hand-outs and entitlements. Part of our Christian ethic relies on rugged individualism. People must learn to care for themselves and not wait for the government to intervene. Therefore, this bill will bring an end to Medicaid in Arkansas. It won't take effect immediately to give hospitals, nursing homes, and doctors time to adjust. So, for the folks afraid they can't afford doctors, they have until Labor Day this year to find a job."

* * *

Jesus, this woman is off-the-fucking-chart crazy. This is unbelievable.

Jon was so angry that he shut off the TV after the governor handed the ceremonial pen to the Arkansas Secretary for the Department of Health, Lauren Goforth. Secretary Goforth struggled to maintain a smile, looking like someone had just shot her dog. She had recently gone to California for a clandestine abortion, knowing it must remain hidden at the risk of losing her life.

Thoroughly disgusted, Jon knew he must turn to other things to get his mind off the absurdity and horror of what he had just witnessed.

* * *

On screens across the nation, Governor Landers continued her commentary.

"My fellow Arkansans, last but not least is HB 5, the Independent Legislature Bill. The bill will ensure proper and fair elections in the future. And no offense to you, Mr. Secretary of State, but it will transfer the power of the secretary of state to certify elections to the legislature. The legislature will be the only authority in the state competent to certify elections and fix voting districts and precincts. In short, the people's elected representatives will be the sole judge of all election issues in the State of Arkansas. Those election shenanigans we saw in the last presidential election will never happen again. And I point out, incidentally, that this same law will be uniform among the other states joining the compact. It is a great day for democracy, my friends. A great day!"

Ironically, the governor handed the final golden pen off to her secretary of state and said, as she did, "Don't worry, Greg, we have plenty of things for you to do!"

When the governor was conducting her presser, an angry mob had assembled at the Capitol Building steps leading up to its bronze doors, and the racket distracted her. Above the din, one could pick out a few phrases, like "Death to Buckshot!" "Fascist pigs!" "Fuck you, Buckshot, Fuck you!" "My body, my choice!" "No hate, no fear, everyone is welcome here!"

The governor paused her commentary and walked over to the windows, looking down on the angry mob. Some of the other politicians in the room joined her to take a look.

"Y'all would think they could be more creative than that," Governor Landers howled. "That group of folks is just a bunch of woke pussies."

The Speaker of the House, Billy Bob Cadell, walked up behind her and said, "Show them who's boss, Governor!"

A handful of other legislators in the room overheard the Speaker's comment, nodded in agreement, and some shook their heads.

"Hopefully," the governor proclaimed, "they will haul their sorry asses out of this state before we round them up. We should arrest them all, try them for treason, or shoot 'em. Law and order must prevail in Arkansas, goddammit!"

As she said so, an aide approached the governor and whispered, "Madam Governor, you are still live on camera."

She gave the aide a frown and glanced back at the cameras.

"Okay, let's cut those cameras off. We have a situation!"

Then she hollered, "Haystack, Haystack!"

Lieutenant Pettigrew had come to despise her as he looked out the window, watching the gaggle chanting while trying to suppress his sign of disgust for his boss.

He turned toward her.

"Yes, ma'am?"

She glared at him.

"Go grab the Director of Public Safety before he leaves and have him send the Capitol Police over to round up those butt nuggets down there. Tell him I'm authorizing him to use whatever force is necessary to shut that shit down. Summon the State Police to assist while you're at it. Get them to clean off the front porch of this sacred building and lock those assholes up or shoot 'em. I don't give a damn how y'all do it. Just do it now!"

Winston Purcell smiled to himself because his phone had been running on audio recording the whole time he was in the reception room, and this last bit was a gold mine since the cameras were shut off.

Little Rock wasn't the only scene of protests. Various groups assembled around town squares and at courthouses throughout Arkansas to protest the New Law. Teenagers, college students, individuals from the LGBTQ community, African Americans, Hispanics, and women of all ages gathered. In most parts of the state, the demonstrations were organized and peaceful, but the scene at the Capitol was beginning to heat up.

The Capitol and State Police assembled with black helmets, shields, and batons while a well-armed contingent of a state militia called The Blade and Shield joined to counter-protest. There were 13 young to middle-aged white men carrying AR-15 rifles and their belief in Jesus. Despite their below-average IQs, they were well-organized and disciplined as they positioned themselves to face off with the protesters.

The crowd grew uneasy, and some went silent. Others refused to step back and continued shouting and marching further up the Capitol stairs. The militia group advanced toward the Capitol rioters and began yelling back.

"Go home, faggots!"

"You will not replace us!"

"Get the fuck out of Arkansas."

"Blood and soil, blood and soil!"

The militia leader, a morbidly obese bearded white man dressed in a khaki long-sleeved shirt beneath a black leather biker vest, turned toward his men and yelled orders. Their chants stopped, and they started backing away from the protestors.

Six men from one end stepped back and assumed positions behind the first row, forming two rows, and each row fixed bayonets to their assault rifles in unison. Buckshot watched the scene gleefully from her window in the Capitol building.

They are squaring off!

"I think that fat bearded guy aims to open fire on those hippies," Buckshot said aloud.

"Holy shit, that is rich!" she broke out above the commotion in the conference room, declaring, "Well, would you look at that fat son-of-a-bitch down there," referring to the Blade and Shield leader.

She turned to Lieutenant Pettigrew. "Haystack, do you have the scene commander on the radio?"

"Yes, ma'am," he replied, reaching for his walkie to switch channels.

"Give me the goddamn radio!" the governor commanded.

Lieutenant Pettigrew handed it to her.

She keyed the mic, "Yessir, lookie here, what's your name? Captain Joe Mallett? Right, Captain Mallett, this is Governor Landers. Listen, pull your officers back. Do you see that group of redneck boys across from you? Yeah, yeah, those guys. Get out of their way right now, goddammit. I think they are going to do your dirty work for ya."

There was a pause on the other end.

"Right now, Captain Mallett, or do I have to come down there and order this myself?" she yelled, thrusting the walkie back at Lieutenant Pettigrew.

Below, the Capitol and State Police contingent began backing away. The governor watched intently as Captain Mallett walked away from the dispersing officers and approached the Blade and Shield leader. She saw the two men speaking and reached toward Lieutenant Pettigrew again.

"Haystack," the governor ordered, "call Captain Mallett and tell him on a direct order by me that he is to deputize those rednecks into the Arkansas State Police right now. Do it!"

Lieutenant Pettigrew radioed the captain while the governor watched Mallett pick up his walkie again. He listened, then he put it down and shook the hand of the leader.

By now, there was a group of two or three hundred protesters raising hell at the front steps of the Capitol. One of them turned his bullhorn toward the retreating police, yelling, "Hey, fuck off, pigs! Cowards! We should have defunded you!" At that second, the Blade and Shield formation stepped forward and opened fire on the crowd of protesters, and every bullet found its mark. Twelve protesters, including the man with the bullhorn, lay sprawled and bleeding on the ground.

Pandemonium. The crowd panicked, and people ran across the Capitol lawn in all directions.

"Son of a bitch, look at those fuckers run!" the governor cheered.

About 20 protesters who lacked common sense rushed the Blade and Shield formation. The governor was beside herself as the Blade and Shield unleashed a hailstorm of automatic rifle fire to repel them while the State Police stood by with their weapons on safe.

As the last protester dropped, the Blade and Shield leader yelled, "CEASE FIRE, CEASE FIRE, CEASE FIRE! RELOAD AND STAND READY!"

Captain Mallett returned to the Blade and Shield leader while a thin layer of smoke drifted skyward. The two exchanged words and shook hands once again. The remaining militia was withdrawing, and Captain Mallett greeted the first line of ambulances and fire trucks that arrived to treat the injured and haul away the dead. As the governor observed the scene below, she beckoned to Lieutenant Pettigrew again.

"Haystack," she declared, "we're safe to go out the traditional way: right through the goddamned front door. I'm not going to sneak out of my own Capitol. Plus, I want to shake the hand of that redneck who took care of business. Now, that's what I'm talkin' about!"

* * *

Jon had left his office to walk off his outrage from the governor's press conference before she had finished her remarks. He walked until he found himself at a flash mob gathering steam at the old post office, a 100-year-old brick building at the center of the town square. He wasn't keen on protests, but his patience with himself and the situation was exhausted, and he was angry.

Time for doing. No more Mister Nice Guy.

Blood flowed on the Capitol steps in Little Rock while Jon, unaware of what was happening, picked his way through the crowd, listening to a local hippie carry on about the evils of the Right. The guy ranted about defunding the police, then launched into how the "man" was destroying the earth. At least whoever organized this mob had the presence of mind to set up a proper microphone instead of resorting to a bullhorn, but the choice of a speaker was lacking.

I am sick of these woke mother fuckers, too. I understand why the Right hates them so much—coming across as though they are more intelligent and better than the rest of us and trying to impose their values on us. I have no use for entitled whiners who don't have a goddamn clue about how the world works and aren't willing to roll up their sleeves and work for anything. I have had it!

Losing his patience, he was compelled by a desire to speak. Jon pushed himself through the crowd and approached the long-haired idiot at the microphone, "Hey, Chief, mind if I borrow that?"

Jon patted Dude on the shoulder and took the microphone. Peering at the crowd through his black horn-rimmed glasses, he searched his furious mind for the words, judging the group as best he could, and thought about what he had to say.

"Hey, y'all, can I have your attention for a second?" Jon asked.

Miraculously, the crowd settled down.

"Here, y'all come up a little closer. Listen up. Many faces here are familiar, some clients, some friends. Regardless of our previous encounters, we must stand united against today's assault on our democracy in Little Rock. This isn't an isolated event but the harbinger of a foreboding era. This turn of events defies comprehension. Protests and fury will surge, but Arkansas has penned an ominous list that labels many of us as endangered or criminal. As night descends, lawyers like me will feel an instinctive urge to retaliate with lawsuits to stop this gross violation of our Constitution. Unjust, inequitable, unconstitutional, un-American, illegal – that's what this is. But I implore you to understand that our salvation doesn't lie solely in the hands of lawyers or courts. Legal battles can hinder this onslaught, but they merely delay an inevitable encroachment on our liberties. I hope today's events ignite within us a realization that rhetoric, attending rallies, or boasting about our progressive stances are not enough. Our situation calls for action. We must rise to the challenge."

"Do any of you believe the federal government will come to rescue this situation? Do you?" Jon pleaded.

The crowd roared, "No!"

"Do you think carrying on about fairness will change the people's minds behind these things without action?

"No!"

"Here's the more difficult question," Jon continued. "Do you believe defunding the police, bitching about global warming, or raging about identity politics will make one goddamn difference or change any minds?"

At that, the crowd was silent, and waiting for the pregnant pause, he said, "Well, do you? We can protest and raise hell, but to what end if we don't back it up with action? We can complain about pronouns, equal rights, a woman's right to choose, marriage equality, trans rights, or why we eat too much meat. But do you really believe that mere complaining will change anything? Trust me when I tell you, it won't change a goddamned thing."

He felt his rage accelerating even though he remained unaware of the developments on the Capitol lawn in Little Rock.

"If you're comfortably labeling yourself as liberal, progressive, or 'woke,' it's high time you moved past that self-congratulatory stage. This is about survival now. It's about each one of us scrutinizing the missteps that have led to half of our country standing in opposition to us. A reckoning is coming, and idle pondering won't suffice. I don't know about you, but to rise to this challenge, we must foster unity among everyone targeted by the New Law. Unity is not rooted in mere rhetoric but in tangible action. Without it, we're nothing more than a pack of toothless dogs."

Jon's voice crackled with ire.

"Our first line of defense is women, particularly single, child-bearing age women, as they sit in the crosshairs of this administration. Consider those who don't conform to evangelical Christianity, people of color, immigrants, and LGBTQ community members. I'm undoubtedly missing others, but we must identify them! Please bring them to the table! If living under the shadow of an Orwellian police state isn't your idea of 'freedom,' we must collectively find our voice."

Someone yelled out, "Man, you sound like a conservative!"

"Oh, come off it," Jon yelled back. "Think about it. Differences of opinion are luxuries. The mistakes of the past must not be our future. Commit these names to memory: Ralph Nader, Bernie Sanders, Jill Stein. Their ego-driven crusades fragmented us at our most critical juncture, birthing a virulent hostility against the Left. Those who supported them were as naive and guilty of this bleak reality as those perpetrating it. Liberals have honed the art of circular firing squads when our aim should be singularly directed at our true adversary. So, gather your strength, set aside your differences, and get ready to fight!"

He heard some boos but continued undeterred.

"Boo all you want, but don't be a dumbass. Shelve your ideologies in exchange for the compromise required to speak with a unified voice that will inspire a singularity of action. If you fail to come together now, I promise you that the country you love so much will cease to exist. Why do you think the Right has been beating our collective ass in almost every election? It is because they are unified, and we are not. It's really that simple."

After briefly pausing to take a breath, Jon continued his speech.

"Look, Liberals and Progressives can't agree on much. We are perpetually fragmented. We are always willing to sacrifice the greater good for an unobtainable ideological purity that will never pass because we cannot act as one. And, sad to say, we lose because we play by the rules. As much as I love the rules, we may have to break some if we expect to make a difference. I'm not talking about mere civil disobedience. I am talking about real sacrifice, and some of you will eventually have to fight these assholes if we cannot stop the flow of fascist ideas from taking root. So, for now, I say this: No more peaceful rallies. Forget pacifism. Arm yourselves. Get organized because if you don't, our state and country will be unrecognizable in months, if not weeks."

There was a quiet moment, and someone yelled out.

"What next?"

Jon replied, "That's a great question, and I have an idea. You'll continue this rally all you want, but when it is over, let's get a group together starting today and plan. I mean, each interest group, whatever it is, whoever it is, should appoint one person to represent its interests, and then we need those people to get together, have a meeting, and decide on how to deal with what we have learned today. Can you do that? Let's see about meeting at the Town Center at 7:00 p.m. tomorrow. There must be a unified movement with real leadership and a willingness to sacrifice. There are leaders among you. I know it!"

Jon motioned to the hippie he took the microphone from and returned it, then stepped down from the podium. He didn't make it far before the crowd was gathering around him. Jon motioned to the assortment of people wanting to talk to him to follow him off to the side while the stoned crier and his dreadlocks resumed his nonsense.

As people collected, he sat on a bench to talk when his phone displayed a news alert. As his phone illuminated, he heard several other phones of the people standing there emit similar alarms. News of the Little Rock massacre had arrived.

9

Lawyers

"Where the hell have you been?"

Martin was frantic when Jon walked through the front doors of Highland House at nearly 6 p.m.

"I've been watching the news," Martin said. "Militia shot a bunch of protesters down in Little Rock, and the police just stood by and watched."

Jon hugged Martin, "Yeah, I heard. I'm scared, but we can't panic. We must plan. This state has become dangerous. We might need to get the fuck out of here."

Just then, Martin caught a TNN report with a video of Jon giving his speech at the protest from not an hour before.

"Holy shit, babe! Look at you! What in the world possessed you to go to the rally?" Martin asked in a state of surprise.

"I'm not sure, honestly," Jon said. "I just got pissed off. I'm tired of hearing Liberals and Democrats complain about how messed up everything is and then doing nothing about it. There's no leadership. All talk, no action. And now, this New Law. We earned this by sitting on our hands. I couldn't stand being part of the problem any longer and had to speak up."

"Let's listen to this," Martin interrupted, reaching for the remote to turn up the volume on the TV.

The anchor played Jon's comments at the Fayetteville protest. After the local reporter finished his segment, the anchor brought on three other

84

guests for a panel discussion.

"The gentleman is a courtroom lawyer from Fayetteville. His name is Jonathan Christian Freeman. His firm has been a fixture there for a long time. He served in the US Army after college before becoming a lawyer. He doesn't have an active political record but has given money to mostly Democratic and Independent causes. But his comments, boiling them down, suggest that the Left should take up arms. I don't know about all of you on the panel, but I have to say I empathize with where he is coming from. But let's hear from the panel."

Miriam Logan was the first panelist to speak up. She was the former chief of staff to Alexandria Ocasio-Cortez, the progressive house representative from New York's 14th Congressional District.

"Seriously, this guy sounds as bad as the Right! And then to blame third-party candidates for losing three presidential elections? That's rich!"

"Miriam, you're missing his point," interjected Reggie Boyer, a reporter for the *Washington Post*. "Maybe his frankness is a 'trigger' for you? I get his point. He's sharing a common frustration Centrists have had for years, that the Left is too over the top to affect real policy change. You must admit that the Left has boxed itself in with its focus on identity politics, putting itself on the fringe. It doesn't make them wrong. It just doesn't win elections. How do you think the Democrats managed to alienate the working class?"

"I have to agree with Reggie on this," said Raj Patel, a panelist from the Democratic National Committee. "Democrats have been wringing our hands for too long, it seems, and this guy is giving a voice to a very frustrated Middle. Look what has happened in the last few election cycles. We have managed to alienate working-class America. Obviously, our message has not resonated, so I'm with Mr. Freeman on this, Miriam. You guys on the Left should take a chapter out of his book and relearn how to connect with the common people."

Jon's s cell phone buzzed. It was Tiny.

"Jesus, dude, what were you thinking getting on TV like that? They're going to be coming after you! It sounds like you might as well have challenged the governor to a duel!"

THE LAST INDEPENDENCE DAY

"Good to hear from you too, dude. I don't know. I wasn't thinking. Hell, I didn't see any cameras there. I'm just sick and tired of all this bullshit, and I won't sit back and do nothing anymore."

"Hell, meet me down at the Pub later. What do you say? Let's talk it out," Tiny suggested.

"Yeah, I'd like that, but I need to talk with Martin first. Let me call you back."

"You got it, Boss!" Tiny replied.

Jon terminated the call.

"So, babe, what about us," Martin asked, ignoring the television. "What should we do? I don't know about you, but I'm fuckin' scared, and I'm pissed at those assholes."

"I think we need to make some plans to get you and our stuff out to the Valle Grande until we figure out what will happen here," Jon suggested. "Is that cool with you? I'll feel a lot better knowing you're safe."

"You talk as if you're not coming if that's what we do," Martin said nervously.

"No," Jon said, "I'll come out there, of course, but I'm not going to do what I just accused a bunch of people of doing by talking shit and doing nothing. I must do something!"

At about the same time, Martin's phone went off. It was his dad, Butch.

"Son, your other half might have let his mouth overload his ass even if I agree with everything he said!"

"I know," Martin replied. "He's always so even, but he told me he just lost his shit about everything. And honestly, I don't blame him. It's like he is too controlled all the time. Until he's not, and this is when he's not."

"Well," Butch continued, "I don't know about all this stuff, son, but I saw the governor's speech, and she aims to make you two criminals along with many other folks. If you need to hide out, get your ass down here, and bring Jon with you. No one fucks with me here on the mountain, you know that."

"Yeah, Dad, I appreciate it," Martin answered. "I'll see what Jon wants to do. He wants to get us to that ranch he runs in New Mexico. I don't want to leave you or Mom, but I don't know if we have a choice. I think they are going to come after us. How the fuck could this happen?"

"Son, those redneck politicians finally got what they wanted. Trust me. I know a bunch of 'em from down this way. Nice to your face, but they've been biding their time for a while now. Anyway, let me know what you decide, okay? The door is always open."

More calls, but one thing was sure by the end of the day. Martin decided to go to the ranch, even though leaving his family behind would be the most challenging thing he'd ever do. Jon grieved moving Martin to the ranch because he knew how much Martin hated being away from his family, and ranch life wasn't Martin's cup of tea. At least the Valle Grande staff would be there at his beck and call, and he would be safe and could be as busy or idle as he chose to be.

The following morning, they hopped in the Cessna 182 and hauled ass to New Mexico.

* * *

It was a windy landing for the fully loaded Cessna on January 19, 2023, and the Little Rock massacre already seemed a hundred years ago. Chee loaded up Martin and his things when they landed while Jon refueled the airplane.

Jon told Chee, "Tell Sam I'll return in a few days."

"What? Hosteen? You're not staying?"

"I can't stay right now. Martin will tell you all about what we've decided."

Chee closed the back of the Range Rover as Jon hugged Martin tightly.

"Don't worry, babe," Jon assured. "I won't be long. Give me a few days, and then I'll be back out here."

"Do what you gotta do, babe," Martin said. "Just be safe, okay? And if you happen to have to shoot one of those fuckheads, take one out for me!"

At 12:13 p.m., Jon and his Cessna lifted off for the five-and-a-half-hour flight back to Arkansas.

* * *

Jon huddled with his brother at his office early the following morning. It was Friday, January 20.

"I'm going to have to take some time off from the practice," Jon said with a look of regret and concern.

His brother, who had a penchant for being a comedian, reclined in his chair with his legs crossed and a furrowed brow as he listened to Jon.

"With the laws that came down, that goddamned governor is going to try to round up people like Martin and me," Jon continued. "I've already flown him to New Mexico because he'll be safe there. But I returned because I won't cut and run without a fight. I'll be lucky to have a law license if they follow through with the commission and tribunal the New Law established. I'm sure they'll strip all the gays of their professional licenses the first chance they get. That's if they don't try to round me up and put me in jail first."

"It's unbelievable," Ira said, "but whatever you need, name it. The Colonel and I will be here, but we need to discuss our financial arrangement because we'll have to contract out the litigation since you won't be around."

Jon knew the "money" discussion would come sooner or later.

"I understand," Jon said, "let's make some time to discuss it soon."

"That's fine," Ira said, "but we can't put it off for too long. We're bleeding money. And what about you? How are you getting by without taking a draw? You haven't taken any money from the office in weeks."

"I've been getting by on my trustee fees with the ranch," Jon replied, "so I'm covered. I think I can make it on the trustee fees, so if you need to take me off the payroll here, so be it. I know that remaining here may not be an option for me with all that is happening."

Ira sighed with resignation.

"Well, Little Brother, you gotta do what you gotta do. We'll make it work. We sure have before."

"Yep," Jon replied. "Why don't I call you if I get in a jam? Until then, the ranch fees will cover me. I know the firm needs the cash flow."

"Okay, but let me know if you need anything!"

Next, Jon walked up the ornate wooden staircase and down the hall to call on a handful of his lawyer buddies to meet him for lunch. He also placed a call to Win Purcell.

It surprised him that Win answered on the second ring.

"I wondered how long it would be until you called me," Win said when he answered. "I'm surprised you didn't call sooner, but holy shit, you made the news! Jesus, dude, I envy your style, but you are a marked man."

Jon conceded, saying, "Oh yes, I'm beginning to figure that out. So, Win, I don't have much time. I'm calling because I need a favor. I can't find the actual text of the bills the governor signed, but I. . ."

Cutting him off, Win said, "One step ahead of you. I have them and can email them to you, but they will arrive from a phantom email, so they can't be traced to me. It will be later today before I can do that. Also, I have some audio I'd like to send you from some off-camera comments the governor made just before those people were shot at the Capitol. Do you have an address you'd like me to send it to?"

"Send everything to my work email," Jon suggested. "And Win, we will be filing suits this coming Monday morning on every single one of those goddamn bills Buckshot signed into law. Thought you should hear it from me."

"Oh, again, one step ahead of you," Win said. "I knew before she touched her fucking red pen to those bills that lawyers somewhere would be lining up. The word on the street is that most of the lawyers in Little Rock are running scared and don't want to be on the wrong side of the governor. Certainly, the big firms won't have anything to do with it, especially since at least half of them helped draft the legislation she just passed. One thing is for sure, that bitch made quite a point when she let those rednecks shoot those protesters at the Capitol. Everybody knows it was her order that got those dumbasses shot. That woman is a fuckin' monster, let there be no doubt. And here I thought you were too smart to get involved with this stuff."

"Well, Win," Jon said plainly, "I think I'm fresh out of fucks to give, and I'm a slow learner. But you, what about you?"

"I don't know what I will do. I'll wait to see the petitions you file. I wouldn't put it past Buckshot to try and take me out, so I'm watching my back. I may not be the attorney general for much longer, but one step at a time. Let's see what you file. I'm sticking it out for now."

"I don't envy you," Jon said. "Whatever happens, you'll have a friend up here in Fayetteville."

After finishing his call, Jon hastily grabbed his jacket. He left his office to head to City Hall for a meeting with the mayor to continue organizing Fayetteville's activist community.

After a surprisingly productive meeting at City Hall with about a dozen community leaders and activists, Jon left the mayor's office satisfied that he'd convinced the diverse interest groups to begin coordinating, building unity, and planning for multiple scenarios. Part of it hinged on convincing the local liberals that the Second Amendment applied to them. They needed to arm themselves for what was surely coming.

Later, Jon and five other local lawyers dined together at the Fayetteville Country Club in a conference room. The food up there was marginal, but the room was private and offered a view of the bucolic 9th tee and the rolling fairway beyond.

Jon asked the group between bites of his hamburger, "Okay, can we get temporary injunctions filed Monday on parallel state and federal tracks?"

The lawyers looked around, across at one another, and then back to Jon.

"We can do it, yeah," said Paul Joseph, a long-time friend of Jon's, "but I think we'll have to choose—state or federal."

"Let's go with the state first," Jon suggested, "because that's right here in our backyard with judges we know. Will you take the lead on it?"

"Sure, I got it," Paul replied.

"Everyone good with that?" Jon asked. "I'll be there when you're ready for the hearings, and you'll have my full support. I have some money set aside in a slush fund from my ranching interests, and I'll funnel some of that to you guys. You all still have to eat. It wouldn't hurt if you could figure out how to raise some funds, too. There's a lot at stake here. For all it can do, I'll transfer $50,000.00 to Paul for you all to defray your expenses. You'll need it. If it helps, I'll match whatever you all can raise dollar for dollar to another $50,000.00."

"Jesus, Jon, where the hell is that money coming from?" asked Paul.

Jon replied, "My trustee fees for the ranch work are pretty rich. I can't think of a better use for some of it than to help fund a fight against the governor and her henchmen. I will have advance copies of the New Law by the end of the day to send you, too."

Jon's mind was also on the money, his firm, and the Colonel.

I should resign entirely from the firm. Fuck. It will upset the Colonel and all that work over 30 years. Gone. Goddammit!

Jon left the meeting and drove down from Country Club Hill back to his office to make more calls, but instead of getting back on the phone, he reclined in his office chair and turned on the news.

God damn, that woman signed two more bills into law!

HB 6 and SB 6. He listened to the broadcast more than watching it as the local news anchor described the new laws.

"Governor Landers signed two more bills into law, House Bill 6 and Senate Bill 6. House Bill 6 follows the same religious themes we learned on the 18th. The governor called it the Free Exercise Law. It allows persons of sincere religious belief, so long as the religion is, as the bill terms it, authentic, to withhold service to anyone in any public business, professional service, or government. Senate Bill 6, on the other hand, follows up with the anti-gay marriage law she signed, except this bill makes interracial marriage illegal."

That woman is relentless. We need to get some suits filed and start this fight.

* * *

It was dark out when Jon returned to Highland House Friday evening. The house was like a crypt.

How long would it be until the governor comes for me?

Jon called the ranch. Chee picked up.

"Curtis, it's Jon."

"Hosteen. Good to hear from you. Do you want me to put Martin on the phone?"

"In just a second, sure. Tell me something, though. How are things out there? How's Martin settling in?"

"Things are just like you left them, Hosteen. Everything is great. I mean, all of us here are worried about you. We know what's happening in Arkansas and are anxious about your safety, but Martin seems right at home."

"Go ahead and put him on if you can find him."

"Sure thing, Hosteen. Give me a second, and I'll get him for you."

The call went on hold for a moment.

"Hey, Sweetheart," Martin said when he picked up.

"Hey there. How are you? It feels like a century since I saw you, even though it has been a day since I dropped you off."

"Everything's fine here, babe. Chee and Chef are great and have been showing me around. Even Carl called to check on me. I think he will come up tomorrow and take me shooting."

"Shooting? You're kidding!"

Jon was shocked.

"Seriously. I've had just a little time to think about everything, and I want to fight those fuckers who want to take away our marriage or make us criminals. I want to hurt them for trying to hurt you, me, and people like us. It's so fucking wrong. I cannot even tell you how angry I am about it. I guess I've become like you. I don't want to sit and do nothing."

"Well," Jon allowed, "besides me, you couldn't find a better firearms instructor than Brother Carl. You'll enjoy the range up there. There's one thing about shooting, too. You can express all your stress and anxiety out of the smoking end of that barrel, then leave it behind."

"Yep, I hope so. How long do you think it will be until you can return?" Martin asked.

"I'll need a few days here, but not much more. I'll resign from the firm, but my brother and I are working that out. I've also organized some lawyers to file legal challenges to the New Law. And hey, you'll never believe this, but I've also gotten some of the community leaders together. Among them is a group of drag queens and trans people who want to do more than protest. They want to fight. So I'm organizing some firearms training for them.

Some used to be a part of the Sisters of Perpetual Indulgence, but this group will be strictly off the books. They are a bunch of bad bitches!"

"Holy shit, that's awesome," Martin said with a smile. "Is it alright if I share this news with Carl? He'll love it!"

"Yeah, go for it," Jon said. "I'll probably ask him to come out here and work with some of them when it's safe. Anyway, babe, I'm gonna try and wind down. It's already dark, and I plan to try and get some sleep tonight so I can get some legal challenges set up to file before Monday. After that, I'll be flying back out to you. Hug the dogs for me!"

* * *

Over a long weekend, Jon and his team of lawyers gathered together and crafted a mammoth lawsuit against the governor and the state to stop the New Law from going into effect.

Promptly on Monday morning, January 23, 2023, they presented the lawsuit to the circuit court and requested an emergency temporary restraining order against the New Law. The judge, Michael Lynell Taylor, granted the temporary injunction, but she insisted it was only temporary.

Jon's team had won the first battle in what would likely be a prolonged war. The next battle would be hearings to take evidence. The judge set hearings over two days so Jon's team could present evidence and allow the state to raise its defenses. She scheduled the evidentiary hearings for February 13th and 14th. Once that was done, she would hear arguments on Monday, March 6, 2023, and decide whether to make the injunction permanent at that time. Meanwhile, Jon was content that he had done his part, so he flew back to the ranch to wait it out until it was time to come back for the decision.

10

Justice Delayed

J ustice moves slowly.

On a blustery Monday morning, March 6th, 2023, Jon and his lawyers filed out of the elevator on the 4th floor of the Washington County Courthouse and walked to the Second Division Court Room. They were early, but the bailiff was waiting and ushered them directly into the courtroom.

Jon and his entourage of suits passed through the swinging gate to enter the well. Jon sat at the counsel table with Paul Joseph, and the other lawyers walked around and took empty seats in the jury box. Just as the rest of the team sat down, the attorney general walked in with an assistant.

"Morning, Jon," Winston Purcell said with a nod. "And Mr. Joseph, good morning to you, sir."

Jon returned the Win's nod but said nothing.

"Morning, General Purcell. Good to see you," Paul responded.

The portly bailiff turned and faced the lawyers, saying, "Gentlemen, I'll let the judge know you are all here."

Moments later, Circuit Judge Michael Lynell Taylor emerged. She wore a black robe with a single strand of pearls around her neck, and her long, straight black hair collected around her shoulders. She was a handsome woman who only spoke to lawyers if they were before her, in open court, and on the record. Her penchant for never having off-the-record conversations frustrated lawyers who were used to the more informal methods of making the legal sausage by visiting chambers for the "trial before the trial." Those informal conferences usually resulted in settled cases, but she was a different breed. Everything had to be on the record with her.

Judge Taylor took her seat at the bench and shuffled some papers. The court reporter walked in from a side door and sat beside the bench. The judge looked upon the assembly of lawyers with her expressionless face and inquired, "Are the parties ready?"

Jon rose from his chair, "Good morning, Your Honor. The petitioners are ready."

The attorney general stood, "The State of Arkansas is ready."

"Very well, Gentlemen. We are here for arguments regarding the temporary injunction I granted previously. I presume your arguments will be brief. I've listened to testimony from last month and read all your briefs and memoranda. So, without objections, let's call it for the record."

After the judge called the case, she focused on Jon.

"Mr. Freeman, you're up, but I want to hear only from one lawyer per side. Also, you all know I appreciate brevity, but there are no time limits. Just don't abuse me up here, okay? I'd like to hear your arguments and issue my rulings soon. Oh, Counsel, one last thing, if you don't mind, just so I can keep all this straight in my head, please address each act in order, starting with the Senate bills, and then you can go to the House bills. Thank you."

Jon rose from his chair and proceeded to the podium.

"Good morning, Your Honor. Jonathan Christian Freeman, for the petitioners." Standing tall in his navy blue suit, he glanced at his notes, looked at the judge, and began his remarks.

"You've tasked us with dissecting the so-called 'New Law,' which comprises a series of bills the General Assembly produced in January. Let's dive headfirst into the turbulent waters of Senate Bills 1 through 3. These chilling bills retroactively dissolve same-sex marriages, transform anyone attempting to officiate such unions into a criminal, and ensnare anyone providing aid as an accomplice. It's as though we've taken a time machine back to before the 19th century. Arkansas is toppling decades of Supreme

95

Court precedent, hurling us back to a time when civil rights were a distant dream. Critics, including myself, argue that these bills reek of *ex post facto* laws, directly violating our Constitution. This is not progress. It is a perversion."[13]

Jon's words sliced through the silent courtroom.

"Senate Bill 4, Your Honor, the infamous bounty hunter bill, is a dangerous overreach pitting citizen against citizen. It is a law that betrays any form of legitimate governance. Then there's Senate Bill 5 - a stinging slap in the face of the First Amendment's Establishment Clause."

After a brief pause, he continued.

"Your Honor, the suggestion to use the Holy Bible as guidance or supplemental law is a constitutional perversion. Let's illustrate the societal chaos this could unleash. Take Leviticus 20:20, which prescribes the death penalty for a man sleeping with his neighbor's wife. Are judges expected to enforce that? Are we supposed to stone astrologers and palm readers, as suggested in Leviticus 20:27? We're on the brink of converting our courts into religious tribunals! What possible compelling state interest would be served to stone people accused of divination? And blasphemy - who determines its definition? Are we supposed to gather blasphemers and publicly stone them out back in the parking lot as recommended by Leviticus 24:14? The sheer absurdity of it is impossible to overstate."

"Lastly, Your Honor, we have Senate Bill 6, which invalidates and outlaws interracial marriages. With this bill, the General Assembly and our governor brazenly challenge the Supreme Court landmark decision of *Loving v. Virginia*" and ask you to ignore it. It is astonishing!"[14]

Jon stood momentarily to collect his breath while the judge made notes.

"Turning to the House bills, Your Honor. House Bill 1 is nothing short of legislative brutality. It is the most oppressive anti-abortion law in our nation, prescribing the death penalty for any abortion. It gives zero guidance or mercy in cases where medical intervention is a matter of life and death. Are we expecting women to die amid pregnancy complications, unable to find a medical professional brave enough to risk their life to save hers?"

Next, Jon addressed House Bill 2, the notorious interstate compact.

"The interstate compact agreement is a flagrant violation of state and federal constitutions. It authorizes a separate, unregulated, militarized law enforcement agency with unrestricted power to trample Arkansans' rights. It eradicates the privilege of extradition, creating a constitutional nightmare that eviscerates due process. Moreover, it signs over our state's sovereignty, an act dripping with irony. Like its compact partners, Arkansas parades its love for state's rights until it suits an agenda to sacrifice those cherished rights. The audacity is staggering, Your Honor."

Jon's voice reverberated with righteous indignation as he pressed on with his argument while the judge looked down at her notes through her reading glasses.

"Now, House Bill 3 creates an extrajudicial entity capable of criminalizing actions and thoughts. The commission and tribunal created under this scheme obliterate fundamental due process. It trespasses against the principle of separation of powers by letting an executive agency usurp the roles of both the legislative and judicial branches."

As he moved on, the severity in Jon's tone deepened.

"Then there's House Bill 4, Your Honor, an insult to humanity. It tears away the Medicaid safety net from children and the poorest of Arkansans. It is merciless, especially when the same legislature that bestowed certain benefits upon our citizens now seeks to snatch them away. In real terms, this law threatens to strip over half of our state's population of access to meaningful healthcare."

Judge Taylor was still buried in her scribbles.

"House Bill 5," he continued. "This bill is a political golden goose for the Right. It is a direct path to unchallenged reign over the legislature. It seizes control over congressional redistricting, effectively neutering judicial oversight. It is a brazen, disgraceful challenge to the very fabric of our judiciary. Truly, the resulting evils are too numerous to count, beginning with a wholesale disregard for the 14th Amendment that ensures our citizens equal protection by an equal vote. You and I know, Your Honor, while this and cases like it wind their way to the Supreme Court, irreparable damage will already be inflicted on the nation if this law stands."

"And finally," Jon began with grim resolve, "we have House Bill 6, which, in its audacity, weaponizes the First Amendment's Free Exercise Clause. Is it the state's intention to establish a state religion? I will not insult the court by delving into that preposterous notion."

Concluding his fiery oration, Jon moved center stage, away from the podium, directly addressing the bench, and the judge continued her note-taking, hardly lifting her head to listen.

"Your Honor, these laws are a manifestation of mob rule. They strike at the heart of our state, her citizens, and the rule of law. There was a time in this nation when rules mattered. We adhered to principles, no matter how arduous. Society sought out fundamental fairness with an understanding that liberty and duty are inseparable. The rule of law separates us from despots and dictators, but if these laws are enacted, those cherished ideals will disintegrate and cast us into the abyss. Civil strife and lawlessness will ensue, pitting neighbor against neighbor, sibling against sibling, friend against friend, parent against child."

"My remarks are concluded, your honor," Jon said. "Does the court have any questions?"

"The court does not, Mr. Freeman. Thank you."

Oh, shit, Jon thought while sitting down, *that is a terrible sign. No questions. We're cooked. And she hardly looked up from her notes. This is bad.*

"General Purcell, do you have any remarks?"

At that moment, Jon's eyes locked with Win's, and then Win stood at the table to say, "No, Your Honor, the State of Arkansas rests on her briefs."

"Very well. Let's take a recess for a few minutes so I can get my remarks together."

She lowered her gavel and announced, "The court is in recess."

"All rise," the bailiff called as the judge pushed back from the bench and disappeared behind a panel into her chambers.

After the judge left the room, all the lawyers remained standing aimlessly. Win's decision to make no comments and to let the judge decide without the benefit of argument left Jon with a feeling of surprise.

No argument?

The two had agreed that Attorney General Purcell could do better if he stayed close to the governor than if he resigned, and Jon expected a fight.

An hour passed, and the bailiff was nowhere to be found. The court reporter, an efficient woman in her thirties, finally came out and told the lawyers, "Judge Taylor would like to see you in her chambers. Follow me."

Jon, Win, and Paul exchanged that surprised look familiar to lawyers. Some refer to it as the universal "what the fuck" look.

Chambers?

The reporter led the lawyers into Judge Taylor's chambers. She was sitting behind her oak desk, drained of her usual fire. Jon pulled up a chair on one side of her desk, and Win took the other. The other lawyers filed in and stood behind them, leaning against the bookshelves on one side to listen.

"Gentlemen. I cannot remember when lawyers were in my chambers to talk off the record. But I don't see a way around it. What you have put on my desk to decide might seem easy for the court to do, Mr. Freeman. But I hate to disappoint you. This is bigger than you, your clients, the people of Arkansas, or the state. There are forces at work here, gentlemen, forces that are way beyond my grasp as a trial judge. As you pointed out in your remarks earlier, Mr. Freeman, I'm afraid my decision in this case could spark civil strife and violence no matter which way I go."

"Wait a minute, Your Honor, if I may be plain," Jon interjected.

"I expect you to live up to your reputation, Mr. Freeman. Don't disappoint me now," said the judge, looking over the top of her glasses. "That's why we're in here. Say what you've got to say. Integrity and courage are contagious. So, let's have it. I think we could all use more of that these days."

"Judge, you're not seriously considering lifting the injunction on these laws, are you?"

"Well, Jon, let me be plain. Yes, I am considering it," she explained, "and I'll tell you why. We are all damned if I do what your clients want and damned if I do what the state wants. Do you think I like any of this crap the General Assembly conjured up? I don't, not any of it, but I do not believe this is the proper forum to decide these things. Fundamentally, no matter how evil these things might be for many people, the legislature is where the buck stops, not this courtroom. You may not like it. Hell, General Purcell, I presume you don't like what your client is asking. Speaking of, General Purcell, you have been rather quiet throughout."

"As long as we are off the record, Your Honor," Win began, "I'll be plain, also. I don't entirely agree with my client's actions, but that said, I have nothing to add to the argument already made in the State's briefs," he said.

"Nevertheless," she continued, "here's what we will do. As much as I love the phrase, 'often in error, never in doubt,' I'm not deciding this case today. I'm in great doubt about what to do. I'm sorry, but this is too big. I need to get this right. If I'm going to make the world mad, I had better own it. So, I will not decide this today. The temporary injunction will remain in place until I do. Thank you, gentlemen."

* * *

The beginning of a blustery March 6th ended with a whimper in the judge's chambers. March 7th, then 8th came. No decision. The rest of the week came and went, and the week after that. No decision.

There was no use waiting in an empty house, and Jon was all but finished with his work at the firm. He flew back to the Valle Grande at the end of that week.

On Wednesday, March 29th, Judge Taylor was in her chambers drinking a coffee when her phone buzzed.

"Judge Taylor, I have the governor on the line for you," the judge's assistant said over the line.

"Top of the morning to you, Judge. Is this a good time?"

"Of course, Governor Landers. What can I do for you?"

"Well, Judge, I'll get to the point," the governor said. "I've run my traps on you. I understand you appreciate straight talk. Hell, that's why I won the governorship because people like straight talk. So, I see no reason to make an exception for you. But to answer your question about what you can do for me, Your Honor. Are you aware that a federal judgeship in the Eastern District remains open since the chief judge retired?"

"I am aware of the vacancy, yes," Judge Taylor said.

"Well," the governor continued, "I think you'd be a good fit to fill that vacancy, and both Arkansas Senators agree and endorsed you as the nominee to fill it. I asked them to consider you instead of that other limp dick they had picked out. Here's the catch, and Judge, I won't shit ya. There's always a catch. You need to resign your judgeship today, just as soon as you hang up the phone with me, and right after that, call Senator Bledsoe's office, and you'll be on a greased rail to that federal judgeship. You've already been vetted, and even the president agrees to nominate you. And don't worry about that case you've been struggling with. We'll have a judge appointed who can finish that up for you. How's it sound, Judge?"

Judge Taylor had only two thoughts running through her mind: her fear of deciding the case, followed closely by relief that she would be excused from it. So, without hesitation, "Governor, it sounds like you'll have a new federal judge for the Eastern District. I'll submit my resignation effective immediately."

Buckshot was genuinely surprised.

Holy shit, this is a dream come true. That woman doesn't fuck around!

"Judge, why don't you fax your resignation to my office," the governor suggested.

"I'll have it to you in just a few minutes," Judge Taylor said before whirling around in her chair to type out her resignation.

"I hereby resign the office of Circuit Judge for 4th Judicial Circuit, Washington County Circuit Court, 2nd Division, effective immediately."

She hit print, walked out to her secretary's desk where the printer sat, pulled it off the printer, signed it, and asked her assistant to fax it to the governor's office.

Darlene Cranston, her assistant, was stunned.

"Judge?"

"Darlene, don't you worry about this," the judge said. "I'm accepting a nomination for a federal judgeship. I'll need a case manager where I'm

THE LAST INDEPENDENCE DAY

going, and I'll hire you if you want to come down to Little Rock. Please get me a couple of banker boxes. I'm done here."

Judge Taylor walked straightaway back into her chambers and began to organize her things while Karen, the court reporter who overheard the conversation from her office, called Jon's cell phone – they had known each other for many years.

* * *

Jon was at the HQ going over spreadsheets with Sam Hernandez when the call came in. He recognized the number as the one from the judge's chambers, so he excused himself.

"Jon, it's Karen Baker. "You didn't hear it from me, but Judge Taylor resigned. Something about taking a federal appointment. Her resignation is effective immediately."

"What? She did?" Jon was incredulous. "Karen, thank you. Thank you for the heads up."

"Jon," Karen said, "you're a good man and one of the better lawyers I know, but I don't think any lawyering will change things. I fear for what is happening, and I fear for you. I'd better go. Take care of yourself."

As soon as Jon hung up, he called Win, but Jon went to voicemail: "Win, it's Jon. Call me back. Judge Taylor resigned. She will not be deciding the case."

Jon slid his phone into a coat pocket and walked back into Sam's office.

"Hey Sam, unless you need anything more from me, I must cut this short and return to La Hacienda. Something has come up in Arkansas."

"We're good here, Jefe," Sam said. "We need to finish going over some issues we are having with predators in one of the interior paddocks, and it's time to bring the Cimarron Herd back up to the Valle. Anyway, can we pick this up tomorrow, Jefe?"

"Sure thing, Sam. See you in the morning." Jon said.

When Jon arrived at La Hacienda, he walked into the kitchen, where Martin and Jennifer were having tea at the counter.

"Oh shit, there's trouble!" Jon exclaimed as he removed his canvas jacket and laid it over the back of an empty counter chair.

"You should expect trouble when I am involved," Jennifer said playfully. "We have been running story on you, Little Brother."

Jon responded with a wry grin, "I'd expect nothing less!"

Jon loved that Martin fitted in, especially with Jennifer, who could be tough on strangers and was oddly possessive over Jon's attention.

Jon kissed her on the cheek and hugged Martin.

"Why don't you join us," Jennifer asked Jon.

"I'd love to," Jon said, "but I just received some bizarre news I must deal with. The judge on the case in Arkansas to stop the New Law suddenly resigned. Something is afoot. I can feel it. I need to go up and call around to see what I can find out. Keep a chair saved for me. I'll be back down in a bit."

11

Justice Denied

On Friday morning, March 31, 2023, Jon sat at his desk looking out on the snowy mountains with Chef's coffee. Martin was asleep downstairs.

At 7:31 a.m., Jon's phone lit up. It was the number from Judge Taylor's chambers. Jon picked up immediately.

"Good morning, this is Jon Freeman."

"Good morning, Jon. Hal Ledger here. How are you this morning?"

"Senator Ledger?" Jon exclaimed with surprise.

"Judge Ledger, now. The governor appointed me to complete Judge Taylor's term after she resigned. Let me get the attorney general on the line if you have a second. Hang on."

The "on-hold" music played the same version of the *Brandenburg Concerto No. 3 in G Major* for as long as Jon could remember.

Maybe they ought to change it, Jon thought, then his mind shifted to the contradiction of a right-wing governor like Buckshot appointing a lefty from Northwest Arkansas to assume a judgeship. It made no sense to select Ledger to hear this case, of all cases.

Absolutely zero sense.

"Jon, you still with us?" asked Judge Ledger when he came back on the line.

"Yes, sir," Jon said.

"Win. Are you with us?" asked the judge.

"Yes, sir," Win replied.

A text to Jon from Win came through to Jon's phone that read, "WTF?"

"Gentlemen, I'd like to wrap up this case that started with Judge Taylor. I read the case file and transcripts and am ready to rule. Now, Jon, when I called your office, I was told you were in New Mexico. That right?"

"Yes, sir, that's correct," answered Jon.

"Well, this is the sort of thing we should do in open court. Can you all appear next week? Is Monday too early? Jon, you're furthest away. Can you make it?" asked the judge.

"Sure I can, Your Honor," Jon confirmed.

"I'll be there," Win said, "the State has no higher priority."

"I'll see you two in court on Monday morning. Be there at 8:30 a.m. I'll announce a decision then."

As soon as the call ended, Jon saw Win ringing in.

"Hal-fucking-Ledger? How is that even possible," Jon said without even saying hello.

"The governor must have cut a deal with Ledger or has something on him," Win replied. "There's no way she would appoint him just for him to enjoin the statutes permanently. You should have seen him during the legislative session. No. Fucking. Way."

"I honestly don't know how you've stuck in as long as you have," Jon offered, "but I want you to know I've appreciated the information you've been able to give me. It's helping us properly organize resistance to what is coming down the pike. But I don't think this is going to turn out for us. Something isn't right. Right before the case is decided, Judge Taylor resigns to become a federal judge, and then the governor appoints Hal Ledger. There is something we are both missing here."

"True," Win said, "well, listen, prepare yourself. If this goes south for you, the governor will move quickly to implement those statutes. She has had several meetings with different militia groups and the adjutant general. This is going to get crazy quickly, my friend."

"See you on Monday, Win," Jon said.

Jon chartered a flight to pick him up in Los Alamos instead of flying himself on Saturday morning. He couldn't shake a bad feeling and didn't want to risk his plane being detained in Arkansas if something went wrong.

* * *

After landing in Fayetteville Saturday morning, he took a cab to Highland House. It wasn't home anymore. The house didn't smell like piñon or sage. It wasn't surrounded by ponderosa pine or the tall grass of the valles. It felt more like a hotel. So, rather than spend time alone in a shell of a house, Jon spent the rest of the weekend relaxing and catching up with his brother, Ira, the Colonel, Tiny, Paul, and some other friends.

After the weekend, he flew into action early Monday morning. Before walking to the courthouse a few blocks away, Jon called the landline at La Hacienda, and Chee answered.

"Curtis, it's Jon."

"Good morning, Hosteen. Is everything all right?" Chee asked.

"Yes, listen, I need you to wake Martin up and get him on the phone for me. It's important."

"Of course, sir, give me just a few minutes," and Chee put him on hold.

A sleepy-sounding Martin picked up the phone in less than a minute. "Hey, babe, what's up? It's early."

"Hi there, look, I don't have much time. I've got that court hearing soon, and I'm afraid it will not go well. I'm going to ask Chee to come here with a couple of the cowboys to load up everything left at the house and bring it back to the ranch. I mean everything, including the Range Rover. I don't want anything here that could be seized, held over our heads, or used against us if they decide to come after me. Would you put him on the phone, and I'll tell him, but I wanted you to know."

"I understand. Love you, sweetheart," Martin said. "I'll get Chee. Keep in touch with me and tell me what's going on. I'll know to call Will if there's a problem."

"Right, if something goes down and you can't find me, call Will. Okay,

106

love you. Put Chee on, please."

Chee picked up.

"Curtis," Jon said, "I need you to drive to my house in Arkansas and pack what is left of it up except furnishings. Take everything else. Leave now, take a couple of Caballeros, and come directly here. One of you will also take my Range Rover back to the ranch. Let Sam Hernandez know. I'll be in touch later today. If, for some reason, I am out of contact, have Sam call Mr. Thomas. You got all that?"

"Yes, sir," Chee confirmed.

"I know it is a long day for you," Jon stated, "but it's important. I'll expect you all here early this evening. Check in with me along the way."

Jon knew it was a lot to ask to have Chee come and load up things at the house, but it was something that had to be done. He only wished he had thought of it sooner.

* * *

It was a fresh and bright spring morning for Jon's walk to the courthouse as hundred-year-old maple and oak trees cast long shadows along his path. Walking up to the courthouse entrance, he noticed three black SUVs parked side-by-side in the spots where the sheriff's deputies usually parked their cruisers. He observed a symbol on the front doors of each vehicle: a black shield with a flaming red sword in its midst, hilt up, sharp end down. He also noticed the vehicles did not have license plates and the windows were blacked out.

Jon cleared through the security checkpoint at the courthouse at 8:13 a.m. After clearing security, Jon proceeded up the elevator to the fourth floor and walked directly to the judge's chambers to check in with the judge's assistant. The AG, she said, was already in the courtroom, waiting.

Jon walked into the courtroom and saw Winston Purcell sitting at the counsel table on the far side of the well closest to the windows. Win rose to greet him, and as he did, he glanced at Jon and then shifted his gaze beyond him. Jon's eyes moved toward the jury box, where six men dressed in black fatigues and red berets sat. Some of them were armed with assault rifles. On the berets was the same symbol he saw on the doors of the black SUVs parked outside. He didn't recognize any of them.

Jon sat at the counsel table to await the court's judgment when Judge Hal Ledger came out from behind the panel and sat behind the bench.

"Good morning, gentlemen. Thank you for being here on such short notice. The court must rule on important matters here, face to face, and on the record. I want you and your clients to understand that I have familiarized myself with the case. I have read every filing, every affidavit, the transcripts of the hearings, and, in particular, the closing arguments that the plaintiffs made. I note the state rested on its briefs and made no closing."

Judge Ledger continued. "Being satisfied that I have been furnished with everything, it is the judgment of this court that the plaintiff's petition to declare various acts of the General Assembly unconstitutional should be, and hereby is, dismissed with prejudice.[15] The court will file a reasoned letter of opinion in due course, but the time for an appeal will begin today after the precedent is filed. We are adjourned."

Jesus, all that way for what, so he could summarily kick it?

Jon was stunned. Win was motionless. Jon collected himself after the shock of what just happened began to wear off. There was nothing else left to do but leave, so Jon waved at the attorney general as he left the courtroom when one of the men in black fatigues approached him.

"Excuse me. I need to talk with you for a moment," said the man in black fatigues.

Jon wheeled around when the man touched his shoulder to get his attention.

"Who are you, and what do you want?" Jon responded as he jerked his shoulder away from the man.

"I'm an officer with the Compact Task Force," was the reply.

"What? There's no such thing."

Jon walked away from him toward the elevator.

"Sir, stay where you are. I won't ask again," commanded the man in fatigues.

Jon felt his temper take hold and wheeled around to face the man.

"Or what, you're going to do what, exactly?" Jon demanded.

"I'll arrest you, sir. If you refuse to cooperate, I will place you under arrest," said the man in fatigues.

Jon snarled, "Fuck off. I have nothing to say to you, and you have no authority here. Compact Taskforce. That's not even a real thing. Go fuck yourself."

Jon continued to push the call button for the elevator when the man in black grabbed him by the left wrist, pulled him around, and shoved him against the wall face-first. It created such a commotion in the hallway that the bailiffs from both courtrooms at the opposite ends of the corridor came out to investigate. When they saw the man in black fatigues putting handcuffs on Jon, both drew their side arms and rushed the man.

One bailiff yelled, "Release Mr. Freeman, sir, release him now."

The man in black hesitated, and the bailiffs rushed both men, separated the man in black fatigues from Jon, and wrestled the black-clad man to the ground. The man in the fatigues was face down on the floor with his hands cuffed behind his back, and in a flash, one of the bailiffs triggered an alarm that flashed lights in the building and sounded a klaxon. Suddenly, sheriff's deputies, about eight in number, were gathered around Jon.

"There are four or five more armed subjects in black fatigues in the second-division courtroom!" one bailiff yelled.

Another deputy stayed with Jon and the subdued man who assaulted him. At the same time, the rest of the bailiffs and court security split into two groups to enter the courtroom from the main door and through the chamber entrance simultaneously. Outside, local sheriff deputies parked their rigs behind the three black SUVs to block them in. As the two groups of sheriff's deputies stormed the courtroom, the sound of gunfire erupted. The muffled pops in quick succession were unmistakable. The first officer inside was a young deputy armed with a 9mm service pistol. When he entered the courtroom, he was met with an explosion of assault rifle fire by one of the other men in the jury box who remained in the courtroom after the proceedings ended. The men inside the courtroom had turned over the two counsel tables to make a barricade to guard the attorney general.

"Stand your ground, brothers!" Yelled one of the men in black. "We have the attorney general. Back off, lower your weapons, and we will leave this place without bloodshed."

The courtroom bailiffs and sheriff's deputies were at a profound disadvantage because the two entrances formed a narrow kill box. As the standoff continued, the man outside who tried to interrogate Jon rolled over, looked up at Jon, and said, "You and your kind are going to be eradicated along with all the other ungodly filth in this state and country. Once we are freed, I will be coming after you. It is just a matter of time. We are the Arkansas Defenders. There will be no place safe for you to hide."

"Go fuck yourself, you piece of shit," Jon growled, fighting off the urge to kick the man in his teeth.

"Mr. Freeman, get out of here. It isn't safe." Said the bailiff standing there with him. "We can get a statement about what happened here from you later. Take the stairs and exit through the bottom floor into the garage."

Jon hastily made his way to one of the stairwells, pulling open the metal fire door that clanked shut behind him. He bounded down the stairs until he reached the bottom floor, where an unattended exit led to a basement parking deck.

Who were those men in their uniforms? The new interstate compact force? And how did they bring automatic weapons into the courthouse? And what the fuck was this with Hal Ledger?

Sirens in the distance grew louder as the questions in Jon's head multiplied. Jon looked around and saw a discrete stairwell at a corner of the parking deck opposite him. He knew that stairwell because he used the same escape route from the courthouse to avoid angry police and press after a not-guilty verdict from a notorious murder trial he had won years ago.

He ran crouched low toward the stairs. Leather on metal, up the stairs, and he emerged at the street level of the parking deck and poked his head above the surface. He saw a collection of emergency vehicles at the courthouse entrance. Local police cruisers, sheriffs, state police, and the fire department were there. Ambulances and numerous press vans rushed to the scene. Then he heard a familiar sound: several M939 heavy military trucks. Commonly referred to as "Five Tons," there was more than one by the sound of the diesel engines powering them.

National fucking Guard?

His curiosity got the best of him, so Jon quickly climbed over a retaining wall. The cedar trees planted along the top gave him cover so he could go undetected to an exterior staircase on one side of a neighboring church that offered a view of the courthouse.

He called Will. "Will, you are never going to believe this," Jon whispered over the phone. "All those laws I told you about are in effect. We lost the injunction. We had the notice of appeal ready to file, but a paramilitary dude dressed in black assaulted me on the way out of the courtroom. There was a standoff. Shots were fired. I managed to sneak out of the basement. And something else, that guy who assaulted me, he said 'they' will be coming after me."

"Can you get out of there?" asked Will.

"Maybe." Jon replied, then said, "Wait, holy fucking shit. Three five-ton National Guard trucks just pulled up with troops in the back and some Humvees. What the fuck is the National Guard doing here?" Jon was breathing too fast.

"I got to figure out how to get out of here. Hey, Will, can you call the manager at Bentonville Airport and see if they have a pilot available? Tell her to charter me anything she can find. And I'll try to be there by six this evening. That should give me enough time to get there without being noticed. If they are looking for me, hopefully, they won't be looking there. Better yet, ask the charter to meet me at the Springdale FBO. They won't think to look for me there."

Will listened, and then Jon's phone dropped the call.

At the courthouse parking lot, three dozen National Guard troops leaped out of the back of the military trucks. They assembled in formation, dressed in riot gear with full-face helmets, heavy metal shields, and batons.

Jon recognized the "gas" officers and the detachment commander from his army days and training. There was a soldier dressed in a simple army combat uniform with a green web belt holding his holstered sidearm.

That must be the detachment commander.

He also recognized arrest teams, two men per team, and the muscle armed with M4A1 carbines. Jon saw additional National Guard hummers pull up at the three exits/entrances to the courthouse complex to seal off all three avenues of ingress and egress. Then, the commander made an announcement.

"Officers, I am Captain James Hadley Riddick of the Arkansas National Guard. I am here on the orders of the adjutant general and the governor to take command of this scene. Stand down immediately, holster your weapons, and leave the area. Do you understand?"

An Arkansas State Trooper dressed in his blue uniform, complete with his campaign hat, stepped forward.

"Trooper, are you the ranking officer on this scene?" asked Captain Riddick.

"I am, yes, Captain," replied the trooper.

"Then stand these officers down now and leave the area," the captain ordered.

The trooper hesitated, and the captain sternly commanded: "Trooper, do it now."

The trooper turned and faced the array of local police, sheriff's deputies, and the rest, "You heard the man. Stand down. Safe your weapons and disperse."

One of the bailiffs called out, "What about us? We are assigned to the courthouse."

The trooper turned, and Captain Riddick answered: "That means bailiffs, too. Leave the area. We will secure the courthouse, and when it is secure, we will contact the sheriff and allow you to return to your posts."

All the assembled law enforcement began to withdraw. Jon remained glued to his position and watched the arrest team break ranks and enter the courthouse led by an equal number of armed soldiers. While those individuals entered the building, the remaining guardsmen formed a perimeter around the main entrance to the courthouse. Then Jon saw two guardsmen walk around to a stairwell to post up at the remaining doors leading into the building.

In a few moments, civilians began filing out of the courthouse. One person he saw leaving the building through the main entrance was Circuit Judge Hal Ledger, who was in the company of the Arkansas Defenders, including the one who assaulted Jon as he left the courtroom earlier. Slowly, cars started and left the parking lot to disappear into what was once the quiet, peaceful City of Fayetteville.

As the parking lot cleared, Jon looked for his friend Win, but there was no sign of him. Judge Ledger exchanged words with the National Guard captain while one of the older-looking Defenders appeared to join the conversation.

Where the fuck is Win?

* * *

In Little Rock, the governor was behind her desk in her second-floor office at the Capitol, known by those at the Capitol Building as "250" because of the large painted gold numbers above the door leading into her office. The adjutant general was there with her, and they had Captain Riddick on speakerphone.

"Captain Riddick," began the governor, "I'm here with the adjutant general. Were you able to get things under control up there?"

"Yes, ma'am, I'm still at the scene, and everything is under control," the captain replied.

"What about my Defenders? And Judge Ledger?" asked the governor.

"All present and accounted for, Governor," Riddick replied.

"And the attorney general?" The governor inquired, almost as an afterthought.

"No sign of him, Governor," said the captain.

I wonder where that squirrely son of a bitch wandered off to, she thought.

"Well, go in there and see if you can find him. But first, the adjutant general has a question for you. Hang on."

"Captain Riddick, General Hampton here. How did your boys do up there? Any problems?"

"No, sir. They were here with me to restore order and did so without hesitation," said the captain.

"Well, that's good. Are there any issues with morale in your unit? Any problems with the Defenders?" The adjutant general asked.

"Not that I could tell with this group," the captain replied."

"All right," said the adjutant general. "Thank you. Anything you observe that shows a lack of will to follow the governor's orders or mine, you report that directly to me, will you?"

"Yes, General, of course. Directly to you," the captain said.

"Good. Governor, you have anything else for his young man?"

"No," she replied, "I think that does it for me, and thank you, Captain," she projected from across her desk, "I appreciate your work this morning. Once the courthouse is secure, call the sheriff and let the circuit's chief judge know that the courthouse is back in business. And while you're at it, have the senior Defender call me after you hang up on my landline here."

"Yes, ma'am, Riddick out."

Turning to the adjutant general, the governor asked, "You think these kids are up to what we are about to ask of them, General?"

"I do, Governor, I do," he said with a confident grin. "We won't have 100% of them, but most of our guardsmen are Arkansans first. We noticed this trend over the last couple of years. Many of them have become disenchanted with the federal government, and we've been weeding out the ones who place loyalty to the federal government over allegiance to the state. We haven't gotten them all, but most are already out."

"What about the women," the governor asked.

"We've decided to reduce our female ranks through attrition, and recruitment of women has stopped. We have a few more years for the last of them," the adjutant general said.

"Well, General, you may think this is ironic coming from me, but women

114

have no place in the military. Let's be sure to get them out as soon as possible. Accelerate the process without drawing too much attention to keep the fucking lawyers out of it."

The phone rang on her desk, interrupting the rest of what she planned to say.

"Jesus," she said as she picked up the phone.

"This is Governor Landers."

"Yes, ma'am, I am Commander Dennis Clayton of the Defenders. You asked to speak with me?"

She smiled. "Yes, I did, Commander. I did. Thank you for the call. Thank you for showing up today, even though we may have been jumpin' before we were shot with the New Law only being in effect for less than a day. But it's okay. I will have General Hampton help me organize a meeting with all the Defender Districts this afternoon in Little Rock. I want to go ahead and swear all of you in. We're going to do this at War Memorial Stadium. Tonight! There is something I need from you, though. That lawyer, that goddamn lawyer, Freeman. I need you to round him up, take him into custody if you can, and give him a home on indefinite hold in the Washington County Jail. So, if you can find him, lock him up, but whatever you do, don't be late tonight. The General will be in touch with the details."

"Roger that, Governor. See you this evening." The commander ended the call.

12

Prey

Jon remained concealed at his perch adjacent to the courthouse when he called Tiny.

"Tiny, can you meet me at the Confederate Cemetery?" Jon asked when Tiny picked up. "There was a gunfight at the courthouse after my morning hearing on the governor's new legislation. Guys with weapons claimed they were part of a new interstate police force. One tried to arrest me, but I escaped. They will be looking for me."

"I got you, partner," Tiny said. "Where are you now?"

"I'm hiding out across from the courthouse, but I can run through the Holler toward the cemetery undetected."

"Got it. See you in 15," Tiny said.

Jon descended the stairs and jogged toward Conner Street, an alley leading downhill to a wooded hollow next to a creek. Jon headed to the Holler, where many of Fayetteville's African-Americans lived. The term "Holler" had given way to the "Tin Cup" in these modern times, and even though gentrification was seeping in, the area was still poor and run down. He hoped the people hunting him wouldn't be searching down there.

He made it to the Tin Cup, picking his way along the sidewalk and watching for black SUVs. Jon walked briskly past ramshackle wood-frame shotgun houses, one with a tree poking through the roof. On one corner, the crumbling brick Methodist church had foot-tall weeds growing through cracks in the asphalt parking lot.

No sign of them.

Jon came to the Tin Cup's heart. He decided to cut through the center courtyard of a neglected public housing complex and angle up a grass-covered hillside leading to the Confederate Cemetery. A plastic sack floated by him in the breeze. He noticed people peeking through their curtains at the well-dressed white man jogging through the area.

The irony of hiding out at a memorial to the Confederacy was pretty rich since these "Defenders" seemed intent on recreating it. He passed through the squeaky wrought-iron gate into the cemetery, where the tombstones lined up in neat rows. The graveyard was perched on the southwestern shoulder of Mount Sequoyah amid a stand of mature oak, maple, and hickory, affording a view of Downtown Fayetteville on the opposite hill through their branches. This time of year, the dogwoods and redbud trees bloomed underneath the umbrella of towering old growth. He might have taken a moment to enjoy the scene, but the view had lost its luster today.

Tiny arrived in his Jeep to collect Jon about five minutes after Jon had taken a seat on a bench under a gazebo. Jon waved at Tiny when he pulled up.

"Tiny, let's do a quick drive by my office and the house – I just want to see what we can see."

"No fuckin' way," Tiny said. "I heard what happened on the radio, and it's pretty scary. Let me drop you at my place. I can check for you. Let's keep you under the sheets for a minute. "

Tiny was being serious, for a change.

They planned a roundabout way to get to Tiny's house. Still, they had to cross College Avenue to get there. When they reached College, a black Defender Suburban was at the corner of Rock Street and South College Avenue. It was too late when Jon acquired the presence of mind to duck below Tiny's dashboard. He had locked eyes with the passenger in the Defender vehicle.

"Shit," Jon shouted. "Drive, Tiny. Drive!"

The Defender Suburban made a screeching U-turn in the middle of the busy street. Tiny jammed his foot on the accelerator, and his Jeep Cherokee lunged across College, barely missing traffic from both directions as they crossed. A block away was the police station and, beyond that, the public library with a multilevel parking garage. The library would be an excellent place to hide.

"Drop me at the library, Tiny," Jon suggested, "then keep driving. Maybe that will throw them off."

Tiny sped by the local police station with one block to go—no sign of a Defender vehicle.

"Fuck it, drop me here," Jon said.

There was an alley near the library. Tiny slammed the brakes, and Jon leaped out.

"I'll send you a text," Jon yelled over his shoulder, and then he disappeared down the alley, where he hid behind a dumpster and sent a text to Tiny that read, "Call Will Thomas, my lawyer. Call the FBI. Tell them I'm an eyewitness to what happened at the courthouse this morning and that armed militiamen are after me."

The local FBI Office telephone rang off its hook that morning with calls from the media and concerned citizens who saw the National Guard at the courthouse and heard the gunfire. One of the calls was Tiny's, which prompted the local Watch Officer who took Tiny's call to notify Washington because the reports looked like domestic terrorism. When word made it to the Director of the FBI, he phoned the senior special agent in Charge at the Fayetteville Office.

"This is Special Agent Edward Babbit."

"Special Agent Babbit, good day to you. This is Director Flint. I wanted to be sure you heard it from me. I want you to take those militia people into custody, but I'd also like you to keep an eye on the lawyer they are chasing, Mr. Jon Freeman. Learn what you can about him, will you? Do a workup. The Defenders targeted him, and I want to know why."

"Will do," Special Agent Babbit replied.

Meanwhile, Tiny led a pursuing Defender vehicle away from Jon as he headed over to Dickson Street's entertainment district through narrow

118

side streets and then toward the university campus. The Defenders did not fall for the decoy. They circled back, with three other SUVs joining in as they began working a grid pattern at the police station and fanning out, slowly driving every street looking for Jon.

The local FBI Field Office was only three blocks from Jon's hiding place, something the Defenders had not considered as they patrolled through the adjacent streets. Jon considered making for the FBI offices, but then he realized he had been so busy trying to run from the Defenders that he hadn't thought to call the FBI himself.

After several rings, someone answered.

"Federal Bureau of Investigation, Fayetteville Field Office. How may I direct your call?"

"Hello. My name is Jonathan Christian Freeman. I am a lawyer in Fayetteville who witnessed the paramilitary group shooting at the Washington County Courthouse earlier today. The militiamen are armed with assault rifles. One of its members tried to take me into custody. Those people are now pursuing me in flat-black recent model Chevrolet Suburbans with a shield on their vehicle's front doors. I believe the State of Arkansas is cooperating with them, and I think their actions violate federal law. I need help."

"Sir, please hold," came the reply.

Goddammit!

"I don't have time to hold," Jon yelled. "I am a few blocks from your office, hiding behind a dumpster in an alley south of Mountain Street, a block east of School."

"Hang on, sir. Hang on," the person on the other end said.

The person who answered Jon's call put his hand over the microphone, and Jon heard the muffled speaker say, "Special Agent, we have a situation here."

"Sir," the person said when he returned to the conversation, "we are sending a team to your location. Where are you, exactly?"

"I am hiding behind some dumpsters in an alley between Rock and Mountain Street," Jon gasped, "just east of School. Fuck, they are coming.

Please hurry. Black Suburban. No plates."

Jon was frantic. Two SUVs approached, and the occupants opened their doors simultaneously after catching a glimpse of Jon in the alley. They rushed him from two directions, blocking Jon's escape. Jon hit redial on his phone so that it would ring the FBI and secured it in his front pocket. Jon figured his only chance was to delay, so he sprinted toward one of them, who drew his sidearm, and then Jon ran in the opposite direction. At 56, he was active but not fit enough to evade his more athletic pursuers. The tackle came from his right, dislocating his left shoulder when he hit the pavement.

"You are coming with us," one young-looking Defender said through uneasy breaths. He couldn't have been much older than 21.

"Over my dead fucking body," Jon strained with his cheek against the pavement. You have no jurisdiction here. You can go fuck yourself!"

His left shoulder was in a world of pain. The two men in black fatigues lifted him by his armpits, tied his hands with zip ties in front of him, and then wrestled him into the back seat of the SUV, sitting him behind the driver.

"Where are you taking me?" Jon demanded.

"We're taking you to the Washington County Detention Center," replied the young man who tackled him.

"Good luck with that, Chief," Jon said through clenched teeth. "Maybe you should ask them to make space for you because this is a kidnapping."

"We got orders," said the younger one.

"From fucking' who?" Jon demanded.

"The Governor," the younger one replied.

"On what fuckin' charge?" Jon insisted, "as if she has the power to arrest anyone. I can't wait to see how this turns out."

"The New Law gives her the power," said the other captor.

"We shall see about that," Jon huffed.

These guys were amateurs, failing to frisk Jon or seize his phone.

"Don't pull out onto Mountain Street, you dumbasses, unless you want to get caught," Jon yelled.

"Shut your mouth before I shut it for you," responded the younger Defender sitting in the passenger seat.

The first Defender SUV pulled out onto Mountain Street, unaware of its proximity to the FBI Field Office and that the FBI was listening in. Oblivious to the FBI tactical unit speeding toward their location with its complement of SWAT Vehicles, the Defenders were in for a surprise.

"Why didn't you put me in the first SUV to drive me down Mountain Street rather than this one? Are you suffering from a rectal cranial inversion? Seriously! What the fuck is wrong with you," Jon bellowed.

The Defender driving Jon followed the first SUV. Jon realized those idiots had made two other mistakes. One, they tied his hands in front of him rather than behind him, and the second mistake was seating Jon behind the driver. When he realized this, Jon reached up with both arms and lunged forward from his rear seat to get his tied hands around the driver's neck. The pain in his left shoulder was exquisite, but it didn't prevent him from trying to choke the mother fucker to death. As he pulled back on the driver's neck, the SUV swerved across Mountain Street and collided with a fire hydrant at the corner while FBI vehicles screeched onto the scene.

"You'd better run like a scalded hog before you're double fucked!" Jon yelled as he pulled as hard as he could choke the life out of him. The driver's partner in the passenger seat stared, frozen in fear, as an FBI armored van collided with the defender vehicle's rear passenger side quarter panel, shattering glass. In moments, FBI agents in tactical gear had trained no less than half a dozen automatic weapons on the driver and his companion.

"Show us your hands! Now! Don't be a hero." Yelled the FBI scene commander.

Jon lifted his arms and released the driver's neck, falling back into his chair behind the driver. Then, two pairs of Defender's hands went up as a lone agent with his assault rifle raised crept toward the vehicle to open the rear passenger door. He reached for Jon to help him out of the car while two additional agents on each side approached to take the driver and his companion into custody.

"Sir, are you hurt? We have a medic here," said one of the FBI men.

"Hang on, man," Jon yelled, "I gotta see this."

Jon wrenched himself away from the supportive grasp of his escort. He marched over to the passenger in his black fatigues, his former captor, now face down on the pavement. Before any other agents approached him, he called out to the young man on the pavement.

"Hey, you piece of shit, looks like I'm not going anywhere with you," Jon hissed.

The young man stared back at Jon as Jon spit in his face and kicked him as hard as he could in his chest. Jon was about to kick him again before another FBI agent grabbed Jon in a bear hug and pulled him away.

"I hope you become a poster child for prison rape, you fuck!" Jon yelled through his gnashing and spitting teeth.

"Maybe someone can shove a broomstick up your ass and break it off so you can shit in a bag for the rest of your miserable life! Fuck!"

"Sir! Sir! I need you to calm down," said his escort.

"Oh, I am the picture of calm, Agent," Jon said sarcastically. "Here, let me kick that fuckstick once more, and I'll be the calmest mother fucker you ever met."

The agent grabbed Jon around his waist to pull him further away.

"Can't let you do that, sir," the agent firmly said. "Let's get the medic to check you out, okay? Sir?"

Jon's furor continued erupting.

"I'm not fucking done with that asshole, goddammit!"

"Sir, please. Take a deep breath. Just breathe. Come sit over here and let the medic see you," the agent urged.

A young African-American woman dressed like a medic approached Jon, who was sitting on the curb.

"Oh man, you dislocated your left shoulder," the medic said. "It might not be too late to fix it, but it will hurt like a muhfucka when I pop it back in."

"Do it," Jon said. "Just do it."

"All right, give me your arm and straighten it for me. This is going to hurt," the medic said.

Before Jon could yell out, the medic, who had done this many times before, wrapped her hands around Jon's straightened arm, pulled, and then push-twisted the arm back into the socket with an audible click.

"Fuck!" Jon yelled out. The medic stood over him for a moment.

"Sir?" the medic asked.

A look of relief passed across Jon's face.

"Goddamn, thank you, my friend. I feel better already," Jon said with equal measures of sincerity and sarcasm.

The two laughed, and Jon remained sitting on the curb in a daze as a flatbed wrecker hauled off the Defender SUVs. The FBI shoved the two captive Defenders unceremoniously into the back of a black unmarked FBI van. Jon secretly hoped they'd drive the two assholes off to a quiet place and put a bullet in their heads.

In Jon's heart, even though he was profoundly compassionate and had his share of experience defending criminals, he had no tolerance for thuggery or violence. He profoundly and truly hoped these men who abducted him would roast in the pits of a hellish fire stoked by the burning Bibles they claimed to cherish.

"Excuse me, are you Jon Freeman?" came a man's voice directed at Jon.

Jon looked up.

"Yes?"

Before him stood Edward Babbit, a pugnacious-looking middle-aged man who peered at Jon through oddly thick eyeglasses.

"Mr. Freeman, my name is Special Agent Edward Babbit. I am the special agent in Charge of the Fayetteville Field Office. I want to ask you a few questions if that's all right. Are you willing to come down to our field office with me? The coffee isn't very good, but it is free. I want to learn what I can from you about today and these men who abducted you."

"Yeah, I can do that, but I need to make some calls to let people know I'm all right."

"You're welcome to do that from the office if you like. We have rooms there if you need some privacy. When we finish up, I can drop you wherever you want," said Agent Babbit.

"Sure," Jon replied, feeling more at ease.

They arrived at the federal courthouse. The field office was at the end of an antiseptic government hallway on the second floor of the building.

"Do you know if the attorney general was harmed," Jon asked at the beginning of their session. "When I left the courtroom, he was still in there, and I never saw him come out."

Agent Babbit replied. "We assume he eventually left the building. We have tried to reach him for a statement, but we have not been successful. We are taking a close look at this, but believe it or not, our jurisdiction is limited."

"I understand that. I do." Jon explained. "The US Attorney should be able to find federal crimes that merit an indictment. The weapons those morons carried were modified, and it sure felt like an attempt to take hostages. I also recall one of the men saying, 'You and your kind are going to be eradicated.' That sounds like terrorism. But I think it is because I have a husband, so it starts to look like a federal hate crime."

Jon continued unprompted.

"I'll tell you something else. This morning, the National Guard detachment commander cooperated with those 'Defenders' as they are being called. Once the National Guard took control, the commander excused all law enforcement who left the building and the scene. After that, the Defender dudes came out. All six of whom I saw there this morning, and they made time for a friendly chat with the National Guard detachment commander in front of God and everyone."

"Jon, may I call you Jon," Babbit interrupted.

"Sure, of course," Jon said.

"Jon, I'm curious about something off-topic. We checked on you this morning, and beginning in 2011, your public records and credit began disappearing. Up until that point, your credit report was current. You had your home here in Fayetteville and several bank accounts and credit cards. Then, after 2010, poof. All the accounts that were there before disappeared except a Visa card, an American Express card, and one local bank account. Everything else, even IRAs, vanished. Aside from what disappeared, we noted that you acquired a private pilot's license. Care to help me understand with whom I am dealing? And mind you, you are not under investigation, and I assure you, Jon, that what you tell me here will stay with the Bureau and me. We could use your help, but we want to know who we are dealing with. Can you help me out here?"

Jon paused, leaning forward in his chair opposite Babbit's side of the desk. He said, "How much time do you have, Special Agent? Because this could take a while. I can see how the sudden absence of a credit, financial, or public record coupled with the recent acquisition of a pilot's license might concern you. Hell, I look like I work for a cartel."

"Why not give me the *Reader's Digest* version," Babbit suggested.

"Well, Special Agent," Jon told him, "To make a long story short, in 2010, my best friend, a man named Cullen Dunigan, died, and just before he did, he signed every single thing he owned over to me which consisted of a huge working cattle ranch in the mountains of northern New Mexico. The Valle Grande Land and Cattle Company, LLC operates the ranch. I own the land and the company that runs it through a series of trusts. If you want to learn more about the ranch, a simple Google search will explain a lot to you. Safe to say, on public record, I am a trustee of the ranch and its company. With the sudden ownership came generational wealth, and I wanted to keep my true relationship with the ranch a secret. Since then, I have lived as I always have, as a lawyer here in Fayetteville. Only a handful of people know the extent of my wealth or interest. Even my spouse does not know the half of it. But in the process, I reduced my public financial profile. Does that answer your question?"

Special Agent Babbit looked at him and asked, "But why keep it such a secret? Why stay here and slug it out as a lawyer?"

"Three reasons. Number one, I didn't want the wealth to go to my head and kill me. I used to be an alcoholic, so there's that. Number two, I enjoy being a lawyer. Number three, my family is here. My husband is here, my brother and I practice law together, and my elderly mother still comes to the office daily. It affords a pleasant and simple life."

Special Agent Babbit studied Jon, and after a long pause, Babbit said, "Seems reasonable. Do these Defenders here know anything about you or your ranch?"

Jon replied, "No, I don't know how they could, honestly. It would take some digging to find out more. I am sure there is a record, an article, or a photograph of me with dignitaries in New Mexico. Maybe my husband has a photo of me. I didn't catch that he posted on social media of the ranch. But, no, I don't think they know about the ranch or my resources. I suspect that will be short-lived because I've royally pissed those rednecks off. I'm sure an outspoken gay man grinds their gears."

"Well, about that, Mr. Freeman. I want to assign a detail to keep an eye on you. Is that all right? We believe there is a lot more we could learn from you. Answer me this, though. What are your immediate plans today and over the next few days? Will you remain here, or are you planning to what, go back to your ranch?" Special Agent Babbit asked.

"I had planned to have my house packed up to bug out today, but I'll be honest, I want to fight these cocksuckers, Special Agent. I do. My whole adult life, I have been a lawyer. I believed in something more significant than even the outcome of a particular case because I believed in the rule of law. I took oaths, too," Jon emphasized, "to support and defend our constitution."

"Unfortunately," Jon continued, "all I see today is our corrupt governor, every legislator in league with her, and these so-called 'Defenders' taking a giant shit on our law, our Constitution, and our sacred rules. I didn't earn a Purple Heart during my service in the Army, but I served with soldiers who did. And I'll tell you this, Special Agent Babbit. They bled because they believed they were fighting for an idea in our Constitution and Declaration of Independence. Ideas, Special Agent, ideas. I hate that these people seek to destroy what our Founders envisioned in 1776 and after."

The meeting lasted much longer than Jon or Special Agent Babbit planned because they adjourned at five o'clock in the afternoon. Special Agent Babbit introduced Jon to a two-man security detail, and both young men seemed genuinely interested in Jon's safety, which was something Jon sensed and appreciated.

* * *

During Jon's visit with the FBI, about ten thousand white men of different ages, shapes, and sizes gathered in the bleachers at War Memorial Stadium in Little Rock. In their collective midst stood Governor Suzy Brandy Landers, red cowboy boots and all, behind a microphone in the middle of the field at the fifty-yard line.

The governor began her speech to the assembled men in the bleachers.

"All you here, God is with you. I am with you. That you are here tells me you will fight to return us to the state and country we once knew. We must take our country back because the United States of America is no longer a Christian Nation. No. Our once beloved America has become a nation of weak, homosexual, child-porn-addicted perverts run by spineless liberals. It is now home to baby killers and race traitors who corrupt our precious Anglo-Saxon blood and heritage through interracial marriages. We are under the heels of money-grubbing, Christ-killing coastal Jews and liberals who take, take, and take. So, I ask you, are you ready to serve our great state as my deputies?"

Shouts of affirmation erupted from the bleachers as the voices of ten thousand men chanted, "God is with us! We are your Army! God is with us!"

"All of you, repeat after me!" announced the governor as she began the oath.

I solemnly swear before God/
that I will faithfully execute the duties of an Arkansas Defender/
on behalf of my state/
and behalf of all the member states of the Red State Compact/
and that I will faithfully and dutifully enforce, preserve, protect, and defend the
New Law/
and that having been appointed to serve as an Arkansas Defender/
that I will obey all orders of the Governor of the State of Arkansas and her
successors/

and that I will follow the orders of the officers appointed over me according to the
New Law/
and the regulations promulgated thereunder, so help me, God.

Governor Landers smiled broadly, "Congratulations, boys," she exclaimed.

"Now, therefore, as Governor of the State of Arkansas, I declare a State of Emergency to exist within the State of Arkansas, and according to existing law, I am calling upon and deputizing every one of you reputable citizens of the state for assistance. I grant you authority to act through the Arkansas Military Department Chain of Command, the Arkansas State Police, and the Arkansas Defenders to enforce the law according to your orders under the New Law, which is now in effect."

"May God give you the power because I sure have!" she declared. "Now, report to your assigned section commanders for further instructions. Have a good weekend, and we will see you at work bright and early beginning Monday morning."

13

Safety

Chee arrived at Highland House after sundown with two Caballeros the same day Jon escaped his Defender pursuers. Chee and the two cowboys who joined him loaded up what was left of Highland House except for the furniture. Jon asked them to take special care to remove books, technology, computers, memorabilia, photographs, and documents. After that, Chee went to the firm and packed Jon's office, including his computers and files. They were on the road by midnight after a quick chat with Jon by phone.

"I have everything packed up, Hosteen," Chee said.

"Thank you, Curtis. I know it's been a long day, and it's late, but you need to get on the road. We can discuss what happened here when I return to the ranch. Highland House is surely being watched, so I am staying with a friend in town. I expect to fly back tomorrow. If we time it right, maybe you can pick me up at the airport in Los Alamos. Meanwhile, watch your back."

"Do you think someone is going to follow us?" Chee asked.

"Maybe, but a dually with New Mexico plates and a horse trailer at the house might throw them off. Just watch your back," Jon said. "I made sure to call my neighbors to let them know I've sold the place and am having it packed up to avoid one of them calling the police."

"What do you want us to do if we get pulled over?" Chee asked.

"It depends on who pulls you over. Local or state police are probably okay but don't give them a reason to pull you over. Mind the speed laws. I presume you received Will Thomas's email with a bill of sale showing that the ranch owns everything you are hauling. So, if you're questioned about any of it, you'll have some evidence." Jon said.

"Sounds good, Hosteen."

"But Curtis, listen to me. Do whatever you must to avoid being pulled over by a black SUV. I'd drive north from here on I-49 to Missouri to get you out of Arkansas as quickly as possible. Then, you can make your way to New Mexico through Kansas. It adds a bit to the drive time, but going north will have you out of Arkansas in less than an hour. All I'm saying is this: don't get pulled over by a black SUV."

"Yes, sir," Chee affirmed.

"Thanks, Curtis," Jon said. "Drive safely."

* * *

After a restless few hours of sleep on Tiny's couch, Jon rose early Saturday morning and called his mother and brother. They agreed to meet at his mother's house in town, where the three sat down over cups of Folgers, the only coffee the Colonel would drink.

"Son," his mother began, "I saw what happened at the courthouse yesterday on the news. Were you caught up in all that?"

"Yes, I was. It was horrifying."

"Those men," the Colonel asked, "did they want something with you?"

"If you've watched the news, Mom, you've heard about the New Law. I am opposing it with other lawyers, and the governor doesn't like it, so she sent her new goons after me," Jon said.

"That's crazy, son. She can't do that!" The Colonel exclaimed.

"Well, Mom, she can. And she did. We lost the case, so the New Law is in effect. I can't stay here because if I do, they will eventually arrest me and Martin. It won't stop there, though. I'm afraid they will come after anyone close to me, including you and Ira."

Ira listened, saying, "I just can't get my head around all that. Surely, the federal courts will stop it. Or an appeal of the state judge's decision at least."

"Maybe, " Jon said, "but these people actively pursued me, and I'm not going to wait around to be arrested or worse. That's why I need to get out of here, and we need to get the two of you out of here, too. I have a plane chartered and ready to go. There's plenty of room for you, Elaine, and your boys if you want to bring them. Plenty of space on the plane, okay? But I have to leave now. They will be coming. I promise you."

"Wait," Ruth said, "the ranch, aren't you just a trustee?"

"I am the trustee, but my word is law there. Trust me on this. There is no issue." Jon replied patiently.

With a look of concern, Ruth asked Jon, "Well, is it going to be all right with the owner, and is there enough room for us?"

"To answer your question, yes, and yes," Jon said. "There is a large vacant home on the property with plenty of room. The owner has no problems with it. I've already worked that out."

Jon hated lying like that to his mother, but there was no time to explain it all today.

"Well, son," Ruth replied as she placed her coffee cup on the table, "I appreciate your concern, but I'm not going anywhere. I'm 90 years old. My house, my things, and my people are here. I've seen political swings before, and this is just one of those swings. I remember when the blacks couldn't eat in the same room as us, but that time passed. This situation will pass, too. After things calm down, you can come back. We have made do without you in the office so you can care for yourself."

There is no reasoning with her. She isn't going anywhere.

"I agree," Ira said. "This stuff isn't lasting long. All of it is illegal. I bet the feds end it before it gets too far down the line. Go, though. I get it. Everything will sort itself out in the courts. How about money? You haven't been on the payroll. Are you getting by alright?"

Jon didn't need the money, but he kept his secret. Perhaps it was time to tell them about the Valle Grande and the truth of it, but not today. Instead, Jon pleaded unsuccessfully with them to join him, finally leaving his mom's house in the same Uber that brought him over there with the FBI security a block away, keeping watch.

* * *

"Where do you want me to take you now," the Uber driver asked as Jon stepped into the back seat of the spotless Toyota Corolla.

"Springdale Airport, please. I'll put it in the app for you. I need to go to the FBO." Jon said.

"No worries, I know where it is," replied the Uber driver.

Along the way to Springdale Airport, Jon called Special Agent Babbit to tell him he was returning to New Mexico.

Jon hopped out of the Uber and gave the driver five stars and a generous tip before stepping through the glass door and into the grey corrugated metal building. The fixed base operator at Springdale Municipal Airport didn't have a fancy facility with its plain waiting area and plastic chairs, but the Pilatus PC-12 parked outside on the ramp was a welcome site because it would fly him to safety.

"You ready, Jon?" asked the pilot, Rex Earl Bosworth, as he greeted Jon. Rex was a commercial pilot for the charter service and a flight instructor when he wasn't flying charters.

"Yeah, Rex, I'm ready. Let's get the fuck out of here," Jon said.

"Hey man, hop up front with me," Rex suggested. "Get in the left seat. On the way, you're going to do most of the flying. It's about time you got checked out on this beast."

"Right on. My left shoulder is a little jacked up, but I can still use it!"

Jon settled into the left seat behind the controls as Rex secured the cabin door. Rex climbed into the right seat, "Man, all you have to do today is worry about flying. I'll handle everything else. Hell, I'll even do the radios for you. After we taxi out, we'll fly a northerly heading that I've programmed into the flight director, so get us to altitude, and then we'll hook a left and get you to Los Alamos."

"What a deal," Jon agreed. Every bit of him loved flying, even the procedural aspects of flight. It might be nice to focus on something completely unrelated to what had happened to him the day before. Rex made the radio calls, and they proceeded to run up with departure clearance. Everything was green for immediate departure on Runway 36.

Jon taxied away from the ramp along Taxiway Alpha when he noticed three black SUVs pulling up on the other side of the chain link fence between the aviation area and the car park on the other side. Jon increased the power to get to the end of the taxiway a little quicker. He reached the hold-short line and instinctively depressed the mike, "Tower, Pilatus Niner Four Yankee Victor Echo, holding short of 36, ready for departure."

Tower responded.

"Pilatus Niner Four Yankee Victor Echo cleared for take-off runway 36, Spring Five Departure. Pick up Razorback on 126.6 once airborne."

"Clear for Departure, 36, Spring Five Departure. Contact Razorback 126.6. Niner Four Yankee Victor Echo."

Jon swiftly guided the airplane onto the runway and pushed the throttle forward, instantly feeling the force pressing him into his seat. Observing the SUVs approaching the fence, he knew he had to take off quickly. He added a notch of flaps for extra lift, and the lead SUV crashed through the gate, closely followed by the second one.

"Airspeed is alive," Jon called out.

"V1," Rex called out.

"Rotate," Jon called out after.

Jon made his move. The Pilatus lifted off at a steep angle, leaving the Defenders holding their dicks 1,000 feet below and a half mile behind.

Rex radioed the tower, "Tower, Pilatus Niner Four Yankee Victor Echo. We are well clear of the temporary runway obstruction. You might want to update your NOTAMS."

"Pilatus Niner Four Yankee Victor Echo. That was a good piece of flying. I guess those guys missed theirs! Contact Razorback on 126.6."

When word got back to Special Agent Babbit that Defenders pursued Jon to the airport, Babbit wondered how they knew to follow him. They must have had a man on him the whole time, who escaped the security detail's observation. The Defenders he encountered yesterday were not overburdened with intelligence, but at least some were smart enough to avoid detection. Babbit realized the Defenders might not give up so quickly. If they followed Jon to the airport, what else would they try? Would they go after Jon's mother or his brother, Ira?

The flight to Los Alamos lasted about two hours. When Jon landed, he called Chee to see where he was. To his delight, Chee wasn't far from Los Alamos, so he wouldn't have to wait long for a ride. While he waited at the Los Alamos FBO, Jon called his mother. All was well. Ruth acted as though she didn't want to be bothered because she was into whatever sports were playing on ESPN at about 1:00 p.m. on a Saturday. Good. Next call to his brother, then to Paul Joseph.

"I guess you saw what happened on the news yesterday," Jon said when Paul answered.

"For whatever reason, Judge Taylor suddenly resigned," Jon continued. "Then, of all fucking people, Hal Ledger, who I assumed would be on our side, fucked us. Hell, he voted against the legislation and then denied the injunction."

Paul said, "The deal with Taylor's resignation had to be a setup. I'll investigate Hal Ledger, but rumor has it that he has a gay grandson who is not just gay but super-duper gay, like former Miss Gay Arkansas gay. The governor might have used that to get that ruling out of him in exchange for, I don't know, protecting the grandson from the New Law. I'll see what I can turn up."

"Jesus. Well, take that money I left with you and file every goddamned thing you can," Jon suggested.

"Jon, keep your money," Paul said. "The lawyers and I haven't spent a dime of it. And we won't. We've pooled together quite a war chest ourselves. We're going to go federal next. Just stay out of Arkansas for a while. We'll be in touch. Let's have a daily call."

"Yeah, that's fine," Jon said. "I had everything packed up and sent out here to New Mexico. Keep an eye on my brother and mom, will you? I begged them to come with me, but they had their heads in the sand. And you need to watch your ass, my friend."

* * *

Jon safely returned to New Mexico, and Governor Landers remained busy churning the butter with more laws pouring out of the legislature weekly. The initial temporary injunction Jon won in court only bought the governor time to fine-tune her treachery.

The New Law erected the equivalent of a fourth branch of state government, its most notable feature being what became known as the Commission for Standards, Morality, and Education. The commission possessed powers to create rules, regulations, sanctions, and punishments under the New Law.

The New Law also erected a tribunal with all the powers of a court of general jurisdiction. Governor Landers appointed Pastor Lawrence Lee Huckabee, her cousin with no legal training, to lead the commission and set her friend, the unhinged Tom Hardy Blasingame, over the tribunal. Even though the combined Full-Scale IQ between Pastor Lawrence and Judge Blasingame could not have been more than 175 on the best days, those two would be efficient agents of the governor's plan.

The tribunal's judges were called chancellors, who were all gubernatorial appointees. The New Law provided the governor could appoint one chancellor for each of Arkansas' 75 counties. It would be up to the county quorum court to give each chancellor chambers, a secretary, and a courtroom. The state would provide court security through the Defenders. The task was monumental, but the governor had the candidates preselected. So, once Judge Hal Ledger's order dismissed Jon's temporary injunction, the governor's appointments were made effective. The New Law machinery could then begin its grind without further delay.

One of the significant challenges for Governor Landers was coordinating between her Military Department, the Defenders, and law enforcement. There were glitches while the governor and the military department secured the cooperation of law enforcement departments throughout the state, and the governor knew courts and lawsuits would challenge her. Part of her strategy was to ignore federal decisions. At the state level, she would secure the cooperation of the Arkansas Court of Appeals and the Arkansas Supreme Court by intimidation. If the Court of Appeals or Arkansas Supreme Court refused to do her bidding, she'd refer them to the new commission or the tribunal for a hearing and potential removal from office. She would not tolerate any more delays with the New Law's implementation.

Governor Landers learned a lot when Judge Ledger's ruling came down before she could coordinate the Defender's activities with the Fayetteville City Police and other law enforcement agencies in Washington County. Had she achieved that coordination beforehand, perhaps the scene at the Washington County Courthouse would have been less chaotic. In all likelihood, the chaos is what allowed Jon Freeman to escape. Her error taught her an important lesson, and she would not make that mistake again. The Defenders needed the complete cooperation of all law enforcement in Arkansas, from the head of the Department of Public Safety down to beat cops.

* * *

After the governor signed the bills making up the New Law, she ordered that a new title be added to the existing Arkansas Code so the New Law could be found in one place. On the surface, Title 29's code sections looked like the rest of the statutes, with all sorts of legalese and official-sounding terms that only lawyers could decipher. None of it seemed particularly evil, but one might come to a different conclusion on closer reading.

Section 103 proved to be one of those benign appearing statutes when it was a herald for a legion of evils that would pour out upon the people of Arkansas. The section entitled "Statutory Construction to Promote Purposes and Policies - Applicability of Supplemental Law Principles" read:

This subtitle shall be liberally construed and applied to promote its underlying purposes and policies, which are:

(a) to promote standard norms of behavior in civic, business, public, and private life that are consistent with the fundamental Judeo-Christian values and the Race of White Anglo-Saxons and their descendants, traditionally observed within the United States;

(b) to enforce, through the application of these norms, a variety of legislative and regulatory measures consistent with these purposes herein described that will elevate and advance matters of public health and society; and,

(c) to reestablish, reclaim, and enforce adherence to the traditions and moral standards that prevailed throughout society by applying legislative, regulatory, and law-enforcement means.

On Monday, June 19th, 2023, Tom Hardy Blasingame, the newly appointed Chief Judge of the Tribunal for Causes of Standards, Morality, and Education, was beside himself with joy as he read through the freshly codified sections of the New Law for the tenth time. He had waited a lifetime for the government to realize that all the problems in the world could be solved if people lived by the Bible and traditional Christian values. And even though Judge Blasingame wasn't very bright when it came down to it, he did have good instincts. He wasn't about to let the opportunities go to waste when there was an overabundance of political will for the first (and only) time in his adult life to pass laws putting things right. So, as he read, he harbored a particular fondness for what he considered to be the crown jewel of all the New Law's achievements: Section 104.

Section 104 read:

The King James Version of the Holy Bible, as well as the Authorized Version, is composed of 80 books, including 39 books of the Old Testament and 27 books of the New Testament, excluding the intertestamental sections known as the Apocrypha, and shall be considered the law of Arkansas. Any duly appointed judicial

137

officer of the state may choose to apply the Bible as defined herein to any case or controversy before him. It is, moreover, the express desire of the Arkansas General Assembly that the prescriptions set forth by the King James and the Authorized Versions of the Holy Bible, not be merely considered supplementary but that its use should be promoted and may be utilized to supplant or supersede existing law if so described with particularity in any decree or judgment to supplant existing law at the discretion of the judicial officer.

Pastor Huckabee, the commission's newly appointed chairman and commissioner, matched Blasingame's appetite for old-fashioned biblical justice. Likewise, he gloated over the New Law's provisions by his umpteenth rereading. Still, it would be in the tribunal where the rubber would meet the road with the slew of cases and controversies that would surely test its authority.

14

Gerry the Veteran

On the sweltering summer day of June 30th, 2023, a Friday, the air was thick with humidity. Tiny made his way towards a local all-you-can-eat Chinese buffet on College Avenue, anticipating an early lunch. Even with his air conditioner working overtime, the heat was stifling. As he neared the intersection, he spotted Defenders creating a blockade, with cars queued for a block toward Baba's, Jon's favorite coffee hangout. Impatient, especially when hunger struck in the urban jungle, Tiny sought an alternate route. However, Defender SUVs had cordoned off the side streets. Progress was slow. Nearing the main intersection of North and College, he noticed a black van stationed at one corner. Uniformed Defenders were ushering a group of disheveled individuals into the vehicle while others managed the crawling traffic.

What the fuck is going on?

Tiny picked up his cell phone and called 911.

"911. What's your emergency?"

"Yeah, I am stuck in traffic on College just south of the intersection with North Street, and a bunch of guys dressed in black army-looking costumes are rounding up the homeless people at that intersection. You need to send the police over here or somebody."

"Sir," the 911 operator responded, "everything is being taken care of. Thank you." Then, the line went dead.

Well, shit, he thought. *I guess we're not rid of those Defenders after all.*

Traffic inched forward. Tiny got a better look and recognized one man being conducted into the back of the black van. It was a guy Tiny knew only as "Gerry," who often panhandled at that intersection with a sign that read "Will work for food." Gerry was clad in dirty, off-brand jeans 3 or 4 sizes too large for his withered frame and a red thread-bare Arkansas football tee-shirt. Gerry's balding head was bowed, and his tangled beard hung below the grimace on his face. Tiny didn't know much about Gerry beyond his name and that he was a veteran of the war in Afghanistan who probably suffered from PTSD.

A uniformed man in black directed traffic while some others checked the IDs of drivers as they proceeded through the intersection.

Tiny rolled down his window when he pulled up.

"Hey, excuse me, what's going on here?"

"Hello, Citizen," the man in black said. "Everything is fine here. Mind if I check your identification and car registration, please?"

Tiny complied.

As the uniformed man examined the ID and registration, he asked Tiny, "Are you employed?"

Tiny was taken aback for a second.

"Excuse me?"

"Are you employed, sir?" the Defender asked.

"Well, yes, of course," Tiny said with a smirk. "How the hell do you think I can afford this Jeep?"

"Sir, I have to ask. Here you go," the Defender responded.

He returned the documents to Tiny and continued to answer Tiny's original question.

"We are helping get these citizens a place to stay so they can get on their feet—no need for you to worry about them. We are here to help. It is part of the New Law's full-employment provision. Now, sir, I need you to move it along to keep traffic going. Have a blessed day."

Tiny pulled forward through the checkpoint, looking over his shoulder as the van doors shut.

Where are they taking those people?

Tiny decided the buffet could wait, so he found an unguarded side street behind the old Evelyn Hills Shopping Center after cutting in front of someone in the lane to his right. He drove up the hill with College Avenue behind him, through a neighborhood lane, and then circled back down the hill. The intersection was cleared by now, but on a hunch, he decided to drive south on College Avenue toward the county jail.

Where else would they be taking these people?

It wasn't long before he caught up to the black van. Tiny kept his distance. Following block by block along South College Avenue, he passed the Freeman Law Firm to his left, the old courthouse, and then headed down Archibald Yell with its wide and sweeping turns.

The van continued south toward the county jail, a complex of drab, military-grey cement government buildings. The convoy turned on the access road to the unmistakable site but didn't stop at the jail. Instead, it drove toward a collection of military-style tents on the opposite end of the county complex.

Off on the far north end of the complex was a vacant field with about 50 canvas tents set up in an open area. The tents were arranged in neat rows, with old military-style mess tents and their cylindrical chimneys at the far end of each row. While the presence of the tents themselves might not have been a cause for alarm, the tall chain-link security fence topped with coiled razor wire was.

"What the fuck is going on here," Tiny pondered, thinking out loud.

Tiny pulled into the coroner's office driveway to turn around when he saw a black SUV pull out through a chain-link gate. It pulled onto a service road, coming directly at him at speed.

Jesus.

He turned off the ignition and walked into the coroner's office's front door as if he owned the place.

The building was constructed of the same jail grey cement as the other county buildings. There was a small waiting room with a reception desk placed atop sterile white tile underneath garish fluorescent lights. No one

141

was at the desk. There was a strong smell of bleach. To his right was a hallway that led down to more doors. To his left was a shorter hallway with restrooms. Simple enough. He chose the right hallway and walked down, hearing a vehicle door shut outside as he did. He picked the first door and went in. It was a small office occupied by the coroner himself.

"Can I help you?" an elderly white-haired man in a lab coat asked with some degree of consternation.

"I'm sorry to barge in," Tiny said, "but I need a place to duck in for a minute. I don't know who they are, but a guy in a black SUV drove this way, and I think he is looking for me."

The look of consternation on the man's face turned to one of concern.

"Yeah, those guys," the coroner said. "Here, you follow my lead, okay? Your mother just died, and she's back there on ice, so leave it to me. I don't like those guys. Anything they are up to isn't good. So, follow my...."

The door opened abruptly, and a Defender stood there, his hand on his sidearm.

"Hey, hold on a goddamn minute, son," the prickly coroner demanded. "Don't they teach you how to knock? I'm conducting an interview."

"I need to ask this man some questions," said the officious Defender.

"No, you don't, son," the coroner told him. "Listen, I have his mother on ice in the back here. Whatever it is you must ask him, it will have to wait. I'm about to go with him to identify the body and continue my death investigation. On these matters, I outrank you, the sheriff, and just about any other goddamn official in this county. I'm a constitutional officeholder. Did you get that? Now, remove yourself!"

The young man in the black uniform was strangely intimidated by the old man.

"I'm sorry to disturb you. I just needed to ask this gentleman why he is down here."

"Jesus, son, isn't it obvious?" The coroner was growing more impatient as if speaking to a petulant child, "He is here because his mamma cashed in her chips, and I asked him to come to my office to find out about the circumstances of her death. As the county coroner, it's my job to investigate deaths in this county. You're getting in the way of that, so get out of my office and try using some common-goddamned sense next time."

"I'm, I'm sorry, sir," the Defender said as he excused himself and pulled the coroner's office door behind him.

The coroner held up his hand with his palm facing Tiny while the sounds of the Defender's boots receded down the hall until they heard the front door open and shut. After a few seconds, the coroner dropped his hand and resumed his aggravated expression as he addressed Tiny.

"It seems I just saved your ass," he said. "What the hell are you doing down here, anyway? That one was as green as they come, but let me tell you, most of them are not all that easy to get along with, and they have hardly any restrictions on what they can do. So, don't come poking around down here again, you hear me? There's no telling what will become of you!"

"I saw those guys pick up some homeless people at North and College, so I wanted to see where they were taking them. Now, I know." Tiny told the old man.

The coroner looked at Tiny and said, "They are a new law enforcement agency for the State of Arkansas and the Red State Compact. It's been on the news."

"I don't watch much TV, but I had a run-in with them earlier this spring," Tiny said.

"I suggest you broaden your interests and catch up on some news, my boy," the coroner said, "because these Defenders outrank local police, state troopers, and even sheriffs. You name it. They can arrest anyone at any time and for any reason. Consider leaving this state if you know what's good for you. Things are changing, son. I'd get myself out of Arkansas if I weren't so damn old, but lucky for me, there's not much about me that they care about. I'm an old white man carrying a coroner's badge and attending a Baptist church."

* * *

Tiny departed the jail complex. Gerry, the veteran, did not because

Gerry remained at the camp. He was among the first detainees at the Washington County Rehabilitation and Reeducation Center erected by the Commission for Standards, Morality, and Education. Gerry was confused and dehydrated when he arrived, having been off his anti-psychotic meds for several days. At least Gerry had the presence of one of his minds to appreciate a few things: a hot meal, a shower, and a roof over his head. He wasn't free to come and go as he pleased, like at the homeless shelter, but this might be better than he had had in a long time with hot food and a routine.

Two Defender escorts brought Gerry into the tent encampment through a sally port constructed of barbed wire with a gate on either end. From there, they took Gerry into a large tent with a placard over the doorway that read "Welcome Center." Going through the canvas flaps, two rows of folding chairs were inside. Beyond the first row of chairs were folding tables with one chair behind each table, a stack of forms for each, and a label maker. The inside of the tent would have been dark but for the naked light bulbs rigged up and hanging from the support poles inside the tent. A portable air conditioner blew cool air inside but did little good to staunch the heat. His guard escorted him to a desk behind which a middle-aged man sat wearing the same black uniform as all the others.

Gerry's escort sat him down in the folding chair before the table.

"Hello, sir. I have some questions for you so we can get you situated," said the black-clad Defender.

"Where am I?" Gerry whispered through a blank stare.

"You're safe, sir," was the reply. "We are here to help you, okay?"

"Okay," Gerry responded.

The Defender behind the desk asked several questions such as name, can you read and write the English language, gender, last address where you lived, current occupation, previous occupation, married, single, gay, straight, bi, trans, children, no children, military service, education, property, religion, church membership, and a slew of other questions about health and family history. Once the Defender finished his inquiries and filled out his form, he reached over to a keyboard and entered some data.

After checking it, he pressed a button. The black label-making machine whirred to life, producing a blue wristband with a barcode named Gerry Lyndon Barksdale.

With his wristband on his left wrist, a different Defender accompanied Gerry through an open end of the processing tent where the flaps had been pulled aside and tied back like drapes. Walking out into the midday sunlight, the Defender took Gerry to an open space between the rows of tents on either side. Each tent had a placard with a number above its front door. On the opposite end of the walk from the welcome tent was a similar-looking tent with a large white cross mounted on top of it in the center.

It wouldn't be too long before the encampment south of Fayetteville would be full of detainees who were unemployed, undesirable, or in need of "reeducation."

15

Smith v. Smith

T he Tribunal for Causes of Standards, Morality, and Education was open for business, consisting of Chief Judge Blasingame and 12 other judges who acted through a majority vote. He intended the tribunal to be patterned after the ancient Hebrew courts the Torah describes in the Book of Judges. Blasingame named each seat on the tribunal after one of Israel's original judges: Othniel, Ehud, Shamgar, Deborah, Gideon, Tola, Jair, Jephthah, Ibzan, Elon, Abdon, and Samson. Even though Judge Blasingame was a committed misogynist, he conceded that a woman must fill the shoes of the "Deborah" judgeship. After all, the Bible said so. Beyond the governor and the "Deborah" judgeship, he had no use for women other than as breeding vessels and someone to keep his house clean or offer sexual comforts.

The tribunal took a particular interest in domestic relations law. According to the New Law, individuals seeking a divorce were allowed to file in state circuit courts or before a tribunal chancellor in their county of residence. The New Law also permitted a local chancellor to take jurisdiction over a divorce case from the local circuit judge.

It was August of 2023 when the first case went to chancery court. It was a case of adultery in Lafayette County, Arkansas. The petitioner was a 45-year-old God-fearing man named Hansel Smith, who accused his wife of having an affair with a man who lived in the trailer next to theirs at the

Easy Pines Trailer Court in rural Lafayette County.

Over the objection of Jenny Smith's otherwise capable attorney, Chancellor Edwin Rippon called the case of *Smith v. Smith* on Monday, August 21st, 2023, at 9:00 a.m. He listened to Mr. Smith's witness, who testified that he could hear a man and a woman "going at it" in the single-wide trailer next door to Mr. Smith's residence. When asked what he meant by that and how he knew it was Smith's wife, the witness testified he was walking past the trailer when he heard a man say in ecstasy through its paper-thin walls, "Jenny, stick that thing up my ass and make it count!" Hearing the nocturnal activities and the man's excited utterance, he ran over to Smith's trailer and woke him to tell him what was happening.

On the stand, Mr. Smith recalled getting up and running next door after being supplied with the news.

Mr. Smith's lawyer asked him, "What did you do when you got next door to your neighbor's trailer, Mr. Smith?"

"Well, sir," testified Mr. Smith, "I was pretty worked up, so I beat that door like it owed me money until that sorry son of a bitch came and opened it up."

"What happened next?" asked Mr. Smith's lawyer.

Smith leaned forward in the witness chair and pointed at his wife's paramour, who was in the courtroom and likewise accused under the Biblical law. He raised his voice, declaring, "That piece of shit opened the door and started hollerin' at me. And my wife was standing behind him, lookin' like she had been rode hard and put up wet. I swear, if you'd throw'd her panties against a wall, those damn things would have stuck to it they was so wet."

The lawyer said, "I think we get the picture, Mr. Smith. So, she was dressed in panties? Is that it?"

"Panties and a t-shirt," said Mr. Smith. "That was it. Looked to me like she had her ashes hauled."

It is said that hell hath no fury like a woman scorned, but in *Smith v. Smith*, the reverse was true. Petitioner Smith, the spurned husband and self-proclaimed "Bible-believing" Christian, intended to exact his revenge.

Inspired by a lifetime of hackneyed sermons, snake handlers, and country preachers, Mr. Smith fancied himself a biblical scholar. After all, he had taken his learning in sacred scripture at tent revivals and vo-tech Bible seminars with his grandma, Etta Mae Smith. Despite his sixth-grade reading ability, his Bible was well-worn, especially the Old Testament pages. So, despite his intellectual shortcomings, Smith was sure of one thing: he wanted that bitch to pay.

Mr. Smith's lawyer, a like-minded "Christian" from the same small town, wasn't burdened with a good reputation or many clients. Still, when he had heard the scuttlebutt going around Lewisville about Mrs. Smith and her extramarital adventures, he went to Smith's house and volunteered to be his lawyer free of charge. A free lawyer, even a bad one, was fine with Mr. Smith. Besides, how hard could it be? The lawyer was undoubtedly bright enough to prove adultery, but the legal *coup de grace* would be the penalty. Even that wouldn't take a work of genius according to the dictates of the Good Book.

In court, Mr. Smith's lawyer proposed Leviticus 20:10 as the penalty, ably quoted from his copy of the King James Version: "And the man that committeth adultery with another man's wife, even he that committeth adultery with his neighbor's wife, the adulterer, and the adulteress shall surely be put to death."

The chancellor agreed and sentenced the unrepresented neighbor man to death, but he reserved the sentence of death for Smith's wife so the tribunal could decide her fate. In other words, the chancellor was content to kick Mrs. Smith's case to the tribunal while the order to dispense with the neighbor man would be carried out immediately and in secret.

Mrs. Smith's attorney, Roscoe Bender, was a distinguished 70-year-old lawyer renowned in those regions. His snow-white hair and Southern drawl perfectly mirrored his affable nature. However, despite his amiable demeanor, he couldn't hide his disdain after being outwitted by a questionable "lawyer" with a string of bar complaints long enough to wallpaper Bender's living room.

Bender's arguments fell on deaf ears, so he appealed. After filing the notice of appeal, Mr. Bender returned to his two-room office across the street from the county courthouse. The court's consideration of stoning his client, much less the unsuspecting neighbor, seemed unimaginable. Fueled by frustration, he began making calls to tell anyone he could about what happened. He called his wife, his best friend, the sheriff, and anyone he could think of, all the way up the chain to the governor's office.

The exasperated lawyer faced dead-ends until he finally connected with someone who suggested calling a local news station. The station, in turn, directed him to TNN's Washington News Bureau. When he got through, a producer introduced him to the reporter who broke the news on Jon Freeman's lawsuit against the State of Arkansas. It was imperative, Bender believed, to tell somebody, anybody, about the events that transpired in that Lafayette County courtroom, even if no one would believe it.

* * *

A day later, a fax arrived on Mr. Bender's fax machine, which read:

BEFORE THE TRIBUNAL FOR CAUSES OF STANDARDS, MORALITY AND EDUCATION

JENNY SMITH, APPELLANT,

v.

HANSEL SMITH, APPELLEE.

CAUSE A23-001

On appeal from the Chancery Court of Lafayette County, Arkansas, Chancellor Edwin Rippon, Presiding

<u>NOTICE OF HEARING</u>

NOW, THEREFORE, on this 22nd day of August 2023, the

tribunal, being well and sufficiently advised, hereby gives notice that a hearing on the appeal of *Smith v. Smith* shall be heard by the tribunal on Monday, August 28th, 2023, commencing at 9:00 a.m., at its courtroom in Little Rock, Arkansas, or at another time to be ordered by the tribunal. Counsel is advised to contact the tribunal's clerk a day before the hearing for further instructions.

IT IS SO ORDERED.

PER CURIAM

Roscoe Bender wasn't one to use harsh language because his long-since-dead mother's words haunted him every time he cursed. "Roscoe Erasmus Bender, I'm going to have to wash your mouth out with soap," she'd say. But if there was ever an exception to his reflexive disdain for the vernacular, this was it. Even then, the most he could utter was, "Jesus Christ, what kind of kangaroo court is this? Less than a week's notice for a hearing?"

He picked up the phone and called the clerk of the tribunal in Little Rock. Like any officious bureaucrat, she utilized the word "no" brutally. "No, you may not speak with the chief judge." "No, you can't delay the hearing." "No, there will be no briefs filed."

After the call, Mr. Bender dictated a petition for an emergency *writ of certiorari* he intended to file with the Supreme Court of Arkansas to wrest jurisdiction from the tribunal. He asked the Supreme Court to vacate the tribunal's hearing scheduled for the 28th.[16] He argued in his petition that the tribunal had no jurisdiction or authority to hear an appeal because it was unconstitutional. An even more officious Supreme Court clerk rejected it with a simple phone call to be followed by a *per curiam* order denying the *writ*. And sure enough, within an hour after his call with the Supreme Court clerk, Mr. Bender received an electronic notice that the Arkansas Supreme Court rejected his emergency writ.

* * *

It was Wednesday, August 23rd, 2023, at 4:00 p.m., New Mexico time. Jon was still a few miles north of La Hacienda on a horse when his cell phone vibrated. He had been checking fences with Sam Hernandez and some of the Caballeros all day. He didn't recognize the number, but it was an Arkansas area code. Jon answered, overcoming his temptation to let it go to voice mail. He tied off the reins on the horn of his saddle. Maybell knew the way home better than he did, anyway.

"Hello, is this Mr. Jon Freeman?" asked Roscoe Bender.

"Speaking," replied Jon.

"Mr. Freeman, my name is Roscoe Bender. I'm a lawyer from Lewisville. Quite a ways down south from you. You're Fayetteville, yes?"

"I used to be in Fayetteville," Jon said, "but in April, I had a case in Washington County to challenge the New Law. We lost the case. The Arkansas Defenders intended to take me into custody, so I fled."

"Good Lord," Bender said. "I read about your case. Things have gone south over here with the New Law. Anyway, I spoke with a TNN reporter who connected me with you. Does the name Levi Pincus ring a bell?"

"Yes, I know Levi," Jon said.

"Well, I need some help, Mr. Freeman. After my talk with Levi, I did a little checking on my own, and there doesn't seem to be anyone who knows more about this New Law than you."

"Well, I wish that wasn't the case. Attorney General Purcell knows quite a bit about it, but he has dropped off the face of the earth. Until we hear from him, I'll step up and be the next best thing. So, Mr. Bender, how may I help?"

"I tried a divorce case before one of those new chancellors yesterday, but I don't think they have jurisdiction. The whole darn thing is unconstitutional. So, anyway, my lady was accused of adultery. The evidence was clear, and the chancellor found her guilty of it. He granted the divorce and suggested that the New Law would fix a punishment for her adultery, but he referred the punishment to the tribunal."

Mr. Bender continued.

"And the petitioner's lawyer, a local clown named Eddy Runyon, quoted

Leviticus and asked the chancellor to order that she be stoned to death."

"What happened after that?" Jon asked.

"The chancellor reserved ruling on the stoning, and I filed a notice of appeal. The next morning, the tribunal set a hearing seven days out. I mean, that's this coming Monday. Not only that, but I also filed a *writ* of *certiorari* with the Arkansas Supreme Court to try and stop the appeal and toss the case."

"Let me guess," Jon said. "The Supreme Court rejected your petition."

"That's right, that's right. So, what are my options?" asked Mr. Bender.

"Tell you what," Jon said, "I am on a horse in New Mexico. I'll get back to the house and call you to go over this in more detail, but let me offer this because it will be another hour before I get home. I want you to call a guy named Paul Joseph. He's a close friend leading a group of lawyers I've worked with since this all started. His number is easy to find online. When you call him, tell him I said a writ needs to be filed in federal court, not state court. The state courts are useless. If you want to have a chance of stopping or delaying a tribunal proceeding, you'll have to file it in federal court. I have to go for now. I'll follow up with you shortly after I get home."

As instructed, Mr. Bender filed a federal lawsuit the next day in the United States District Court for the Eastern District of Arkansas in Little Rock to stay the appeal for Mrs. Smith. Under federal venue laws, it was the only option. The judge appointed to hear the case was none other than Michael Lynell Taylor, who scheduled an emergency hearing the following day, Friday, August 25th, 2023, at 9:00 a.m.

Jon decided attending the hearing was a risk worth taking. Martin did not want him to go at first but relented, acknowledging it was time for Jon to go and make a difference.

* * *

The following morning, a Thursday, Jon's chartered jet touched down in Little Rock at 8:14 a.m. The cabin door opened as soon as the engines powered down. Two men with military haircuts in black dress coats and ties stood beside an unmarked grey Ford Explorer at the bottom of the stairs. Jon walked straight away to the waiting car.

The drive to the federal courthouse was smooth along Bond Street by old railroad tracks through the industrial and warehouse region by the river. Along the way, Jon observed a couple of Defender SUVs as they neared the federal courthouse, but his anxiety faded when they pulled into a secured underground parking garage.

Jon walked into the spacious old courtroom at 8:30 a.m. The "two worlds" Waha warned about were nagging him as he entered the empty courtroom, knowing he would have no peace until he brought down Buckshot's treachery. Jon sat behind the polished bar on the first row of oak pews and waited until the two heavy courtroom doors burst open as Paul Joseph walked in with Roscoe Bender and the accused adulteress, Jenny Smith.

"Jesus, man, you came," Paul exclaimed, reaching out to hug. "Meet Roscoe Bender and his client, Jenny Smith."

Jon extended his hand, "Pleasure to meet you, sir." He approached Mrs. Smith and extended his hand to her, "Ma'am. Nice to meet you, too."

Jon asked the lawyers, "So, gentlemen, what's the plan?"

"Plan?" Mr. Bender said. "I don't have one other than the hope we obtain an injunction against this so-called tribunal. This whole thing is outrageous. A tribunal with concurrent, if not superseding, jurisdiction over state circuit court judges? And the fact that the Bible is now part of Arkansas law? I don't think it takes a constitutional genius to argue about the separation of church and state!"

Paul Joseph was one hell of a lawyer. He was relentless, with a stratospheric IQ and a comprehensive understanding of law and procedure. He also knew Judge Taylor well. It was hard not to know one another among Arkansas's relatively small roster of attorneys, but those two were law school classmates. If anyone could get through to the judge, it would be Paul Joseph. Hopefully, Paul could succeed where Jon failed with Hal Ledger.

Paul and Bender sat at the counselor's table in the grand old courtroom, but Jon remained seated in his front-row pew. Suddenly, a lawyer from the Attorney General's Office appeared, the double doors swinging behind her as she walked in. Paul looked over at her as she sat at the counsel table and then turned in his leather swivel chair to look back at Jon, who shrugged his shoulders.

"Who the fuck is that," Jon said silently with his lips.

Paul, like most trial lawyers, was an excellent lipreader. No one knew this woman.

Newly appointed Federal District Judge Michael Lynell Taylor entered through a hidden wooden door and ascended the imposing bench. Underneath the district court seal and flanked by the flag of the United States to her right and the Arkansas flag to her left, Judge Taylor took her seat. She looked taller than the last time Jon saw her when she was a circuit judge in Washington County. Two United States Marshals joined the collection of people through side doors. The judge's court reporter and a young woman, probably her law clerk, followed behind and took their seats.

"All Rise," the bailiff called. "The United States District Court for the Eastern District of Arkansas is now in session, Judge Michael Lynell Taylor presiding. All persons having business before this court draw near, and you shall be heard. May God save these United States and this Honorable Court. You may be seated."

"Good morning, counselors. Well, well, if it isn't Jonathan Christian Freeman. Good morning. Will you be joining the fray this morning, Mr. Freeman?"

"No, Your Honor, I'm just a part of the interested public today," Jon replied.

"Morning, Mr. Joseph. So good to see you. Who do you have with you?" the judge asked.

"Good morning, Your Honor. My client, Jenny Smith, and associated counsel, Roscoe Bender, from Lewisville, join me today."

"And madam, I presume you represent the State of Arkansas?" The judge asked, looking at the young lady lawyer who rose awkwardly from her chair, unsteady in her four-inch heels.

"Good morning, Your Honor. My name is Vivian DeShields. I am here on behalf of the State of Arkansas and the attorney general."

"All right, well, not that it matters to me, Mrs. DeShields," said the judge, "but I'm a little surprised General Purcell isn't here today since this is, I take it, a matter of some importance to the State of Arkansas. Tell that rascal I expect to see him here next time."

Vivian smiled nervously, "Yes, Your Honor."

"Counselors, will there be any testimony today? And who will be presenting arguments?" the judge asked.

"We will present Mrs. Smith to verify her petition and answer your questions," reported Paul Joseph, "And I will argue for our side."

"Very well," the judge stated. "We can swear her in when you decide to call her."

The judge then looked at a notepad she had brought and a manila folder she opened and examined through her ruby-red reading glasses.

"So, this is the matter of Jenny Smith versus Judge Tom Hardy Blasingame, Chief Judge of the Arkansas Tribunal for Causes of Standards, Morality, and Education, and the Tribunal for Causes of Standards, Morality, and Education, and John Does 1 through 12, Eastern District Case 23-cv-1452."

Then, the judge looked upon the lawyers, "Are the parties ready?"

"Petitioner is ready," voiced Paul Joseph.

"The respondents are ready," replied Vivian DeShields.

"Mr. Joseph, do you desire an opening statement, or do you just want to get to it," asked the judge.

"Unless the court desires an opening, I'd just as soon call my first witness and get on with it," he replied.

It's an interesting tactic. Paul Joseph understood courtroom dynamics and the often-overlooked prize that brevity can purchase. If there was ever a mark of confidence in one's case, it was to waive an opening statement.

Paul Joseph called Mrs. Jenny Smith to the stand, and her testimony was brief. Her federal petition was because the divorce was filed in an unconstitutional court with no jurisdiction. Moreover, she feared an appellate body could order her death by stoning, another constitutional

155

violation.

Her testimony was followed by a brief cross-examination by Attorney DeShields, who asked whether the trial judge had passed a sentence under the New Law. Mrs. Smith answered truthfully that the trial judge had not handed such a sentence but had reserved the decision for the tribunal.

The direct examination and cross took less than 15 minutes. Judge Taylor had no questions when it was done.

"You may stand down and return to your seat, Mrs. Smith."

When Mrs. Smith sat down, Paul Joseph addressed the court.

"Is the court ready for argument?" he inquired.

"Indeed, the court is, Mr. Joseph. How much time would you like?"

"20 minutes, your honor, with 5 for rebuttal. If there is a rebuttal, Mr. Bender will present that."

"I have no problem with that. You don't have a problem with it, Mrs. DeShields?" asked the judge.

"No, no objection, Your Honor," said Mrs. DeShields.

Paul Joseph forcefully argued that the New Law violated the Constitution's separation of powers doctrine. He pointed out that creating the commission and tribunal through enabling legislation rather than a statewide constitutional amendment created an unconstitutional new arm of the judiciary in Arkansas.

Regarding the First Amendment Establishment Clause violation, he specifically highlighted the incorporation of the Holy Bible into the state's body of law.

"The New Law represents the most significant attack on civil liberties in the history of this state and the nation," Paul Joseph argued. "It is inconceivable that a legislature can delegate to a constituent body like the tribunal the authority to impose capital punishment for conduct that is not even an enumerated crime, let alone subject individuals to a penalty that clearly qualifies as cruel and unusual punishment under the Eighth Amendment. We, therefore, request this court to enjoin the New Law immediately, suspend the proceedings scheduled for Monday in Mrs. Smith's case, and prohibit any further unconstitutional actions."

Before he sat down, he asked: "Does the court have any questions?"

"No, I do not, thank you," said the judge.

Then, turning toward Mrs. DeShields, Judge Taylor asked, "Ma'am, do you have anything?"

"No, your honor, I will, as instructed, rest on the government's brief."

The judge took a moment on the bench to study her notepad, and then she looked up and said the following:

"I have carefully studied the petition, response, and briefs. I listened to the testimony and arguments presented today, aware that the petitioner seeks extraordinary relief. It is no small thing to ask a federal court to enjoin a state from enforcing its laws. As counsel knows, the enactments of a legislature receive a presumption that those enactments are constitutional. My ruling today rests on the notion that the acts of the General Assembly must benefit from that presumption. But before I get to the meat of the arguments, I acknowledge that the Lafayette County Chancellor did not issue a ruling on whether Mrs. Smith ought to be stoned to death for her adultery. You are here today because you are afraid of something that has not happened yet. On that basis alone, I must deny the injunction."

Jon jumped up, "Come on, Judge, are you kidding? You can't be serious!"

"Sit down, Mr. Freeman," the judge commanded. "We might go back a long way, but remember your place in this court of law."

The judge continued as a chastened Jon Freeman sat back down.

"As I said, I will not grant your petition, Mrs. Smith, because the issue is not ripe. I cannot forbid something that hasn't happened yet. The tribunal must issue a ruling first. Once it does, perhaps this court could reconsider your petition. But let me continue to give you an additional reason for my opinion. One of the issues I must consider when granting injunctive relief is to decide whether the underlying case has a reasonable chance of success on its merits. And while I appreciate your anxieties, I cannot make such a finding—quite the contrary. I do not believe it has much chance of success. Let me tell you why."

Shifting in her chair, the judge continued lording over the chamber. "Your case has little chance of success for two additional reasons. There is no "due process" issue here. Your "due process" argument overlooks Supreme Court precedent, thanks to the *Dobbs* Opinion from 2019 and its progeny.[17] The concept of substantive due process is non-existent because of *Dobbs* and the cases following it. To repeat what Justice Barker wrote in his concurring opinion in *Dobbs*, "substantive due process is an oxymoron." Instead, due process analysis asks if customary procedures are allowed and followed. You could cross-examine witnesses, make arguments, and even file an appeal. Again, as best I can tell, Mrs. Smith, you had a hearing and a lawyer with all the trappings of process."

The judge continued and declared, "Number two—the First Amendment Establishment Clause. I reject the idea that adopting the Holy Bible violates the Establishment Clause. While it may adopt the contents of a book called the "Bible," it does not endorse the requirement of any religion anywhere in the particular act or its application to your case. To have it your way would mean that we cannot have any laws rooted in belief, yet many laws are rooted in faith, religious texts, etc. Where do you think the concept of adultery comes from? Try the Sixth Commandment, phrased differently throughout our divorce laws. So, with respect, I cannot accept your argument based on a violation of the Establishment Clause."

"Finally," she said, "I have one last word about substantive due process. Much has been said and written about it. I suspect my comments here today will be the subject of criticism or accolades by courts above this one. But substantive due process invites judicial policy-making, which is not the judiciary's job. Instead, it is up to the State of Arkansas General Assembly to make policy. In your case, Mrs. Smith, the state spoke directly about marriage, family, and divorce by enacting a policy to discourage adultery. I will not pass judgment on what was on the General Assembly's collective mind when it created the New Law, its commission, or tribunal. It simply is not for this court to decide that. Therefore, I deny the petition for injunctive relief for the reasons I have given from the bench. This court is adjourned."

Jon and the other lawyers silently sat while Mrs. Smith cried uncontrollably: "They are going to kill me! They are going to kill me! They are going to kill me!"

16

The Command Room

Mrs. Smith's hearing adjourned at 9:37 a.m., and Vivian DeShields beat an awkward retreat through the courtroom's side door, leaving the US Marshals, Mrs. Smith, the lawyers, and Jon's security agents alone in the immense courtroom.

"Mr. Freeman, we need to get you back to the airport," said one of the agents with him.

"Give me just a second, agent," Jon said, motioning to Paul, who was consoling his client and Mr. Bender.

"Hey, you guys need to go to an office and get something up to the Eighth Circuit today. Even if it's shit, get something on file. Do you have someone's office you can borrow down here to do a notice?"

"Yeah, we can go over to the Arkansas Bar Center. They have a spare office for visiting lawyers," Paul said.

"Get to it, my friend," recommended Jon. "And hey, is there any warrant or anything making it illegal for Mrs. Smith to leave the state?"

Mrs. Smith was listening in and looked at Jon and then Roscoe Bender and said, "Y'all, I got no money. I ain't got nowhere I could go if I did, and I'm not going to leave my babies to that sorry ass ex-husband of mine. If I could go, I'd have to take 'em with me."

Jon looked over to Mrs. Smith.

"Well, ma'am, you have smart lawyers, but I'd get the hell out of Arkansas today if you can."

"Jon, we'll figure something out," Paul said. "I'll call you later today when we file the notice of appeal. We could use some help with a little press. Can you get in touch with someone?"

"Let me go with these guys. Once I'm airborne, I'll stir up some press!" Jon said as he started for the courtroom doors with his escorts.

* * *

The group poured into the hallway to follow the marble staircase down and out the courthouse's front doors onto Capitol Avenue. Jon thought he would see them off, but his security agents gently grabbed his upper arms from either side and steered him down the hall and away from the staircase instead.

"Sir, it's best not to go down to the street," one agent told him.

Jon waved goodbye, "Adios, guys. I'll see what I can do with the press. Get that notice of appeal filed! Today!"

Jon disappeared down the hallway with the agents to a utility elevator. They pulled out of the basement garage onto the street. With the courthouse on the right, they rounded the corner to a stop light when Jon recognized four black Defender vehicles pulling up to the Federal Building security barriers, blocking westbound traffic on Capitol Avenue. Suddenly, a swarm of black fatigues and guns encircled Roscoe Bender, Paul Joseph, and Mrs. Smith. Federal Marshals ran down the front steps of the Federal Building with guns drawn, but it was too late. Two Defenders grabbed Mrs. Smith and shoved her into the back of a nondescript van while other Defenders held her lawyers at gunpoint. The van doors slammed shut, and the Defenders left the scene, tires screeching.

"Guys, we gotta go over there and find out what happened," Jon demanded.

"With all respect, sir," said one of his agents, "we're driving you back to the airport and putting you on your plane. Babbit will have us for lunch if anything happens to you. Sorry, sir."

Jon called Paul's cell phone, and Paul picked up immediately.

"You guys all right," Jon asked.

"Yeah, roughed up, but we're okay. They took Jenny. They gave me a 'red warrant' and said they would hold her until her hearing on Monday. I spoke with some dude who called himself a captain, and he told me if I didn't like it, I could call the head of the tribunal to see if I could get the warrant lifted. We both know how that will turn out. There is no way the tribunal's chief judge will let her out."

"Understood. I'll get on the press thing. You guys get the appeal notice filed."

Jon terminated the call and immediately looked up Levi Pincus's number.

"Come on, come on, answer your damn phone," grumbled Jon as the car weaved its way through Little Rock's bustling downtown toward the airport. He left a voice mail.

"Levi, Jon Freeman. 911. A woman will be stoned to death for adultery here in Arkansas. Call me."

Jon's phone vibrated a few seconds later. It was Levi.

"Levi, Arkansas Defenders arrested a lady after a federal court hearing to prevent a state tribunal from having this woman stoned to death for adultery. I am in Little Rock, but I have a plane and can come to you. Once airborne, I can call you back and give you more details. I gotta call attention to this."

"Okay, yes, Mr. Freeman. I am in Washington, DC, at TNN's offices. Can you come here?"

Jon replied, "I can arrive at Dulles or National within a few hours. This is important. I gotta go. I'll call you back when I am in the air."

Jon hung up and called the pilot.

"I'm about five minutes out. Fire up the plane. We are going to Washington, DC. Dulles or National, but National would be better."

He didn't wait for goodbye and ended the call.

The agents pulled through the security gate onto the airport ramp and drove right up to the awaiting aircraft.

"Thank you, gentlemen," Jon said over his shoulder as he disappeared into the cabin of the waiting Citation 526, its stairs folding right behind him.

Jon poked his head into the flight deck, "Fellas, sorry about the change of plans. I presume we have plenty of fuel to get to DC. Can we fly to National? Dulles is too far out."

"We're good," said the first officer over his shoulder. "We should have a hell of a tailwind at altitude, so we could have you on the ground by 12:30 Eastern, if not before. Are you going to want us to stay with you after we land? It doesn't matter to us, sir."

"Yeah, stick around, please," Jon told him. "With a little luck, I'll have you get me back to Los Alamos tonight, and I can put you guys up at the ranch."

Jon returned to the cabin, picked a seat, and latched his seat belt. The plane was already moving, and he could hear the pilots on with the tower at Little Rock getting their clearance through to National.

Jon called Levi, not waiting for take off. Levi suggested they meet at the studio for a live interview. The two spent nearly the entire flight reviewing everything Jon had learned about the situation in Arkansas and other states, along with the morning's events. The news of the stoning would be staggering, and a live interview was precisely the thing to do to make the public notice.

While Jon was in the air, Paul Joseph and Roscoe Bender had zero luck getting anyone with the tribunal to answer the phone, much less call them back. They had no idea where the Defenders took Mrs. Smith, so they focused on cobbling together an emergency appeal with the Eight Circuit Court of Appeals, which it promptly denied in a one-sentence *per curiam* order within an hour of receiving it.

After the Eighth Circuit denied their appeal, they applied for an emergency stay with the United States Supreme Court in a last-ditch effort to try and save Mrs. Smith. Justice Theodore Cartright, the "circuit justice" of the Supreme Court assigned to hear requests for stays out of the Eighth Circuit, denied the application without comment. With appeals exhausted, they would be trying Jenny Smith's case before the tribunal on Monday morning without the benefit of any rules of evidence or procedure. They were going to have to wing it.

* * *

Jon's plane touched down at Ronald Reagan National Airport at exactly 12:24 p.m. Eastern Daylight Time, and a car was waiting for him at the private terminal. This would be a historic interview, preempting everything on TNN. Jon quickly called Martin to check in as he descended the stairs from the plane.

"Hey babe, I am in Washington, DC, to give an interview over at TNN. It's going to be a whopper!"

"What?" Martin exclaimed.

"Yep. This morning's hearing in Little Rock was a disaster," Jon said. "The federal judge refused to stop the tribunal proceeding that will end up getting that poor woman killed. It's unbelievable."

"Jesus, those fucking people, Jon. Those fucking people!"

"I know. It is difficult to wrap my head around it all!"

"Hey, so when will the interview air?" Martin asked.

"I don't know, but I suspect this afternoon. TNN's reporter told me I'd be on Connor Blackledge's show and that it would air live and preempt everything on TNN. I will try to get a text to you before we start if you want to watch." Jon said.

"So much for staying behind the scenes, huh, babe?" Martin joked.

"No shit. Well, hey, I gotta go. A car is waiting for me. I'll get in touch later. Love you."

Jon hung up just in time to step into the car Levi sent to pick him up.

The jet-black Mercedes Sedan moved smoothly over the Arland D. Williams Jr. Memorial Bridge, crossing the Potomac River into the DC Metro Area. TNN's Washington DC Bureau was only a ten-minute drive from Reagan. Traffic going into town was forgiving compared to the bumper cars lined up to escape DC for the weekend. Levi was out front waiting for Jon when he pulled up. Walking toward the curb, Levi extended his hand to shake Jon's.

"Afternoon, Jon. Welcome to DC. The studio is ready. We need to get you into makeup and go over a few things. We'll get you on with Connor Blackledge in the *Command Room* for a live broadcast this afternoon.

Jon was dressed in the same suit he wore in court that morning, sitting across from Connor on the brightly lit set of the *Command Room*. Connor looked at him as he stood up and asked, "Are you ready?"

Jon smiled and nodded. Then Connor glanced at a man behind one of the many cameras arrayed on the set with its bright lights. The cameraman held up his hand with three fingers, counting down. Three, two, one.

"Happening now in Arkansas is an outrageous assault on democracy. Jenny Smith is on trial for her life in a divorce case where a special court under new Arkansas laws could sentence her to death by stoning. This afternoon, we have a special guest from Arkansas to help us understand what is happening. We want to welcome our viewers in the United States and around the world. I'm Connor Blackledge, and you're in the Command Room."

Connor turned in his chair toward a different camera and then over to Levi, seated on a stool beside Jon.

"Let's start with our correspondent who broke the story about several red states that banded together and created uniform laws stripping away the civil rights of minority groups, women, people of color, LGBTQ persons, non-Christians, and immigrants. Levi Pincus. Levi, tell us what's going on."

"Thanks, Connor," Levi said. "On January 18th of this year, the Governor of Arkansas called a press conference at the Capitol Building in Little Rock, and she signed several bills termed the 'New Law.' Connor, these laws ignore federal law and destroy the civil rights that many in this county take for granted. For example, the New Law adopts the Christian Bible as supplementary law in the state. The New Law retroactively nullifies all same-sex and mixed-race marriages. It criminalizes abortion from the moment of conception. It makes contraception in just about any form illegal. It sets up a particular type of Christianity as an official religion. And tonight, we are joined by a man who spoke against these laws. He's a lawyer from Fayetteville, Arkansas. Let me introduce Jonathan Christian Freeman, who fled Arkansas with his husband for their safety."

The camera turned back to Connor.

"Good evening, Mr. Freeman. You have had quite a ride over the last several months. Let's play the footage from the January rally in your hometown, where you became somewhat of a lightning rod."

Connor continued after they displayed the clip of Jon's appearance on the Fayetteville square the day of the Little Rock massacre.

"Jon," Connor began, "tell us what has happened in your state with the New Law and what you have been doing to combat it."

"Thanks, Connor. I don't know where to begin except that I deeply believe in our federal republic. I served in the US Army and now serve as a lawyer. I cherish democracy and the rule of law, but democracy cannot thrive in the face of unchecked political extremism like in America today."

"You are definitely on record attacking both Right and Left extremes, but do you believe one is worse than the other?" Connor asked.

"Indeed. I believe extreme ideologies on both ends of the political spectrum are divisive, hinder progress, and are dangerous. However, I see the right-wing extreme as more concerning. I mean, look what is happening in Arkansas." Jon replied.

"What are those reasons, Jon? Then let's get to what is happening in Arkansas." Connor said.

"First and foremost, Connor, like we are seeing in Arkansas right now, the extreme right embraces exclusionary and discriminatory policies that harm marginalized communities. In the last election, the Right ran on a platform of xenophobia, Christian nationalism, racism, homophobia, and transphobia. Those policy objectives always lead to the mistreatment and marginalization of vulnerable groups."

"I don't think you'll get an argument from anyone here because it is a valid concern," Connor commented. "So what of the Left? Some might argue that extreme Left policies, such as high taxation on the wealthy and significant government intervention, might also have unintended consequences. How do you respond to that?"

"You're right, Connor. Extreme policies from the Left have unintended consequences, and that's why it's essential to avoid any extreme ideology. However, while the Left might advocate for policies that increase government involvement, these measures are often intended to address social inequities and provide essential services for all citizens. On the other hand, the extreme right's emphasis on minimal government intervention can lead to neglecting social safety nets and necessary regulations, which can exacerbate disparities and undermine the well-being of the most vulnerable in our society."

Connor cut in.

"You got a lot of attention from both the Left and the Right with your comments that day in Fayetteville. I mean, you aimed at Progressives as well as the Right. You blamed our current situation on a collective unwillingness to compromise."

"I did," Jon said. "It isn't that I disagree with liberal or progressive values. I find myself at odds with the approach taken to promote those values. For example, I remember a friend who was an ardent Bernie Sanders supporter during the Democratic primary against Hillary Clinton. When Bernie didn't win the primary, my friend, and many others like him, refused to support Hillary. I told him that withholding support for Hillary Clinton for the sake of his 'principles' would land Donald Trump in office. And we all know what happened after that! Trump appointed enough conservatives to the Supreme Court to lock in a right-wing court for a generation. We now have a Supreme Court that is beyond repair. It isn't merely conservative. It is reactionary, and the Left can do nothing to counterbalance it. As we have already begun to witness, evils from the Supreme Court will pour forth, making the *Dobbs* case seem like child's play as the court moves ever closer to embracing constitutional originalism. And this says nothing of the harm the ultra-conservative super majorities did in the red state legislatures."

"Well, so tell me, Jon," prompted Connor, "what has happened in Arkansas since the New Law?"

"Since Arkansas adopted the New Law, we have seen the deployment of a new law enforcement agency called the Arkansas Defenders. They have unchecked authority. And they work for a commission and tribunal that are creatures of the New Law with regulatory powers. For example, everyone with a same-sex partner, including me, received a notice in the mail that their marriage would be nullified retroactively and that we had so much time to get a divorce before it would be a crime to remain married. The same notices went out later to interracial couples. So, my marriage, and thousands of other same-sex marriages, no longer exist in Arkansas. They are illegal now, along with mixed-race unions. And, of course, the list of evils that ushers in is hard to comprehend. The state is now undoing adoptions and removing children from their former homes, creating a humanitarian crisis that will impact a whole generation of children stripped away from their families."

Jon continued.

"We also learned that the State of Arkansas erected internment camps, for lack of a better term. The Defenders have been rounding up the homeless, disabled, the unemployed, and other 'undesirables' or morally 'unworthy' people as defined by the New Law through its commission and tribunal."

Connor interrupted.

"Internment camps?"

"Oh yes," Jon replied. "I think a better word for it is 'concentration camps.' According to the regulations, the state can round up anyone they don't like. Anyone single and unmarried that they don't like. Gays, lesbians, trans persons. Immigrants. Racial minorities. People who are not Christians. There is no telling where this will end. Think about another law that passed, the Free Exercise Law. That law protects someone acting according to his 'sincere and authentic' religious belief. So, think Jim Crow, except Jim Crow at a level never seen before. I also have information from my sources within the state that the Defenders will round up persons who tolerate, protect, or aid 'undesirables.' They will be rounding up and detaining all immigrants, whether here legally or not. So, if you have a gay son and shelter him or an undocumented worker you pay, you may be subject to arrest and detention. But the worst thing yet to happen is what is happening with Jenny Smith."

"Tell us about Mrs. Smith," Connor asked. "You flew here today from

Little Rock, where you and two other lawyers representing Mrs. Smith tried to get the federal court to put a hold on her adultery case to prevent her from being stoned to death. And the tribunal reviewing her case is scheduled to meet on Monday, right? And possibly sentence her to death by stoning?"

"Connor, that's right," Jon told him. "This morning, I was in federal court with lawyers who argued unsuccessfully that the New Law, in general, and Mrs. Smith's case, in particular, should be enjoined."

"And what happened," asked Connor.

"The federal judge denied our application for a stay. She borrowed her reasoning from the *Dobbs* opinion, where Justice Barker said that 'substantive due process is an oxymoron.' As in, there is no such thing as substantive due process anymore. I cannot begin to tell you what violence that reasoning will do to America. Whatever civil liberties exist today could be rolled back when seen through that eighteenth-century lens."

"What will happen with Mrs. Smith's case now?" asked Connor.

"As I was leaving the federal courthouse in Little Rock, a contingent of Defenders arrested and took Mrs. Smith into custody. They held her at gunpoint, forced her into the back of a van, and sped away. I presume they will take her to her court appearance before the tribunal on Monday morning. But here's the thing, Connor. There are no published rules for this tribunal and no written procedure. There wasn't even a week's notice or briefing schedule. There is no telling what will happen on Monday morning."

"Take me back to earlier in the spring for a minute, Jon," Connor said. "You tried to defeat the New Law with a state injunction in state court, right?"

"That's right, and the court denied it. Right after that, there was a standoff at the courthouse in my town, and a Defender tried to arrest me. They eventually chased me down, but the FBI intervened and arrested them. They were after me, Connor. I escaped Arkansas. I didn't leave. I fled. I am surprised they didn't try to arrest me when I returned this morning, but I couldn't miss the Jenny Smith hearing."

"Where are you now," Connor inquired.

"I am a trustee of a cattle ranch in Northern New Mexico," Jon answered. "I decided to focus on my trusteeship and ranching. It is as if I am a refugee, but I remain committed to helping organize resistance to the New Law through legal challenges and, if necessary, an armed counterinsurgency. Because, in all honesty, that is what will happen, Connor. Armed conflict. Once too many people are put in internment camps. Once enough, everyday Americans are hauled before some judge because they are not the right kind of Christian or not a Christian at all. Once enough Americans' lives are interfered with, it will boil over. You will witness civil strife and conflict when ordinary Americans have nothing to lose. I hope Americans realize what is happening in Arkansas before it spreads to other states."

"What is next for you, Jon?" Connor asked.

"I'll go back to the ranch where I work and focus on that, but I am worried about my family and friends who I left behind in Arkansas. It was my home, and the governor and her New Law are destroying it. What could happen if left unchecked is unthinkable, so I will continue to do what I have done since our first court case to help encourage resistance in every way possible. I'm probably past running in the streets and raising hell at my age. But I can help organize others who will do that, who will arm themselves, if need be, and who will fight not just with information but with bullets."

"You know, Connor," Jon continued. "The last time I checked, the Second Amendment, the one amendment these right-wingers exalt above all others, goes in more than one direction. One day, the Left will arm itself and contest the Right's abuse of power. Sadly, our country, Connor, our country is sick. We've lost our way. On the one hand, left-leaning people with good ideas unwittingly alienated the middle class and rural people living in the 'flyovers,' as coastal people are so fond of saying. I mean, we are seeing a result of that alienation. I am from one of those 'flyover' states, and even though I am educated, even progressive-minded, I understand the sentiment. I am often offended by coastal elites' penchant for looking down upon those of us who are from rural America. I resent the hell out of it. Honestly, I do. The difference between me and many where I'm from is that I've benefited from a classical liberal education, traveled widely, and experienced different cultures. But imagine, for a moment, how many others might feel the same if someone like me feels this way?"

"By the same token," Jon continued, "the red-state people need to get over it, take some interest in real education and tolerance, and adopt portions of the Bible that speak to the love of one's neighbor, even if their neighbor is different. Meanwhile, Red and Blue must learn to coexist before this country wages war with itself. There must be a true, honest, national conversation, but that isn't happening. We are already seeing the beginnings of it, and I dare say, if they stone poor Mrs. Smith, it won't be just her blood that flows. A truth-telling and reconciliation time will be much more complicated after that happens, and the blood of many will run in the streets until we have that conversation and achieve mutual respect."

The interview continued with Connor and experts in constitutional law, federalism, and even an advocate for state's rights, with all sides debating the ramifications of states refusing federal jurisdiction over efforts to restrain the New Law short of armed conflict.

Later, as the lights turned off and stage crews cleaned the set, Jon and Connor shook hands.

"Jon," Connor said, "I'd like to keep in touch with you. I hope you have a safe trip home to New Mexico. As a journalist, I cannot think of a higher calling now than illuminating what is happening in Arkansas and elsewhere. Take care of yourself, and let us know how we can help. Here's my direct line. Use it."

"Thank you for having me on your show, Connor. I fear a fight is coming, and our country is in for tough times ahead. It will take all of us to do what we can to get back on track. I hope I live through it."

17

The Wages of Sin

On Monday morning, August 28th, 2023, Paul Joseph and Roscoe Bender waited in a dim basement hallway at the Capitol Building until a middle-aged man approached and introduced himself. He wore a formal black uniform with brass buttons, red epaulets, and a black leather Sam Browne belt. He said he was an officer of the tribunal.

"Gentlemen, it's time. Follow me."

The uniformed man led the lawyers into the courtroom that had once been a fallout shelter. On the opposite end of the stark room was a semi-circular bench and a podium with a witness box off to one side. The room smelled of freshly varnished wood mixed with old, musty basement.

"The tribunal will convene in just a minute, gentlemen," the man said before disappearing through a side door.

Paul spoke up as the officer retreated, "Excuse me, sir. Where is my client, Mrs. Smith?"

"She is here, sir," replied the officer. "I will retrieve her momentarily."

Moments later, Paul Joseph and Roscoe Bender reflexively came to their feet as the tribunal judges entered dressed in red judicial robes. From right to left, they walked to their tall leather chairs behind the bench. Neither Paul Joseph nor Roscoe Bender recognized the judges except Chief Judge Tom Hardy Blasingame. As soon as the last judge stepped in behind his chair, they all took their seats in unison.

A second later, another man in a black dress uniform called the case.

"Good morning. The Tribunal for Causes of Standards, Morality, and Education is called to order, Chief Judge Tom Hardy Blasingame presiding. Please be seated."

"Bring out the accused," Judge Blasingame commanded, and a door behind the witness box opened. Mrs. Smith appeared. She was pale, dressed in an orange jumpsuit, and her hair was askew as she shuffled in with shackles clinking. The officer pushed her abruptly into the single chair within the box, and he stood behind her. Then, Judge Blasingame focused his attention on Joseph and Bender.

"Gentlemen, I presume you are here on behalf of the accused, is that right?"

"Yes, sir," the two said in unison.

"Very well. Which of you will present an argument?" asked the chief judge.

"I will," said Paul Joseph.

"Very well, and your name?" prompted the chief judge.

"I am Paul Joseph, a lawyer from Fayetteville, Your Honor."

"I don't care where you're from, but being from Fayetteville won't help your client's case much," he said with a perverse chuckle. "At any rate," continued Judge Blasingame, "we are here on your client's appeal from Lafayette County on account of adultery. Is that your understanding, Mr. Joseph?"

"Yes, sir, it is, and if I may," Paul Joseph said, "I have some objections to make."

The chief judge bristled.

"Make all the objections you want, Mr. Joseph, but that will not change anything here today. I'll give you a chance to speak in just a moment, but you agree that we are here today to hear an appeal of the chancellor's decision by your client, Mrs. Smith, the lady in that box over to my right?"

"Yes, sir," replied Paul Joseph.

Judge Blasingame continued, "Now, the judge's transcript from the case and docket sheet indicates he reserved a ruling on punishment for the alleged adultery. Is that also your understanding?"

"It is, yes, but how can the judge reserve a ruling for a sentence he has no authority to impose?" pressed Paul Joseph.

"I told you, sir, this is no time for objections, but you'll get your chance," declared the chief judge. "However, I will take the liberty of telling you that the chancellor has every right under the New Law to impose a whole range of punishments, including death by stoning, and so does this body. I mean, you have read the provisions of the New Law, have you not?"

"I have, Your Honor," Paul Joseph stated.

"And you have done everything in your power to stay the application of the New Law and to stay a judgment in this case, have you not?" the chief judge inquired.

"I have, Your Honor, yes," Paul Joseph replied.

It feels like this asshole is just getting warmed up, Paul Joseph thought to himself.

"And it further seems that your efforts were unsuccessful, efforts you made by filing for an emergency stay in federal court on Friday, right?"

"That's right," Paul Joseph stated, his patience tested.

"I will save you the time, Mr. Joseph," said the chief judge. "According to the New Law, this tribunal does not recognize the federal government's authority in what is strictly a state matter. Remember that if you are ever before us again. Nevertheless, I'd say you did everything in your power that you thought appropriate to forestall these proceedings. When you didn't get satisfaction from the federal judge, you took it to the Eight Circuit. You didn't win there, either, so you applied for a stay with the United States Supreme Court, which was likewise summarily denied. True? It looks like you had three strikes there, counselor, and here we are. So, my question for you is this: do you dispute that there was a trial in front of the Lafayette County Chancellor?"

Paul was red-faced.

Fucking mouth-breathing cretin...

"I do not dispute there was a proceeding, but I wouldn't call it a trial."

"Watch your tone, Mr. Joseph," the imperious chief judge demanded.

"Do you dispute that a witness appeared, a neighbor of the aggrieved party, Mr. Smith, who testified about the sexual activity between Mrs. Smith and the neighbor?"

"I do not dispute there was testimony," Paul Joseph relented.

Pushing further, the chief judge persisted.

"And further, do you refute the chancellor heard testimony from Mr. Smith that when he went and rapped on the neighbor's door, he saw, with his own eyes, the neighbor and the accused, standing aside one another, in comparable levels of undress?"

"I do not refute that testimony," Paul Joseph replied.

Paul Joseph's thoughts were becoming a dramatic monologue.

What a son of a bitch that sanctimonious asshole of a judge is. And not that smart, either.

The chief judge continued his inquisition.

"Well, sir, it seems that on the important points, we agree. So now, the moment you have been waiting for, hell, us too! Your objections, pray tell us will you, what are your objections? What do you say we give you what, five minutes? That sufficient?"

"Thank you, Your Honor, but five minutes is insufficient."

Looking perturbed, the chief judge commanded, "The clock is ticking, Mr. Joseph. I recommend you make the most of it."

"Jesus," Paul Joseph muttered to himself.

"Very well. Number one, Your Honor. The so-called chancery court cannot exist without a constitutional amendment. The legislature or the commission did not have the power to create it. Number two, the chancellor did not have jurisdiction to usurp the Circuit Court domestic relations division. Number three, I could not find published procedures for the chancery court, much less this assembly, so I object on due process grounds. Number four, I object because this body's existence violates the separation of powers doctrine. Number five, the fact that the Commission for Standards, Morality, and Education, not the legislature, issued an enactment allowing capital punishment is beyond the pale. Only the legislature can specify capital punishments through the criminal code.

Finally, imposing the death penalty by biblical stoning is cruel and unusual punishment, violating the Eighth Amendment to the U.S. Constitution."

"You're about out of time," interrupted Chief Judge Blasingame, "but indulge me, is that all?"

"Oh, no, I'm just getting warmed up, Your Honor," Paul Joseph said, raising his voice. "What you all are doing here is an abomination, and you and all of you up there know it. You should be ashamed of yourselves. This legal charade is detestable."

"I'm going to stop you right there, Mr. Joseph," the chief judge boomed, raising his voice to match Paul Joseph's.

"Unless you want to find yourself in Mrs. Smith's shoes, I'd recommend you bite your tongue and bite it right now."

"Are you threatening me, Judge Blasingame," yelled Paul Joseph. "Are you?"

The judge sitting to the right of Judge Blasingame leaned over and whispered something indecipherable in his ear. Then, ignoring Mr. Joseph's outburst, the chief judge turned to either side of him.

"Fellow judges, do you have any questions for Mr. Smith?"

They all shook their heads.

"Hearing no calls for questions, then I believe we can proceed. Sit down, Mr. Joseph."

The chief judge turned to face Mrs. Smith's crumpled form in the witness chair.

"Mrs. Smith, you are accused of adultery because you had relations with your next-door neighbor, a man you are not married to. Do you deny you had sex with that man who is not your husband?"

She was silent.

"I take it by your silence that you do not dispute the accusation," the chief judge told her.

"Fellow court members," the chief judge said, "I will call the role, and you will each answer as prescribed.

"Othniel," he called.

"Ad sum," was the response.

"Ehud," he continued.

"Ad sum."

He finished the roll call with each judge responding with "ad sum" to their biblically inspired title.

Continuing, the chief judge said, "The roll call is complete. Is there anyone of you who disagrees with the judgment of the Chancery Court of Lafayette County, Arkansas? If so, speak your disagreement now."

Deafening silence. The chief judge shifted in his chair and, with sharp eyes, looked at Mrs. Smith, then said in a commanding voice: "According to the enabling legislation set forth within Title 29 of the Arkansas Code, otherwise known as the New Law, this body invokes Leviticus 20:10 and imposes the penalty of death by stoning upon you, adulteress, according to the undisputed testimony of two witnesses. Therefore, I move the accused, Mrs. Jenny Smith, of Lafayette County, Arkansas, to be put to death by stoning."

Judge Deborah spoke up, "I second the motion."

"All in favor," intoned the chief judge, "say 'aye.'"

Every member of the panel repeated "aye" in unison.

"The decision is unanimous. Therefore, this tribunal affirms the chancery court's ruling that Mrs. Jenny Smith is divorced from the appellee due to adultery and should now be taken to a place to be put to death by stoning. The sentence shall be carried out immediately."

Mrs. Smith wailed and collapsed as the red-robed judges filed out. The officer standing by her took her from under both arms and pulled her out of the chair, causing it to tumble with a clatter as he dragged her through a side door. The other officer, who escorted the lawyers into the courtroom, went to Joseph and Bender and gestured toward the doors to usher them out. Not that Paul Joseph or Roscoe Bender wanted to stick around, but they were stunned by the spectacle.

They found the ornate elevator in the basement, which moved like a glacier to the ground floor.

Paul reached for his cell phone to call Jon, but it went to voice mail.

"Jon, it's Paul. The tribunal ruled against us and ordered Mrs. Smith's execution. Call me back when you can."

The elevator doors parted with Roscoe and Paul entering a frantic Monday morning at the Capitol. They briskly walked shoulder to shoulder down a crowded hallway toward the rotunda and then out through the colossal bronze doors to face media trucks pulled up to the drive encircling the building.

"Holy shit, Roscoe, here's our chance," Paul Joseph exclaimed.

The two approached a skinny blond lady with an NBT ball cap.

"Excuse me, ma'am. What's going on here?" Paul Joseph asked.

"We're here to find out about a stoning if you believe it," the woman from NBT said. "TNN did a piece on Friday afternoon about a tribunal and a woman named Jenny Smith, who was supposed to have a court hearing today over a divorce. The issue was whether she'd be stoned to death for adultery under the Arkansas New Law. As soon as the news broke, I think every network in the United States, no, in the world, is here - Jesus, even Al Jazeera sent a reporter."

Paul Joseph looked at the lady and asked, "Are you a reporter?"

"No, producer," she replied.

"Well, Madam Producer, go get your reporters and your cameras. I'm the lawyer for the lady you described. Her case was just tried in the basement of the Capitol Building. We lost, and it was a farce. When it ended, armed men dressed in black uniforms took our client out of the courtroom. They mean to stone her today. If you want a story, here it is. If you want to try and save her, get every one of these reporters out here looking for her right now!"

The producer paused momentarily and said, "This story is too big for one network."

She then yelled out, "Hey, everyone, gather around. This man here is Mrs. Jenny Smith's lawyer, and the State of Arkansas plans to stone her this morning."

Suddenly, there was a crowd of reporters, lights, and cameras three deep encircling Paul Joseph and Roscoe Bender.

Paul Joseph stood in their midst, saying, "Roll your cameras because we don't have time for me to say this more than once. If you have spare crews, send them to hunt around the Capitol Building Complex while I give my report. Look for a black van, men in solid black uniforms, red berets, and black SUVs. You see it, you follow it. They will take her someplace to execute her."

Back at the Mansion, the governor's phone lit up. It was the Chief Judge Blasingame.

"God damn, you bastards didn't waste any time," the governor said. "It's not even 11 a.m. So what next?"

There was a pause.

"You are fucking kidding me," the governor said. "I'm on my way."

She ended the call and hollered out for Lieutenant Pettigrew.

"Haystack, we need to get the fuck out of here. Come on, let's go!" she yelled.

"Where too, Governor?" he asked.

"War Memorial Stadium," she answered. "That's where the tribunal intends to execute that woman."

* * *

A lone reporter named Shel Spivey from a local ABC affiliate had a commercial drone in the trunk of his car and a hunch. He ran to his 15-year-old faded red Volkswagen Jetta and peeled out toward War Memorial Stadium. Being the recovering Pentecostal that he was, he knew the Bible. If there was a stoning based on biblical principles, he presumed it would have to be in a prominent area but still closed to the public.

He departed the Capitol, wove through an alley, and made it to Markham Street and its late morning traffic, driving as fast as he could toward War Memorial Stadium. If he were lucky, he'd catch up to the black vans ahead of him. He pulled onto Stadium Drive, which led to the north entrance.

Spivey turned into a long parking lot that paralleled a little park next to the stadium to avoid calling attention to himself, but he noticed two men in black uniforms standing on either side of the north gate. Spivey found an open spot in a row of cars parked at the drab government building housing the Arkansas Public Health Laboratory. He figured he could fly his drone around the stadium's south end to delay detection. With some luck, he hoped to fly it to the roof of the press box on the stadium's west side.

He carefully launched his drone and guided its climb into the blue Arkansas sky. Keeping the drone just below the elevation of the stadium's bleachers, he flew it around the south side clockwise to reach the west side. Then, he climbed the drone to level with the roof of the press box no more than six inches above it and slowly advanced the drone toward the edge. He slowed the drone, hovering, and carefully advanced it to the edge, balancing the skids so he could power it down while keeping the camera trained on the field below.

Jackpot. He switched a setting on his controller to "live stream," and then he texted the access to his stream to a list of the reporters he knew, which numbered half a dozen. He asked them to share the link with anyone and everyone, and within five minutes, his video was streaming live on the World Wide Web.

Through the drone's camera, the world watched two men in all-black uniforms escort a shackled woman in an orange jumpsuit to the middle of a football field. The two uniforms pushed the woman down to her knees on the 50-yard line, bound her hands with rope behind her back, and tied them to her ankles. To one side of the kneeling and bound woman stood 13 people in red robes along the 45-yard line. In front of them was a pile of stones.

Across the field from the 13 figures in the red robes were two men wearing jeans, white t-shirts, and red ball caps, standing on the 55-yard line. In front of them was a smaller pile of stones. Looking back along the 50-yard line, beyond the condemned woman, Spivey could see a husky-looking woman wearing jeans, bright red cowboy boots, and a red cowboy hat. It looked like she was making a speech. Suddenly, she lifted her arm and pointed at the two men. They each stepped forward, picked up a stone, and solemnly stood on each side of the pile. Across from the two men, each judge picked up a stone and stepped back in line.

THE LAST INDEPENDENCE DAY

All was motionless for a moment. Then Ball Cap Man reached up and threw his stone at the bound woman as hard as he could, hitting her on the side of her head and knocking her over to her side. The drone's camera captured blood erupting from the woman's head, showing her helpless cry. Then, one of the red-robed persons stepped forward with a stone and threw it at her back, hitting her directly between the shoulder blades. The condemned woman writhed on the ground as if having a seizure.

The other ball cap man hurled his rock, hitting her neck and tearing her skin in a jagged fountain of red. Then, each red-robed figure closed in, one by one, on the victim and pelted her with their stones until she lay dead on the fifty-yard line of War Memorial Stadium, her red blood, bits of skull, and chunks of grey matter cast upon the green.

Spivey heard approaching sirens, so he hurried to push a small lever on his controller, and the drone lifted off. He maneuvered it forward in the airspace above the field and then dropped it down slowly with his camera trained on the crumpled body of what was once Mrs. Smith. Maneuvering the drone closer and scanning the scene revealed the expressionless faces of each judge, a dour Hansel Smith, his lawyer, and the witness who secured Mrs. Smith's conviction. Spivey refocused the lens to zoom in on the face of Governor Suzy Brandy Landers, cowboy hat and all, smiling and clapping proudly at the spectacle.

Outside the north gate, local and state police pulled in with lights and sirens screeching their tires as they screamed onto the scene, piling out of their vehicles. Seeing this, Spivey lifted the drone to get a better view. Besides, he could see muzzle flashes from Defenders on the field trying to shoot down his drone. By now, he remembered that his video was being streamed to the world, and he knew three possibilities besides that a woman lay dead existed: his video would make him famous, get him killed, land him in jail, or all three.

Shel shut off the live feed, flew his drone due south up and over the stadium's south end zone, then dropped it to a level just above the treetops, looking for an obscure place to set it down and allow him a chance to escape unnoticed. The entire area was a sea of flashing lights and sirens. He could always retrieve his drone later after he landed it on top of a featureless parking structure while lying low in the front seat of his Jetta.

* * *

Jon sat alone in the courtyard at La Hacienda with a cup of coffee, enjoying the silence surrounded by the scents of lavender and rosemary. His cell phone was on the kitchen counter when Paul called with news about the tribunal.

Martin walked out with Jon's phone to get Jon's attention.

"Hey babe, your phone went off in the kitchen. It was Paul Joseph on the Caller ID. I figured you'd want to know."

Oh shit, a decision can't be this soon!

"Thanks. I am a little surprised he called this early," Jon said. "I'd better go check."

"I saved you a trip, sweetheart!"

Martin handed Jon his phone.

"You, sir, are too kind!" Jon said while standing to hug Martin. "Here, let's see what's happening."

Jon listened to the voicemail on speaker with Martin.

"Jesus. What in the fuck is the world coming to." Jon muttered.

"Are you going to call him?" Martin asked.

"Oh yeah. Let's go in and hear this together."

Once inside, Jon called Paul Joseph.

"I heard your voicemail. So, the tribunal is going to execute her? Did they set a date?" John asked.

"Jon, the tribunal was a joke," Paul said. "It ordered her execution to take place immediately following the hearing. People are trying to look for her to see if we can somehow stop it. You might want to turn on the TV because there's no time to file anything."

Martin exclaimed, "Oh my God, they will kill that lady? Those fuckers. I hate them! We've got to do something!"

"Paul, I could try to bang out an emergency petition for rehearing in federal court for all the good it will do. I could file something from here," Jon offered.

"Anything you do would be better than nothing, but I am afraid it is too late," Paul said.

"Let me get off the phone and see if I can pull something out of my ass and get a petition filed," Jon said.

"Go. We are going to look for her. There is a media swarm here, and all of them are out looking."

Jon and Martin went up to Jon's study. Jon sat at his desk and opened his computer while Martin turned on the TV to see what the news was saying.

Jon started typing.

"IN THE UNITED STATES DISTRICT COURT FOR THE EASTERN DISTRICT OF ARKANSAS, LITTLE ROCK DIVISION," but before he hit the return button to continue drafting the petition, the TV showed the live footage streaming from Shel Spivey's drone.

"Oh my God," Martin's voice trailed off to silence.

Jon watched with tears streaming. His chest was tight, and his stomach churned. He clenched his fists. Martin was paralyzed while Jon's mind dashed between dismay and wrath in the no man's land of madness.

Mrs. Smith. That poor woman. I could have done more.

As it often does, grief can turn to anger and rage. This would take some time to sink in, but one thing was clear.

These people must be stopped at all costs.

* * *

The news cycle ran Spivey's video for several days, and the press relentlessly sought out Jon Freeman and Paul Joseph for appearances on every show to discuss it. In contrast to Shel Spivey's newfound fame and Jon and Paul's increasing popularity, Governor Landers had been transformed into a worldwide pariah. Still, right-wing talk radio pundits helped mitigate her tarnished reputation by promoting her folksy fascism. She leaned in and doubled down because of the strong correlation between her core supporters and their beliefs. She was confident the MAGA Movement was a fight for the soul of Americana, with enough people duped into believing it.

Capitalizing on the momentum from the stoning, Buckshot called for rallies throughout Arkansas to host coliseum-style entertainments to shore up her support because she had an idea. Twenty-nine souls languished on death row in Arkansas, so the governor hatched a plan to conduct public hangings at her rallies. Executing the condemned in the county where the crime was committed would be a spectacle, and the masses would eat it up.

As autumn leaves began to fall in 2023, so too did the number of the condemned. The cold embrace of nooses cast shadows across the state. Mrs. Smith's judicial execution became a haunting whisper, lost in the spectacle that took center stage. Buckshot, once again the champion of public sentiment, stoked the flames of the Right's fervor, directing it towards new depths of hatred against those they deemed unworthy.

* * *

There was one pressing item on the governor's to-do list that fateful Fall season, and she announced it in a morning meeting with Adjutant General Hampton.

"General, I have something I need you to arrange," she said from behind her desk in 205.

"What is it, Governor?" he replied.

"I need you to arrest three people. Jon Freeman's mother, brother, and his brother's wife. Do it as soon as possible. Have them taken to the camp in Washington County until I decide what to do with them. I think they'd be prime candidates for "reeducation," if you know what I mean. Plus, I could use them as leverage to bring in Jon Freeman in exchange for letting them go."

"Governor, you are aware that Mrs. Freeman is elderly, right? Are you sure you want me to arrest her?"

"I'm damn sure, General. Don't doubt my resolve. I couldn't care less if his kin are on ventilators in nursing homes. Arrest them, and when you've done that, let's start figuring out who's close to him and take those people, too. I will make that mother fucker pay for all the shit he's stirred up!"

18

Moves

T hanks to Shel Spivey's video, for a short time, the world could not ignore the evils wrought by the New Law, and public protests erupted throughout the compact states. But even with Mrs. Smith's execution, and later the public executions, polling in Arkansas revealed the general public was beginning to accept the Defenders as part of their daily lives. The public's increased acceptance made the initial resistance lose momentum, and the lack of resistance allowed for the accelerated detention of Arkansans at the commission's various internment camps. As a result, Gerry, the veteran, wasn't alone at the Washington County Rehabilitation and Reeducation Center entering the Fall of 2023.

Gerry had been there the longest, making him the unofficial dean of the camp, now organized into different communities. The camp commandant, following the commission's instructions, segregated detainees into groups: unemployed and homeless, "out" or "obvious" LGBTQ persons, children, the elderly and disabled, and "undesirables" imprisoned there for other reasons, including voicing dissent to the New Law.

One evening at dusk during the third week of September, the assistant to the camp commandant summoned Gerry to the welcome center because there were new detainees to be processed. Even though Gerry's start at the center was harsh, it had become a home and a place where he found usefulness. Sober and far removed from his pre-detention diet of Schlitz

Malt Liquor, Marlborough Reds, and Ho Hos, Gerry had become an asset, especially when processing new detainees.

"Gerry, come over here, please, sir," asked a camp guard respectfully. "We have some new detainees."

"Glad to help them get settled," Gerry said.

Gerry moved the canvas door flap aside and entered the welcome center tent.

"Wait here," the guard said. "We have an elderly woman, a lawyer, and the lawyer's wife who are just arriving. I'm told they won't be here long."

Gerry waited inside the reception tent with the guard for a few minutes, smoking a cigarette the guard gave him until he saw the lights of the approaching van and the sound of the gate opening. The van doors opened, and he heard people walking across the gravel between the chain-link fences. When the guards brought them in, he saw an elderly lady with thinning white hair dressed in silk pajamas with slippers limping along, her hands zip-tied in front of her. A taller man of medium build in his sixties followed along in a tracksuit with a woman of slim build and pageboy style haircut casually dressed in jeans and sneakers. All three were silent as guards escorted them in. Gerry knew better than to react, but he recognized two of them.

Gerry remembered Ruth from the Freeman Law Firm. He had once been a client, and she always took the time to listen to him even when he was off his nut. He felt indebted to Ira and Jon because those boys helped him get his VA and social security benefits after Operation Enduring Freedom.

Why are they here?

He knew better than to let anyone know he recognized them, but he was confident he could help them. Now wasn't the time, though.

Seeing a bedraggled Mrs. Freeman limping into the tent moved Gerry underneath his poker face. Despite her frailty, Ruth was still sharp. She scolded the young, uniformed man behind the desk, asking questions, commenting that this was all silly, and concluded, "What in the hell do you think you can do to a 90-year-old woman living on borrowed time?"

A horrified and indignant Ira was watching from behind Ruth, who said,

"You know this will not end well for any of you! For fuck's sake!"

The guards remained silent as Elaine, Ira's wife, became hysterical.

After the guards processed the three, one guard motioned to Gerry, "Go ahead and take them back to Number 13. There is room in there for all of them. If it doesn't work out for the old lady, you can put her in with the disabled ones."

Gerry nodded in the affirmative, then walked up to Mrs. Freeman and offered her his arm, "Ma'am, you can come with me."

Mrs. Freeman looked at him angrily for a second, then a flash of recognition appeared in her eyes, and she replied, "Thank you, at least you are polite!"

She gave him her arm, turned back to Ira and Elaine with her free arm, and waved them as if to follow her.

One never had to guess where one stood with Ruth Freeman. She had not earned the nickname, the Colonel, for nothing. She remained a tough customer, ruthless in business, supremely ethical, and disarmingly direct.

On the way out of the tent, she looked at Gerry and said, "I know you. You used to come by the office. My sons represented you."

"Shhhhh," Gerry said while holding an index finger to his lips.

They walked further down the central pathway between the tents through the quiet camp. No detainees were outside. Only two guards walked up and down "the line" between rows of tents with flashlights.

After Gerry and the three with him were roughly twenty paces away from the welcome center, he said, "Follow me a little further down to where you'll be staying, and we can talk there."

Arriving at No. 13, he turned to them, looking up and down the rows of tents on either side of the line.

"I remember you," Ira said. "You look a lot different now. How did you end up here?"

Gerry answered Ira.

"One day, I was out trying to pick up spare change, and these guys picked me up at North and College along with some others. When they picked us up, they said they were there to help us, help get us back to work, and give us food and shelter. I was homeless and glad to have a roof over my head. I have to say, they have treated me well here. I've gotten off all the drugs I was on, and the food has been decent. So yeah, I'm all right, but I haven't been let loose to go to work yet. They keep telling me they're working on getting me a job assignment. Anyway, yeah, I'm okay. But you, why are you here?"

Ira spoke first.

"All they said was that they were detaining us for a review of our compliance with the New Law and that we were sympathizers with traitors. They mentioned my brother Jon."

"Where is Jon?" Gerry asked. "I remember him. Jon was the one who took me to my disability hearing. He was something. I'll never forget it. I think he knew more about it than the judge on my case."

"Yeah," Ira responded, "Jon is like that. He lives for the fight. I remember how happy he was that you won your case."

Gerry suddenly displayed profound concern, his lips tightening and a frown appearing, "Look, we don't have much time. The guards will be coming back to do their checks. You all have been assigned to No. 13, so you won't be here long. Maybe a week or two. Then they will take you somewhere else, but I don't know where. We need to get you out of here. I have managed to help a couple of people escape since I've been here. Is there anyone you want me to get a message to? It will take a day or so, but I can get a message out, and then we can work on getting you out of here."

The Colonel spoke up, looking at Ira, "We need to get word to your brother."

"I agree," Ira said, "but he's out of state. There is a friend of his, Paul Joseph. He's also a lawyer who practices here in Fayetteville. Can you get word to him? He's easy to find. He used to have billboards all over town."

"I know who he is, yep. What's the message besides that you all are in here?"

"Tell him to get a hold of Jon and that our mother is locked up with us."

"Copy that," Gerry replied. "Now, let's get you two folks settled before they see us talking like this."

188

No. 13 was a military "GP Large" with bunks on either side and a large box air conditioner at one end with fans to help circulate the cool air. At the end of each bunk was a footlocker. There was also a stove toward one end, but the nights were still warm.

Gerry left and walked down the line back toward the reception area. The camp was quiet most evenings because there was a strict sundown curfew. Initially, the guards had been brutal to detainees who resisted, killing two of them, a man and a woman. Having learned its lesson, the camp population collectively understood that resistance would get you killed, and curfew was strictly enforced.

"Can I talk to you for a minute," Gerry asked one of the guards he worked with to get people out.

"Sure, what's going on, Gerry?" the guard replied.

"Those people we just processed in, I want to get them out. Can you help?"

"It's going to cost, but yeah, I can help." said the guard.

The guard's name was Randall. He knew Gerry from a VA-sponsored AA Meeting on Saturdays at noon. Even though the "Program" didn't keep Randall (or Gerry) off the sauce, it somehow instilled some of its principles. The problem for Randall was that one of those principles presented an ever-increasing conflict with what he was doing. The focus of "live and let live" was becoming a rare concept compared to what he thought when he took a job with the Defenders early on. So, slowly, over time, the thinning veneer of "patriotism" made him more willing to be an agent of the opposite side, working from within as long as some money came with it.

* * *

It was Tuesday morning, September 19, 2023. Jon was on the phone with Special Agent Babbit in his study, discussing a task force seeking volunteer counter-insurgents from Fayetteville and Eureka Springs to combat a notable uptick in violence against people of color, women, and LGBTQ citizens. The federal government was willing to deputize volunteers and allow them to carry out counter-insurgency operations against known militia groups as determined by the Director of the FBI. Once intelligence sources identified a group, the FBI put it and its sponsors on a list of Domestic Terrorists. This list and the operations were highly classified.

After the call with Babbit, Jon's phone displayed Paul Joseph's number, who called to relay Gerry's message that the Defenders had his mother, brother, and sister-in-law.

Trying his best to suppress panic, he called Special Agent Babbit again.

"Ed, I've got some news," Jon said.

"The Defenders picked up my mother, brother, and his wife. A former client of mine is a detainee at the internment camp in Washington County who got a message passed on to me. I am expected to reply tomorrow through an intermediary about whether and when we can retrieve them, but it will require a tactical operation. I need to act on this. I can't let them keep my family there, especially my mother. Jesus, she's 90 years old."

"I understand," sympathized Babbit. "What do you have in mind?"

"I want to organize an operation to free them and get them to New Mexico as soon as possible. My mom surely cannot survive long in a camp like that. I need to know if you can assign some guys to me or if you'll at least look the other way if things get messy and I do it on my own."

"I believe the Bureau will assist you," Babbit said. "I have a couple of guys who already have eyes on the camp who can help. I have to phone it into Washington for approvals, and we'd have to deputize you as a federal agent like we intend to do with the counter-insurgency operation, but we already have an interstate task force set up for things like this. Let's see, what county are you in out there?"

"Sandoval," Jon said.

"How soon do you want to do this?" Babbit asked.

"The sooner, the better, Ed. If we could get a plan together yesterday, that probably wouldn't be soon enough for me." Jon said.

"Give me some time. I will call Washington and then contact our field office in Santa Fe. Let's see. It's about noon your time. Okay. I will call you back this afternoon." Special Agent Babbit ended the call.

An hour later, Special Agent Babbit called Jon.

"Okay, Washington is all-in, and we spoke with the Sandoval County Sheriff. This is what's going to happen," Babbit said.

"We're sending out the Sandoval County Sheriff himself because we need him to deputize you and anyone with you first. Then, the special agent in charge of the Santa Fe Field Office will be with him to deputize you into federal service as part of a task force. You're a New Mexico resident now, right?"

"Undoubtedly," Jon replied.

"Good. They will come to you, and I asked them to pull it together today. I wouldn't be surprised if they flew up there. Don't you have an airstrip? Send me the coordinates, and if there is anyone else you want to have to help you, you better get them there."

"I can already tell you who I want on this thing with me," Jon said.

"Shoot. Who are they?" Babbit inquired.

"Curtis Chee," Jon said. "He's 19 years old and competent. Also, Carl Joseph Clack, who is 60, but he's meaner than a snake, in good enough shape, and has a crazy bone."

"Done. I'll call to update you on when you can expect them."
Special Agent Babbit hung up.

Carl was in his garage at home in Corrales working on his '57 Bel Air when Jon's call came in. He was underneath the belly of the car and slid out on a dolly to grab his phone. Jon didn't even say hello when Carl picked up.

"Brother, I think I have something you're going to enjoy. We will be deputized as federal agents to go to Arkansas and get my mom and brother out of an internment camp there. Grab your best guns and get your ass up here!"

"Holy shit, I'm in," Carl said enthusiastically. "I want to fuck up some rednecks! Let me gather my shit and get on the road."

"Don't fuck around! We need you here ASAP."

Jon ended the call with a smile on his face.

It's time to get some fucking payback.

Brother Carl Joseph Clack was as loyal a friend as anyone could hope for, a loyalty matched by his willingness to vindicate it by violence if necessary. He was in good shape for a man his age and didn't give a fuck about much other than his friend, Jon. He was indeed a study in contrasts. This man, who was built like a tank with a buzz cut and bright blue eyes, talked a lot of shit and was as gay as gay could be. He'd think nothing of wearing combat boots, a kilt, and a wife beater to a biker rally to spark a reaction and start a fight, which he was equally glad to finish. How he remained free from prisons and hospitals proved that God takes care of fools and drunks.

But Carl was no fool and wasn't drunk all the time, but it was as if he had spent his whole life waiting for a day like today. He had a bug-out bag with fatigues, a gas mask, ammo, and a selection of firearms, not all of which were legal. He threw the bag and an assortment of other weapons and ammo into the back of his other car, a converted red Jeep 4x4, and headed up to the Jemez to meet Jon.

* * *

Jon had been upstairs in his office at La Hacienda for most of the day. He got up from his desk and ran downstairs to find Martin, who, he then remembered, was probably still at the Hot Springs down the valley.

Chee, he thought.

"Curtis, where are you?" Jon called out as he walked down the hall.

"Right here, Hosteen, as the two met in the kitchen."

Jon filled Chee in on the plans and asked, "Do you know where Sam is now?"

"I think he's up at the HQ," Chee replied.

"Good, how about Martin? Is he down in the valley?" Jon asked.

"I think he is," Chee said.

"See if you can find him. He needs to know what's going on. Send someone down there after him if he doesn't pick up his phone or call Officer Parnell in Jemez Springs. If Martin is in town, Parnell can find him." Jon instructed.

"Got it, Hosteen."

"Good, I'll be back in a little bit. I need to meet Sam at Headquarters," Jon said. "Please let Jennifer and Waha know what's happening and prepare a room for Brother Carl. He's coming up and will be here in a couple of hours."

* * *

Jon found Sam in his office.

"Sam, those people in Arkansas have taken my mother, brother, and his wife. I need to get them out, and we'll have some guests here at the ranch soon. But I need a favor, my friend. My mother won't be able to stay up at this altitude if we get her out of the camp. Could anyone down the valley at the pueblo take her in? I suspect my brother and his wife will want to stay with her to keep an eye on her after all she's been through."

"Let me call Governor Toya and see if a family could take them in. They could remain well-hidden there on the pueblo if that is a concern," Sam replied.

"It is, and thank you—one other thing," Jon asked. "Assemble Los Caballeros as soon as you can. I want to talk with them all at once. We will have the Sandoval County Sheriff here later today, and I will ask him to deputize all of them. I am concerned that these people who have come after my family in Arkansas will come after me here, and I want to be sure everyone here on this ranch has the law on his side. Last thing: call the Sandoval County Sheriff. You know him. Tell him what I need regarding Los Caballeros. He should understand."

"Will do, Jefe," Sam answered.

Jon left and drove the short distance back to La Hacienda.

Brother Carl loved to make a grand entrance, and this one did not disappoint because two hours later, Jon saw the plume of dust trailing behind Carl's Jeep as it bounced down the road at excessive speed. As Carl's dust got closer and closer, Jon heard the wop-wop-wop of an approaching helicopter. Behind Carl's trail of dust was another plume. Martin was right behind him.

193

Right on time, Jon thought.

Jon called after Chee, "Curtis, let's go over to the airstrip."

Jon grabbed his cell and phoned Carl.

"Carl, meet us at the airfield."

Next, Jon called Sam.

"Sam, summon Los Caballeros to the hangar."

"Curtis, let's go," Jon called out.

They climbed in the Range Roger, Chee driving, and rolled down the driveway to the perimeter road they'd take to the airstrip. Brother Carl was pulling up right behind them. Chee drove up to the hangar just as the FBI Helicopter blades were coming to a stop. Eight mounted cowboys were riding up in a group from the stables, and two more were arriving on ATVs. While everyone was assembling, Jon walked over to Francisco Villareal, the Sandoval County Sheriff. The two had met before. Jon shook his hand, then introduced himself to the special agent in Charge of the Santa Fe Field Office, a native New Mexican named Ruben Chavez.

"Gentlemen, thank you for coming on such short notice," Jon told the two men.

"You're welcome, Jon," Villareal said. "Do you have everyone here?"

"I do, but I need to ask something," Jon stated.

"Name it," said the sheriff.

"I need you to deputize my cowboys, Sheriff. I'm afraid that the people who took my family in Arkansas will be coming looking for me here, and I'd like to have Los Caballeros deputized so if those people come here, we can defend this place with lethal force if needed and arrest them if possible."

"I'll be glad to do that, Señor Freeman," said the sheriff. "But this is New Mexico, and as far as I'm concerned, anyone who shows up on your property that doesn't belong, you can shoot 'em. But arrest them if you can, that's fine. When I return to the Bernalillo County office, I'll arrange to send up one of our radios and badges."

The sheriff told the special agent, "I need to make these folks Sandoval County Deputy Sheriffs, and then you can do what you need to do, right?"

"Yep, that's how it goes," said Special Agent Chavez.

"All right," the sheriff began, turning to the assembly of cowboys.

"Would all of you who will be deputized step forward and gather around? Raise your right hand and repeat after me…"

The sheriff administered the oath of office.

"Congratulations, everyone," he said after the oath was completed.

"Now, Señor Freeman, you will have the rank of captain. Señor Hernandez, I am giving you the rank of Lieutenant. Give your senior cowboy the rank of sergeant. There needs to be a basic chain of command. Now it is all yours, Special Agent."

Special Agent Chavez approached Jon, Chee, and Brother Carl.

"The three of you raise your right hands and repeat after me."

They completed the oath with Chavez saying, "Congratulations," before turning to Jon.

"Do you have a place where we can talk privately?" Chavez asked.

"Sure, let's go to the house. There is plenty of privacy, but first, I must say a few words to my people here."

"Go right ahead," Chavez allowed.

Jon yelled to everyone, "Excuse me, please give me your attention. Come on, gather around. I have a few things I need to say to you."

Carl, who couldn't help himself, yelled, "Listen up! El Jefe is speaking!"

Martin jammed his elbow playfully into Carl's side, and Carl returned a grin.

"Sometimes you gotta be a dick to get people's attention," Carl whispered with a smile.

Los Caballeros and everyone took off their hats, and Jon began a speech, his cowboy hat in hand.

"I know you all know the events unfolding in Arkansas, my birthplace. Evil individuals took my mother, brother, and his wife hostage. The Governor of Arkansas is making war against me, attempting to silence me and dismantle our Constitution. I could have avoided putting my family in danger by staying silent and leaving long ago, but I didn't, and now they face the consequences. I must rectify that situation. But there's more. When Cullen Dunigan passed away, I didn't understand why he left me the ranch and its magnificent valles. Nevertheless, I fulfilled his wish, even though I never believed I deserved this place. Yet, here we are, together. I've tried to balance my life between my legal career in Arkansas and this life with you in these ancient, living mountains and valleys. But what was once my second home has now become my only home. I want to see this ranch thrive for another century, supporting your families, children, and future generations after I'm gone. I was born on Arkansas soil but chose this land for my rebirth. As the head of this great family, I see you all as my sons and daughters. Today, I'm asking you to protect this land, this ranch, and each other because we are La Familia de Valle Grande."

One of the Caballeros yelled, "We won't let you down, Jefe!" And the group of Caballeros cheered with their hats held high.

Finishing his speech, Jon gazed past their cowboy hats and horses toward the tree line beyond the airstrip where Jennifer Romero and Alfonso Waha sat cross-legged at a campfire, singing prayers about making war.

19

Counter Moves

After the swearing-in, Sheriff Villareal and Special Agent Chavez met Jon, Martin, Chee, and Carl at La Hacienda. Their visit lasted a few hours, with Special Agent Babbit patched in on a video call. As a result of the call, they assembled a special weapons tactical team of FBI volunteers and special operations soldiers to support the mission. Jon's team included breachers, assaulters, a medical tech, a sniper for overwatch with a spotter, Jon, Chee, and Carl. Jon's role was to enter the compound and identify his family members. Plus, Jon was familiar with the area. Carl's job was to back up the assaulters with firepower. Chee's job was to stay with the medic and help evacuate Mrs. Freeman.

Jon's family needed help, and he was grateful the FBI was willing to give it. Although Jon knew he couldn't match the stamina of his younger teammates, he was confident he could keep up because he had gotten himself in good shape since moving to Valle Grande. Jon rarely took a day off, and the daily ranch work caused him to shed about 30 pounds.

The operational plan was simple. The team would deploy by parachutes to approach the camp under the cover of darkness to bust out the Freemans. Propositioned Blackhawks nearby would swoop in to collect everyone before the Defenders could respond with enough force to foil the extraction. One helo had a hoist because Mrs. Freeman likely could not walk fast or far. One significant advantage was that the Defenders didn't have barracks nearby and no rapid-response team, which meant it would take some time to muster enough manpower to repel an assault.

The plan was all set to go down at midnight. Jon and Carl met with the team at sundown on the Los Alamos Municipal Airport ramp. They boarded the FBI Task Force C-130 Hercules and took off for Arkansas. Once on board, the team leader, a former SEAL Team Member, briefed the crew on the plan. Fly in, parachute into a nearby field just south of the jail complex, and approach through a dense, undeveloped forest. Not only did they have the advantage of Jon's familiarity with the territory, but the inside man, Gerry, had the assistance of his AA buddy within the camp who, for the price of $1,000.00 per head, was more than happy to give them intel on the best route in and the exact location of Tent No. 13. For an extra $1,000.00, he would cut the power and create a diversion on the opposite side of the camp with some pyrotechnics.

It had been almost 30 years since Jon separated from military service, but his last assignment with an airborne ranger unit remained a clear memory. Jumping out of a perfectly good airplane at any age, even at his age, wasn't his idea of a great way to spend an evening. At least the parachutes they used for this operation were paraglider chutes, so they could jump out at a relatively high altitude, open the chute, and fly it to the ground using night vision gear. The only challenge was Carl, who had never parachuted before, but he'd go out in tandem with another operator—a piece of cake.

There might be one thing that Jon hated more than waiting for a jury to return a verdict: sitting in the back of a flying tin can on nylon webbing with red lights, waiting for the one-minute warning. To suffer the wait, Jon dozed off to the drone of the four Allison AE2100DS turboprop engines. It surprised him when the operator beside him poked his shoulder and said, "Sir, it's time to get ready."

The team used a modified high altitude, high opening, or HAHO insertion. They would deploy a few miles from the target point and fly their chutes using GPS to the landing zone they selected near the encampment. Meanwhile, the C-130 would proceed to land at Drake Field, a local municipal airport nearby, to be ready for a rapid departure.

As a precaution before the jump, the jump master had all the team members breathe 100% oxygen through masks. With a 57-year-old and a 60-year-old, the jump master wasn't taking any chances. Five minutes until go-time. He looked at Carl sitting across from him and gave him a thumbs up.

Carl briefly pulled his mask down and said to Jon, "Brother, I hope I get to take one of those cocksuckers out for you!"

The jump master looked over, "Mask up!"

Carl complied with an evil grin.

This C-130 was outfitted similarly to the ones Jon had jumped out of when he was in the service. The jump indicator light was still red, but he knew it was moments away from turning green.

Then the jump master yelled out, "Get ready!" as he punched a button to cause the ramp on the back end of the plane to open. Jon was buttoned up. The lights in the cabin flickered, and he switched on his night-vision goggles. Everything was set.

Jon reflected on past jumps before the green light came on. Jumping from an aircraft at night was intense, with wind, engine noise, and stomach-churning drops. The fear of parachute malfunction always lurked in his mind, but the jump master interrupted his fear when he yelled, "Stand up!"

Carl was in a tandem harness with his jumper. The tandem jumper nodded, and the jump master moved to one side and clipped himself into a safety harness near the opening ramp. Jon checked his GPS tracker one more time. Waiting. The jump indicator turned green, and the master yelled, "Go! Go! Go!"

They all walked to the edge of the ramp and flew out the back.

Jon pulled his rip cord and watched his feet go below the horizon through his night vision goggles. He thought it would be colder at this altitude, but this had been a warm September.

With the prevailing winds out of the west and northwest, the pilot dropped them about 7 miles northwest of the landing zone. The wind did the rest. All they had to do was fly. According to Jon's GPS, they would be on the ground in a few minutes.

* * *

The team leader checked in for a roll call after everyone was on the ground in the dark field.

Jon was momentarily disoriented after touching down, but he scanned his surroundings through his night-vision goggles. There was Carl, unbuckling his harness. The team leader was a few yards away. Breachers. Assaulters. Sniper. Spotter. All present.

Then the team leader whispered, "On me."

Each man gathered his parachute and brought it to the team leader standing by some brush in the middle of the field. It was pitch-black outside. They shoved their chutes underneath the brush and covered them with some branches. Then the team leader whispered, "Weapons on safe but ready. No fireworks unless they shoot at us first!"

Through the humid night air, they formed a squad wedge formation of black-painted faces. Jon was in the middle with the team leader and the medic. One of the breachers was on point, and back behind, a few meters apart, were the assaulters and Carl. They advanced from the field to a tree line and then into a wooded area with underbrush that slowed them down as they moved through it, step by step, slowly, carefully avoiding making noise.

They neared the edge of the wood after about 300 yards and saw the unlit fence of the County Road Supply Complex that ran perpendicular to their approach angle. The yard was littered with bundles of metal pipe, stacks of concrete barriers, piles of gravel, and parked vehicles. It provided excellent cover as they moved silently along. They crept east toward the taco factory in the distance. Still, the internment camp was a little further ahead, placed in a large open field between the factory and the Razorback Greenway Bike Trail. The team narrowed its wedge formation, staying within the tree line adjacent to a subdivision they were sneaking past. The leader held up his fist in the air. The team froze in place. Two kids on bicycles came up the path the team had just crossed. The top of Jon's assault rifle was less than 6 inches away from them as they rolled by on their ten-speeds. It was safe to move again.

A fist was up once more. They were at their staging point, and it was time to wait. Tent Number 13, where the Freemans were, was on the north end of the encampment, next to the fence. It was 2349, and the operation was to commence at midnight with a power outage followed by a diversion of pyrotechnics south of their position.

As he checked his watch, Jon thought the summer cicadas were louder than he remembered, and for a moment, he recalled how much he missed late fall evenings in Arkansas.

Go time, and at that exact moment, what few lights were on in the camp went dark. The darkness was followed by loud explosions south of the camp.

"Go, go, go, go, go!" came across his earpiece.

Jon held his position momentarily while the breachers moved across the open grassy area between the tree line and the darkened fence, then he made his move. The assaulters were close behind. The sniper found a perch with his spotter on the roof of an adjacent building next to the trail, affording a decent field of fire to perform the sniper's overwatch function.

Jon waited with the team leader as Carl and the breachers made a giant doorway in the fence with wire cutters.

The spotter called out, "Breacher one, at your twelve o'clock. Tango walking in your direction."

While the rest of the camp converged on the pyrotechnics, this moron walked in the opposite direction.

"Wait, one. Wait. He's friendly," reported the spotter.

Just as the sniper was about to put a bullet in him, the friendly flashed his light three times in the direction of the insertion team. Then he turned around and ran in the opposite direction.

"Time to go," the team leader said, and Jon ran with him across the opening from the tree line, through the hole cut in the fence, to Tent Number 13. There was his mother, his brother, and his sister-in-law, huddled together, waiting. Jon motioned to them with his hands in a hurried fashion, whispering, "Let's go. Mom, this man here will help you. Ira, Elaine, follow me. Keep low, and don't make a sound!"

Elaine was frantically looking about in a state of shock and terror.

"What if they catch us? What if we don't make it?" she pleaded.

"We don't have time for this! Jon whispered. "If we don't leave now, they will kill all of us. Now, let's go!"

Then the team leader came up with Jon to Mrs. Freeman, "Ma'am," the team leader said, "I'm here to get you out of here, and I'm going to carry you."

For the first time in her adult life, Mrs. Freeman was speechless as the team leader bent down, picked her up gently, and positioned her across his shoulders in a fireman's carry. Jon motioned emphatically for them to leave the tent, and as they did, he could hear two approaching UH-60 Blackhawks.

The two Blackhawks came in low from the northwest, just over the treetops. One was to land in an open space closer to the north end of the camp, but the other was to hover and drop a hoist for Mrs. Freeman as close to the fence as possible. As they approached, Jon could see the hoist through his night vision goggles being lowered while the other helo was landing. The gunner on the hovering Blackhawk opened fire on some Defenders who began advancing on Jon's group. Carl trained his automatic shotgun toward the threat and opened fire from his hip.

"Eat shit, you cocksuckers!" He yelled. "I bet you don't like having your ass handed to you by a faggot! Burn in hell, mother fuckers!"

The anger from a lifetime of ridicule blew through the smoking barrel of Carl's fully automatic drum-fed shotgun.

In less than two minutes, Jon's team had entered the compound through the fence and secured Mrs. Freeman, Ira, and Elaine. Half a dozen Defenders were running toward them as the extraction team retreated toward their assigned Blackhawk, but Carl stopped to take out two of them before the gunner on the Blackhawk yelled, "Get your ass on board!"

Meanwhile, Mrs. Freeman was in the hoist, and her Blackhawk was climbing as she dangled from the cable above the ground. There was no time to wait to pull her into the helicopter.

The Defenders kept up the pursuit, with only two out of the six taken down. As they neared their Blackhawk, Jon flung himself on the ground and assumed a prone position in the grass to give covering fire along with the door gunner. One more fell. Then another. Two left.

His brother and Elaine ran past him with the remainder of the team. Elaine tripped and fell along the way, but Ira reached down and helped her stand back up. She stood momentarily paralyzed, with gunfire erupting around her in a daze.

"We can't kill all those people," Elaine cried to Ira.

"Run, goddammit," Ira yelled at her. "Those 'people' are trying to kill us! Get your fucking priorities straight."

Ira was white-hot, enraged, and wished he had a gun to shoot his former captors. He had always avoided conflict with wit or humor, but the smell of gunpowder, smoke, and fear changed everything. He realized in the few seconds it took to escape his captors that he and many other Americans had been naive to believe the right-wing fanatics could be reasoned with. Now, force was the only answer.

Ira and Elaine reached the helicopter, and one of the team members, a young army corporal, helped Elaine aboard. Ira hopped in after her.

"I had no idea it would come to this," Elaine gasped as she collapsed in her seat, "those people in the camp were doing their jobs. They were even nice to us."

"Would you rather we let them kill us?" Ira admonished, "Jesus, stop being a fucking Pollyanna!"

As Ira finished yelling at his wife, he turned and watched his brother squeeze off more rounds at the last two approaching Defenders. One more fell—one left. Jon rose from his prone position and emptied the remainder of his magazine on the hapless idiot, who staggered like a marionette before collapsing at Jon's feet.

Jon glanced down to see if he recognized the dead middle-aged man before turning to run as fast as he could and jump into the Blackhawk as it began to lift off. Carl sat on the floor of their Blackhawk with his legs dangling out the side, taking potshots at black SUVs until the team leader yelled, "Knock it off, goddammit! We got 'em!"

The team leader pulled on a headset and told the pilot, "Radio the C-130 and tell them we are coming in hot and to be ready for an immediate departure. They need to power up now."

The door gunner closed the helicopter door as the helicopter gained altitude and flew toward the awaiting C-130 just a few miles away. Ira leaned over and tapped Jon on the shoulder.

"Where are they taking Mom?" he asked, raising his voice so Jon could hear him over the noise.

"They put Mom on her helicopter to get her out with the hoist. They are taking her to board another military plane in Fort Smith, and we will meet her in Albuquerque."

* * *

It took Mrs. Freeman several weeks to recover from her harrowing extraction, which, miraculously, only resulted in a torn rotator cuff and a sprained knee. However, she found peace and safety in the welcoming home of Jemez Pueblo Governor Fred Toya. Despite being an outsider on a reservation normally closed to non-natives, Mrs. Freeman quickly became a beloved figure among the Jemez People, many of whom visited her daily.

As with many operations, the military and FBI used tactical cameras on the team's helmets to review the footage later in their debriefings. Such footage was always classified, but in this instance, the President of the United States wanted the extraction videos declassified and released to the media. One unintended result of releasing the video to the press was that it catapulted Jon to international fame. The footage depicting his family's dramatic rescue on the heels of Mrs. Smith's chilling execution fomented opposition to the New Law from all corners, but people were still afraid.

After the bold rescue, recruitment for counterinsurgency groups formed in the compact states accelerated. However, recruiting and training were still too slow to stop Buckshot's push toward dystopia. As opposition grew, the Defenders arrested and detained more people, and as they vanished, many became too scared to oppose the New Law openly.

In Arkansas, for example, the commission initially focused on people it deemed "gender non-conforming." They were easy targets with a broad definition of gay, lesbian, and transgender individuals. Even rainbow flags were made illegal. Displaying a rainbow flag, even on a bumper sticker, resulted in an arrest. Arkansas didn't stop there, though. Arkansas initiated a program of systematic removal of children from the homes of same-sex couples, placing them with "upright" families or sending them to "re-education" facilities—repurposed dorms at university campuses overseen by commission appointees. The Defenders' tyrannical tactics didn't end with LGBTQ persons, however.

Buckshot pushed the commission to develop a state-wide registry that would catalog each person's declared religious belief so it could begin revoking the professional licenses of non-registered persons or persons whose registration did not fit into an accepted category of religious belief. The state restricted public library access by requiring permits issued by local chancellors before visiting a public library, much less checking out books. State officials confiscated and destroyed unapproved books deemed criminal to possess. The state also embarked on a scheme of seizing the homes and property of nonconformists and reallocating the seized property to ruling elite members of the state government. Among the homes taken in this program were Mrs. Freeman's residence and Ira's, among many others. In a spiteful display, Buckshot ordered Highland House to be razed, taunting Jon with photos of the burned-out shell of a home delivered in a box wrapped in Christmas paper.

* * *

By the Fall of 2023, Washington, DC, was a political war zone under the leadership of President Timothy Hedges, a spry but elderly man in his 80s. The Republican-controlled 118th Congress sworn in after the midterms had a stranglehold on the Democrats, but the Republicans did not have a supermajority as they did in several states. The result was a gridlock that left the Democratic president and his party with few options to combat the dramatic swing to the right in American politics.

The White House was hunkered down, determined to protect the rights of people living in the compact states, but without a cooperative Congress, the president had few options. With a majority of federal legislative powers out of reach, the White House was cornered, left to consider the drastic measure of federalizing the National Guard—a decision the president was reluctant to make. Without the Supreme Court, the nerve to utilize military intervention, and a recalcitrant Congress, his arsenal was pared down to financial interventions implemented through executive orders.

Money influences politics, and that reality struck a nerve when the president issued Executive Order 15068. EO 15068 ignited a firestorm by mandating the Comptroller of Currency and the Federal Reserve Board to freeze all compact state funds held in federal institutions until it could be verified the state was complying with federal law, regulations, and court orders. His sweeping order also halted electronic and paper check transactions involving compact state governments. He also suspended federal highway funding and agricultural subsidy payments. A debate raged within the White House on whether he should also freeze Medicaid Block Grant payments and Medicare payments to providers to force the affected states' people to rise against their legislatures. But in the end, the president was unwilling to take actions that would punish people rather than the state actors.

While some may have seen EO 15068 as a masterstroke to corner the compact states, it only steeled their resolve. As a result, tensions reached a fever pitch on Independence Day, 2024.

* * *

In the center of it all was Wilson Brannigan, the president's chief of staff. He was a retired army three-star general, a former congressman from Montana, and the consummate Washington insider. Under his smooth-shaved bald head, he was a grizzled and ruthless political warrior.

One evening in late October 2023, Brannigan was having dinner with President Hedges and the First Lady in the Executive Residence, discussing the situation with the compact states.

"Wilson, what the hell am I going to do with those compact states?" Asked the elderly president, who was sharp even at 79 years old.

"The Democrats are too disorganized and fighting among themselves," Hedges continued, "and the moderate Republicans are running scared. I can't pass any federal legislation to bring those states to heel. The Supreme Court gives the states free rein under its new-found 'originalism' doctrine. And, of course, the states have ignored the few federal court orders that stuck. I'm relegated to using force through the Insurrection Act, but I won't turn our military against our people."[18]

"It's a good question, Mr. President," Brannigan said. "Part of the problem is that neither you nor I understand the people down there leading it, much less the culture behind it. I might be a crusty old warrior, but I'm no Southerner. I'm hard-pressed to find anyone in this administration who does understand them. It is as if those Southerners down there have their special language, and no one gets it but them."

"But Wilson, it isn't just the southern states," he observed.

"True, true. It is more of a rural versus urban disconnect. I get the rural part because I grew up in Montana, but a Southerner is leading it. Hell, this whole mess started in the South. It is like those rednecks want to relitigate the Civil War again and have co-opted the rest of the rural states into believing it was their war, too."

The First Lady, pretty and much younger than her husband, spoke up. Some thought she was the brains in that duo.

"Have either of you thought about getting someone to come up here who is from the region? Maybe get a different perspective than what you get inside the beltway. Most of these insufferable beltway liberals are out of touch."

"Wilson, you can see why I married her. Why didn't we think of that!" The president leaned over and kissed his wife on the cheek.

"That's a splendid idea," Brannigan remarked. "Now that you mention it, I think I might have a suggestion. Do you remember the lawyer from Arkansas who shot his mouth off the day the Arkansas governor signed the first New Law at her press conference? TNN picked up on it, and ever since he's made his rounds on several news shows."

"Wait," Hedges paused, "you mean the lawyer who got himself deputized and participated in that recent FBI raid against a detention camp in Arkansas?"

"That's him."

"And now he's a rancher in New Mexico, that guy," the president said.

"Yes, sir, that's who I mean."

"Why don't you invite him to meet us, honey," the First Lady offered, turning and putting her hand on her husband's shoulder.

"What do you say, Wilson?" The president said.

"I'll make it happen, Mr. President."

20

Misty's Journey

It was October 2023, and Misty had made up her mind. Her Uncle Frank raped her, and she was pregnant with his child. She could not have a baby, much less HIS baby. She had just turned eighteen and was a straight-A senior at Morrilton High School. She was brilliant, pretty, and able to keep high marks despite her position as the cheerleading captain for the Devil Dogs. Having achieved top scores on her college entrance exams, she wanted to study molecular biology and attend medical school. All she had to do was get through the Fall semester and graduate in the Spring, but now, she was in trouble. One thing was clear: her aspiration to be a scientist to help cure or prevent the cancer that killed her sweet granny would never come to pass if she had a child at eighteen. She had to go through with an abortion. The only thing was where, when, and how much.

On Monday, October 30th, 2023, when his phone rang, Tiny was adjusting an insurance claim at his desk. At first, he didn't recognize the number but thought again.

That's a prefix from back home.

It was his second cousin, Misty.

"Tiny," she said when he answered. Her voice sounded small.

"Misty! I haven't talked to you in a long time. What's new?"

"I'm in trouble, and I didn't know who else to call," she said.

"Whoa, whoa, wait up. What's goin' on, Darlin'?" Tiny asked.

He could hear her sniffle through the line.

"I, I, I don't know what to do," she said weakly, her voice barely audible, "and I don't know who to trust."

"Misty, it's me, Cousin Tiny. Take a deep breath and tell me what's going on."

"Uncle Frank raped me," she whimpered.

"Oh no, he didn't, that mother fucker! Do your parents know about it? How about the police?" Tiny asked.

"There's no way I could go to the police. Going to them would ruin everything. My parents don't know, but my mother suspects something happened," Misty replied.

"Honey, can you at least tell your mom what happened?"

Misty held her breath for a moment.

"I can't tell her or Dad because..." she paused. "I'm pregnant. You know how religious they are. They'll never understand, and I cannot, cannot, cannot have a baby! I'm supposed to go to college! And with Uncle Frank? I think they would blame it on me."

"Jesus. I don't know what to say, Misty. How can I help? Do you want me to talk to your folks? Is there anything I can do?"

"There is, but please, please, please don't tell anyone about this, OK? I need an abortion. I can't have a baby. There's no way. What I need is money to get one," she said.

"Honey, abortion is impossible with the New Law in Arkansas," Tiny said.

"I know, I know," Misty said. "But I found a clinic in Albuquerque, New Mexico. I checked it out online, and I called. It's anonymous. But I have to get it done before I start to show."

"Honey, you know I'll do what I can for you. How much money do you need, and how will you get to New Mexico without your parents knowing?"

"The Clinic in Albuquerque says it will cost $750.00, but I'll need that and enough money for gas and a hotel," she said.

"But how will you be away from home without your parents knowing?"

"I told Mom and Dad that I'm going on a field trip to Fairfield Bay with

210

my science class and plan to stay over with my cheer squad."

"Wouldn't they call the school and check?" Tiny asked.

"You know my parents. No way. They are not involved with my school at all." Misty said.

"Tell you what," Tiny said, "I can send you $1,500.00. More if you need it, but that should be enough to get you there and back. When do you plan to go?"

"My appointment is this Friday morning, but I have to call them before the end of the day to keep it," Misty said.

"OK, I'll send the money to you now. Please be careful. I love you, kiddo." Tiny signed off.

* * *

Misty left the house at 7 a.m. on Thursday, November 2nd, for the 12-hour drive west on I-40.

At about 8:30 in the morning, Misty was approaching the Arkansas/Oklahoma state line when she saw traffic slowing for a roadblock. She slowed her 2018 Altima and joined the line of cars. Ahead, reflective cones funneled the traffic into one lane as she approached a checkpoint next to a portable building on the shoulder. Uniformed men were stopping every car and checking IDs.

Her heart pounded relentlessly in her chest as the line of cars inched forward for several minutes. The very sight of the Defenders looming ahead sent a cold shiver racing down her spine, her palms growing clammy and her breaths short and shallow. Every fiber in her screamed tension, her eyes darting and her fingers trembling. The weight of their presence was almost palpable, and the overwhelming nervousness threatened to consume her.

Oh my God. What if they know? I can't get caught. I can't get caught. I can't get caught.

After what felt like an eternity in line, her turn arrived. The oppressive atmosphere tightened her chest, clashing with the sheer will to move forward. Hesitantly, she pressed the button, and the window descended, and the cold air spilled inside the car. A middle-aged man with hardened features stood outside her door dressed in black military fatigues. His eyes, cold and emotionless, bore into hers, and the black stocking cap he wore seemed less for the cold and more a symbol of the darkness he embodied. The silence was suffocating, every second stretching painfully long as he neared her.

"Good morning, young lady. May I see your license, registration, and insurance papers?"

Misty handed the officer her documents. Her hands trembled violently, causing her to drop her license on the floorboard.

"Young lady, are you alright? Is there something going on? Anything you should tell me?"

"No, I'm OK." Her voice cracked.

She bent forward, picked up her license, and handed it to the Defender through her window.

"Wait here just a minute, please," he said.

He lowered the gate and motioned for other cars to pass around her. He walked to the portable building on the shoulder and went inside.

After a few moments, he emerged with a woman who looked to be in her 50s with short red hair and dressed in similar-looking black fatigues. The two approached the car.

"Have I done anything wrong?" Misty asked with a quivering voice.

"Oh, not at all, Miss, but I need you to accompany us. We have some questions to ask, and then you can get back on the road," the female officer told her.

Misty's heart raced as she obediently pulled off the highway to find a parking spot beside the nondescript portable building. This wasn't right.

Drawing in a shaky breath, she stepped out of the car, her legs feeling unsteady beneath her. Drizzle began coming down on this freezing and grey November morning. The sterile appearance of the portable building did little to ease the tight knot in her stomach. Once inside, the stern-looking woman from earlier beckoned her into a cramped room barely large enough to hold a desk and another chair. The walls seemed to close in.

"Miss Jenkins," the woman began, her voice holding a false warmth that did nothing to comfort Misty, "my name is Matron Tipton. Relax. You are not in trouble." The words should have been reassuring, but the situation's oddity did nothing to assuage her anxiety.

"We are stopping you to check to see if you are pregnant. If you are, we want to be sure we get you on the state registry. Any woman of childbearing age has to register if she's pregnant. We'll do a little pregnancy test right now, and then you can be on your way."

Misty felt her mouth go dry, a lump forming in her throat. She was overwhelmed by thoughts of being registered, categorized, and monitored. And what would happen when she retested and was not pregnant anymore? Utterly suffocated, her eyes darted around the room, searching for some semblance of normalcy but finding none.

Misty was still shaking as her fear erupted into tears.

"Don't cry, hon," the matron said. "We just want to be sure you get proper care if you are pregnant. The registry helps us do that. But before we do the test, I have a form for you to fill out and some questions to ask."

The officer withdrew some papers out of a desk drawer and a pen and gave them to Misty.

One of the questions was, "What is your final destination and the purpose of your trip?"

Misty's mind rapidly went through all the possible lies she could write down on the form. She hesitated.

"Ummm, well..."

"Where are you going, young lady," the matron asked again, but this time with a sharper tone.

"I'm going to visit a cousin in Albuquerque. He's been sick, and I wanted to go see him for the weekend," Misty stammered.

"Then write that down, but aren't you supposed to be in school?" the matron asked.

"I got an excuse from the principal," Misty said.

"I see," the matron replied. "Mind if I call your cousin?"

"Sure, I guess," Misty said.

Oh fuck, fuck, fuck. I hope Tiny isn't home!

Misty read off Tiny's number for the matron.

"That's an Arkansas number, but you say he lives in Albuquerque." the matron stated with a raised eyebrow.

"That's right, he's from near where I live, but he recently moved out there," Misty said.

The matron used the phone on the little desk and punched in Tiny's number.

"Hello, this is Tiny Jenkins."

"Hello, Mr. Jenkins. My name is Matron Tipton of the Arkansas Defenders. I'm sitting across from your cousin, Misty. She says she's coming to visit you. I wanted to call and verify if that is true."

"She's not in trouble, is she?" Tiny asked.

"No sir, she's fine, no trouble at all. I just wanted to verify that she's coming to visit you."

"That's right, she is," Tiny said.

"And where might you be, sir?" The matron asked.

"Albuquerque," Tiny said. "I moved here not too long ago."

"Well, that's great, Mr. Jenkins. Thank you for your time. Bye-bye."

The matron hung up her phone.

"Alright, Miss, I have everything I need. Let's go down the hall. There is a restroom down there. I have to observe you take the test, so let's go and do that. After I check the result, you can be on your way. I have to say, though, you seem awful nervous. Do you think you're pregnant?"

"I don't think so," Misty said. "I have a boyfriend, but we are always careful."

"Alrighty. If I were guessing, I'd say you're pregnant, deary. You have that look about you. Let's go see, OK?"

Misty produced barely enough urine to complete the test. She silently handed the cup to Matron Tipton and returned to sit in the chair to wait for the results, hoping the test would be negative by some miracle.

Today was not a day for miracles of the sort Misty needed.

"Congratulations, Miss! You're going to be a mom. I'm so happy for you. Better get with the child's father when you get back. He's going to help you with this baby, right?"

Misty looked up and nodded, tears welling in her eyes.

"Now, now, don't cry. It will be OK, I promise you. Women younger than you have been having babies since the dawn of humanity, with or without the help of men. You'll be fine."

Misty nodded "yes" again as the matron typed some information into a computer on the desk.

"I'll be right back. I have a paper to give you, and you can be on your way," the matron said.

Misty considered telling the matron about her uncle raping her, but the rumors of the New Law scared her out of it. If she told on her uncle, wouldn't she be in trouble, too?

When the matron returned to the room where Misty sat, Matron Tipton handed Misty a printed form with her name, address, and registration number at the top of the document. The paper also featured instructions printed in bold capital letters:

A TEST ADMINISTERED BY THE ARKANSAS DEFENDERS INDICATES THE PRESENCE OF HUMAN CHORIONIC GONADOTROPIN (HCG) IN YOUR URINE THAT DEVELOPS IN A PERSON'S BODY DURING PREGNANCY WHICH INDICATES YOU ARE PREGNANT. AS A PREGNANT WOMAN, YOU MUST REPORT TO YOUR HOME COUNTY HEALTH DEPARTMENT WITHIN 60 DAYS OF THE DATE ON THIS FORM AND SUBMIT TO A FOLLOW-UP PREGNANCY TEST. FAILURE TO REPORT FOR A FOLLOW UP TEST IS A SERIOUS FELONY PUNISHABLE BY UP TO 10 YEARS IN PRISON AND/OR A $10,000.00 FINE, OR BOTH.

Underneath the first statement was a second statement that read:

IF A REGISTRANT'S SUBSEQUENT PREGNANCY TEST
RETURNS A NEGATIVE RESULT, THEN THE REGISTRANT
WILL BE SUBJECT TO A REBUTABLE PRESUMPTION THAT
SHE HAS VIOLATED THE ARKANSAS UNBORN CHILD
PROTECTION ACT CODIFIED AT A.C.A. 5-61-401 ET SEQ
(as amended), A VIOLATION OF LAW THAT COULD RESULT
IN SEVERE CRIMINAL PENALTIES INCLUDING DEATH.

Misty left the building with the paper, determined to continue her journey to New Mexico. She passed through similar checkpoints, leaving Oklahoma into Texas and again leaving Texas at its border with New Mexico. Officials stopped her at both borders but allowed her to proceed when she produced the registration document the matron gave her in Arkansas.

* * *

The following day, Misty drove to the clinic for the procedure. She parked in the back parking lot of the stand-alone stucco building and went to an entrance where she could avoid a small crowd of right-to-life protesters across the street from the front of the building. She felt a strange mixture of shame, guilt, fear, and relief as she walked toward the check-in counter for her appointment. All of it at once swam in her head while she signed the papers and paid the money.

Vacuum aspiration terminated Misty's pregnancy, and after, Misty grappled with more whirlwinds of emotion. Relief was her most immediate feeling because the procedure was over. However, intertwined with that relief was an overlay of profound sadness and fear, perhaps stemming from the circumstances that led to her decision.

Moments of anxiety occasionally surfaced as she headed east up Tijeras Canyon on her way home, but it was done, and all she wanted to do now was to get home. Along the way, Misty made three personal resolutions. One, to never tell another soul. Two, to put the whole thing out of her mind. Three, never to be in the same room alone with her Uncle Frank again as long as she lived.

* * *

No one other than Tiny knew Misty's secret. Thanksgiving came and went. Then finals. Misty had put the entire affair out of her mind by Christmas, and because Christmas was her favorite holiday, she was busy with her friends. This year was super special for her because it might be the last one she could spend with her girlfriends before college. In the weeks leading up to Christmas Day, she spent all her free time with her friends shopping, making silly videos for social media, and staying up late talking about boys. Then there was the New Year celebration. Time passed, as did January 2nd, 2024, the deadline for Misty's follow-up pregnancy test.

A knock was at the door on a cold and dark January afternoon. It was January 4th, 2024, and Misty was home with her mother. Her dad was off hunting ducks over on the Delta. Misty thought nothing of it when she went to open the door where two Arkansas Defenders stood in their trademark black fatigues with overcoats and black stocking hats.

"Are you Misty Jenkins," asked one of the Defenders.

Then she remembered. Her mother came around the corner to see who was at the door.

"What's going on?" Mrs. Jenkins asked.

Misty could not move or speak.

One of the Defenders came inside, took Mrs. Jenkins by the hand, and led her back into the living room. Misty stood motionless in the doorway, her face white with fear.

"Are you Misty Jenkins?"

This time, the Defender was demanding.

"Yes," Misty whispered.

"You have to come with us. We have a Body Attachment Order from the

217

Conway County Chancellor to bring you to the county health department for a follow-up pregnancy test under the New Law. Turn around, please, and put your hands behind your back."[19]

The cold handcuffs pinched her skin.

Misty heard her mother's raised voice coming from the living room as the one Defender led her to a black SUV parked out in the front yard.

"You can't take my daughter. She hasn't done anything wrong!" Mrs. Jenkins screamed. She had no idea.

Misty's pregnancy test yielded a negative result later that day. After that, the Defenders took her to the Conway County Rehabilitation and Reeducation Center, where she was to await a detention hearing on the criminal allegations against her.

Misty's case would be the first in a series of firsts under the New Law. To ensure the case would be tried properly, the chancellor appointed a special prosecutor from a list of "approved prosecutors" the tribunal provided. It was no secret the chancellor sought a special prosecutor who could make an example of Misty by testing the limits of the law.

* * *

On Monday, January 8th, 2024, Chancellor Jefferson Beauregard "Beau" Caldwell III mounted the bench in his repainted courtroom at the Conway County Courthouse in Morrilton. Two Defenders, a man, and a woman, brought Misty into the courtroom through a side door and sat her down at one of the tables in the well. When the judge walked in, the special prosecutor, a younger man in a dark gray tailored suit, approached the bench.

"Your Honor, I wanted to introduce myself before we get started. I'm the Special Prosecutor assigned to this case. My name is Liam Montgomery."

"It's a pleasure to meet you, Mr. Montgomery," the chancellor said. "Thank you for coming up from Little Rock."

Right about that time, a plump man wearing rumpled khaki pants capped with a poorly knotted tie and a blue sports coat hurried in and sat beside

Misty.

The chancellor raised an eyebrow.

"Mr. Lawson, nice of you to join us."

Bubba Lawson, Misty's court-appointed public Defender, was late. This judge wanted all the lawyers assembled and ready to go in his courtroom before he came out.

"Sorry, Judge," Bubba replied.

"Let's get started," Chancellor Caldwell said, ignoring the lawyer's insincere apology. Bubba Lawson had a reputation for always being late for court.

A clerk came in through the same side door Misty entered and handed the chancellor a thin manila folder with some papers. He rifled through them, withdrew one sheet, and closed the file.

"Let's get on the record. This is Tribunal Case TCCR-24-001, State of Arkansas versus Misty Jenkins. We are here for the defendant's initial appearance. Counsel, is there any reason we cannot proceed?"

"No, Your Honor," Bubba Lawson said. He was rattled.

"Very well," said the chancellor. "Miss Jenkins, you are here because the State of Arkansas has charged you with two violations of the New Law. One, that you failed to report for a follow-up pregnancy examination at your county health department within 60 days, and two, that you violated the Arkansas Unborn Child Protection Act by terminating a pregnancy without the legal right to do so. Do you understand why you are here?"

Misty didn't say anything.

"You have to answer him," Bubba whispered.

"Yes," she whispered.

The chancellor paused and pursed his lips.

"Miss, this will go much faster if I can hear you when you speak. Speak up."

"Yes," she said louder, then bowed her head.

"Is there anything that would prevent you from understanding or answering my questions, Miss? You are not on any medication or under any mental strain that would prevent you from understanding these

219

proceedings, are you?"

"No," she said.

"What does the state have for me?" The chancellor asked.

Mr. Montgomery rose to his feet.

"The state filed a two-count information against the defendant, Misty Jenkins. Count One alleges the defendant violated the New Law provision requiring her to follow up with the county health department after a positive pregnancy test on November 2nd, 2023, that the Arkansas Defenders administered at the Arkansas/Oklahoma border checkpoint on I-40 West. Count Two alleges the defendant violated the Arkansas Unborn Protection Act by unlawfully terminating her pregnancy."

"Does the defense wish the court to read the formal charges as filed, or does the defense waive formal reading?" The chancellor inquired.

"We waive formal reading, Your Honor," Bubba replied.

Lawyers often waived the reading of the formal charges, seeing little value in it. Some lawyers, perhaps the more meticulous or ambitious, insisted on hearing every word. But not Bubba Lawson. With his perpetually rumpled suit and a demeanor that oozed lethargy, Bubba was the epitome of slovenliness. Why waste precious moments in court when he could be relaxing at home? So, true to form, Bubba waived the reading—every single time.

The judge flipped open the little manila folder again and pulled out another document.

"Miss Jenkins, I am required by law to advise you with your counsel present that you have certain rights unless you waive reading of those rights. Mr. Lawson?"

True to form, Bubba Lawson rose from his chair and said, "We waive the reading of rights, also, Your Honor. I advised Miss Jenkins of her Constitutional rights."

"Alright," the chancellor continued. "Miss Jenkins, I must advise you of the potential penalties if you are found guilty by plea or trial of the offenses charged against you. Do you understand?"

"Yes," she said.

"If found guilty of count one, the penalty ranges from 3 - 10 years in the Arkansas State Penitentiary, up to a $10,000.00 fine, or both. If found guilty of count two, the penalty ranges from 10 to 40 years, or life, unless the state seeks the death penalty."

The judge opened his folder again and looked through it.

"I don't see a notice that the state seeks the death penalty in my file, Mr. Montgomery."

Mr. Montgomery rose to his feet.

"I apologize, Your Honor, but the state intends to seek the death penalty in this case. We will have a *Notice of Intent to Seek the Death Penalty* on file with the Clerk of the Court by the end of the day."

Misty's face turned white. Mr. Lawson's mouth opened, and he looked at the table.

"I will proceed on that information, then," the chancellor said.

"Miss Jenkins, you have been advised of the charges against you and your rights. I find nothing before me to suggest you are incompetent to continue. So, I must ask for your initial plea. How do you plea to the charges against you?" The chancellor inquired.

Bubba said, "The defendant pleads not guilty to all charges, Your Honor."

"Very well. I will enter a plea of not guilty to the charges. Now, Mr. Montgomery, what about bail?"

"The state opposes bail. Given that the defendant had the means to leave the state, which is why she was identified in the first place at the border checkpoint, the state believes she is a flight risk. Furthermore, the state has additional reasons why the court should deny bail. These are serious charges, plus the defendant poses a danger to the community. If free on bail, she could get pregnant again and repeat her alleged crime a second time. This doubles as a reason to hold her out of concern for public safety and the potential life of another yet-to-be unborn child. Finally, Your Honor, the state also believes it has a solid case backed by uncontroverted physical evidence and reliable eyewitnesses."

Mr. Montgomery sat down with a look of self-satisfaction on his face.

"Mr. Lawson?" The chancellor inquired.

"May I have a moment, Your Honor?"

"A moment, Mr. Lawson, just a moment."

"Misty," he whispered, "You've got to give me something here. Anything. Any reason why they shouldn't lock you up before a trial."

The two conferred in whispers.

"I don't have all day, Mr. Lawson. What's it going to be?" The irritated chancellor said.

Mr. Lawson stood up, looked down at his crumpled client, and addressed the court.

"Your Honor, the defense opposes bail. The court should release her on her recognizance because she has few resources to travel and no job. She has life-long ties to this community and no other place to go. Her family lives here. She's not going anywhere. But there is one more thing. There are extenuating circumstances. She tells me the pregnancy was positive because her uncle raped her. Surely, that places this case in a different category than what is charged."

Mr. Montgomery was already on his feet.

"I presume you have a response to that, Mr. Montgomery," the chancellor inquired.

"Your Honor, it doesn't matter how she got pregnant. It only matters that she was pregnant. The law recognizes no exception to aborting a fetus due to the cause. Perhaps the cause might be argued in the sentencing phase, but whether the defendant got pregnant willingly or because of alleged rape is not a recognizable exception to the law."

"I've heard enough," the chancellor remarked. "Mr. Lawson, I will deny bail and remand the defendant to the custody of the Arkansas Defenders, who may, at their discretion, house the defendant at the county jail or detention camp while she awaits trial. You, lawyers, see my trial court assistant for the next hearing date in this matter and a scheduling order. The court is adjourned."

Chancellor Caldwell retired to his chambers to read some emails and check his docket for the rest of the day. He was relieved that he had nothing else on the calendar so he could leave early. Then his phone buzzed.

"Who is it, Marlene?" He yelled through the door to his trial court assistant.

"It's Judge Blasingame," she reported.

"Tom's calling, huh? Thanks, Marlene. I'll pick up."

The chancellor punched the blinking button on his phone, putting it on speaker.

"Tom! What are you doing, you irascible son of a bitch?" Caldwell said with a smile as he leaned back in his swivel chair.

"Morning, Beau, better pick up the receiver for this call," Blasingame said.

"What's going on, Tom," Caldwell asked after he picked up the handset.

"Beau, the governor is interested in your case with that Jenkins girl. You know she's pushing for the death penalty on it. Today was her first appearance. Can you tell me how it went?"

"Sure, Tom," Caldwell replied. "We had the initial presentment by the book. The state's lawyer did a fine job. He's a sharp fella, that one. Anyway, I denied bail, so she'll be bound over awaiting trial. But there was something of a surprise in the hearing."

"What's that," Blasingame asked.

"Her lawyer, a complete dipshit, argued against bail because she claimed an uncle raped her, which was why she was pregnant. If you could call it an argument, he argued, 'extenuating circumstances' that justified the unwanted pregnancy."

"What did you do?"

"I overruled the objection and denied bail, of course. You and I worked on that statute together, so I know there is no exception for a rape victim terminating her pregnancy."

"What about the press? Was any press there?" Blasingame inquired.

"No press."

"I appreciate the update, Beau. Let me get with the governor on this. If that little girl was raped, the governor would want to know. You know she has a real bee in her bonnet about rapists. Last thing. When is a trial set?"

"I've got a trial date set two weeks out for the guilt phase—January 22nd. I suspect the trial on her charges will not take more than a day. Then, we'll go right into sentencing. I am confident the case will be concluded by the time that week is out."

* * *

On January 22nd, 2024, Chancellor Caldwell found Misty Jenkins guilty on both charges after a trial that took less than a day. It was an easy case for the state to prove, with only three witnesses to prove its case. The Defender who first encountered Misty at the checkpoint. The matron who administered the pregnancy test at the border and the county health administrator who testified that Misty did not appear for her follow-up test. The administrator also testified that she supervised obtaining the negative pregnancy test when the Defenders brought Misty into the county health department.

"I want to thank the lawyers for their work," the chancellor announced from the bench at the close of the evidence. I especially want to thank Mr. Lawson for his passionate defense of his client in his closing argument."

"Nevertheless, I am charged with the solemn duty to determine whether or not Miss Jenkins is guilty. Based on the evidence and testimony, I have no hesitation in finding her guilty on both counts. We will be in recess for the rest of the day to allow the attorneys to prepare for the sentencing phase that will begin tomorrow morning. The court is in recess."

"All rise," the bailiff commanded.

The fate of Misty Jenkins was all but sealed as two matrons escorted her from the courtroom.

Later that evening, a jailer visited Misty's cell at the Conway County Detention Center.

"Come with me," the tough-looking female jailer said.

Misty lifted her emaciated frame off the concrete bench that served as a bed and followed the woman to a secure "contact room" where lawyers could talk in private with their clients. The jailer opened the door and asked Misty to sit at a table with a chair on either side. She secured Misty's hands to a restraint fixed on the tabletop and cuffed her ankles to the legs of the chair.

"Wait here," the jailer said before closing the heavy door behind her and leaving Misty alone.

A few moments later, a different door opened, and Governor Landers entered. It was just the two of them alone in the naked room. When she walked in, Governor Landers had a plastic trash bag with her and set it on the table across from Misty.

"Miss Jenkins, do you know who I am?"

"Yes. You're the governor."

"I am."

"Do you know why I am here?"

"No, but I hope you will pardon me. Governors can do that, right?"

"Oh, Misty, I'm sorry, dear, but I'm not here to pardon you. I can't do that. Well, I could, but I won't. I have to make an example of you, and I suspect the court will sentence you tomorrow. If the court sentences you to death, I promise I won't make you wait long, and I promise it won't hurt. OK?"

Tears fell from Misty's face.

"Then why did you come here?" Misty asked.

"I came here because I heard your story from the court about your uncle raping you. I believed you, Misty. I came here because I wanted you to know there's a special place in hell for someone who would do that to a little girl. And I brought you a present."

The governor reached down, grasped the plastic bag, and turned it upside down. The fresh and bloody scalp of Misty's Uncle Frank fell out onto the tabletop.

Misty gasped in horror.

"Uncle Frank will never bother you or any other little girl again, Misty.

21

Little Green Pills

It was getting dark when Tiny called Jon on January 12th, 2024. Jon and Martin were driving home to the Valle Grande from the Cimarron Unit in an epic snowstorm. It had been Jon's turn to check on the herd he had relocated there for the winter, which had to be done regardless of the weather. The softball-sized snowflakes were piling up, and visibility wasn't far beyond the hood of the Range Rover when Jon and Martin approached the closed Los Alamos gate along Highway 4. Jon knew the officers and convinced them to let him through even though he wondered whether Martin and he would have been better off finding a room for the night to wait out the storm.

"Hey, babe, your phone's going off. It's Tiny," Martin said as the Range Rover slowly rounded a tight mountain corner in foot-deep snow with a steep drop off to one side. Jon was white-knuckling the steering wheel and leaned forward in his seat to see through the falling snow.

"Talk about bad timing," Jon said. "Tell him I'll have to call him back. I don't think I can drive and have a conversation at the same time right now."

Martin nodded his agreement and answered Tiny's call.

"Hey Tiny, it's Martin. Jon's driving, and we're in a bad snowstorm. He'll call you back when we get to the house."

"Yeah, sure. It's important. I have news from back home," Tiny said. "Just make sure he calls me as soon as possible, okay? It won't matter how late it

226

is."

Jon and Martin pulled into the circle drive at La Hacienda an hour and a half later. It was still coming down on top of the foot of snow that was already on the ground. The sheer volume of this snowstorm alone was all Jon needed to know that his decision to move the herd down the mountain in the Fall was right.

Thank God Chee had a fire going in the Great Room. Jon pulled a chair closer to the hearth, threw a Navajo blanket over his lap, and called Tiny.

"Hey, Tiny, what's up?"

"Jon. Things have gone from bad to worse here. Alexander is missing, and so is Pretty. But that's not why I called."

"Wait, Alexander and Pretty? Missing? What could be worse than that?"

"My little cousin, Misty, well, second cousin. The Arkansas Defenders arrested her a few days ago. She got pregnant after her uncle raped her and kept it a secret. She decided she couldn't keep the baby and asked me for help. I sent her some money so she could pay cash for an abortion at a clinic in Albuquerque."

"Don't tell me that she got stopped on the way out of Arkansas," Jon said, cutting him off.

"Yeah. They stopped her at the Arkansas/Oklahoma line and made her take a pregnancy test. It was positive. Then, when she got back home, she didn't do a follow-up pregnancy test even though the law required it. She blew the deadline, and a few days ago, Defenders came and got her. Her mother called me half out of her mind because no one would tell her where the authorities were holding Misty."

"Tiny, I'm so sorry. I was afraid Arkansas was going to implement that policy. Have you tried calling the local chancellor in her county? Every county has one. If she were arrested, even under the New Law, a chancellor would have to issue a warrant or a 'body attachment.' Try logging in on the Arkansas judiciary website. You might be able to find it there if they are letting those types of things be public yet."

"Man, I tried calling and checking the website. Nothing."

"Why don't you call my friend Paul Joseph? He's been out with us several times and has experience with the New Law."

"Yeah, I remember him."

"Call him," Jon suggested. "He might be able to help track her down. But don't delay. The New Law is hardcore on abortion. The penalties are severe, including death. Anything else I should know?"

"Yeah, there is one thing," Tiny said after a brief pause.

"What's that?"

"When they stopped her, she gave them my number. They called me to ask if I was the relative she was visiting in Albuquerque. I couldn't blow her cover, so I said yeah, I was."

Jon took his phone away from his ear for a second, looked to the side with a frown, and shook his head.

"Fuck. Has anyone with the Defenders been by?" Jon asked with concern in his voice.

"Not yet, no."

"My friend, you need to get the hell out of town. The Defenders are slow, but I understand they are getting more organized by the day. The New Law has severe penalties not just for women who get unsanctioned abortions but for those who help them. You don't want to get caught up in that brother."

"I didn't think those assholes would ever take things this far. What the fuck!"

"Listen to me," Jon urged. "Call Paul. He might help. Then pack your shit and get the hell out of there. Take Rick with you. Let me know what I can do to help. And don't go sniffing around for Alexander or Pretty. Let me see what I can do from here to find them, but if you go looking for them, that will only expose you more. Just get the fuck out of there. You have a place you can go?"

"I have some good friends in Burlington."

"Then Burlington, it is. Don't fuck around, Tiny. It is only a matter of time before they come after you. If they come, there will be very little anyone can do."

* * *

Paul Joseph couldn't gather any information about Misty Jenkins in time. The Conway County Chancellor would not return his calls, there was no public record of the case, and the Conway County Circuit Clerk denied it existed. The one person he could get on the phone with was Bubba Lawson after he called the Conway County Public Defender on the morning of January 23rd.

"Man, I can't talk about her case, Mr. Joseph. I'm sorry," Bubba said over the phone.

"Why not? We're both on the same side here. I'm trying to help your client."

"The chancellor put a gag order on it, and it isn't just me. It's the entire public Defender's office. I'm surprised they even gave you my name."

"Can you tell me anything?" Paul asked.

"Only that she was arraigned on January 8th, and her trial, if you want to call it that, happened yesterday, and the judge found her guilty."

"What next?"

"The judge scheduled a sentencing hearing for today until he canceled it. Something came up that was more important, he said. So he postponed the hearing until tomorrow."

"What do you think the judge will do?"

"I think he will sentence her to death. At least, that is what the special prosecutor wanted. This whole fuckin' thing is rigged anyway."

"Jesus," Paul said. "Thank you for the information. Does her family know? Were they allowed to participate in the trial?"

"No. The judge closed the courtroom and ordered me to shut my mouth so I couldn't call her parents. And you, you can't tell anyone we talked about it. The judge clarified that he'll lock up anyone violating his gag order."

Not to be deterred, Paul cleared his calendar and drove the two hours or so it took to get to Morrilton. He figured he'd show up and start asking around. He went straightaway to the Circuit Courthouse and parked his car out front. He walked into the stately old building on the square with its stone columns and encountered the court security checkpoint.

"Are you a lawyer?" The deputy asked.

"Yes."

"What case?"

"I need to go to the clerk's office to see about a filing."

"Step through, sir."

By now, Paul Joseph knew better than to say too much. He went to the clerk's office as he said he would and made an excuse to ask her about an e-filing. After a few minutes of small talk, he walked out and looked to see if the coast was clear, and it was. He walked around and up the stairs to the floor where most of the courtrooms were, going from one to another. At last, down the end of an empty hallway, he saw a small desk with a man in black fatigues sitting at it. Paul approached.

"Excuse me, sir. My name is Attorney Paul Joseph. Is the chancellor in? I want to introduce myself."

"The chancellor isn't in, sir."

"May I leave a message with his secretary, then?"

"No. I am happy to take a message for you, though."

"That's fine," Paul said. "I'll drop by another day. Good day to you, sir."

He turned and started walking away when the Defender at the desk called to him.

"Sir, excuse me, can you hold up a minute?"

Paul turned.

"Sure, what can I do for you?"

"I thought I'd show you a quicker way out. There is a stairwell right around the corner. Here, I'll show you."

Paul suddenly felt a chill down his spine.

What the hell does this guy want?

"Oh, that's okay," Paul said. "I need the exercise."

"Nah, sir, you need to come with me."

Reluctantly, Paul waited, and the Defender, a younger man in his 30s with blue eyes, good teeth, and a short haircut, walked with him down a side corridor to a corner stairwell. The Defender opened the door for Paul, and Paul walked through. The Defender followed him and took Paul by the arm.

"Listen to me, sir," the Defender whispered. "You seem like a decent guy, but you don't want to be poking around here. I'm not supposed to tell you this. They'd kill me if they found out, but as I said, you seem like a decent guy. Terrible things are happening. Tomorrow, they will hang a little girl because she got an abortion. People all over town are whispering about it. Word is her uncle raped her, but he got his. He turned up scalped and dead in a ditch near Point Remove Creek by the old bridge. But they are still going to hang the girl. It's crazy. I've been all for the New Law until this. So, if I were you, I'd get the hell out of here, you hear me? If they saw me talking to you, they'd lock us both up or worse. One other thing. The chancellor you wanted to see? He's here, but if I let you in there and you didn't have a damn good reason to be there, he'd probably have you arrested. He's a true believer and was one of the people who helped write these crazy laws."

Paul listened carefully. Quietly. Appraising the younger man as if he were a good son, he said, "You are kind to tell me this. Thank you."

"It's best you be on your way, sir. Go down to the basement and take the long hallway out. There are no guards down there. Just exit the building and leave as fast as you can before someone starts wondering who you are and why you're hangin' around."

The Defender left and walked swiftly back down the hall to his desk.

Paul left the building as instructed, got to his car, and pulled away from the courthouse. Before leaving town, he drove around the corner to see what he could see. He drove past the back of the courthouse, and nothing looked out of the ordinary. Then, he decided to head toward the county jail on a hunch. He figured if there were going to be a hanging, there would have to be a gallows set up somewhere. Maybe he could take a photo.

Driving toward the jail complex, set out on a field at the bottom of a wooded hill, everything looked like it should - a grey concrete building with chain link and concertina wire encircling it. Beyond was a collection of tents, much like the detention camp in Washington County. It had to be the Conway County Rehabilitation and Reeducation Center. But one thing caught his eye as he maneuvered to turn around and leave: a glimpse of a newly constructed gallows placed discreetly next to the jail complex and tucked away in the back up against the little hill.

Paul felt a pit develop in his stomach.

They are really going to do this.

If he were going to do anything to stop it, it would have to be today, but he wasn't the attorney of record. He decided to call Bubba again to see if there was anything he was going to do, but Bubba didn't answer. He called back to the chancellor's office, but there was no answer. He called again. No answer. And once more, there was an answer this time, and Paul recognized the voice of the Defender he encountered at the courthouse.

"Mr. Joseph, you really shouldn't be calling here," the young Defender said. "Not long after you left, the guards at the checkpoint phoned me to ask if I had seen someone who meets your description. Look, they could be hunting for you."

Just then, Paul noticed a black SUV in his rearview mirror as he turned off the road that led him to the county jail complex.

Fuck.

Paul kept driving, and the SUV kept following.

Paul called Jon's number. No answer. He left Jon a message.

"Jon, it's Paul. Defenders are following me. I'm down in Conway County looking around for Tiny's little cousin. If you don't hear from me in a while, you can bet that they've taken me. If I'm lucky, I can talk my way out of whatever happens."

A second SUV joined the first one in Paul's rearview mirror. Paul made it to the interstate on-ramp and accelerated to highway speed to merge with the other traffic. The SUVs followed him. It wasn't very long before he'd cross into Pope County, and hopefully, the Defenders following him would peel off, but they didn't.

It was about 3 p.m. when he came upon the border with the Defenders behind him. Right before he reached the county line, the two vehicles accelerated and pulled beside him on the freeway, with the passenger in the lead vehicle pointing for Paul to pull over on the shoulder.

This is it.

Paul pulled his Mercedes sedan onto the shoulder, parked his car, and waited. He didn't dare get out of his vehicle. The two Defender vehicles pulled up, then one pulled around and positioned itself in front of his car. Then nothing. They sat there. 3 p.m. turned to 3:30. At 4 p.m., Paul was still boxed in and couldn't escape. At 4:30 p.m., a door opened in the vehicle in front of him, and a uniformed Defender approached Paul's car. He was a sturdy-looking older man in his 50s, about Paul's age, with a neatly trimmed grey mustache.

He tapped on the window, and Paul rolled it down.

"Good afternoon, officer," Paul said respectfully. His palms were sweating. He hated the police because they were often sloppy and gratuitously rude, but these guys were dangerous.

"Good afternoon, sir, license and registration please," the Defender stated.

Paul complied and handed him the documents. The officer examined both and returned them to Paul.

"Is there something I can help you with, officer?" Paul asked.

"No, sir, just a routine ID check. Court staff in Conway County ran your plates when you visited the courthouse because they didn't recognize you. You're not from Conway County. Mind telling me why you are down this way?"

Paul realized he'd better not tell a lie unless it was a good one.

"I am a lawyer, and I have a client from Northwest Arkansas who wanted me to come down here and check on a probate filing," he lied.

"Then why were you out driving by the jail?" The Defender asked.

Busted. That lie wasn't good enough. Try again and make it better this time.

"You got me. My client thinks his son might have been arrested and placed in the reeducation camp. She can't find him, and there is no way to search for him online, so I thought I'd go to the courthouse to see what I could find. And failing that, I figured I might drive by the jail to take a look for myself, but there was nowhere to go to ask anyone."

"Mr. Joseph, the names of people in the camp are private and protected by law. You, being a lawyer, should know that. I could arrest you for even inquiring. Did you know that?"

"I did not know it was illegal to inquire about a detainee's identity or status, officer. My apologies." More lies.

"Mr. Joseph, we know who you are, and let me give you some friendly advice. Go back to your home. Stick with your clients in Northwest Arkansas, and don't come back down this way again unless you have a legitimate reason. You are free to go."

"Is that it?" Paul asked.

"That's it, sir. Have a good day."

The Defender returned to his vehicle and pulled away. Paul looked at the clock in his car. 4:44 p.m. All the courthouses in the state were closed. He had no options to file anything to help stave off Misty's execution as if a legal filing would do any good.

Paul's phone rang. It was Jon.

"I just got your message. Are you alright?"

"I'm shaken, but I'm fine. They pulled me over and held me at the side of the road for over an hour."

"What? That's it?"

"They asked me why I was down there when I had no cases in Conway County. Jon, I think they meant to delay me from getting anything filed or calling anyone to delay the execution."

"Those Defenders are getting smarter, it seems," Jon said. "Anyway, I'm glad you're okay."

"Yeah, I am. I was shocked a little bit, to be honest. Those fuckers scare the hell out of me. I'm surprised they didn't take me in," Paul said.

"I'm surprised too, but they didn't. I suppose someone up the chain didn't want to call too much attention to the execution just yet by arresting you. Do you think there is anything we can do to stop it?"

"I don't think so," Paul said. "The lawyer representing her says he can't do anything, and I am not counsel of record. A gag order on the whole thing prevents even the lawyer from doing anything. We'd be shut down before the petition sees the light of day, and nowadays, it is likely a crime

234

to interfere with an official chancery proceeding."

"What about the press?" Jon asked.

"These days, the Defenders arrest any press who show up and ask questions," Paul said.

"Well, shit. Look, get home and be safe. I'll call Tiny and tell him we are fresh out of options. I feel terrible about this. I will call Babbit, too. Perhaps the FBI can do something, but he has told me the FBI has pulled back assets in the compact states. Let me check on that, and I'll get back to you. For now, get home, and be safe!"

* * *

Jon and Paul were correct. They were fresh out of options. The press couldn't do much on unconfirmed reports, and the FBI was down to a skeleton crew in Arkansas. So, on Wednesday morning, January 24th, 2024, a male Defender and a matron entered Misty's cell early and without warning.

Before Misty could completely wake up, they handed her two little green pills and a cup of water.

"Take this," the matron said.

"What is it?" Misty asked in a shaky voice.

"It will help you relax. We'll be back in an hour."

Misty did as she was told and laid back on the concrete slab.

One hour later, the same two Defenders who came before were back.

Misty felt woozy, but she sat up.

"Hands," the male Defender ordered.

Misty extended her hands in front of her.

"No, behind you," he instructed.

She felt the zip ties tighten around her wrists. It hurt, but she didn't care.

It was still dark outside when they brought her through a door that led out to a courtyard. It was cold, and she could see her breath through the bright lights behind her. They brought her around the side of the building, and that is when she realized for the first time what was about to happen.

235

"Wait," she said as the two Defenders hustled her up the gallows stairs.

The Defenders ignored her and carried her up the stairs to the platform where the chancellor stood in a black robe with a paper next to another man holding a black hood.

"Hood her, and let's get this done," he ordered.

"No, no, no, no, no, no, no," Misty stammered.

Everything went black as the hood was yanked over her head.

"Misty Jenkins, I have found you guilty of terminating a pregnancy without legal justification in violation of the Arkansas Unborn Protection Act. After reviewing the record from your trial the day before yesterday, I determined that a sentencing hearing under your circumstances was not warranted because the evidence in your case makes it clear that you should be sentenced to die by hanging. The sentence will be carried out immediately."

She felt the heavy, rough rope against her tiny neck and the rushed, calloused hands manipulating the coiled hangman's knot pressed against her left ear.

A second later, she heard the latch give way.

Misty fell through the trap door, but the executioner had mistakenly allowed for too much slack in the rope so that when she came to the end of it, her head snapped off and rolled several feet from her body after hitting the ground like a bloody soccer ball. Steam rose from her severed head and headless body into the morning air. What was left of her blood supply oozed out of her raggedy neck onto the brown Bermuda grass.

"Goddammit," Sergeant, the chancellor, said. "I thought you had this figured out. Get it right next time, or we'll have to test this rope out on you. Now, clean this goddamn mess up while I call the governor. I need that body cremated before sunrise."

It took less than 26 seconds after the chancellor started reading the death warrant for the hangman to cut Misty's life short.

* * *

The thought of Misty's execution left Jon with a sorrow he had never experienced before, but his friend Tiny was inconsolable. Adding to Misty's shameful murder, the Defenders sent a letter a month after Misty's execution to her parents. The terse letter advised them that she had been executed, that there were no personal effects to return, and that her cremains had been disposed of. The grief and sadness of the whole affair also transformed Martin, and Jon sensed it.

"We haven't talked about things in a while, have we, babe," Jon said.

"No, we haven't. You've been doing your thing between this place and Washington DC, and I've been wrapped in my podcast live-streams," Martin replied.

"What do you say we go for a ride, just the two of us," Jon suggested. "It's beautiful out, and the snow has melted off the perimeter road, so we can take that. Maybe go over to the spring and back."

"That's a great idea. Want to go down and saddle them ourselves?" Martin asked.

"Yeah, let's go and bring the dogs."

The two headed out into the winter. The giant ponderosas were the only witnesses to their conversation as the two walked their horses slowly, side by side.

"I suppose you're beginning to understand why I treasure this place so much, huh," Jon said.

"Yeah, I see it. I didn't know what to think at first. It was such a shock to leave Arkansas. But now, this is home. I can't imagine living anywhere else."

Jon listened as their horses' hooves clapped along the road.

"Has it changed much since you and Cullen ran around as kids?" Martin asked.

"No, not really. It's still as wild as it was then. The difference now is that we have a few more creature comforts. La Hacienda, for example. I don't think Cullen's dad would have allowed such an extravagance, or Cullen, for that matter. Cullen was a chip off the old block. The geothermal plant is new, of course. Beyond that, it's the same as I remember: raw, wild, and mysterious."

"You miss him, don't you?"

"Every day."

Jon and Martin continued with long periods of silence under the canopy of blue while the surrounding snow-covered peaks watched them. Martin spoke up after a few minutes.

"This place has changed me," he said while staring ahead.

"It has," Jon said, "but in what way do you think?"

"I don't know exactly, but when I first came here, I was content, I think, to do my streaming and be a good house husband. Now, I don't know. I feel restless. I'm happy, content, but restless."

"The ranch has a way of forging a person, or in my case, reforging a person," Jon said.

"I suppose so," Martin said. "It was hard at first. I didn't want to come here, and I don't know if I would have if all that stuff hadn't gone down in Arkansas the way it did with the New Law."

"Are you glad you came?" Jon asked.

"I am. I feel more confident than ever. It is like I have something more to offer than just a weekly show or the podcast."

"Tell me more about that," Jon suggested, always keen to ask questions to see how much he could get out of a person, even his husband.

"There you go again," Martin chuckled. "But I'll bite."

Martin knew the drill. Jon always wanted to learn more.

"Well, I have been working with Carl and the task force to plan a raid in Arkansas. It's coming up soon. Babbit is in on it, too," Martin said.

"How the hell could I not know about it?" Jon asked with surprise.

"Everyone knew you'd say 'hell no' to protect me," Martin said. "That shouldn't come as a surprise! Seriously, babe!"

"So, I don't have a say in this, do I," Jon said.

"I love you, you know I do, but no, you don't."

"I can't imagine you getting hurt or worse."

"I know, but I have to do this for some of the same reasons you got involved. I can't let them get away with it, and Tiny's little cousin clarifies to me that we have to fight those assholes to stop what they are doing to our friends and families."

"So, what's the operation you're working on?" Jon asked.

"Remember the shootings that took place on New Year's Eve?" Martin asked.

"Yeah, I do," Jon replied. "Militias shot up gay clubs in Fayetteville, Eureka Springs, and Little Rock. They also attacked St. Paul's Episcopal Church during the New Year's Mass. We both lost some friends. It makes me wonder if Alexander and Pretty were caught up in all that. They used to attend St. Paul's, you know, but no one's heard from them."

"Yeah. It's funny that we haven't talked about that, either. Did you know we lost a dozen people between us that we knew well and at least another dozen acquaintances? It's horrendous," Martin said.

"It is. It is hard for me to get my head around it. So tell me about the operation," Jon said.

"It's pretty simple. Carl and Special Agent Babbit have planned a raid to kill or arrest the people responsible for organizing and carrying out the New Year's attacks. It was a militia group with a compound near Mena. The Defenders helped them, but Babbit says Washington won't let us attack the Defenders outright, but we are free to attack the militia. Anyway, Babbit put together a team, and Washington is all in. We're supposed to meet in the next few weeks to review plans and recruit more locals to help."

"Locals. This ought to be good. Anyone in mind?" Jon asked.

"Oh shit, babe, you'll never believe who stepped up and were the first to volunteer after we put the word out."

"Tell me!"

"The first people to step up were three drag queens from Fayetteville. Each of them has been a client of yours in the past."

"Jesus, which ones?"

"From the Sisters of Perpetual Indulgence. Remember them? So, get this. Sofonda Buffet signed up, and right after her, Anita Cox and Bella Bonbon."

"Not Bella! That bitch is at least 300 lbs!" Jon laughed.

"It's true, and those queens have had it. I am told one of your TV interviews inspired them."

"What's that?" Jon asked.

"Your comment that the Second Amendment goes both ways inspired them. They got your message, Jon! In fact, we plan to fly them out to Albuquerque for some firearms training. They are out for serious blood."

"It seems I have been out of the loop!" Jon exclaimed.

"Nah, you've just been focused on other stuff, babe. How often have you been to Washington, DC, since this all started? You've been busy with meetings, traveling, and everything the ranch requires of you. And no one is criticizing you for it, trust me. We all know you are focused on the big picture."

"I felt bad that I couldn't help Tiny with his cousin. It breaks my heart. When all this stuff kicked up initially, I was in on everything. Now, I feel like I'm just trotted out from one news program to another when I'm not going to Washington to advise."

"Babe, you don't know it, but those people at the FBI revere you. You've even got the ear of the President of the United States! I was talking to Babbit about it. The FBI terrorism joint task force work you have been doing, your advice to them, everything, has impressed them. Babbit thinks you'd be a good director if you were ever inclined to government service."

"That's nice to hear, but I did my time for the government in the Army. Other than helping defeat the compact, my place from here on is this ranch," Jon said.

Jon and Martin continued their quiet ride along the perimeter road until it was time to turn back, leaving Jon with more questions than answers. Was Jon doing enough?

And what about Martin? Now, he wants to get into the fight. At what risk to him? What happened to my quiet life? Is it worth it to continue? Why not just draw the line and let others do the fighting?

22

Continuity of Government

High noon on July 4th, 2024, was a steam bath in Little Rock fed by an oppressive dome of high pressure combined with the humidity coming off the Arkansas River. The day was as auspicious as it was hot while the governors from 21 compact states stepped up to a long banquet table set on a bier in the ornate Capitol Hotel Grand Crystal Ballroom to sign the *Joint Declaration of Secession.*

The irony of the date was the natural brainchild of Governor Suzy Brandy Landers. Given her flare for the dramatic, she made sure every network in the country televised it. In her parlance, it was time to "shit or get off the pot," especially with a national election coming up that fall. She hoped to use the occasion as leverage to force a constitutional convention to free the compact states from Washington's oppression, but if not, a declaration of war might suffice.

The President of the United States was tethered to the televised coverage. Buckshot Brandy's declaration set him as hot as the sun beating down on Little Rock that day. The president called his chief of staff, who picked up on the first ring.

"Wilson?"

"Good afternoon, Mr. President. I guess you're watching the news," his chief of staff said.

"I am. And it looks like the compact states have lost a few members. Only

21 governors are signing that declaration.[20] That's still 21 too many."

"What can I do for you, Mr. President?"

"Get the Speaker of the House and the vice president on the phone. Pronto. Tell the Speaker I am summoning Congress into a special session tomorrow at 8 a.m. under the authority given me by Article II, Section 3 of the Constitution.[21] I might not be a legal scholar, but I can read. It says that a president may, and I quote Wilson, may 'on extraordinary occasions, convene both Houses, or either of them and in case of disagreement between them, concerning the time of adjournment, he may adjourn them to such time as he shall think proper.'"

"That's what it says, Mr. President," Wilson agreed.

"I want you to arrange for a resolution in both houses to expel from Congress the congressional delegations from all those goddamned compact states whose governors just signed that declaration. Democrats may not have a majority right now, but there will be enough reasonable Republicans outside those states who will see this as an opportunity to reclaim their party. This is an opportunity, Wilson! And I'll tell you something else: get White House Counsel and the AG dialed in because if Congress doesn't act and get it done by noon tomorrow, I will have a suit filed in federal court expelling the Representatives and Senators from those states under the 14th Amendment, Section 3. Do I need to read that to you?"[22]

The president was hot.

"No, sir, Mr. President. I understand. I'll get to it."

"Wilson, I will go for a joint session when it's done. I've had it. Things have gotten out of control. We have to take the bull by the horns."

The following day, with all Members present in response to the presidential summons, both Houses of Congress went into special sessions to expel members from the compact states according to the 14th Amendment.

The Republican Speaker of the House strode into the chamber at exactly 8:00 a.m. Speaker Paula Gaston rarely agreed with the president on politics but still believed in "country over party." Members milled around as she walked toward the Presider's Chair, and when they saw her, they moved toward their seats. She sat down and slammed the gavel three times. She was sick and tired of the extreme members of her party hounding her, and today, she would exact her revenge by sending most of them home. It was even more delicious to her that all the January 6th insurrection deniers would be among the expelled representatives.

"I call to order this Special Session of the House of Representatives according to a presidential order and Article II, Section 3 of the United States Constitution."

As she said the words, the Sergeant at Arms, a robust man in a grey suit with a buzzcut, walked forward with the Mace of the Republic and planted it next to the Speaker Gaston as the chamber marched through its opening rituals.

"The Speaker recognizes the Honorable Member from the New York, House Majority Leader Morgan Carter."

"Good morning, ladies and gentlemen. I rise to introduce and move for the adoption of House Resolution 69, a resolution to expel the members from the states who signed the declaration of secession. The resolution calls for their expulsion under Section 3 of the 14th Amendment to the United States Constitution. Furthermore, the House Parliamentarian ruled that the members identified for expulsion would not be entitled to vote on the measure. Madam Speaker, I yield back."

"The Speaker thanks the gentleman from New York and recognizes his motion to take up the measure. The Clerk of the House shall compute the votes based on the parliamentarian's ruling, which is adopted and made a part of the record. There must be a vote of two-thirds of those eligible for the measure to pass. "

The Speaker asked, "Is there a motion to suspend the rules?"

"So moved, Madam Speaker," Carter announced.

Then, another member could be heard shouting from the back of the chamber, "I second the motion!"

Speaker Gaston continued. "We have a motion to suspend and a second. All in favor, say 'aye.'"

A roaring response of "aye" mixed with some "nays" and boos erupted.

"This House will come to order," Gaston thundered, "and the Clerk of the House will conduct a roll call vote on the resolution."

After the vote was complete, she announced:

"The following members whose name the Clerk calls are expelled. When your name is called, peaceably leave the chamber. The Sergeant at Arms will see your immediate ejection as the clerk reads your name if you do not go voluntarily."

The husky Sergeant at Arms walked directly to the Well of the House, turned to face the membership, and shouted, "The members who are expelled should leave this chamber when their name is called and do so in an orderly manner, or you will be forcibly removed."

The Clerk of the House of Representatives began calling the names of the expelled members. Uniformed Capitol Police entered the chamber, three walking toward the well down each of the five aisles leading from the back. Some expelled members stood up, walked toward the aisle, and left. Some stood fast.

Gaston banged her gavel again. "For those who refuse this lawful order to leave, you risk being held in contempt."

The Capitol Police wrestled with the handful of recalcitrant members before dragging them out of the chamber after they attempted a "sit-in." The Speaker enjoyed the spectacle as her revenge manifested itself.

Despite the scene on the floor of the House of Representatives, it was all over by 11 a.m. A similar procedure unfolded in the Senate but with more decorum. Once each Chamber adopted its resolution, Speaker Gaston invited the remaining senators to join the House of Representatives in its chamber for a Joint Session of Congress. She then phoned the president, who was waiting for her call.

President Hedges walked tall through the North Portico and climbed into the Beast. They pulled onto Pennsylvania Avenue through the northwest appointment gate en route to the Capitol. The motorcade proceeded along Pennsylvania Avenue's broad boulevard between the massive government buildings on either side.

The president phoned his wife in the car on the way. "Honey, don't worry about me. This is last minute, so I don't think anyone would have had time to plan my demise, at least not today. I'll be back before you know it."

FLOTUS was worried, and so was the Secret Service.[23] She begged him to address the nation from the Oval because the Right despised her husband, and there was increased chatter about an imminent threat from compact state-sponsored sources, according to current intelligence reports. But the feisty president remained undeterred because, in his mind, the declaration of secession might as well have been a declaration of war. Come hell or high water, Hedges was resolved to deliver his message to the nation and the world before a Joint Session of Congress.

The motorcade pulled past the Peace Monument and the imposing west side of the Capitol Building before angling up along the narrower Northwest Drive, rounding the north end toward the East Entrance to the Capitol Building. There is hardly any more reassuring entrance than a president walking up the steps of the Capitol Building toward the East Entrance in broad daylight. There they were, the Speaker of the House and the vice president, flanked by the majority and minority leaders of each chamber and, of course, the cameras. All awaited the president's grand arrival at the hallowed building.

The motorcade pulled up the steps to the bronze Columbus Doors and the awaiting entourage. The heat rushed into the Beast as the Secret Service agent opened the door. With a spring in his step, the president emerged from the limousine nimbly and looked at the agent, "Son, I hope you brought your jogging shoes. Let's go!"

About that time, an anonymous call came into the FBI National Command Information Center indicating there would be an attempt on the president's life while he was addressing Congress.[24] The agent who fielded the call forwarded the recording to his supervisor, who, in turn, reviewed it skeptically.

"Do you think this is real? If so, we need to notify the Secret Service," the supervisor told a coworker.

"Kick it up to the director's office, and let's see what they say," his colleague responded before returning to his cup of coffee.

President Hedges turned toward the steps with his security detail and the officer bearing the nuclear football. He then spirited up the steps to grim faces at the top.[25] Nearing the last step, the president's lead security agent received a priority call from the Director of the FBI. He listened to the message as Hedges extended his hand to greet the vice president, a spunky Hispanic woman from Reno, Nevada, standing 5'4" tall and dressed in a black skirt and matching blazer. Before his hand touched hers, her mouth opened, and her eyes widened with surprise.

"¡PUTA MADRE! EVERYBODY, GET DOWN!"

The president's lead agent turned suddenly, and with a look of terror and astonishment, he watched a trail of white smoke coming toward them from the Supreme Court.

"RPG! RPG! RPG!" he yelled.

Another agent tackled the president to get him away from the inbound munition while a second trail of smoke flew at the group from the roof of the Russell Senate Office Building. There was a flash, and the president and nearly everyone else on the Capitol steps were blown apart by the first RPG, quickly followed by the second that left them unrecognizable by the explosions, shock, fire, and smoke. None of the nation's leadership standing on the stairs of the United States Capitol at 11:14 a.m., July 5th, 2024, survived.

* * *

White House Chief of Staff Wilson Brannigan sat at his desk with his feet propped up on its edge, watching the live coverage of the president's arrival at the Capitol when he saw the explosions. He pursed his lips and stared at the ghoulish scene unfolding on national television. After a few moments, he reached for his desk phone and called the White House switchboard.

"Get me the Director of the Secret Service," Wilson commanded and hung up the phone.

The switchboard operator quickly rang him back, and Brannigan picked up.

"Director, there has been an attack on the Capitol. I presume the president and vice president are dead, along with the others standing with him, including the Speaker of the House. According to the Presidential Succession Act, the secretary of state is the next in line for the presidency. Go find him, bring him to the White House bunker, and bring a federal judge."

He pressed the receiver button for a new dial tone and called the White House switchboard again. "Get me the secretary of defense, the secretary of homeland security, the attorney general, and the Chief of the Capitol Police on a secure conference call. This is a Snap Count call.[26] Contact me in my office as soon as they are on the line. Tell the secretary of defense we may have lost the nuclear footballs with the president and vice president."

Several minutes later, the operator called Brannigan.

"I have the conference call set up for you, sir."

Brannigan picked up and began.

"Ladies and gentlemen. This is a secure line. This call is classified under Snap Count protocols. We must assume the president and vice president are dead, along with key congressional leaders. We are retrieving the secretary of state and bringing him to the White House Bunker to be sworn in as president because he is next in line. What just happened at the Capitol must be taken as a decapitation strike on this government, so we must enact the Continuity of Government Plan immediately.[27] I also believe we should go to DEFCON 2.[28] Once the secretary of state is sworn in, as a precaution, I recommend putting him aboard the presidential plane and getting him airborne. Mr. Secretary of Defense, alert Andrews to get Air Force One ready. Do we have another E-4 at Joint Base Andrews?"

"We do. We always have one on standby," replied the defense secretary.

"Where are the remaining two? We have four, correct?" Brannigan asked.

"Yes, we have four total. The remaining two are at Offutt Air Force Base in Nebraska.

"Good," Brannigan said. "Call Offut and be sure those other two are serviceable, but I recommend you board the standby E-4 and get airborne as soon as possible."

"Yes, sir," the defense secretary affirmed.

Brannigan continued. "Listen, everyone, according to the Continuity of Government Plan, the rest of the government must relocate to predesignated bunkers. Do any of you have any objections to this? Say so now if you do. Otherwise, we need to enact it until Washington is secure."

Wilson Brannigan's patience with this lot was characteristically thin, but he exercised enough forbearance to field some questions before terminating the call at 11:27 a.m.

The nearest federal judge was at the district courthouse two blocks from the Capitol. The courthouse was locked down, and the judges were secured in their chambers when a Secret Service Agent arrived to retrieve a federal judge.

"We need a judge to swear in a new president at the White House," the agent told the Federal Marshals who met him at the doors where they stood guard.

Not long after that, at 12:21 p.m., Eastern Daylight Time on Friday, July 5th, 2024, Secretary of State Rashid Bashir Aidun took the oath of office as the 48th President of the United States. Immediately afterward, the Secret Service rushed him out of the White House to an awaiting Marine Corps helicopter for transport to Joint Base Andrews, where he would board a Boeing E-4 Advanced Airborne Command Post.[29]

The new president's first official act was to initiate Operation Fast Pace and officially declare DEFCON 2. The order put all military forces worldwide on their highest alert status short of war. According to the Continuity of Government Plan, or COG, the Pentagon and what was left of Congress were to be relocated to secure sites outside Washington. While the president and the secretary of defense would be airborne in flying command posts, the rest of the executive branch and the Pentagon relocated to Site R, also known as Raven Rock, in a massive airlift operation. Members of Congress boarded white buses that took them to the bowels of Mount Weather, a separate facility about an hour away.

* * *

The United States Government hadn't escalated to such a heightened defense readiness since 9/11. However, facing a bold attempt to destabilize the government, the president followed the COG and elevated the country's defense condition.

President Aidun was a capable diplomat after spending nearly forty years as a career-commissioned foreign service officer. Though diminutive in stature, he was a giant within international diplomatic circles. He had a long resume, too. He was Chief of Mission at several high-profile posts worldwide, including the United Nations, the United Kingdom, Iraq, Saudi Arabia, Russia, and Canada. Given his close ties to diplomatic affairs, he called the deputy secretary of state from aboard Air Force One.[30] He instructed her to send a message to all diplomatic missions worldwide, assuring every nation on the planet that the American Government was secure, there was a president and a functioning government. He also wanted the move to DEFCON 2 to warn potential aggressors like the Russian Federation and North Korea that the United States was ready and willing to conduct even a nuclear battle at a moment's notice.

"How long until Congress will be secure," President Aidun asked the Administrator of FEMA in a call he placed from Air Force One.

"Give it another two hours, sir, and we should have them in place," replied the FEMA administrator, adding, "There are now 244 Members of the House of Representatives and 56 Senators to account for, and we have them all. It's a little over 60 miles by bus from the Capitol to Mount Weather. But they are on the way as we speak."

"And the Pentagon?" asked the president.

"The joint chiefs are secure, and their respective military department heads are with them. The rest of the Pentagon's essential personnel will arrive by bus to their site a few hours later."

"What about the footballs?" the president asked. "Have we recovered the two with the former president and vice president?"

"The Department of Defense sent a recovery team to Capitol Hill as you were being sworn in," the FEMA Administrator replied. "Capitol Police sealed off the area, but we have no word on the recovery of the footballs.

Sorry, sir."

"Thank you," the president said, turning to an aide. "I want to get on the phone with congressional leadership as soon as they have selected replacements for their colleagues killed at the Capitol. Now, I need to talk with the secretary of defense."

Vice Admiral Samuel (Sam) Ironwood, long retired from the Navy, was the secretary of defense and was already aboard the E-4 assigned to him when President Aidun called.

"Mr. Secretary?" the president began.

"Yes, Mr. President," Ironwood responded.

"Mr. Secretary, I need you and your staff to devise a plan and be prepared to present it to me within the hour with recommendations about securing our federal facilities in the compact states. I also want you to prepare to federalize the National Guard and to call up all the active reserve forces, if necessary, to help secure our facilities wherever they may be. Can you do that?"

"Consider it done, Mr. President," the secretary replied. "I'll loop in the joint chiefs as soon as we are off the phone, and we will give you some options."

"Very well, thank you. That will be all for now, Mr. Secretary."

"Yes, Mr. President," said the secretary. "Out here."

I have to get a vice president, the president thought as he hung up the receiver.

* * *

President Aidun sat in the war room aboard the VC-25 with overhead monitors playing different news networks and read over the COG contained in three large three-ring binders. Wilson Brannigan was with him, and the two knew each other well, which gave the new president confidence since he had never aspired to high political office. Aidun was a policy wonk and not cut out for command, and he knew it. It was one thing to wrangle diplomats and carry out policy but another to create it. This was not his game but an everyday affair for Wilson Brannigan.

"How are we doing, Wilson?" asked President Aidun.

"You mean, how are you doing, Mr. President? If that's your question, I think you're doing fine, sir, under the circumstances. You've made prudent moves, and perhaps after things settle down, we can return everyone to Capitol Hill and get back to business as usual."

"I don't think there will be business as usual ever again, my friend," offered the president as he flipped through pages of the COG and occasionally looked out his window to the earth below, "but we will do the best we can."

"Mr. President, we need to consider a vice president," Brannigan stated plainly, "the urgency of selecting a vice president is emphasized in the most recent revision of the COG. Preferably, we need to do that as soon as possible before you have to scrap it out with Congress. You could nominate a milkman right now, and Congress might agree, especially because it is in such disarray. All kidding aside, you need to nominate someone because the stability of our government depends on it. To make it stick, you'll need a majority vote of both houses of Congress."

The president looked up from the binders and asked, "Do you have someone in mind?"

"I do," Brannigan answered. "It's unconventional, but it might be just what we need to jump-start things and buy you some political cover because you, Mr. President, will need it. Congress is a pit of two-step killing vipers. You only thought Congress was difficult when you briefed them as Secretary of State. But as the president, you have entered a blood sport. And it will get gory. You need someone to buy you some cover."

"Well, all right, what's your idea, Wilson?" asked President Aidun.

"Mr. President. We need someone who doesn't need or owe any political favors. Someone you can use to be your frontman with these compact states. Someone who speaks their language and isn't afraid to take one for the team. In short, someone who can be a punching bag, a potential fall guy, and, if we're lucky, someone who can act as a hatchet man. If I may be blunt, Mr. President, there is no way you can unify this country because you are a Muslim. You represent a good deal of everything the Right hates.

You and I know it shouldn't matter, but you and I know it does. So, the man I have in mind, I think, would fit the bill."

"Well?" shrugged the president.

"By now, you have undoubtedly heard of that lawyer from Arkansas who made headlines in the Spring after those people were shot in Little Rock. Jon Freeman. He was the guy who later ended up on TNN after Arkansas stoned that woman down there."

"Right, the lawyer from Arkansas. Why him?" President Aidun asked.

Brannigan replied, "I got to know him because the former president had him up to Washington to consult with us on many occasions. He's been tremendously helpful and an advisor to the FBI and their Counter Terrorism Task Force. He's proven to be quite capable. He knows the political landscape of the compact states by now better than anyone."

"But he's not a politician. He's never held any public office," Aidun said.

"Exactly! That's right!" offered Brannigan. "And that's why he's perfect for the job. Plus, he's wealthy and doesn't need anything regarding a favor or payout. He has a serious ax to grind, has been vocal, and used his rise to fame to get his message out. He's an effective communicator, and I believe his message is one this country needs to hear, but no typical politician would ever have the cajones to say what he's saying."

"Have you floated this with anyone else on the staff?" Aidun asked.

"There's been no time for that, but I can tell you the former president liked him, and he's popular with the Defense Department and the FBI. I mean, this guy is, on the one hand, a progressive thinker, and he's even got a same-sex partner, but on the other hand, he's a rancher. He's ex-military. He even sympathizes with the compact states because he claims progressives and liberals have alienated them. His ideas and plain speech have earned him massive support among independents, centrists, and moderates, that much I know. One might say he has radicalized moderates while blaming them for their complacency. He doesn't drink, but he curses like a sailor. By some reports, he is a devoted Catholic despite being married to a man. There is a lot to like about him. So, if you want someone who speaks the language of the Right, he certainly does, and trust me, they will get over the gay thing in a hurry if that's a consideration."

"You know, Wilson, it's no wonder the former president was keen on you. I'm sold. Let's get him on the phone before we throw him to the wolves, and why don't you circulate his name around the senior staff to get their impressions," the president remarked.

"I'll track him down and get it done," said Brannigan.

23

The Long Caliche Road

Blissfully unaware of the catastrophe in Washington DC, Jon left the Valle Grande early that morning to drive down the valley to the Jemez Pueblo to visit the Colonel. His mother had become a beloved fixture there, listening and helping. Being an honored guest at the pueblo had softened her. Her eyes shone with a new light, and Jon was glad. As far as he was concerned, nothing on the ranch needed his attention so urgently that he couldn't be left undisturbed for a few hours, so he turned his cell phone off to enjoy some uninterrupted time with his mom and relish the silence of the drive from the Valle Grande down to the Jemez Valley to see her.

After he visited with the Colonel, he departed from the hot desert scrub of the pueblo for the drive back up the valley, passing the Red Rocks along Highway 4 with its ramshackle stalls on the side of the road where pueblo members sold fry bread, pottery, and other souvenirs to passing tourists. He wound his way past the turn-off to the Gilman Tunnels toward the Village of Jemez Springs, keeping to the main road. He was tempted to drive to the tunnels instead and sit by the Rio Guadalupe, which rushes down through the narrow canyon.

It was nearing two o'clock under the hot New Mexico sky while he drove slowly through the Village of Jemez Springs. He looked up to the top of Holiday Mesa as he went along and dreamt of his adventures with Brother

Carl when they were in college at UNM. It never occurred to Jon then that he'd one day be a permanent neighbor to these mystical mesas where he had spent so much of his youth exploring the dirt tracks through high meadows and aspen groves. It was the stuff of childhood dreams he still held close to his heart.

While passing by the old Jemez Bath House, Jon decided it was time to end his phone vacation, so he reached over and turned it on. His phone lit up, ending his nostalgic moment. The screen displayed a number he didn't recognize, but it was a Washington, DC, area code.

This ought to be good, he thought as he answered, *probably another interview request.*

"Jon Freeman," he answered.

"Mr. Freeman, my name is Wilson Brannigan. Do you have a moment to speak with me?"

"Hello, Mr. Brannigan, it's been a while. How are you? How's the president?" Jon inquired.

"You haven't seen the news today," Brannigan said.

"I haven't seen any news, not today," replied Jon, but just as he said it, news alerts started to pop up in his notifications.

"Mr. Freeman, the president, the vice president, the Speaker of the House of Representatives, and several in government were assassinated today by a terrorist attack. A new president was sworn in shortly after that. Former Secretary of State Rashid Bashir Aidun is now the President of the United States. Anyway, Mr. Freeman, I am calling on his behalf to ask if you would accept his nomination to serve as Vice President of the United States."

Jon gasped.

"Hold on just a damn minute, sir. You'll have to run that by me one more time."

"Mr. Freeman, for continuity of government, we must appoint someone to fill the office of vice president, and we think it ought to be you. Congress will meet later this afternoon or early this evening, and I'd like you to say yes so we can get a vote and swear you in."

Jon was further up the valley and away from the hot desert flat of the pueblo, near La Cueva, a little mountain community adjacent to the Jemez River. The narrow canyon opens into a verdant meadow with some houses dotting the landscape. Jon pulled into a vacant parking lot off the side of the road.

"Mr. Brannigan, you'll have to give me a few minutes. Do you realize I operate one of the largest cattle ranches in the United States? It isn't as if I can up and leave," said Jon.

"I do," Brannigan replied, "but I also know you haven't always been running it, at least not like you are now. I'm sure you have an able manager. We need you. The country needs you. The president needs you."

"Why me?" questioned Jon.

"Because you don't aspire to higher office or a political career." Brannigan answered, "And because, honestly, you don't need the money or the power. Those are two things you already possess. We have come to know you, Mr. Freeman, and we believe you may be the person who can help the president deal with the current crisis."

"Sir, you'll have to give me a few hours. I need to get back to the ranch and talk to my husband. You realize I have a husband, right? Not a wife?" asked Jon.

"No one cares about that, Mr. Freeman," Brannigan stated bluntly. "Take two hours, but no more than two. We cannot afford to let the office go vacant for very long. Listen, get to your ranch, talk to your husband, but call me back at this number in two hours. Will you do that?"

"I can do that, Mr. Brannigan," Jon said. "I'll call in two hours. But what job does the president want me to do? Don't vice presidents sit on their asses, cut ribbons, or do little else except break ties in the Senate? If so, I'm probably not your man even if I decide to take the job."

"Mr. Freeman, I'll be frank. The president needs someone to run point on restoring domestic peace and security. He needs someone who is politically expendable, who doesn't need or seek high office, and who is not afraid to make some hard calls. He needs a compact state czar, for lack of a better term. It would be your job, Mr. Freeman, to take charge and help restore order and deal with these compact states. The president is not cut out for it, and trust me, he would tell you that himself. You would have his full backing. Call me in two hours."

The phone went silent.

"Jesus," Jon said aloud. "Jesus. Fucking. Christ."

Jon pulled out of the parking lot and back onto Highway 4, climbing up the slopes of the great caldera, and passed Jemez Falls with lodge pole pines whizzing by.

* * *

Wise Waha had always known that Jon lived on the edge of two worlds: Arkansas's familiar embrace and Valle Grande's call to Jon's soul. Once, Jon had chosen family ties over New Mexico's allure. But now, as his nation crumbled from the weight of ignorance and extremism, too many looked away because it was someone else's battle. He stood at that crossroads, wrestling with competing allegiances, furious that he had a choice to make. Would he remain settled at the Valle Grande and let his nation's call go unanswered, or would he return to service?

Speaking at the Fayetteville town square following the Little Rock massacre, he sharply revealed his disdain for extremists and complacency. Now, faced with the call from the U.S. president, he had to act on his words. Every fiber urged him to stay at his ranch, but deep down, he knew he must accept the invitation. Meanwhile, Martin, deeply attached to the ranch, would face a similar dilemma - remain settled at Valle Grande with the freedom to fight with the counterinsurgency or go with Jon to Washington.

I can't displace Martin again. I won't do it. He must remain free to follow his path.

Jon's Range Rover rolled towards Valle Grande's grand entrance off the scenic Highway 4. As the vehicle neared, the gates—imposing steel masterpieces—recognized the RFID tag and slowly opened. Before him unfurled the long, dusty, winding caliche road, shimmering under the sun, snaking its way through the undulating grasslands of the Valle Grande Caldera. Far away stood La Hacienda, a faraway speck in the tree line. While this journey had become a familiar drive for Jon, today felt different. The raw beauty of his surroundings rekindled memories of his first encounter with this road as an awestruck teenager visiting the ranch for the first time. A deep sense of wonder washed over him as the magnificent caldera stretched out vast and endless, capturing his breath and imagination again. Every turn of the wheel drew him closer to the choice of home or an uncertain new chapter of his life.

* * *

The swift execution of the COG was a testament to the federal government's efficiency in this crisis because by sunset on Friday, July 5th, 2024, POTUS and SECDEF[31] were flying their respective holding patterns on opposite sides of the continental United States. Congress was snugly tucked away in the bowels of Mount Weather, and the executive branch and Pentagon were secure at Raven Rock. Even nukes could not take any of them out.

Before the day was out, Jon called Wilson Brannigan as promised after speaking with Martin, who was surprisingly supportive so long as Martin did not have to leave Valle Grande.

"Hello, my name is Jon Freeman," Jon said from his study at La Hacienda on Friday evening. "Please connect me with Mr. Brannigan."

"Hold, please."

Wilson Brannigan picked up the phone.

"Mr. Freeman, I predict you are calling to accept the president's invitation."

"Against my better judgment," Jon said flatly, "I am. So, what happens next?"

"Sit tight," Brannigan responded. "We still must get the new majority and minority leaders of the House and Senate on the phone. Congress remains in disarray, and nature abhors a vacuum, Mr. Freeman, but you will receive a call tomorrow, so keep your phone nearby. You don't need to pack your bags until we know we have Congressional support. In this scenario, the 25th Amendment requires both houses to approve your nomination by a

THE LONG CALICHE ROAD

majority vote."

Later that evening, Jon received another call from Wilson Brannigan.

"We've got to stop meeting like this," Jon said when he picked up Brannigan's call.

Brannigan laughed, saying, "You're a smart ass, too, and I like that, but listen, we are having a problem getting your Congressional approval without formal hearings. Given the situation's urgency and our dire need for a functioning government, including a vice president, we reached a compromise with congressional leadership. Instead of taking weeks for live hearings, weeks we cannot afford, congressional leadership agreed to have you appear now by secure video conference so they can ask you questions. It would be considered under oath. If they like you enough, they'll vote tonight. If not, this thing could drag on for a while."

"Alrighty, but it's already close to 9:00 p.m. here," Jon said.

"Leadership is ready to get on a call with you now, so they are waiting," Brannigan said.

"Wow. Alright. Tell you what, I need just a few minutes to comb my hair and put on a dress shirt. You can send me a link to join the video conference."

"The link is on its way," Brannigan said.

A few minutes after 9:00 p.m. local time, Jon sat down for the video call in his study. Dressed in a blue button-down dress shirt without a tie, he entered the code into his laptop and watched the little green camera light turn on.

His screen suddenly divided itself into several boxes, one for the Speaker of the House, another for the president *pro tempore* of the Senate, and four more for the majority and minority leaders of the House and Senate. Neither Brannigan nor the president were present on the call.

The first voice was Speaker of the House.

"Mr. Freeman, good evening. My name is Bernice Atwood. I am the new Speaker of the House of Representatives. I want to introduce everyone else on the call. I'll continue with the House Members. House Majority Leader Vernon Iverson is with us, along with House Minority Leader Claire

Turner. I'll pass this over to the Senate president *pro tempore*."

"Good evening. My name is Natalie Harrison. I am the majority whip. Majority Leader Desmond Clarke is with me and Minority Leader Brian Kuroda."

"Hello everyone, I am honored to meet you, especially under the circumstances," Jon said.

"Mr. Freeman," began Speaker Atwood. "As you can imagine, we are still in shock after what happened today. We have been scrambling to reassemble the Congress. We are calling you from within a hollowed-out mountain and will be here until it is safe to return to Washington. I don't need to tell you that today's loss is incalculable."

"Yes, Madam Speaker. I am in shock."

"Despite the unbelievable events, we have a job to do, which is to discharge our constitutional duty and decide whether to approve your nomination as Vice President of the United States despite the pressures of circumstance," Atwood said.

"Madam Speaker, it warms my heart to hear you say that," Jon replied.

The Senate Minority Leader, Brian Kuroda, entered the conversation.

"Mr. Freeman, Brian Kuroda. Why does it warm your heart to hear that we intend to discharge our constitutional duty while, at the same time, we are making an accommodation for you instead of deferring the matter of your nomination until we can hold proper hearings in Washington?"

Jon sipped his teacup and set it on its saucer before answering the question.

"Leader Kuroda, your question is a good one because it touches upon a fundamental belief of mine. We must govern ourselves based on principles rather than blindly following a rigid ideology. One of these principles is respecting the rule of law and the legacy enshrined in our democratic institutions. Therefore, I firmly believe that you must abide by your constitutional duties, one of which is to agree or disagree with the president's nomination for a new vice president. You cannot fulfill this duty without meeting me. Fortunately, we are doing that now. Your question implies that you doubt your ability to fulfill your obligations without holding hearings in Washington, DC. I respect that, but I disagree that you are precluded from discharging your responsibilities under the circumstances."

"You are correct that I have doubts that we can, or should, approve your nomination without having hearings in Washington, Mr. Freeman," Kuroda said. "So, how do you reconcile the problem we face, which is that the president asks Congress to agree to your nomination without following normal procedures?"

"To begin with," Jon offered, "President Aidun fulfilled his obligation under the 25th Amendment by nominating me to assume the vice president's office after it was vacated. The Amendment mandates that the president 'shall' nominate someone but does not specify why or when. The COG, however, does emphasize that in the event of a threat to the continuity of government, a nomination should be made forthwith. It is up to Congress to confirm the nomination. Although the 25th Amendment does not outline the process for reaching this vote, our current situation demands a sense of urgency. It may be preferable to hold hearings over a longer period, but I believe the circumstances require a faster response. I am grateful for the opportunity to meet with you and provide the information necessary for an informed vote."

Kuroda looked mildly satisfied with Jon's answer, as much as one can tell through a video.

"I believe we need to be more rigorous with such an appointment under ordinary circumstances, Mr. Freeman," Kuroda added, "but I agree that this is no ordinary situation. I was mainly interested in your thought process since this does have the feeling of being rushed."

"It is rushed, Leader Kuroda," Jon allowed, "but that does not mean it falls short of the Constitution. We have never had a situation where all the elected leadership was taken out at once, and I believe this situation demands an immediate solution."

Natalie Harrison, the Republican Senate whip, asked, "Mr. Freeman, you are nominated by a Democratic president, so am I safe to assume you are a Democrat?"

"Madam Senator…"

"Please, Mr. Freeman, let's dispense with titles so this can go faster," she interrupted.

"Senator Harrison," Jon said, slightly put off by her rebuke, "you are not safe in your assumption because I do not belong to one party. I vote independently, as demonstrated by my voting record. If you can see the records of my political giving, I have given money to candidates of both parties and Independents."

"Then how would we know what side you are on," Harrison prodded.

Jon's left eyebrow raised a little with the Senator's prickly question.

"Side? Senator Harrison? I am only on one side, America's side."

Undeterred by his answer, Harrison poked further.

"Well, Mr. Freeman, it seems that if you had to choose sides, you'd choose to be a Democrat because that is where most of your giving and voting patterns have landed over the last few years. So, I'll ask you again: what side are you on?"

"Senator, I will answer again. I am on the side of America. I will answer any questions you may have about my political persuasions or why I voted for this candidate over another one. What I won't do is have my loyalty to one party or another questioned. So, once more, I am only on one side - the side of the American people. But if you might indulge me a moment, I can tell you why I feel this way. I feel this way, Madam Senator, because many politicians appear to prioritize their party over the country. Speaking personally, I have had enough of watching that transpire to our nation's detriment. As the Preamble to the Constitution implies, my goal as a vice president will be to promote the general welfare of our nation within the rule of law if Congress confirms my nomination regardless of party affiliation."

"Well, it sure does seem you favor Democrat policies and politics, Mr. Freeman. What will I tell my mostly Republican constituents if I vote to approve you as vice president?" Harrison said.

Jon shot back, "I have no idea what you should tell your constituents, and I honestly don't give a damn what you tell them so long as it is the truth.

If you're asking me for political advice, why don't you tell them that their new vice president will serve all of them regardless of party."

Senator Harrison appeared to squirm in front of her camera.

The House Minority Leader Claire Turner, a Democrat, was next. She was a Progressive who won her seat in Virginia by a slim majority.

"Mr. Freeman, we obtained clips of your public statements since the advent of the New Law, and we have seen some of the video footage of the raid that freed your family from the internment camp in Arkansas. I'm not concerned with the raid but about your public statements about how the 'Second Amendment goes both ways.' Are you advocating a violent response to the New Law?"

"Representative Turner, thank you for that question. I've been grilled about my statements on the Second Amendment on a lot of news shows. If Congress approves my nomination, you ask whether I would advocate for a violent response to the New Law. Did I get that right?"

"You did, Mr. Freeman, yes. That's my question," Turner replied.

"The short answer is 'no,' I do not advocate a violent response to the New Law. So, if you'll indulge me, a little background for that answer. I served in the U.S. Army. I was in the 82nd Airborne, and I was in special operations. I saw combat. Those operations were classified at the time and still are, so I will not discuss them, but I can tell you that having lived through battle and lost soldiers, I believe that violence should be a last resort."

"But what about your statements suggesting that the 'left' should arm itself and fight back? Isn't that what you mean when you say the Second Amendment goes both ways?" Turner pressed.

"Do I believe violence should be a last resort? Yes, absolutely. Believe me when I tell you, being in battle is something I wish for no person. But do I believe doing battle might be necessary in some instances? Yes, I believe that one hundred percent."

"I was afraid you were going to say that, Mr. Freeman," Turner said. "I just do not know whether I can endorse your nomination for that reason, and I believe I speak for all the progressive caucus members when I say that, which is enough to prevent you from becoming the vice president."

"I understand, Leader Turner, and to vote against my nomination is your prerogative, but I would ask you this before you make that decision," Jon said as he leaned forward in his chair and brought the palms of his hands together, forming a little tent beneath his face.

"Do you believe there is anything worth fighting for?" Jon asked Turner. "Because I do. I believe the New Law must be ended by using military force if necessary. I believe preserving the integrity of the United States, all 50 of them, whether rural or urban, liberal or conservative, red or blue, is worth fighting for. American citizens in the compact states are being wrongfully arrested and killed because of the unspeakable evils wrought by the New Law. And it is spreading to other compact states. Arkansas, where it all started, is only the beginning. Think of it as a pilot program. So, would I endorse or advocate using force against the perpetrators of the New Law in the compact states if they cannot be brought to heel any other way? My answer is an unequivocal yes."

"I appreciate your honesty, Mr. Freeman, but I simply cannot agree with your worldview. Surely there is no place for violence even in the face of the New Law or a declaration of secession," Turner said.

Speaker Atwood interjected, "I'd like to remind my colleague that this is not the time to discuss votes. We are here to learn from Mr. Freeman. The time for discussing votes will be after this call is ended."

"Respectfully, I disagree, Madam Speaker," said Kuroda. "This is precisely the time to hash this out because we may not get another opportunity to discuss it with Mr. Freeman present. What do you think about that, Mr. Freeman?"

"Senator Kuroda, I respect that you and the others in Congress have a job to do. My job is not to try to sway your votes one way or another. My job is to answer your questions honestly, which I am trying to do. What you decide to do is none of my business so long as you are honest in what you do and how you carry out your duties."

It was nearly 2:00 a.m. when the call ended. Jon walked down to the master suite and climbed into bed without trying to wake Martin, who was fast asleep.

Perhaps I may not be the right man for the job, which would suit me just fine.
Then he shut his eyes and fell fast asleep.

24

Oaths

J on had been asleep for about four hours when Chee opened the drapes. Before Jon could get to his morning tea that Chee brought, his cell phone received a call from area code 202. Puffy-eyed, Jon picked up, but it wasn't Wilson Brannigan.

"Good morning, Mr. Freeman."

It was the president.

"I hope I'm not calling too early. This is Rashid Aidun. Wilson Brannigan, my chief of staff, says you agreed to accept my nomination for you to become the vice president. Is that still the case?"

"Yes, Mr. President," Jon said. "I've decided to put my money where my mouth is, so you have called, and I am answering that call, sir."

"Well, good because the House and the Senate just advised me that you are confirmed. Ironically, your support was stronger among Republicans, with most of the Progressive Caucus voting against you. The Progressives thought they could scuttle the nomination assuming you lack Republican support."

"Well, leave it up to the liberals to vote against their interests. So, what happens now, Mr. President?" asked Jon.

"Well," replied Aidun, "we are following a protocol to assure the continuation of government, which is why your ascendancy to the vice presidency is so important. I'm still aboard Air Force One, and the secretary of defense

266

is aboard another of our E-4 flying command posts. We will remain airborne until the Department of Defense and Homeland Security certify that Washington, DC is safe and secure. Now that I know you will accept, I will scramble one of those same aircraft to your location. They tell me you are near Santa Fe. Is that right?"

"Yes, sir, I am," Jon said.

"Very good, very good." said the president. "Look, I know this is short notice, but let's see, hang on, let me see how long it takes until we can have an E-4 arriving in Santa Fe. In anticipation of your decision, I ordered one to depart its location at Offutt Air Force Base and fly to Santa Fe. Wait just a minute, will you?"

The call went on hold.

This was all happening too fast, but at least Martin was understanding and supportive so long as Martin didn't have to leave the valles. That was the deal. He'd come and go when needed but wouldn't leave the ranch permanently. Martin had found his place and voice at the Valle Grande, and there was no debating the point.

President Aidun came back on the line.

"Mr. Freeman, they tell me the E-4 is about an hour out. I understand if you have to get some things together. Listen, we'll send someone to your location to pick you up. I'm designating you as a Secret Service Protectee and your husband, who will become the Second Gentleman of the United States once you're sworn in."

"Yes, sir," Jon replied, "but there's something you should know. My husband supports me in this 100% but does not intend to leave our ranch here. Is that going to be a problem?"

"We'll make it work, Mr. Freeman, we will make it work," the president stated. "For now, get your things together. We'll have someone reach your location, swear you in, and get you to Santa Fe. Once you are airborne, I'll have them patch you in with me, the secretary of defense, and congressional leadership. You better put on a suit and tie. I look forward to working with you."

Jon set his cell phone down and then called again for Chee.

"Curtis? Where's Martin?"

Chee spirited down the hallway to the master suite.

"Yes, Hosteen," Chee said, "Martin rode out early and headed toward the Hidden Spring."

"Goddammit. After a lifetime of sleeping in, today, of all days, he gets up early to go riding. And he didn't bring his phone, did he?" Jon commented in his frustration.

"Does he ever?" Chee said.

Since moving to the Valle Grande, Martin had drastically changed some of his previous life habits. For one, he didn't stay up at all hours anymore. He stopped doing a late evening live stream, deciding instead to produce a podcast debating contemporary political and social issues. Another difference was that he no longer had an umbilical cord connecting him to his phone. He often left it on his nightstand, much to Jon's frustration because he instinctively worried when Martin went alone for long rides, violating a ranch rule that "nobody rides alone."

Jon thought momentarily and then said to Chee, "I need you to go get him. Tell you what, get over there to Hidden Spring as fast as possible and ask him to meet me at the geothermal complex. We are about to have people coming up here to pick me up and take me to Washington, and it will be soon."

"Yes, sir!" Chee said.

In a fleeting moment, Jon contemplated his imminent move to Washington, DC, wondering what he would do without Martin by his side every day. Since the move from Arkansas, Jon had come to rely on Martin more and more, whereas before, Jon was always self-contained. Some might say he was self-centered. But Martin was transformed. Despite Jon's imminent departure and fear of the unknown, seeing Martin blossom was glorious.

Then there was Chee, whom Jon had grown particularly fond of, seeing him much like a son. Chee was an old soul. Even though he was Navajo, Waha loved him and Jennifer, too. Jon thought about all the other persons on the ranch who made the place work. Waha. Jennifer. Sam. Los Caballeros. They had become his family of choice, but soon, he would have to say goodbye for a short time.

At the house, Jon took his time to pack two bags, one his typical overnight bag with his waxed canvass jacket, even in summer, a pair of black oxfords, a pair of brown oxfords, a pair of chinos, and two shirts, one long sleeve button down and a short sleeve polo shirt along with miscellaneous necessities. The other was a hanging bag for a blue suit, a khaki suit, more dress shirts, and a red and blue necktie. Whatever else he needed, he'd figure it out later. He brought the bags up to the foyer of La Hacienda, dropped them there, and drove to the geothermal plant to meet up with Martin and Chee.

The sun was rising over the east edge of the caldera ridge as Jon drove along the perimeter road, looking out on the Valle Grande with hundreds of cattle grazing upon the expanse. He would miss moving the cattle with the Caballeros to other pastures this summer, but those rituals had been performed for generations before without his help. Chee called, interrupting Jon's thoughts. He'd found Martin, and they were at the geothermal plant waiting.

A few minutes later, Jon rolled up to the site, and there Chee and Martin were with Martin's horse tied up to a picket line. Chee stood silently as Jon hopped out and jogged over to Martin, who opened his arms into a big hug.

"Babe, don't worry about it," Martin said. "Chee told me. We both knew it was coming, but this was a little sooner than we thought! You need to do this. I love you. I know you don't want to leave, but this ranch isn't going anywhere, and neither am I."

Jon remained silent, but his quietness spoke volumes as he hung on to Martin's bear hug. Then he whispered: "Martin, I don't want to go."

Martin released his hug and held Jon at arm's length by the shoulders, looking at him directly into Jon's watery eyes.

"Jon, you are a good man. If you don't go, you'll always regret it. Don't be like the guys you complain about who can and then don't. You can, so go. Do what you are called to do. Don't worry about me. I'll come out wherever needed, but my home is here. You understand that. I will be fine. Besides, I have Carl, Jennifer, Waha, Sam, and Chee. And trust me. I'll see your mom. She'll be fine, too. Okay?"

"Tell Mom I'll be down to see her on my next trip out, okay?"

Jon's phone beeped with a call from Sam Hernandez.

"Jefe, a flight of two helicopters called on the CTAF. They are on approach. It is a military flight from Kirtland."

"Okay, thanks, Sam," Jon replied. "Please go clear the field. I'm on my way."

"I got to go, babe," Jon said to Martin.

Martin and Jon exchanged another squeeze, then parted.

As Jon drove back toward La Hacienda, he lowered the driver's side window and heard the wop-wop of approaching helicopters. He saw them, two Sikorsky HH-60 military helicopters approaching the field from the south.

Here we go.

Sam was already there with a pair of aviation wands waving down the approaching aircraft. A stout man jumped out of one of the helicopters dressed in an Air Force Service Dress Uniform, about 6'2", as far as Jon could tell, and right behind him were two other Air Force Security Police dressed in USAF battle uniforms. One looked to be an officer with a sidearm. The other, an enlisted man, judging by the stripes on his sleeves, was armed with an M4A1 carbine. Last out of the Sikorsky was a grey-haired Hispanic man in a dark suit with a briefcase. Jon thought he recognized him but wasn't sure.

The man in the dress uniform was a full colonel, and when he came up to Jon, he extended his right hand, "Hello, Mr. Freeman, I am Colonel Brandon Westfield. I am the base commander of Kirtland Air Force Base. I'm here with Judge Manuel Gabaldon from Santa Fe, who will swear you in. The President of the United States asked me to accompany you to an airborne command post arriving in Santa Fe to pick you up. Are you prepared to come with me, sir?"

"Hello, Colonel, I am," Jon said, "but we don't do anything on this ranch without first having breakfast, and you're just in time. You and your boys come with me to the house for a few minutes. Let's have a bite to eat, then we can go after I speak with my staff. Is that all right? Because I'm not getting on that helo with you until I've had breakfast!"

"Whatever you say, sir," Colonel Westfield replied with a friendly smile.

"Let's go, then," Jon said, "Sam will drive you guys. We're just going up the road to the house. Why don't you tell your crew to join us? Your helos are safe."

The colonel motioned the Sikorsky crews to cut the engines and waved them to follow. When they all made it inside, Chef Wiles whipped up some New Mexico-style huevos rancheros with green chili and blue corn tortillas. Everyone spread out between the kitchen and dining room to accommodate the Air Force crews and everyone else, including Sam, Waha, and Jennifer, who joined in.

With a cup of coffee in one hand, Jon said to Sam, "The ranch will remain in your capable hands, my friend. I am sure the government will afford me plenty of visits back here, and we will get this chapter behind us. Soon, I will be back for good."

Silence settled upon the crowd, and Jon addressed it.

"Everyone, look, things will be busy. The president has called on me to do a job, and I will do my best. When my job is done, I'll be coming right back here, and this is where I'll remain until you put me in a box!"

Jennifer and Waha looked over at Jon, nodding their approval. Martin approached Jon and hugged him. The room erupted into clapping as Sam approached Jon to shake his hand.

"Everything's gonna be fine here, Jefe! Let's get this done."

Jon asked Colonel Westfield, "Am I missing anything, Colonel?"

The smiling colonel looked back, "Just that you need to be sworn in. And once you are, the Secret Service will send a detail for your husband's security. They know this is a working ranch operation and have instructions to make no intrusions on the ranch operations, but I am sure their presence will take some getting used to."

"Right," Jon said, "thank you for reminding us of that. I recommend they interface directly with Martin and the ranch foreman to coordinate their integration into ranch life."

"One other thing," the colonel said. "The Secret Service will give Martin and Sam instructions on contacting you because you won't be able to use your cell phone anymore once you're sworn in."

Colonel Westfield continued. "Now, we need to tend to a critical piece of business," and then he gestured to the judge. "Judge, you ready to swear him in?"

Judge Gabaldon sat at the opposite end of the dining table in the kitchen, opened his briefcase, and withdrew a folded black robe. Underneath it was a Bible.

Jon stood back and observed, "Your Honor, you've thought of everything."

"As I expect the lawyers coming before me, I come prepared," the judge said with a grin. The judge donned his robe, took the Bible with him, and handed it to Martin as he walked toward Jon. "Why don't you step over here, Mr. Freeman?" the judge suggested, motioning for Jon to come closer.

"All right, sir, stand here, raise your right hand, and place your left hand on the Bible. Repeat after me:

I, Jonathan Christian Freeman/

do solemnly swear/

that I will support and defend the Constitution of the United States/

against all enemies, foreign and domestic/

that I will bear true faith and allegiance to the same/

and that I take this obligation freely/

without any mental reservation or purpose of evasion/

and that I will well and faithfully discharge the duties of the office/

on which I am about to enter/

so help me, God.

"Congratulations, Mr. Vice President," the judge said, extending his hand to shake Jon's. Then, Sam walked up and shook Jon's hand, looking at Jon squarely in the eyes: "Jefe, the Valle Grande will be fine. Go and saddle up!"

The colonel said aloud, "I need to make a call. I'll meet you out front. Walking toward the front door, he pressed a saved number for the Desk Officer at the National Military Command Center.[32] There was one ring and then a click with silence on the other end. Then, the colonel spoke:

272

"Westfield. Authenticate Victor Papa. Ranch Hand secure. Westfield Out."

Without realizing the colonel's phone call was to confirm Jon's place in the chain of command that would generate his launch codes if the president were incapacitated, Jon stood there looking at the crowd, took his Greeley hat off the kitchen counter, and hat-in-hand, hugged Martin.

"Keep an eye on this place, will you? I'll call once I'm able. Love you," Jon said.

"Love you, too," replied Martin.

Waha and Jennifer slipped out of the house through a side door off the kitchen. They stood silently at the Grand Portal of La Hacienda, Waha holding the same old Jemez clay pot he handed Jon on Cullen's deathbed with its old-style designs containing a pile of smoking sage and sweet grass. Following the colonel, who had just come out, was the rest of the crowd, all walking through the smoke drifting from Waha's clay bowl. As Jon walked through the smoke, he stopped and looked at Waha.

"Waha," Jon said, "I now understand what you meant that day on the mountain."

"Ho'ok'iya ahmantu'ne," Waha said in his native tongue. "Go with the Great Spirit."

After making their way to the helos, Jon climbed aboard the lead Sikorsky with two airmen. The sliding door closed, and he put on a headset hanging above his seat.

The left-seat pilot looked over his shoulder at Jon, "Are you ready, Mr. Vice President?"

"Ready as I'll ever be, Captain," Jon said.

"Valle Grande Traffic. Air Force 2 departing to the south," announced the co-pilot over the common frequency. Jon peered out to the ground below as the Sikorsky flew over a lava dome after a low pass over La Hacienda, picking up altitude as it crossed the Valle Grande and its expansive grasslands, flying south toward Peralta Ridge at an altitude low enough that Jon could count the branches on the pine trees covering its slopes.

Less than ten minutes later, the Sikorsky approached Santa Fe Municipal Airport. He observed the E-4B at the ramp, a converted Boeing 747-200. Once aboard the E-4B, its call sign would change to Air Force 2 and take up a pattern over the center of the United States until the president ordered otherwise. It was an intelligent plan. SECDEF on the West Coast, the East Coast, POTUS, and VPOTUS in the middle. It would be easy for the aircraft to disburse even further if there was a plan afoot to follow with another attempt to decapitate the federal government.

* * *

Colonel Tartaglia stood at attention in the bright morning sun as Jon approached the stair leading to the aircraft door. She was a decorated combat pilot in her forties who was the first female aircraft commander of a flying command post.

"Good morning, Mr. Vice President. I am Colonel Tartaglia, the aircraft commander. Welcome aboard."

"Good morning, Colonel," Jon replied with a broad smile.

Jon stepped up the stairs to the open aircraft door leading into the main cabin, and a steward directed him to his right along a narrow hall as Colonel Tartaglia made a left behind him toward the stairwell leading up to the flight deck. Before heading up, Colonel Tartaglia stopped and turned around to address Jon.

"Mr. Vice President, once we are airborne and at cruising altitude, the Joint Chiefs of Staff vice chairman will brief you. Your aide on this flight is Air Force Major Aaron Sims. He'll get you squared away and situated in the Executive Suite."

A bright-eyed Major Sims stood in his dress blues in the hallway that ran a short distance to a door along the aircraft's port side.

"Come with me, sir. I'll get you squared away," the eager major said as he motioned for Jon to follow him.

A steward closed the aircraft door, and Jon heard the high-pitched whine of the four turbofans power up. They would be airborne in a matter of moments.

How do they get this done so fast and on such short notice - sending up two Sikorskys from Kirtland, launching an E4-B to my location, all within a couple of hours of the order to get me sworn into office and plugged into the National Command Authority. It is remarkable.

The steep ascent pushed Jon's body weight back into his chair. Jon estimated they must be climbing at over six thousand feet per minute. A few minutes later, Jon felt the plane leveling off at cruising altitude. There was a phone on the desk in the Executive Suite, and it rang. Jon picked it up. It was Colonel Tartaglia.

"Sir, we're level at 41,000 feet. Major Sims will escort you back to a briefing room so you can get on a video conference with the National Command Authority and congressional leadership."

Jon handed Sims the phone, and Sims listened momentarily before placing it back in its cradle.

"Sir, would you follow me?" invited Sims.

Sims led Jon through a narrow hall to the galley and then into a conference room with a table that had eight command chairs, a speaker on the table, and a large flat-screen monitor with a camera mounted in front of it. Jon sat at the head of the table opposite the camera with Sims sitting next to him, and then he was joined by an Air Force brigadier general, a full colonel, and a senior master sergeant. They were all part of the permanent crew and battle staff assigned to this aircraft in the event of a national emergency. Sims stood up and made introductions to the team.

Everyone was then seated. Sims reached for a remote control mounted on the conference table and turned on the monitor. The monitor briefly showed the Air Force seal, then flickered. The President of the United States from Air Force One appeared in one of several sections, and then the other officials appeared. The secretary of defense came on from his plane. The chairman of the Joint Chiefs of Staff from Raven Rock appeared. Speaker Atwood of the House of Representatives and the Congressional majority and minority leaders appeared from Mount Weather.

President Aidun began the call.

"Good morning, everyone. Let me get right to the point. Now that we have a vice president and Congress has filled its leadership, we are back in business as a fully functioning government. All of us on this call comprise the United States' senior leadership, and I remind you that we are in a *de facto* state of civil war. We still do not know precisely who is responsible for the attack at the Capitol Building, but we know it was from domestic rather than foreign actors."

"Mr. President," Atwood interrupted. "How do we know the attack on the Capitol was by a domestic actor?"

"Madam Speaker, right before the attack, a call came into the FBI National Command Center warning of an imminent attack. The NSA intercepted it, and the FBI examined the call and its origin and compared it with ongoing chatter.[33] The FBI determined with high confidence that the attack was of domestic origin. I'll give you all more details soon."

"Thank you, Mr. President," Atwood replied.

"Meanwhile," the president continued, "on the domestic front, we have 21 states attempting to withdraw from the Union. There are significant federal interests and property in those states. We must protect those assets and the citizens whose civil rights are at risk. But we may also face international threats from countries like Russia or North Korea, who might seek advantage of the chaos. Does anyone have any questions so far?"

"What about Washington DC," inquired the House Majority Leader Vernon Iverson. "Is Washington safe?"

"Good question, Leader Iverson. Before we were outside Washington's airspace, I issued an order to federalize the National Guard to secure the District. As soon as it is deemed safe, we will return."

"Thank you, Mr. President," Iverson said.

"Given my previous job," the president continued, "I will head up the efforts to maintain our international relations. On the domestic front, I am asking the vice president to take charge of securing our federal interests located in the compact states and try to begin a dialogue with the rebelling state governors. I intend for the vice president to operate with my full authority. Whatever he needs, he gets. Does everyone understand?"

There was a chorus of "Yes, Mister President" from every box on the screen.

"Let's go over that again. I will not tolerate typical Washington, DC, backbiting. I chose Jon particularly because he is NOT from Washington, DC. He doesn't aspire to higher political office but speaks the language of those red-state rebels. He has progressive values, but he has little patience for coastal tofu-eating vegans and hand-wringing. I'm hoping his brand of unvarnished straight talk will convey our message in a way that everyday people understand. When this is all over, he can return to his ranch, the politicians can return to business as usual, and we can move forward as a country. But make no mistake, he is here to do a job, and I expect everyone's unwavering cooperation."

Goddamned politicians will muck this up if Jon doesn't move fast, the president thought.

"The last thing I have is that we will remain airborne for at least another 24 hours while the Defense Department and Homeland Security secure Washington DC. The FBI is investigating the attack on the Capitol, and they are especially curious how an RPG could have been fired from the Supreme Court building of all places, much less the Russell Senate Office Building. The attack on our government will not stand, my friends. I will stop at nothing to capture or kill whoever is responsible and whoever helped them. Good hunting, all. Maintain your stations. I'll send an order out when it is time to return to Washington."

25

The Easy Way, or the Hard Way

As soon as the call with the president ended, Jon faced everyone assembled in the conference room and stood up.

"You heard the president. We have work to do."

Turning to Sims, Jon said, "Get me the secretary of defense, please."

"Yes, sir," Sims replied.

Sims disappeared for a few minutes and returned.

"I have Secretary of Defense Ironwood on screen for you, sir."

The screen flickered again.

"Mr. Secretary," Jon began, "I require your assistance."

"Yes, Mr. Vice President," Ironwood answered.

"My first concern, Mr. Secretary, is securing all our federal property within the compact states. That means we must secure all military equipment, bases, and anything that could be used to wage war. So, unless you disagree, we should federalize the National Guard and call all our reserve forces to active-duty status to have those forces available."

"I agree, Mr. Vice President. The COG has extensive guidance on this subject. Would you like me to put together a plan?"

"I would, yes," Jon replied. "Tell me where things stand by 1800 hours Central Time. I'll also work through the COG to get up to speed."

"Yes, sir," Ironwood answered. "We can at least have the contours of a plan together by 1800."

THE EASY WAY, OR THE HARD WAY

"Thanks, Mr. Secretary," Jon said, ending the call to continue with the next one.

"Sims, next on the list is Homeland Security, then Treasury after that. After those calls, I want you to get me on the phone with the Governor of Arkansas."

After his calls with Homeland Security and Treasury, Sims tried contacting the Arkansas Governor. At the same time, Jon looked over maps showing where US bases and assets were situated in various compact states until Sims came in and interrupted him.

"Mr. Vice President," Sims said, "she's dodging."

Jon smiled.

Of course, what a bitch that woman is! If it is the last thing I do, I will make her pay for what she has done.

"Keep trying her. Next time you call, be sure she knows exactly who it is that is calling. Use my name, and spell it out if you have to."

* * *

Jesus! What could that son-of-a-bitch possibly want from me?

"Tell him I'm unavailable, goddammit," Buckshot commanded her aide when the sixth call came from the vice presidential plane.

"Ma'am, I have been. The vice president's assistant, Major Sims, said the vice president would not take 'no' for an answer. He suggested that you might regret not taking his call."

"Jesus, vice president? Some no-name numb nut? I thought you said Jon Freeman was calling."

The governor's aide paused.

Holy shit, she doesn't know! This is going to be good!

Buckshot's expression turned to surprise.

"You said what? Vice President Jonathan Christian Freeman? You have got to be fucking kidding me. That mother fucker keeps turning up like a lingering fart under the sheets. Jesus, OK, put the pole-smoking faggot on."

Sims returned to the airborne briefing room where Jon had set up shop.

"I have her on the line, Mr. Vice President."

"Good morning, Governor Landers. I presume you are unpleasantly surprised to be hearing from me. It's a pity we haven't been formally introduced until now," Jon said sardonically.

"Mr. Freeman," Buckshot replied, "I thought you had run off to your ranch in New Mexico to hide."

"Not quite, Governor. Let me get to the point of my call. You, madam, are in a pickle. If you want to save yourself from being captured, taken into custody, prosecuted, and executed for treason, you'll listen to what I say."

"Fuck you, Mr. Freeman," she said with guile. "I don't give a shit if you're the vice president. You're a homosexual and an ex-lawyer. Why should I give two shits? You're just the vice president. You don't have the power to do shit to me."

"Governor Landers," Jon began, his patience tested but his voice remaining calm, "I was counting on you saying that from a position of personal satisfaction. I'd love to serve some good old-fashioned justice on you by seeing your sorry ass hanged for treason. But for the sake of your citizens, I hope you'll hear me out. I can give you a way out of the shitstorm you created by asking you to come to Washington along with the other compact state governors to sit down and see if we can resolve whatever led you all to sign that declaration of secession. The president and I, along with leaders of Congress, believe it would be beneficial to talk before things get out of hand."

Buckshot's voice became violent and shrill.

"You can fuck straight off, Mr. Freeman. There is no way I'd step foot in the cesspool of Washington, DC, a town of niggers, faggots, gender nonconformists, liberals, and false Christians. So, no, you won't get me to Washington, DC. Ever."

Jon let a pregnant, silent pause fill the connection for roughly 15 seconds.

"Fair enough," Jon said, finally. "That option was the easy way. Let's discuss the hard way."

"What's the hard way, Mr. Freeman?" she demanded.

"The hard way, Madam Governor, is military force," Jon replied calmly.

Her voice sharpened and caught a strange pitch.

"Fuck you, you little pencil dick motherfucker. You don't have the balls, and that rag-head Muslim president certainly doesn't either."

"Hmmm, well, Madam Governor," Jon said, "that suits me."

He turned to Sims: "Cut her off."

The abrupt silence on the governor's end and the following buzzing tone left her shaking mad.

That mother fucker hung up on me!

After the call, Jon asked for more coffee and stretched.

"Sims," he called out, "take a walk with me. I need to think through some things, but why not give me the nickel tour at the same time and introduce me to the crew."

"Yes, sir," Sims said.

Jon followed Sims through the passageways and into different work areas during his tour, allowing him to meet the rest of the highly-trained crew. The tour humbled Jon at the thought of how one could conduct conventional and even nuclear warfare from aboard this plane. There was not a place on the planet that could not be reached. After the tour, Jon returned to the conference, where he was working to call the president.

"Mr. President. It's Jon. I thought I'd give you an idea of where I'm headed after consulting with defense and having a call with none other than the Governor of Arkansas."

"Lay it on me, Jon," the president stated.

"Mr. President, the compact states have unofficially declared war on the federal government. We are at DEFCON 2, and the leader of the movement, Governor Landers of Arkansas, pretty much told the federal government and me to go pound sand in my recent call with her. I did what I could to lay it bare for her and invite her and the other secessionist governors to come to Washington, DC, to sit together and sort through a solution."

"Keep going, Jon."

"I'll be honest, Mr. President, I won't make an 'A' in 'Diplomacy 101.' I didn't give her any wiggle room because she only respects brute force. She indicated her unwillingness to explore a peaceful solution, so we must cut the head off the snake and take her into custody as soon as possible. But before doing that, the COG advises that we activate the reservists and federalize the National Guard in areas affected by a national emergency. I reckon the situation in Washington, DC, and Arkansas constitutes a national emergency. The plan is to order the National Guard and reservists to muster and prepare to harden and secure federal facilities throughout the compact states. Starting with Arkansas will get the governor's attention and send a message to other states through our actions in Arkansas. We will learn very quickly where other states stand."

"Tell me more, Jon," the president prompted.

"Mr. President, we should divide to conquer by contacting each governor of every compact state to see if we can start a dialogue before resorting to more extreme measures, military action, or the suspension of *habeas corpus*. Cracks in the damn will appear. As a backup, Secretary Ironwood is preparing a plan to federalize all the National Guard units and call up all reservists in Arkansas and throughout the United States."

"Seems reasonable," the president allowed, "but Jon suspending *habeas corpus*? That hasn't been done since the Civil War. I suggest you contact the attorney general and get him to work on our legal standing."

"Yes, of course, Mr. President. He is on my call list," Jon said.

Several hours later, the secretary of defense presented his plan to Jon to activate reserve troops and federalize the National Guard. At Jon's request, President Aidun issued an executive order calling all federal reserve troops within the borders of Arkansas to active duty. He also federalized all Arkansas National Guard Troops in a separate executive order. Orders for other states were forthcoming.

The EOs were transmitted from Air Force One through secure channels to the National Command Authority staff and the Joint Chiefs of Staff, with a copy of the Federalization EO to the Chief of the National Guard Bureau, a four-star general. Upon receipt, the Chief of the National Guard Bureau relayed the order to the adjutant general of Arkansas.

* * *

The communications officer at the Robinson Maneuver Training Center in North Little Rock received the order from the Pentagon. The order read the following:

> Under 10 USC Section 12406(2) and by Executive Order, all members of the Arkansas National Guard and the Arkansas Air Guard are called to federal service. Each member shall report to his or her local guard armory or base (in the case of the Air Guard), ready for duty and awaiting further instructions through the chain of command.[34]

The National Command Authority transmitted a similarly worded order to the chain of command to mobilize every member of the US Reserve Forces of every branch within the State of Arkansas.

As per procedure, the staff duty officer, or SDO, at Camp Robinson in North Little Rock received the flash traffic and authenticated the order. The SDO then took the order and drove it to the residence of Arkansas Adjutant General Rhys Hampton, who lived at Camp Robinson.

The SDO knocked on the front door of the general's quarters, a red brick salt-box-style home, at 3 a.m. She knocked again and waited. A light came on in an upstairs room. Then, another light came on downstairs. The porch light came on, and a bleary-eyed Major General Hampton dressed in powder blue pajamas opened the front door and peered out at the captain standing before him under his porch light.

"General Hampton, I have an urgent presidential order over the wire from the National Command Center. It is authenticated."

"Give it to me," the general said, and she handed it over.

"Thank you, Captain, that will be all. You may return to your post," the general stated as he shut his front door.

"Yes, General," and she departed in her Humvee through the humid Arkansas dark.

The adjutant general went to his kitchen to get a coffee and then phoned the governor, who answered, much to his surprise.

"Morning, Governor. An authenticated presidential order came in from the National Command Center on behalf of the National Guard Bureau. It federalizes the Guard. I need your agreement to pass the order on to subordinate unit commanders. I'm afraid it is time to fish or cut bait. What do you want to do?"

"Son of a bitch, he didn't waste any time," Governor Landers ranted. "Son of a bitch! Don't give the order yet. I need some time."

"Be careful with that, Governor, unless you want to pull a charge of treason for both of us," the general expressed.

"No, no, I get it," the governor said. "Just give me until 8 o'clock."

She hung up.

After that, she woke up one of her aides and asked him to arrange an immediate conference call with the State Commander of the Arkansas Defenders, the Director of the State Police, the leaders of the state militias, and the majority leaders of the General Assembly. About an hour later, the aide called and said the conference call was ready.

"Thank you, everyone, for getting up so early." Governor Landers began on the conference call. "I am calling because the federal government is about to attack us. I received word an hour ago that the President of the United States issued an order to federalize the National Guard. He also activated all reserve units in Arkansas. To avoid it looking like treason this early in the game, I will issue the order to federalize the Guard, but after that, this is where you come in. I want every militia member and every citizen inclined to do so to show up at every reserve unit, military base, and armory to protest and impede anyone reporting to duty. Don't use force. Just pressure your citizens, friends, and neighbors to resist the feds. My aide will fax you a list of all the facilities in the state, but it will be up to you to organize it. I am ordering the Arkansas Defenders to aid every citizen who wants to appear and protest. I am ordering the State Police to do the same. If there was ever a time for Arkansans to make their views known about the Nazi federal government, it is now. Once I issue the order, these people will take time to reach these facilities. I'll give the order at 8 a.m. sharp, so you have some time to get organized."

At 8:00 a.m., Sunday, July 7, 2024, the adjutant general transmitted orders to the 39th Infantry Brigade Combat Team to muster its troops in Arkansas at their respective armories. Then he worked through the list of other units: the 77th Theater Aviation Brigade, the 87th Troop Command, the 142nd Field Artillery Brigade, the 189th Airlift Wing, and the 188th Wing. The order to muster would then filter down to groups, brigades, battalions, companies, air wings, and squadrons, resulting in a phone call to each guardsman, soldier, or airman.

At about the same time, the Pentagon issued orders through the National Command Center to each federal reserve unit in the state, placing those units on active-duty status with orders for each reservist to report to their respective unit immediately.

* * *

The adjutant general's orders resulted in a call to Mary Bumgarner, the first sergeant of Alpha Company, Second 153rd Infantry Battalion in Harrison, Arkansas. Her unit was federalized and called to active duty.

Even though she was the mother of four, she checked her maternal instincts at the door when she showed up for duty. The unit administrator told her the company commander and executive officer knew the order and that everyone would be briefed when they arrived at the armory. Mary always kept an away bag ready at the front door, so all she had to do was get on her ACUs and head out.[35]

Her husband's phone lit up as she sat on the end of her bed, lacing up her boots. Frank "Flaps," Bumgarner answered.

"Flaps here. What the fuck are you calling me so early for, Jimmy?"

"Hey, Flaps, we have a situation. The governor called the militia commander. This is it, buddy, the feds are coming, and the commander says we have to go and protest the armory because the Guard's been called out," said Flap's friend, Jimmy.

"Hey, my wife's the first sergeant over there. I gotta call you back." Flaps hung up the phone.

"Hey Mary, was that call to activate your unit?" Flaps asked.

"Yep. We've been federalized," she said as she buttoned up her ACU blouse.

"Well, shit, that was Jimmy. He said the local militia commander called us to go to the armory to protest the activation."

"I don't know what to think," Mary replied. "Don't worry. Go on over there with the militia boys. I will head over to the armory and see what's going on. But I can tell you this: most soldiers in my unit will not support the feds. This is going to be interesting! Love ya, hon. See you down there!"

Mary knew her husband was a member of the local militia, a paramilitary arm of the Ku Klux Klan, and she was sympathetic to the cause, as was most of her unit at Alpha Company. Even though she didn't think of herself as a racist, she didn't like the idea of immigrants, blacks, or non-Christians pushing good, hard-working white folks like her to the side. She tolerated homosexuals as long as the men didn't act "gay" around her. And lesbians, she couldn't get on that train. She identified with Christian evangelicals most, even though she didn't attend church. But she had a Bible; she could read, and that was all that mattered.

Mary turned her 1989 Cherry Red Camaro onto the two-lane asphalt road leading up to the armory. She passed along a fence by the county airport and saw two Defender SUVs blocking the road leading up to the armory. She pulled up, exited her car, and approached the black-clad Defenders. Looking further down the road, she saw State Police patrol vehicles.

"What's the deal, boys?" Mary asked.

"Hey Mary, good to see you," a Defender named Ben replied.

"The governor sent us here to stop people from reporting for duty. There was a big meeting about it early this morning. The feds are coming."

Behind Mary's car approached a caravan of vehicles, ten of them in all, and each pulled over onto the side of the road behind her. Every brand of North Arkansas redneck piled out of the cars and trucks dressed in military-like costumes, complete with MAGA hats. Some wore pistols on their belts, and some carried crude signs that read, "Feds, go home!", "Not on my watch," "Lock and Load," and "Don't Tread on Me."

"Look, boys, let me check in with my commander," Mary said. "I want to avoid a court martial for being AWOL.[36] Let's see who turns up. Who knows how this will turn out?"

"Go on, then, Mary, but I can't guarantee things will stay calm out here," Ben, the Defender, stated.

Mary returned to her Camaro and drove to an opened gate at the armory that led her to a parking area in the back. She parked and entered the back door to find the supply sergeant holding the company commander, Captain Francis Tweedy, at gunpoint in the hallway.

"Sergeant Jones, what the hell are you doing? Put that goddamn gun down!" Mary commanded.

"First Sergeant, I heard him. He's going to report anyone who refuses the call-up as AWOL. I won't go against my state, First Sergeant. I won't do it." Sergeant Jones nervously told her while keeping his gun trained on the captain.

The supply sergeant, a local boy, was upset and not much older than the company commander he was threatening, but the difference was that the young captain had pissed his pants. He was new and wasn't from the area, which was a major strike against him, whereas Mary had known Sergeant Jones since he was a little boy. First Sergeant Bumgarner never thought much of the captain anyway.

What a pussy, she thought.

"Sergeant Jones," she said again, "put that fuckin' gun down and secure it back in the weapons locker! God damn! Let me talk to the captain in his office."

She walked over to Captain Tweedy, who was visibly relieved and embarrassed.

"Come on, sir, let's get you cleaned up and talk."

Down the hall, they walked, and Captain Tweedy stepped into his office to change. He stripped off his ACUs and donned his civilian clothes right before Mary.

"I'm done with this right-wing bullshit, First Sergeant," Tweedy said. "There is already a mob out there, and I won't stick around to get killed by a bunch of rednecks."

Mary appraised the handsome young captain standing before her, now dressed in Levi's and a polo shirt.

"Aren't you going to say anything, First Sergeant?" the captain demanded.

Mary studied him for a moment longer, then said with a calm, level tone of voice: "You're new here, sir. I don't know why you moved here, but you had to know that the people you are supposed to lead are proud Arkansans. We place our state above all else. So let me tell you, it is best to leave quickly and return wherever you come from. I didn't sign up to turn guns on my people. I signed up to help out around here or kill me some rag heads. So you can take your federal order and pride out of here."

"What about our oaths, First Sergeant?" the captain asked incredulously.

"Look, sir, my oath, yeah, I took one, but I didn't take no oath to go after my own. And as far as I am concerned, the federal government is the enemy."

The captain decided to flee in contravention of his oath in fear for his life because the scene unfolding outside Alpha Company was getting violent.

As Captain Tweedy departed in his car, one of the men in the mob saw him leaving. "Hey, y'all, that's the company commander! He's leavin'! Y'all know he's a dick sucker, right?"

About 20 men who heard the announcement ran over and surrounded the captain's car before he thought to lock his doors. One man with a bald head and a pair of overalls opened the door and pulled the captain out of the car, wrestling him to the ground with the help of two others. Standing over him, the bald man of about 50 years put his booted foot on the captain's chest. "I knew you was a faggot when you moved to this town. I seen you downtown at the diner with another guy. You two sure were sittin' close makin' eyes."

The captain's young face and wide eyes were contorted with terror.

"Jesus fucking Christ, did you shit yourself?" Mr. Overalls raged.

The group surrounding him closed in and began kicking him until he was unconscious, bloody, and filthy. The State Troopers and Defenders standing nearby on the side of the road did nothing but observe the desecration of the captain's lifeless body on the side of the road as the locals dragged it off and threw it in a ditch.

One mob member produced a can of gasoline and poured the fuel onto the front seat of the captain's car and the rest of the can on the captain. The redneck took a final drag of his cigarette and cast it into the car, setting it alight with a whoosh of flame. He dropped the empty fuel can and lit another Marlborough Red, after which he flicked the match on the unconscious captain, leaving him alive and handsome no more.

News trucks appeared at the scene and broadcasted the ghastly spectacle to viewers around the globe while Mary witnessed her former company commander devoured by flame with black smoke rising from his corpse.

What a waste, she thought, *what a god damned waste*.

She went to the unit's full-time civilian administrator, who was hiding in her office.

"Get up and get me the number for the Sergeant Major," Mary demanded impatiently.

She made the call.

"Sergeant Major, First Sergeant Bumgarner here, Alpha Company. We have a situation. Barely anyone has shown up for the muster, and a mob outside the armory killed the captain."

"I hear you, First Sergeant. I don't know what to say about the captain, but protect the armory. The Guard isn't going to fight. It may look like treason against the federal government, First Sergeant, but I suppose you know that already," the crusty old sergeant major said.

"I do," Mary replied.

The sergeant major continued.

"Many Guard units in the state will probably follow the order, but we will not enforce it. So, do what you need to do to secure the armory. You can send everyone else home."

First Sergeant Bumgarner hung up the landline and walked out the front door of the armory with the supply sergeant behind her. He was armed with a loaded M4 Carbine.

"Listen up, everyone," Mary yelled, addressing the crowd outside.

"Let me have your attention. I am sending everyone home. Y'all had your way with the captain, but no one else needs to be hurt. I will not permit anyone to attack or seize the armory, so if you plan to do that, be prepared for a fight. We are ignoring the federal order. Stay on that side of the fence, and we won't have a problem, okay?"

Members of the crowd stood there for a moment, looking at each other in silence.

"Do I need to repeat myself? This unit will not follow the federal order, but we will not allow this armory to be attacked. Understand?" Mary said again.

A voice yelled, "You heard the lady!" It was Mary's husband, Flaps. "Stand down."

Scenes similar to what happened in Harrison played throughout the day in Arkansas, with some units like Alpha Company rejecting the federalization order and others deciding to abide by it.

* * *

"Mr. Secretary, do you have a report for me on the National Guard and reservist call-up in Arkansas?" Jon asked.

"I do, Mr. Vice President—the long or short version?" asked the defense secretary.

"Bottom-line it for me," Jon suggested.

"Mr. Vice President, the Arkansas National Guard operates over 70 Readiness Centers across the state, housing approximately 8,600 troops. However, seven units, making up around 20% of the force, fully rejected the order. Despite minor skirmishes, those who remained ensured the security of the armories. As for the active reservists within Arkansas, 13 facilities host 38 units and detachments comprised of 2,184 soldiers and 129 civilians. Although we maintained control of all reserve centers, a similar 20% of reservists failed to report for duty, equating to about 400 individuals."

"What about aviation units?" Jon asked.

"We did not lose a single aircraft. All federal and air guard military aircraft in the state were flown out to friendly states and secured."

Jon paused, then said, "Mr. Secretary, my next question is whether we can hold on to our facilities."

"That is a good different question," the secretary replied. "The intelligence provided to me indicates there will be a concerted effort led by the Governor of Arkansas and the Arkansas Military Department to take as many armories by force as possible. It isn't a matter of whether she decides to do that, but when. They are disorganized but will be regrouping and adding numbers to their ranks."

"Thank you," Jon said.

"Get with the joint chiefs, Mr. Secretary, and prepare to defend federal property. Also, I want a plan to arrest the Governor of Arkansas. I will get with the attorney general about that and brief the president. We'll need options."

26

Washington, DC

Jon was stretched out on a couch in the E4-B Executive Suite. A sizeable three-ring binder with the COG lay on the floor beside him, along with some briefing folders. He had been asleep for a few hours when Sims knocked on the door. It was Monday morning, July 8th.

"Mr. Vice President, Mr. Vice President."

"What, what?" Jon muttered.

"Mr. Vice President," asked a polite voice from the other side of the door. "May I come in?"

"Yes, of course."

Sims walked in. Jon sat upright on the couch rubbing his eyes, still dressed in the same suit he wore when he first boarded the plane, only his tie was loosened.

"Sorry to wake you," Sim's said. "The president ordered us to stand down and return to Washington. We are en route to Joint Base Andrews. Congress and the Pentagon are returning to Washington, also. We'll be on the ground in about an hour."

"That's great news. Any idea where I'm going to be staying when we get there? This couch isn't going to cut it."

"Sorry for not mentioning it earlier, sir, but the General Services Administration already arranged a temporary residence for you in the Eisenhower Executive Office Building across from the White House until the Naval Observatory can be ready."[37]

The E4-B touched down at Joint Base Andrews later that morning. A contingent of Secret Service Agents met Jon with a caravan of vehicles parked on the tarmac and whisked him to the Eisenhower Executive Office Building. A busy day was ahead, beginning with a security briefing by the FBI's point man on domestic terrorism, followed by a working lunch with the cabinet and a meeting with his staff.

Sims accompanied Jon to the Executive Office Building to assist in getting Jon settled in. Jon's learning curve would be steep, and there was no time to spare. They walked into the vice president's office with its mahogany paneling, white maple floors, and two fireplaces made of Belgian black marble. Jon noticed the photo of the recently deceased vice president's family still sitting on the large desk in the room.

I have to pay my respects to the family as soon as possible.

"Mr. Vice President, the Director of the FBI is sending a man over to brief you. He should be here any minute," Sims reminded.

"Yeah, I read what I could on the plane before falling asleep. Let's see what he has to say," Jon remarked.

The FBI's point man on the secession movement, Special Agent Dan Jenson, arrived at 11 a.m. The two men met previously during Jon's trips to Washington, DC. Jenson's hair was gray and thinning from a long career working in domestic terrorism. His report confirmed people were disappearing under compact state operations, not just putting them in internment camps. And there was unsettling evidence that a conservative Supreme Court associate justice was part of the assassination plot that killed President Hedges on July 5th.

"You mean to tell me that an associate justice of the Supreme Court was the inside man who made it possible for terrorists to get an RPG into the Supreme Court Building?" Jon asked.

"Yes, sir, that is what our preliminary investigation reveals," Jenson replied.

"And these disappearances?"

"Mr. Vice President," Jenson continued, "compact state governors were

THE LAST INDEPENDENCE DAY

aware of many of them and, in some instances, ordered disappearances. The disappearances included political opponents, liberal activists, and some outspoken members of the NAACP and the LGBTQ community."

"This just gets worse and worse," Jon observed.

"Mr. Vice President, that's not all. Our intel indicates that Texas and South Carolina may attempt to seize nuclear material stored at federal facilities in their states - the Pantex Plant in Texas and South Carolina's Savannah River Site.[38] They want to use nuclear blackmail, if necessary, to influence enough states to join them in a constitutional convention so they can push for major amendments. The compact states don't have the numbers to call for a convention right now, but the implications are immense if they successfully call for a convention, by whatever means."

"Jesus. This is overwhelming," Jon said.

"Indeed, it is, Mr. Vice President. Any questions?"

"Yes, but more questions than either you or I have time. I'd like you to prepare and send me a report detailing your findings. I also want it to focus on the military threats they might pose. Can you do that for me?"

"I can, sir," the agent replied.

"Thank you, Agent Jenson," Jon said. "The president expects a lot from me, so I must be prepared—and one more thing. I want everything you have on the Governor of Arkansas and the missing attorney general of Arkansas. I feel that the Arkansas AG is one of those people who have been 'disappeared.' I'd like that as soon as you can get it to me. Can you do that for me?"

"Yes, sir," Jenson said, excusing himself.

Jon looked over at Sims, who was in the room during the briefing.

"Major Sims, I'd like you to stay as my military attaché. I need someone I can trust to help me navigate all this stuff. Can you make that happen?"

"I'm sure your chief of staff can, Mr. Vice President. Let's get her in here and see what she says."

Sims stepped out of the stately office and into the hallway, where the chief and several other staffers lingered. A few minutes later, Sims walked back in with the former vice president's chief of staff, a lady with short-cropped

294

hair and black horn-rimmed glasses named Beverly Cross.

"How may I be of service, Mr. Vice President?"

"Ms. Cross," Jon began, "it is a pleasure to meet you. I look forward to working with you and the staff here. I'm going to need a lot of help. One of the things I need help with is adding Major Sims to the team as my attaché or whatever title is appropriate. You can handle that?"

"Yes, Mr. Vice President, I can," she replied.

"That's good, Beverly. Let's make it happen. I have a cabinet meeting at the White House shortly, but perhaps we can reconvene after that. One more thing. I'd like you to arrange a time for me to head over to the Naval Observatory to give my condolences to the former vice president's family. I also want to clarify that I have no intention of moving to the Naval Observatory until they are good and ready to move out. It is their home, and that family has just lost its wife and mother."

"Yes, sir, I am sure the family will appreciate that," she said.

"Thank you," Jon said before turning to Sims again.

"Don't we have a working lunch at the White House with the cabinet?"

"Yes, sir," Sims said as he opened the office door and led Jon down the hallway, where they were met by a contingent of Secret Service who had just arrived at the Executive Office Building.

Sims and the Secret Service detail escorted Jon through exit doors leading to a cordoned-off lane. Across the street was a covered walkway leading into the busy West Wing of the White House. Jon proceeded through the door and headed down the busy hall toward the Oval.

* * *

President Aidun rose from his chair behind the Resolute Desk to greet Jon. The Oval Office was full of staffers.

"Hello, Jon!" he said, rising from his chair. "I'm so happy you decided to join the team. You probably haven't had any time to get your bearings. Things move fast around here."

President Aidun then addressed the room full of people, "Everyone, give us the room for a moment, please."

Wilson Brannigan stood to one side of the president, and when he heard the words, he held his arms out toward the door and said, "Okay, everyone, let's go! You heard the president."

"Wilson, why don't you stick around with us," Aidun said.

"Yes, sir," Brannigan said as he ushered the crowd out of the office.

The three men sat down on the plush sofas arranged in the center of the Oval Office, facing each other, separated by a coffee table.

"Jon, I wanted to talk with you before entering that cabinet room. Those cabinet secretaries are too shaken up by all that happened to have come out of the fog, but rest assured, the vying for favor and position will begin very soon. Some of the secretaries may hesitate to invest in you. So, we need to be sure they understand that you and I are a united front," the president said.

"I understand, Mr. President. What do you have in mind?"

"We did not establish an agenda for this meeting in hopes to talk openly, off the record, and see what ideas bubble to the top. I'd especially like to have a free and open discussion about your ideas for how you want to approach the compact states, especially considering the intelligence briefing you received earlier. Are you ready?"

"Yes, I think so," Jon said. "I have been working nonstop to get up to speed on the secession issue, what we can do, can't do, and what needs to happen. I have a general outline of a plan in my head. Some of it may be a surprise, and some of it may not be. But I'm ready to put it out there."

"Good. Good," President Aidun said. "This is not typically how it is done. We usually have an agenda because these cabinet secretaries want to have a plan in writing before they open their mouths. This will be uncomfortable for them, but I say we get in there and see what happens. We'll work on ideas this afternoon with the cabinet, get them involved, and hopefully, we will have some notes to give a speech writer so we can go to the American People tonight or tomorrow. Both you and I need to address the nation. They need to know their government is in good hands. But before we go in there, what are your thoughts about moving forward?"

Jon presented his ideas. Afterward, President Aidun rose, studied Jon, and said, "Jon, your objectives are more comprehensive than I expected. Let's get in there and pitch it. There will be bellyaching, but we'll get them on board. If we do, you and I will chat with congressional leadership right after this meeting. We will need their support."

President Aidun and Jon, followed by Mr. Brannigan, walked down the short stretch of the hallway from the Oval Office toward the Cabinet Room. Aidun stopped short of opening the door to the cabinet room, looking back at Jon: "You ready for this?"

"No balls, no babies, Mr. President," Jon replied dryly.

The three of them strode into the conference room. Everyone began to stand up, but the president said, "Ladies and gentlemen, keep your seats. I want to say a few things before we get started. Just a couple of days ago, I served as a cabinet secretary, just like each of you. Because of the 25th Amendment, the president's job has fallen to me. I cannot do the job alone. So, I want to ask everyone in this room whether you will have a problem serving in this administration moving forward. If you have a problem, the door is over to my left. But if you choose to stay, I will need your loyalty. Challenging days are ahead. Everyone says what I am about to say, but very few people mean it. But hear me when I say this: we must set politics aside if we are going to reunify this country without a civil war."

President Aidun stopped speaking and held his breath momentarily as he looked around the table at the motionless cabinet secretaries: statues, all.

"Okay, then. My next question is whether you will work and cooperate with the vice president. I believe he can make tough calls. That is where you come in. He will need your full support. If Jon asks for something, I expect you to deliver. Again, if you have a problem with this, the door is right over there."

He paused again. Most of the eyes in the room turned to Jon.

Aidun then turned to Jon. "Well, Mr. Vice President, do you have anything to say?"

"I do, yes. Hello, everyone. I'm here because the president asked me to be here, not because I sought the office. There are other reasons I'm here. I have seen the results of right-wing extremism becoming policy. With hardly any opposition, the governor of what was my home state dismantled most, if not all, of the significant protections the U.S. Constitution guarantees Americans. Governor Landers' agenda is murderous and totalitarian. She is turning Arkansas into a dystopian society. What is happening there is now spreading throughout the compact states like cancer, and we must stop it. But I am here for another reason. I realized I was partially to blame since I had become complacent like many Americans. I figured someone else would take care of our country. I remained silent against injustice. Well, I am done with silence. Perhaps some of you figured that out by my appearances on TV, but now that I am here, I aim to take care of business. I have the outline of a plan I want to share with you, and as soon as the president is ready, we can discuss how to tackle the situation before us. In time, we will restore order and heal our nation."

The cabinet meeting proceeded for a little over two hours. The secretaries were surprisingly cooperative and helpful, offering ideas, fears, and suggestions. When the cabinet meeting ended, the president and Jon returned to the Oval Office and sat alone.

"Jon, I've asked the leaders of both houses of Congress to come over here with the chairman of the Joint Chiefs of Staff, the attorney general, and the national security advisor. Let's present the plan to them. It is ambitious, and we'll need Congress and the military to execute it."

27

Constitutional Law

The speaker on President Aidun's desk buzzed. It was his secretary. "Mr. President, congressional leadership is here along with the Joint Chiefs of Staff chairman, the attorney general, and the national security advisor. May I send them in?"

"Yes, please do," Aidun said from his seat on the couch across from Jon.

"Find a seat, everyone," the president gestured as the crew entered the Oval Office.

"Everyone, Vice President Freeman and I met with the cabinet earlier. In that meeting, we discussed a plan to address the current situation regarding the 21 states that declared their intent to secede. I want to turn this over to him now, and he will discuss tactical and strategic options as we move forward. The goal is to prevent a civil war and protect federal property and American citizens residing in the rebelling states."

The president then looked at Jon and said, "Jon, the floor is yours."

Jon looked down at his notes and then cleared his throat.

"Hello. I'm not used to how things are done in this city, but I'll give you an objective and blunt assessment about what I think should take place and our roles."

"On July 4th," he said, "the governors of 21 states signed a document indicating the intention of those states to secede. Remember, of course, that originally, 27 states entered the compact, but not all of them had the stomach to go through with secession. One hope I have is that we can erode the will of the ones who stayed in the compact and convince them to withdraw. Our plan today is to set in motion things that might motivate some, if not all of these states, to abandon secession."

Jon continued his presentation, referring to his notes scribbled on a yellow legal pad. "I presume you received the same intelligence I received before this meeting. We know there have already been attacks on federal properties and violence against minorities by non-state actors, but state actors are intensifying efforts to curtail civil rights. We know states are disappearing people, for example, or detaining some in camps. We also know of horrendous executions in Arkansas, including stoning one woman and hanging another. We believe the lawlessness will devolve into state-sponsored violence, requiring an organized and comprehensive federal response. We have already begun steps to secure federal property, assets, material, and other interests within Arkansas, and we will expand those operations to the other members of the compact. You may also know that the FBI and other agencies have covertly helped counterinsurgency efforts, and these, too, will intensify."

"I don't mean to interrupt you," the House Majority Leader Vernon Iverson said, "but you just suggested that our government has given aid and assistance to counterinsurgency efforts?"

"That's correct, Leader Iverson, but based on solid intelligence, decided on an operation-by-operation basis coordinated with law enforcement. The former president realized there were many pissed-off Americans who wanted to help. But getting to the point is that we must protect and secure federal property. We must also protect the rights and property of citizens. An organized counterinsurgency has helped erode non-state actors' capacity to perpetrate violence, but we want to increase those efforts considerably with proper intelligence. So far, the counterinsurgency work we have sponsored has been very successful over the last several months."

Jon waited for a moment, and Iverson nodded his head in agreement. "But I digress. Our plan must also include activating FEMA after the president declares a state of emergency in the compact states. That has not been done yet. When he declares the emergency, we will need FEMA to prepare for refugees who flee the compact states. That leads me to another issue. Securing land borders in and through these states will be key, along with maintaining a military no-fly zone over all of them to prevent the use of air power for whatever untoward purposes these compact states might consider. We have already contacted the FAA about that and are working on the particulars of that aspect of the plan."

"What about the legalities of all this," asked Elijah Brooks, the Joint Chiefs of Staff chairman, "because it sounds like you are headed toward declaring martial law."

"General," Jon replied, "We consulted with the attorney general about suspending *habeas corpus* and other things to ensure our actions are legal under the Constitution. The suspension of *habeas corpus* will be necessary for the plan."[39]

House Minority Leader Claire Turner was a liberal Democrat from Virginia who emitted an audible gasp. Jon recalled she had won her seat by a narrow margin in the last election.

"Leader Turner, bear with me on this. The president and I realize this could appear drastic, but we will address your concerns regarding suspending *habeas corpus*. General Matheson, do you want to discuss the *habeas corpus* issue?" Jon asked, turning to the attorney general, Elliot Matheson.

"Of course, Mr. Vice President, I am happy to do so."

Elliot Matheson was a product of Harvard Law. His peers nicknamed him "The Professor," who was scholarly even by Harvard standards. He was tall and lanky in his ill-fitting suit and wispy grey hair. Everyone respected him.

"The Constitution permits the suspension of *habeas corpus* in cases where public safety demands it due to rebellion or invasion," he began. "I believe contemporary events meet the criteria by a rebellion matched with the recent attempt to decapitate our government."

"Thank you, General Matheson," Jon said. "To contain the compact states, we must get out front and deploy a deterring force to encourage the rebelling states to back down voluntarily. But to have the option to deploy forces, we must suspend *habeas corpus*. Suspending *habeas* will allow the federal government to target and arrest state political, military, police, or civilian actors who are either participating in the rebellion or actively abridging the rights of U.S. Citizens. For example, the ringleader of this effort is the Governor of Arkansas. Suspending *habeas corpus* would allow us to arrest her, which is necessary.

Jon flipped a page on his notepad. "In addition to suspending *habeas*," he continued, "we need Congress to invoke the Insurrection Act of 1807 and suspend the *Posse Comitatus* Act during the declared national emergency.[40] The reason for this is simple. Even though the National Guard is already federalized, the Guard cannot secure or defend all national interests, property, or citizens alone. We need legal authority to send federal troops to help, and that legal authority must come from Congress."

Claire Turner interrupted again. "Hold on just a minute, Mr. Vice President. In your confirmation hearing, I asked you point blank whether you would advocate the use of violence, and your answer was no. Now, all I'm hearing is a plan that paves the way for using the military against our people. I can tell you right now that I'm not endorsing any of what I'm hearing. None of it."

"Leader Turner, actually, what I said at my hearing is that we should only use violence as a last resort. I believe I also testified that I believe battle may be necessary in some instances."

"Let him finish, please," Aidun demanded.

Jon resumed the discussion. "What is important here is that we prepare for a host of possibilities, such as the governor of Arkansas not responding to reason. I've already given her one chance to talk things out, and the response was, shall we say, vulgar. Anyway, let me be more plain. Intelligence revealed that the July 5th attack was aided and abetted by an associate justice of the Supreme Court and his wife, who was in contact with the Governor of Arkansas, among other right-wing extremists, before it happened. They had a strategy in place for the right moment and seized it when it came. My point is this: that is an extraordinary level of commitment to a cause. It is also a situation that demands we take some people into custody. To do that urgently, we not only must suspend *habeas*, but Congress must suspend *Posse Comitatus* or amend it further along the lines of the Enforcement Acts of 1870 and 1871."[41]

The Minority Leader interrupted again. She looked angry. "Mr. Vice President, you are going to have to give me more before I can endorse this!" she proclaimed.

"Claire, may I call you Claire?"

She nodded.

"I appreciate your concern, Claire. I truly do."

Jon was deploying a simple psychological device he learned when going up against an adverse witness. Use the witness's name. His studies showed that people like hearing their names, which often helps make an angry witness more agreeable. The other side of the coin is that a hostile witness can feel patronized. It was a gamble worth taking, and it wasn't at all clear how Turner would respond. She was cornered and mad as hell.

"Claire, let me approach it this way, and we can ask the attorney general to delve a little deeper into the legalities."

"But with great respect, Claire," Jon said as he plodded along, slowing his speech, "the issue you must first address is the source of your chief concern. Is it potential violence that concerns you? Or is it how the folks at home will perceive it? Think of it like this. This nation has cancer, and it needs some pretty strong medicine. Some people, including you, do not like the suggested medicine, and I get that." He lied.

On what planet does this woman live? Ridiculous.

"I don't appreciate your suggestion that I'm worried about re-election, Mr. Vice President," Turner shot back. "And that medicine you are suggesting? It has some severe side effects!"

"Touché, Claire, touché, I meant no disrespect," Jon lied again. "But I must add one thing that in my mind trumps all over consideration: locking down the rebelling states and protecting Americans is a moral imperative. Come what may, we must act decisively. You must agree with that, don't you?"

All eyes shifted toward Clair Turner, who sat in her chair wanting to be angry, but she was outfoxed. Jon leaned in. "Claire, I'll leave the politics to you, but our nation faces an existential threat, but I sense it will help if we put some more legal meat on the bone. As is the attorney general, I am prepared to do that now."

"Mr. Vice President," Turner said with all eyes on her as she shifted nervously in her chair, looking defeated, "I need more from you on the legal side. I may lose my seat over this, along with probably most of my colleagues. If I am going to gamble my seat, I would at least like to know that we are not breaking the law when I do."

"Of course," Jon said. "I was a lawyer in my previous life, so let me put that hat on for a minute unless the attorney general wants to jump in. General Matheson?"

"I'm happy to discuss it, Mr. Vice President."

"Please, go ahead," Jon said, grateful for the backup.

"Our government has suspended *habeas* before," Matheson stated as he morphed into full professor mode.

"Let's first address the Insurrection Act. The Insurrection Act of 1807 allows the U.S. president to deploy the military and federalize the National Guard to address civil unrest, insurrection, or rebellion. There can be no debate that we already face civil unrest, insurrection, and rebellion. The Act bypasses the *Posse Comitatus* Act, which limits military use in domestic law enforcement. Historically, the federal government has used the Insurrection Act to enforce desegregation and manage riots, but we could rely on the law in this situation."

"Let me interrupt you for a second," Jon said. "What about the Enforcement Acts of 1870 and 1871? Do they play a role in the legal framework?"

"They do," Matheson replied with a smile. "The Enforcement Act of 1870, in particular, does. It used to be referred to as the Ku Klux Klan Act. The law was used to curtail the Klan's and similar groups' oppressive activities by instituting harsh penalties for those infringing upon voting rights or public office eligibility. It criminalized force, bribery, and intimidation as means to obstruct voting, even authorizing the presidential deployment of federal troops and suspension of *habeas corpus* for enforcement. Later amendments targeted the Klan's organizational structure, empowering federal intervention, including using troops, suspending *habeas corpus*, and prosecuting civil rights conspirators. It also sanctioned federal lawsuits against state officials neglecting to protect citizens from civil rights violations."

"Thank you again, General Matheson, if I may," Jon said.

"Look, everyone, I appreciate Leader Turner's apprehension. But we have Americans to protect who live in these compact states, and we have the means to protect them and stop the assault on their collective liberty."

Jon stopped speaking and looked about the room at the small gathering before he started in again on the elephant in the room: politics.

"There is an elephant in this room, my friends, and the elephant is politics, but Congress needs to step in despite the political risk. Congress must declare its full-throated endorsement for the president to address the rebellion because that is what it is—a rebellion. The compact states are actively assaulting Americans' rights and have attacked the seat of government. What I am suggesting here isn't new and is not drastic under the circumstances. It is required. Historical precedent demands we act."

"At any rate," Jon said, "you may want to know what will practically occur. Elements of our government, including the military, will have the power to arrest persons and place them in military custody, subject to a military tribunal for waging war against the United States and its citizens. We are already in a *de facto* state of civil war, which must be treated as such, but there is much more."

"In my discussions with the attorney general before coming here," Jon resumed, "he made it clear the president has the authority to declare a state of emergency under the National Emergencies Act of 1976. Declaring a state of emergency will secure additional executive powers, but all the executive power in the world will be meaningless without Congress. And for the military to be involved, which is a must, Congress must create and authorize military districts to ease administration and assure unity of command."

Suddenly, Senate Minority Leader, Democratic Senator Brian Kuroda, erupted. "Military districts? This is beginning to sound like what happened leading up to the internment of Japanese Americans in World War Two. I won't have it!"

"Settled down, Brian," the Senate Majority Leader, Desmond Clarke, a Republican, reacted. "I think the goal here is to stop the further internment of Americans that is happening right now. Get a hold of yourself, man!"

Kuroda was a hothead liberal firebrand in the Senate with no love for decorum. His acerbic nature had earned him a reputation of being less than a man of his word.

The Speaker of the House, Bernice Atwood, joined the conversation abruptly. "I have a question: Could you boys in the Senate drop your dick-measuring contest for a second?" She was smiling. "The president does not have the authority to declare a military district?"

Senator Clarke grinned at Atwood's remark. Kuroda sulked.

Jesus, is this how policy is made in Washington? What the hell have I gotten myself into? Jon was half amused.

"No," Matheson replied to the question. "He does not. The President of the United States cannot legally declare a military district within the U.S. borders unless Congress authorizes it. During a national emergency, insurrection, or rebellion, Congress may grant the president additional powers to establish military control over specific areas."

"Again," Jon said, "we must have Congressional cooperation. Something that came up in my research, and I hope General Matheson agrees with me, is that Congress passed the Reconstruction Act of 1867 after the Civil War ended. In the Act, Congress divided the former Confederate states into five military districts, each governed by a Union general. Naturally, I would recommend consulting with military leadership before doing so. Still, if we use the military within our borders, there must be a framework for the military to do its work."

"My friends, I know these are some difficult things we discuss. But can we agree that we are all here because we care about our nation?" Jon spoke further while people looked left and right and nodded their heads.

"Let me get to the next subject," Jon said. "Compelling and disturbing intel forces us to act for an entirely different reason than the attack or the rebellion itself. For that, I invite the national security advisor to weigh in."

Celine Delacroix, retired Navy vice admiral, spent her entire adult life working within the national security apparatus in one department or division of government or another. She was fierce but measured. Jon liked and respected her immensely from their first meeting months ago on one of his trips to consult in Washington. During today's briefing, she positioned herself in the back of the room, listening to the conversation and appraising everything quietly. It was her nature to listen first and speak only when necessary, so she laid it out without fanfare.

"What I am about to tell all of you must not leave this room. The federal government has significant nuclear material that resides within the compact states. Intercepted communications inform that Texas and South Carolina state actors intend to seize nuclear facilities and hold the federal government hostage to force constitutional changes or risk secession and civil war."

The people gathered in the Oval Office sat in silence, then, with all eyes turned back at Admiral Delacroix, she continued her presentation.

"In Texas, there is the Pantex Plant. In South Carolina, the Savannah River Site. Both facilities build, refurbish, disassemble, test, and store nuclear devices and the materials used to make them. That's the unclassified part. The classified part is that security provided through the National Nuclear Security Administration cannot repel an organized military assault. We also have information from the Director of National Intelligence that elements sympathetic to the compact states infiltrated the Pantex facility with sleeper agents. We do not have data to suggest whether the Savannah River has been infiltrated, but Pantex has. Aside from what we are learning about Pantex in particular, many strategic national defense sites are sprinkled throughout the compact states. Think about munitions plants, chemical weapons storage facilities, and military bases. The results could be catastrophic if we lost control of Pantex, Savannah, or any number of other critical sites."

Jon studied the faces of everyone in the room as the reality of nuclear blackmail settled in. "Thank you, Admiral. Perhaps all of you with us today see the urgency more clearly now. But I'd like to revisit Claire Turner's concern about the use of force. I hope we can engage these governors and invite them to sit down with us to discover a way out of this, but I am not optimistic about it. We would have a stronger position in a conversation with the compact states if we had it from a position of demonstrated strength."

"By that, you mean you want to negotiate with a gun pointed at their heads," Kuroda shouted.

Jon paused and counted to five silently. "Leader Kuroda, that is exactly what I want. By swift and decisive action, we must deprive the compact states' ability to wage war. An insurgency will be bad enough, and with the actions I am recommending, we will secure the advantage to respond to whatever military action they try and throw at us."

Jon folded the paper back on his legal pad and then placed it on the floor at his feet. "Questions?"

Speaker Atwood spoke up while Kuroda fumed. "The suspension of *habeas* will be seen as extreme. On top of that, the suspension of *Posse Comitatus*? The Insurrection Act? Could that not backfire and drive a bigger wedge between the federal government and the compact states?"

President Aidun cut in. "Is there not already a wedge? Twenty-one states declared they wanted to secede. How much more of a wedge could there be? With respect, the pertinent question is whether we can risk losing control of nuclear material!"

"Let me say this," Jon volunteered. "I agree with the Speaker Atwood. These actions are extreme in isolation but reasonable under the circumstances."

"There is another consideration," Admiral Delacroix offered. "We must also demonstrate to the world that we control our nuclear arsenal. If we do not, we risk destabilizing the world."

General Brooks spoke up. "I am a student of military history. I have a Ph.D. in the subject. From the standpoint of the military, we can look to the Civil War as a precedent for using the military domestically. Recall that the *Posse Comitatus* Act wasn't passed until after the Civil War, and even then, exceptions existed to use federal troops within our borders. I do not doubt that federal troops can legally be deployed. Politically, I presume Congress can muster the will to engage the compact states militarily where necessary. Whether Congress has the intestinal fortitude to see it through is different. These are questions that you in this room must answer. I can assure you that our military will perform its duty. I must also warn that the military is a blunt and cumbersome tool, akin to performing neurosurgery with a chainsaw. It will not be neat. It will not be clean. It will take time, and morale will suffer, no matter how noble the cause."

Atwood spoke again. "Politically, this is a disaster, but the loss of a nation is greater, so I agree with everything proposed here and will support whatever legislation is needed. However, the progressive wing of the Democratic party will resist," she said as she looked over at Claire Turner. "Some left-wing members might be tempted to allow the compact states to withdraw from the Union. Others will categorically oppose any use of military force, even to protect American citizens, if you can believe that. Some are so far off the chain that they will vote against any measure designed to preserve the Union if it means the use of force is contemplated. But let me deal with them in my chamber, and I presume Desmond will deal with his chamber. I'll get the votes from the House one way or another."

The meeting continued with more raised voices and debate. The politics in the country portrayed by the media over the last several years had left Jon with little hope that these politicians could get anything done, even in the face of a civil war or nuclear blackmail. But it was also true that these people were shaken. Perhaps it took the advent of civil war to bring warring parties to a path of compromise, but if a compromise were to be reached, it wouldn't be in the Oval Office, at least not today.

The meeting ended, and Jon returned to his quarters at the Executive Office Building around 6:00 p.m. to a stack of folders and memos, but one had to eat, and Jon hadn't even called home yet.

28

Security Restoration Act

Jon realized he hadn't called home since touching down at Joint Base Andrews, so he called the new number assigned for the ranch. A Secret Service agent picked up on the other end and put Martin on the line.

"Hey, you," Jon said.

"Hey! I have been wondering when you'd call. Is everything OK?"

"Yeah. I'm all right. Exhausted. Sorry, I haven't been able to call sooner. We were in the air until this morning. I've never had a longer Monday in my entire life."

"So you are OK, yes?"

"I am, but the next few days will be crazy. How about you? Are you alright?"

"I'm great."

"How about Carl? Did he get settled in?"

Martin started laughing.

"Jesus, yes. Carl won't let me out of his sight. He's taken charge of the security around here and told the Secret Service they work for him. He's a piece of work! But yeah, all is well. I can do my thing without the Secret Service being too much of a pain in the ass."

"How's Chee? He OK?" Jon asked.

"Chee is great. He never seems too far away, but not in my face like Carl!" Martin replied.

Jon felt relieved.

"So what's it like in DC?" Martin asked.

"It's a different world than what I'm used to. I wasn't prepared for how absurd some of these politicians can be, especially the liberal ones. But I'm hanging in there. Today was my first exposure. I am sure I'll have more to share soon enough! Well, hey, I just wanted to check in, but I am going to hop off of here," Jon said with a tired voice. "I have some reading to do before tomorrow hits, and I'm going to have to get some sleep. I don't think I have ever been this tired. I love you. I'll call when I can tomorrow, OK?"

"Sounds good, love," Martin said.

Jon spent the rest of the evening reviewing notes with his speechwriter, preparing for Congress to deliver on his legislative requests. If Congress delivered, Jon and the president would take the news directly to the American people in a televised address.

It was about 10:00 p.m. when there was a knock at Jon's bedroom door.

"Mr. Vice President, it's Major Sims. Are you awake?"

"Come in, Sims."

Jon was reading an intelligence brief at a small writing desk in his temporary quarters.

Jon wasn't the only one who had a long day. Sims was still in his Air Force blues.

"What's up, Sims?"

"I've heard from the secretary of defense," Sims replied. "A special forces team is ready to deploy and arrest the Governor of Arkansas. The Secretary Ironwood mentioned that they will be in place by midnight tonight and then will await your order to apprehend the governor."

Jon stood up, ran his right hand through his hair, and smiled at Sims.

"Well, well, well. The shit is about to hit the fan," Jon said plainly. "Pass the word back to Secretary Ironwood that I want to contact the team leader directly before go time, but we cannot move until after Congress has sent the legislation to the president suspending *habeas* and *Posse Comitatus*. The president hopes Congress will get it to him by 10 a.m. If it doesn't get hung up in Congress, he'll sign it, and then we will go on national television

311

together at noon. I hope her arrest can be accomplished while we are on TV."

"Got anything else for me?" Jon asked as he walked toward a side table to pour himself a glass of water.

"No, sir," Sims replied. "See you in the morning, sir."

Sims shut the door behind him, and Jon returned to his desk to review more notes before calling it a night.

* * *

Jon woke from what felt like a coma on Tuesday morning, July 9th.

Jesus. 6 a.m. This is going to be one hell of a day.

A steward cleared breakfast from the table, and in a flash, it was just before 10 a.m. when the speechwriter and Jon agreed on Jon's speech to the nation. Just as the speechwriter left, Sims walked into the dining room with a gloomy expression.

"Mr. Vice President, the president asked you to come over and join him in the Oval."

"Has Congress sent the legislative package over?"

"Not yet."

"Oh no. Let's saddle up and find out what's happening."

Jon slammed down the rest of his coffee, donned his suit jacket, and followed Sims out the door and across the lane to the West Wing.

The sullen look on President Aidun's face spoke volumes when Jon walked into the Oval with Major Sims.

"Good morning, Mr. President," Jon said.

"I wish I could say it was a good morning, Jon. We managed to get the House of Representatives on board, but Kuroda blew it up in the Senate. They are about to vote, but it will happen only if the Republicans back it fully. It isn't looking good."

"Kuroda, huh? He was pretty hostile with me during my brief confirmation hearing, but that stuff in the Oval Office yesterday, I seriously thought he was acting."

"He has a terrible reputation for being volatile."

"What happens next?"

"We wait to hear from the Senate Majority Leader to see if he can deliver."

President Aidun's phone buzzed, and he picked it up.

"What do you have for me, Desmond?"

He listened.

"I see. Alright. I'll send him over."

Aidun sat the receiver back into the cradle and stood up.

"You're going to Capitol Hill, Jon. Major Sims, will you go out and summon the Secret Service? Tell them what's going on."

"Yes, Mr. President," and Sims excused himself from the Oval.

When the door shut, President Aidun addressed Jon, who was standing on the opposite side of the Resolute Desk.

"Well, my friend, you will have to go to Capitol Hill and be prepared to cast a tie-breaking vote. You may have to take charge of the chamber. Do what you have to do. Leader Clarke told me that he doesn't think the measure will pass but that it will be a tie if he can turn a couple of members in his caucus and a Democrat or two."

"What happened," Jon asked.

"Kuroda is playing a game to delay and has stirred up a hornet's nest. Go on over there. The Secret Service will take you to the majority's cloakroom, where you'll wait until the Majority Leader or his aide comes to collect you. If there is a tie, you will assume your position as President of the Senate and cast the tie-breaking vote. Don't underestimate Senator Clarke, though. Desmond may be able to pull it out, and don't be afraid to follow his lead."

* * *

The ride to Capitol Hill only lasted a few minutes, but Jon, during the drive over, resolved to take matters into his own hands. So, when he arrived, he asked the Secret Service to escort him directly to the floor of the Senate, where he planned to take over the proceedings as President of the Senate.[42]

Jon stepped into the chamber, and when he did, the Sergeant at Arms announced his presence. "Ladies and Gentleman, the Vice President of the United States and President of the Senate."

Jon walked down the aisle toward the presiding officer's dais, where the president *pro tempore* of the Senate, the junior Senator from Utah, presided over the ongoing debate about President Aidun's legislative package. As Jon made his way down the aisle, he caught a glimpse of Senator Brian Kuroda, huddled with a group of senators off to one side of the well. Jon smiled as he approached Senator Kuroda to greet him.

"Good morning, Brian," Jon said with false cheer.

That mother fucker is going to pay a heavy price when this is over, Jon thought to himself.

Senator Clarke intercepted Jon at the bottom of the stairs leading up to the dais.

"Mr. Vice President, I don't know if we'll have the votes on this, but we're still whipping. My side will come together, but the Democrats are another story."

"Let me have a crack at 'em before the vote is called," Jon suggested. "I am, after all, the president of this body, and I have a right to be heard. If it's not a winner today, I can say I made the president's case."

The president p*ro tempore* banged the gavel, indicating a brief recess in the Senate proceedings to address Jon. "Does the President of the Senate desire to assume the Chair?"

"He does," Jon said in reply, at which point, the Junior Senator from Utah stood up and shook Jon's hand as Jon walked up to the dais.

Jon sat down, took the gavel, and banged it on its pedestal three times. "The Chair will call the Senate back to order and ask the leaders to come forward to address the Chair."

Desmond Clarke walked to the center of the well, as did Brian Kuroda, and the two stood side-by-side.

"The Chair invites the Majority Leader to address the chamber regarding the status of the pending legislative package entitled the Security Restoration Act."[43]

"Good morning, Mr. President. In response to the Chair's inquiry, most

314

of my caucus supports the measure as written that has already passed in the House of Representatives not long ago. However, I am advised by Minority Leader Kuroda that he intends to filibuster the measure."[44]

"Thank you, Leader Clarke. The Chair now invites Minority Leader Kuroda to address the Chair's inquiry. Leader Kuroda?"

Kuroda was fuming at the sight of Jon, his face taking on a reddish hue.

"Mr. President," he began haltingly, "this is most irregular!"

"Are you saying the Vice President of the United States is not also the President of this body?" Jon returned.

"No, um, no, I am not." Kuroda stammered.

"Then kindly answer the Chair's inquiry, if you please, sir."

"Mr. President, my caucus opposes the SRA, and some members informed their intent to filibuster the measure until significant changes are made. I don't believe the measure would pass as-is if it is called for a vote."

"And why is that, Leader Kuroda? Would you not agree that the SRA is an urgent response to answer a clear and present existential threat to our nation?"

"I do, Mr. President, but I believe it goes too far in allowing the use of force to address the threat."

"Alright. Perhaps it would help if the Chair addressed the issue. As President of the Senate, I have a right to be heard. I presume there is no objection."

"The minority objects!" Kuroda stammered.

"The Chair notes your objection, Leader Kuroda, but your objection is overruled. I'd refer you to Article I, Section 3 of our beloved Constitution. I aim to inform this body further of what the Administration intends by the proposed legislation. Of course, the Chair may not vote on a measure unless this body is equally divided, but the right of the Chair to have a voice is implicit by the very position itself. So, if it please you, Leader Kuroda, you may take your seat."

Brian Kuroda's otherwise olive skin turned lobster red as he moved toward his desk. A few Republican Senators sneered at him as he walked by. What little esteem he held among his Republican colleagues evaporated by the second. It was a fluke that the Democrats elected him to lead their caucus in the first place, and some Democrats were beginning to think electing him as leader was a mistake.

Jon watched the somewhat chastened Senator Kuroda take his seat as he began his remarks. "Esteemed Senators, I realize it is rare for a sitting vice president to preside here unless he is here to break a tie. Believe me, I wouldn't be here if I were not convinced that delaying the current legislation threatens our security. The failure to act decisively in the face of what happened is irresponsible. The failure to answer it will only embolden other states to follow suit with what Arkansas has done and is doing. It would be best to see what the Arkansas governor is doing as a beta test. If her actions go unanswered, armed conflict is assured. However, enacting the SRA here and now will allow the Administration to move forward from a position of strength. Do not expect us to reel the rebelling states back without giving us the tools to do it."

Kuroda stood up and yelled at Jon from his chair, "You won't get away with this legislation! We will never pass it!"

Jon banged the gavel once. "Now, Leader Kuroda, we will have order in this chamber, but since you have laid down an ultimatum, perhaps we should explore its roots. Ladies and gentlemen, I believe Leader Kuroda's actions belie his true intent. I believe this because after our meetings in the Oval Office yesterday. I was curious about the source of Leader Kuroda's intense objection to these measures, so I looked into Leader Kuroda. With all due respect to his position, I believe his allegiance to our country is misaligned."

Then, a hush settled over the Senate, and Jon continued his accusation.

"My research indicated Leader Kuroda's belief system is rooted in an offshoot of an anarchist political theory known as 'anarcho-syndicalism.'[45] I even found a thesis he wrote as a Ph.D. candidate that endorsed 'green syndicalism.' His former and current ties make it clear he has no love for the federal government. He's an activist who got elected to the Senate, and his actions today make me wonder if he would be happy if the rebelling states left the union altogether. Such a position would be consistent with the views he has espoused before."

Leader Kuroda stood up and yelled at Jon from his desk in the Senate Chamber while Jon enjoyed his moment. "How dare you accuse me of disloyalty to this country! How dare you! We should have never approved your nomination. You should be impeached for slandering me!"

Jon banged the gavel once and then set it back down as some Senators stood, one calling out, "Point of order! Point of order!"

"The Senator from Washington," Jon ordered, "will restrain himself at once," Jon admonished.

"While the Chair might enjoy a têt-a-têtes with Leader Kuroda over his extreme leftist views, now is not the time or place for that because this body has an act to consider - the SRA. Each of you must set aside whatever regional interests you behold in favor of what is best for the United States. You took an oath to defend the Constitution from enemies, foreign and domestic. This is your chance to fulfill that oath. A civil war is brewing, and the enemy fired the first shots on July 5th. We must now be prepared to put an end to the chaos."

"I am a Senator of the United States, and I will be heard!" Kuroda yelled again.

"You, sir, are out of line, out of order, and unrecognized. If you indulge in another outburst, I will remove you from the Senate Chamber."

Kuroda stood still, paralyzed behind his desk.

"Given the current state of affairs," Jon continued, "the Chair will call for a brief ten-minute recess and ask the Senate Leadership, including you, Leader Kuroda, to meet in the majority cloakroom before moving forward to a vote. We are in recess."

Down came the gavel, and Jon stood up from the chair.

* * *

Kuroda rushed toward Jon in the cloakroom, but a Secret Service agent stepped between them.

"Step back, sir," the Secret Service agent commanded.

317

"You have no right to accuse me like that, Mr. Vice President," Kuroda blasted.

"I have every right, Brian," Jon calmly said, looking around the hulking body of his guard, "but we'll save our debate for another day."

"You know Brian, you're not going to get very far if you don't have the votes," Desmond Clarke said, bluffing.

"I have the votes, you idiot." Kuroda barked.

"Are you sure about that, Brian?" Clarke said with a smirk as he doubled down on his bluff.

"Let me be blunt, gentlemen," Jon said. "I will make it my mission to politically destroy whoever stands in the way of the SRA because we will be powerless to bring the compact states to the table without it. If we cannot check the Arkansas governor, this situation will devolve into civil war. And I'll make you a promise, Brian..."

"You can't promise anything!" Brian stammered.

"Oh, yes, I can. I can promise that I will use every lever of power to make sure your anarchist past turns you into a pariah that will cost you your seat. Or is that not important to you?"

Leader Clarke turned to Jon and ignored Kuroda, who was standing right there. Tripling down on his bluff, Clarke declared, "Mr. Vice President, I think you need to advance this to a full vote of the house right now."

Kuroda rolled his eyes.

"That's your call, Desmond," Jon said. "You are the Majority Leader, so control the agenda. But what about the filibuster?"

"We'll need one Democrat to side with us to invoke cloture, but I'll have to get my caucus together.[46] The fence-sitters will jump on board 100% after what they just heard. None will want to be seen as being in league with an anarchist. We may have to go nuclear on his ass even if we get through this, Mr. Vice President, at least for this type of legislation, because, as you can see, Brian doesn't have much personal restraint. Plus, his grip on his caucus is rather loose. I doubt this will be the last time he tries to obstruct common-sense legislation."

"Is that true, Brian? Are you having a little trouble with your caucus?"

Jon asked with a raised eyebrow at Kuroda.

"I don't have to tell you anything, Mr. Vice President, but we will filibuster."

"OK, Brian," Jon said, turning to Majority Leader Clarke, "Well, Desmond, there's your answer. How much time do you need to get with your caucus before I reconvene the Senate?"

"Mr. Vice President, all I need is five minutes, ten tops. I'm going to lay down the law, and they will follow. I knew Brian could be a problem when his caucus elected him as Minority Leader, so we've prepared for this, but I still have some assurances to give. When we're ready, I'll ask you to recognize me to call for a vote on the SRA. Brian must first raise a point of order if he tries to filibuster. But I came prepared. I have a formal cloture motion. It will be irregular, but I'll ask for a cloture vote right there when I file the motion."

"Let's hope we don't have to do all that. We have a pretty short timetable, Desmond," Jon said with a concerned look on his face.

"The Senate moves slowly, Mr. Vice President, but I hope today will be an exception. Besides, I only need one Democrat added to my caucus to invoke cloture. I think I've got one in the bag. Brian doesn't know who it is and won't have time to whip his party."

"Alright, Desmond. I'll wait here until you come get me."

* * *

In the intervening minutes before going back into session, Jon called President Aidun.

"You'll never believe this," Jon said.

"What happened? I thought they were nearly tied in the Senate."

"Not even close. Kuroda is leading a revolt against the SRA and threatened filibuster!"

"Goddamn, the Senate and its rules," the president said. "It's hard to get anything through there, but I thought in this one instance the Senate would be the adult in the room and the House would be the problem, but this time

319

it is the other way around."

"Mr. President, I had a hunch about Kuroda, so last night I researched him. Something didn't sit right with me after our meetings yesterday. I surmise that he'd like to see the entire union fail so he can foster some paradise in an independent Arcadia in the Pacific Northwest. He wrote a thesis about it while a Ph.D. student at the University of Washington, grounding his thesis in a radical anarchist political theory known as 'anarcho-syndicalism.' In other writings, he advocated anarchist political theories while an undergraduate at the University of Puget Sound. It is clear to me those radical leanings influence his judgment in this situation."

"Those guys from the Pacific Northwest are a different breed," President Aidun said. "They think they are a nation unto themselves. So, what now?"

"I'm waiting for the Majority Leader. He assures me he can get his entire caucus to support the SRA, but to win the day, he needs one Democrat to join in a cloture vote if Kuroda initiates a filibuster."

"I never thought we'd be in so deep with the Republicans," President Aidun said.

"Me neither. Political scientists can debate why the Republicans are siding with the SRA when prior logic would suggest they'd oppose it. Perhaps they want to completely distance themselves from the crazy that led to all this. By joining the SRA, they will reinforce their brand as the true patriots in the Congress."

* * *

A nervous-looking male page dressed in a grey suit walked briskly into the cloakroom. He couldn't have been older than twenty.

"Mr. Vice President, the Senate is ready for you."

Jon and his Secret Service contingent returned to the Senate Chamber through a side door. The Senators sat behind their desks except for Desmond Clarke, who met Jon at the bottom of the dais.

"Mr. Vice President, my caucus will support the SRA, and I have the one Democratic Senator we need to support cloture."

320

"Got it," Jon said. "Let's get to work!"

Jon sat back in the President's chair, grasped the hourglass-shaped marble gavel, and banged it three times.

"The Senate will come to order," Jon called out.

Desmond Clarke, still standing in the well, the podium in the middle of the well below the dais.

"The Chair recognizes the Majority Leader."

"Unanimous consent no longer exists," Clarke stated.

"Very well," Jon acknowledged.

Kuroda approached the lectern as Clarke stood aside.

"The Chair recognizes the Minority Leader."

"Leader Clarke is correct. I withdraw my consent and demand further debate on the Security Restoration Act."

"Then the Senate Floor is yours, Leader Kuroda. You may proceed."

Before Kuroda could open his mouth, Desmond Clarke approached the podium and shouted, "I raise a point of order."

"The Chair recognizes Majority Leader Desmond Clarke."

"Mr. President," Clarke said, "I am filing a written motion for cloture."

When Clarke said those words, the same page who summoned Jon back to the chamber walked forward with a stack of papers and handed them to the Clerk of the Senate, sitting at the lower part of the dais.

"The Clerk will read the motion," Jon directed.

"I, Desmond Clarke, move to invoke cloture on the debate of the Security Restoration Act, S. 210, and that the Senate consider it immediately. Mr. President, the motion appears to be signed by every majority party member constituting 34 Republican Senators."

"I raise a point of order, Mr. President," Kuroda called out.

"We will address your point of order directly, Leader Kuroda."

A few boos emitted forth from the Democrats in the chamber, and Jon banged the gavel down.

"There will be order in the Senate!" Jon called out.

"But Mr. President, cloture normally calls for a wait period before a vote is called."

"Mr. Kuroda, you are not recognized."

"May I be recognized?" Desmond Clarke called.

"You remain recognized, Leader Clarke."

"I would ask the Chair to call the matter of cloture for a vote now."

"Very well. The Clerk will perform a roll-call vote on the pending cloture motion."

The clerk stood from his position and began calling the names of each Senator in alphabetical order by last name. Jon listened while the clerk read the names and recorded each response on a notepad until he recognized an "aye" belonging to the Junior Senator from Nevada, a Democrat. More boos erupted from the Democratic side.

Jon grabbed the gavel and slammed it down.

"There will be order in this Chamber, or you will be removed! The Clerk will complete the roll call vote!" Jon thundered from the Chair.

"This is irregular!" came a voice from the well.

"The Sergeant Arms will remove the Senator!"

Jon had no idea who called out the objection and didn't care as he repeatedly smashed the marble gavel on its pedestal as hard as he could.

"The Sergeant at Arms will remove any Senator who disrupts these proceedings immediately!"

The Senate Sergeant at Arms, dressed in a dark suit and assisted by his staff, walked from the dais toward the Democratic side while an assistant dressed in the same uniform walked down the aisle from the opposite end of the Senate Chamber.

At last, the Clerk of the Senate stood up from his post and read aloud the list of Senators and their votes.

"The motion for cloture regarding the Security Restoration Act is adopted by a vote of 35 votes in favor constituting 3/5ths of the Senate."

Jon banged the gavel again as Desmond Clarke approached the lectern.

"The Chair recognizes Majority Leader Clarke."

"Mr. President, I rise and move for a roll call vote for the passage of the Security Restoration Act."

"The Chair agrees. The Clerk will conduct a roll call vote on the Security

Restoration Act now pending."

The clerk conducted another roll call vote, and the matter passed by the same number of votes cast to invoke cloture. When it was done, the clerk announced: "The final version of the Security Restoration Act, as previously adopted in the House of Representatives, is adopted by a vote of 35 Senators in favor."

"The Chair directs the Clerk to transmit the bill's final version to the President of the United States certifying that the Senate and the House of Representatives have adopted it."

Desmond Clarke stood again at the podium while his colleagues on his side of the aisle stood, clapping and cheering.

"The Chair recognizes the Senate Majority Leader, Desmond Clarke."

"I move for adjournment," Clarke announced from the pulpit.

"The Senate stands adjourned," Jon replied. He finally brought the gavel down before setting it in a large wooden box on the end of the long desk. Then he stood up and walked down to the well to shake the hands of several Republican Senators who came forward to greet him.

* * *

It was nearly 3 p.m. when Jon returned to the White House, where he went directly to the Oval Office to sit and wait with the president for the final version of the SRA to arrive so President Aidun could sign it. While the two remained in the office, Jon called Secretary Ironwood to check on the status of the operation to secure the Governor of Arkansas.

"Mr. Vice President, the Special Forces Team Leader is on standby and ready to deploy from Little Rock Air Force Base to arrest the governor. They have eyes on her at the Governor's Mansion. They will insert from helicopters deployed from the base on your command."

"Thank you for the news, Secretary Ironwood. We'll be legal when the President signs the SRA. Remind the team leader of my signal, which I will give during the press conference."

National news networks buzzed about the action in the Senate, and the

323

White House Briefing Room was packed with reporters when the President signed the SRA into law at 3:45 p.m.

29

The Freeman Doctrine

L ate Tuesday afternoon, Tiny walked into his friends' living room in Burlington, where he was staying. He turned on the TV to watch the president's address. Even though Tiny wasn't keen to keep up with the news, he wouldn't miss the first presidential address since the attacks on the Capitol.

Tiny could red-neck it up with the best of them back in Arkansas, passing as one of "them." No one ever suspected he was gay, but now, he lived where he didn't have to hide. He could be himself even though he hated what was happening in Arkansas and throughout the country. Most of all, Tiny was lonely because Rick never joined him in Vermont as the two had planned. Rick wanted to delay leaving Arkansas until saying goodbye to his mom and dad, but Tiny couldn't wait with him. Staying in Arkansas, even for a couple of days, wasn't an option after everything that went down with Misty.

After Tiny left town, the last person to see Rick was a neighbor who said she had seen him pulling out of their driveway two days before but hadn't seen him since. He wondered if the Defenders had arrested Rick. Already, Defenders had detained dozens of gay and lesbian people throughout Arkansas. No one was safe. Queer bar raids were common, as were arrests for citizen-reported "gay activity" like public displays of affection or even a rainbow sticker on the back of a car window. Alexander and Pretty were still missing, too. It was all so surreal. It was so sad.

Tiny settled into an easy chair with a diet cola in a large plastic cup and clicked on the TV as the Fox News host announced, "We are live from the White House, where the president is to address the nation."

The screen changed to show the platform in the White House Press Briefing Room. President Aidun walked to the podium with a grim expression. Grasping the podium with both hands, he began his address.

"My fellow Americans. A few days ago, on July 5, domestic terrorists assassinated the president, vice president, the Speaker of the House, and several other bystanders at the East Entrance of the Capital Building. Within minutes after the attack, this government followed the Presidential Succession Act, which transfers presidential powers when the Office of the President becomes vacant. I was next in line. I want you to know that I acted to guarantee the stability and continuity of our government and assure our continued security at home and abroad. Part of securing our government included selecting a vice president. Your country and government are safe and secure. We will move forward, bury our dead, and address the crimes committed against the nation."

President Aidun adjusted his eyeglasses slightly as he continued following the teleprompter. "The day before the assassinations, on July 4, the governors of 21 states signed a declaration of secession. In response, I inform every American that this government will not permit any state to secede. It is unlawful and unconstitutional. Our democracy is precious, requiring all states to cooperate in unison to make it work. If we become divided, we will perish as a nation."

The president continued. "To assist me in responding to the secessionist movement and later to help knit us back together, I introduce Vice President Jonathan Christian Freeman. I've asked him to lead a task force to respond as necessary to the secessionists, to protect federal assets, and to protect you, the citizens."

Tiny was mid-sip when he nearly choked at the mention of Jon's name, and there he was, standing next to the president.

Jon shook President Aidun's hand and approached the podium.

"Hello, my fellow Americans. My name is Jonathan Christian Freeman. As President Aidun said, my sole focus will be to stop the secessionist movement. The compact states, as they call themselves, are acting illegally. They cannot just walk away from our Constitution and the precious rights it protects by dressing up their actions in the pseudo-legality of the New Law. I am originally from one of those states, Arkansas, and I have witnessed first-hand the evils the New Law perpetrates on everyday citizens."

"There is also something you should know about me. I did not seek this job, and I do not have political aspirations," Jon continued. "Before this happened, I was concerned with my job, my family, making a living, and the everyday things one does in life. I'll also tell you that I damn sure didn't want the government involved in my private life. At the end of the day, like most of you, I want to be left alone to live my life as I see fit. I don't need government officials telling me how to live, act, or think. But recent developments with the New Law created an enemy of freedom in the false name of liberty, which made me angry. Before, 'liberty' was a word that meant self-determination, privacy, and the right to be left alone. It was a shield against government intrusion into private lives. Now, extreme Republicans in compact states weaponized the term and made it a license to trample minority rights in the name of freedom."

Tiny sat there with his mouth opened wide, watching his old friend who was transformed into a different person than the Jon Freeman he had known for so many years.

Continuing his address, Jon said, "For whatever duration I hold this office, I pledge to you that I will try my best to help end the assault on the fundamental right of Americans to live and be as they please so long as their chosen way of life does not infringe on anyone else. Above all, I will do everything I can within the law to bring the compact states and their leaders to justice."

Jon's voice became more steeled, "So if you live in one of the states whose governor signed the declaration of secession, I have a message for you. This government will not rest until every American can enjoy the fullest fruits of authentic liberty without fear, regardless of where you live. You will no longer have cause for worry if you are not white. You will not fear being arrested if you are LGBTQ or living in a same-sex marriage. You will not need to fear prosecution if you are a woman who requires an abortion. You will not need to worry about discrimination against you because you do not practice Christianity or believe in any religion. On the other side of that coin, if you are religious, you will have the right to your belief without fear of government intrusion so long as your ideas do not harm or impact anyone else or their rights. You see, my fellow Americans, one has as much a right to practice his religion as another has a right to be free from having it practiced on him."

Jon flipped a notebook page on the podium and continued his address. "But there is more to this because the president tasked me to deliver a clear message that leaves no room for misunderstanding. The United States government is taking unprecedented action. Federal troops, drawn from every branch of our military, will descend upon any compact state to uphold our citizens' civil rights. Our military's mission when called upon is to liberate internment camps, safeguard federal property, restore individual liberties, and apprehend any state actor abridging any American's rights."

"Let me give you an example of what I mean exactly. We have credible intelligence that right-wing, state-sponsored actors, in collusion with an associate justice of the Supreme Court, orchestrated the brazen attack carried out on July 5. We possess damning evidence that some state officials are plotting to assault other federal facilities integral to our national defense infrastructure to destabilize our government. Those implicated will stand accused of treason and sedition against the United States. This includes state governors. I solemnly swear we will not rest until every responsible party faces justice. To those state officials involved in harming or unlawfully detaining American citizens, we will relentlessly track you down and hold you accountable. As I speak, operations are in motion to apprehend key actors within the compact states, including the associate justice of the Supreme Court who played a pivotal role in orchestrating the attack on our Capitol."

After a strategic pause in his address, Jon continued his speech. "Once we've quashed the compact states effort to unravel our union, we'll uncover the truth behind this crisis. I'll spare no effort to bridge the divides among us. But the healing won't begin until our nation is secure from these unlawful attempts to tear it apart. I'm well aware that deep-seated cultural rifts have festered for decades, breeding mistrust between rural and coastal communities. Urban and rural, coastal or interior. We are all different but share the same continent and breathe the same air. We care for our children, parents, families, and friends. But sadly, trust in one another has eroded to the point where we expect the worst of one another. We must rebuild trust, and we must learn to coexist peacefully."

"Many people," Jon continued, "follow religions. Some follow none at all. I hope we can repair this nation so that if you are a person of faith, you may practice your faith unhindered by your neighbors or the government. But that umbrella of religious freedom is a right that will not protect you when you inflict your belief on others. The only way this works, ladies and gentlemen, is when religious freedom is met with equal tolerance and respect. We won't follow the path of a former president who boasted of building physical walls. No, we'll fortify the wall our Founders envisioned between church and state, higher and stronger than ever. And as your government, we're committed to making the 14th Amendment's equal protection guarantees a concrete certainty, not something we merely discuss in political science classes. Hate crimes will have no place in our society and will be met with fierce criminal prosecution. Differences in gender, sexual orientation, gender identity, culture, race, or religion will no longer be excuses for harming one another."

Jon grasped the podium and slowed the pace of his speech even further. "So here is another message I want everyone to hear: if you or someone you know has been illegally arrested, harmed, harassed, or otherwise had your rights taken away, come forward. At the end of this broadcast, we will give you various ways to contact the federal government to report such incidents in your area. No stone will be left unturned until every bad actor is removed from power and prosecuted. I want you to realize that some of the actions we will take as a government will seem, at first, to be extreme.

All state militias, police, or other state actors are notified that they will be apprehended and arrested for the slightest abridgment of any citizen's rights."

While Tiny sat dumbfounded with the surprise of his friend addressing the nation, that same friend, through coded speech in his address, had given the order for the special forces team to apprehend and arrest the Governor of Arkansas.

30

Operation Red Boots

"The governor is here. She's in the kitchen," Lieutenant Pettigrew whispered over his cell phone.

"Thank you, Lieutenant," a voice on the other end said. "I recommend you bug out. A tactical team will be inbound in less than five minutes. Go to the location we gave you for extraction."

Lieutenant Pettigrew was finally getting his revenge. Smiling, he slipped through the garage and jogged toward an awaiting FBI vehicle three blocks away. Meanwhile, Buckshot sat in a breakfast nook watching Jon's address while sipping a cold beer with her red cowboy boots propped up on the side of the table. She was unmoved by Jon's promises to get control over the compact states.

What a pussy, she thought. *He doesn't have the balls to come after me.*

The sound of a trio of military helicopters interrupted her thoughts, and the sound grew louder and louder until the noise was a roar, and the trees swayed outside her kitchen window.

"Haystack!" she yelled, getting up to investigate when breaking glass showered around her as special operations soldiers crashed through her kitchen windows.

"Mother fuck!" she shouted as an operative tackled and took her to the floor.

"Gag and hood her, and for the love of God, remove those goddamned boots," the female team leader insisted.

Buckshot called out again for Lieutenant Pettigrew, but he was nowhere to be found. Perhaps one of the worst life choices Lieutenant Pettigrew ever made was to work for that heifer, but he more than rectified it when he decided to cooperate with her arrest.

While the soldiers wrestled the corpulent Arkansas governor to the floor, a certain associate Supreme Court justice and his wife desperately threw personal items in an overnight bag to get out of town. Their efforts were too little, too late, to avoid the FBI Swat Team rapidly advancing on their summer home in Savannah, Georgia.

The associate justice was an African American archconservative in a mixed-race marriage with his white wife, which was a rich irony given that the Supreme Court on which he served was willing to overrule itself in *Loving v. Virginia*, the case that initially legalized mixed-race marriages throughout the United States. His wife was embedded within white nationalist and right-wing conservative groups, and he was a pariah among liberals as a justice-for-hire.

After the president and vice president completed their joint address, they relocated to the White House Situation Room to monitor the arrests of the Arkansas governor, the Supreme Court justice, and his wife. In a one-two punch, the president and vice president had initiated the first response to the attack on the Capitol.

Special Forces dragged the discalced Governor of Arkansas through the mansion's front door to the awaiting Sikorsky with blades turning. Several Defenders in their black Suburbans skidded to stops surrounding the governor's mansion and opened fire, but the Special Forces Team leader anticipated resistance and was ready. So, when the Defenders arrived, two Army Apache AH-64D attack helicopters were already on station far above the mansion, providing overwatch and covering fire.

The first of many bullets flew from a Defender AR-15, and the Apaches answered the shots with two volleys of Hydra 70 Rockets aimed at each Defender SUV, destroying all six of them instantly with brilliant explosions.

In the White House Situation Room, President Aidun and Jon viewed

Operation Red Boots on a military live stream from the air. They both patiently awaited news that the team was uninjured and accounted for. A comforting radio call came in as the flight of helicopters rose on the screens: "Red Boots in custody. No casualties. Returning to base."

* * *

Like ants from an anthill, the Defenders mustered and deployed two convoys of Defender Suburbans that raced along I-40 East toward Little Rock Air Force Base. The Arkansas adjutant general, Rhys Hampton, ordered the Defenders to form a blockade of the main entrance to the Air Force Base, enter if possible, and secure the governor. That wasn't his first act of treason against his country, and it would not likely be his last.

"We are going to show the bastards that we won't take it lyin' down!" commanded General Hampton when he gave the order over the NSA-monitored communications channel. Perhaps he believed he could intimidate the capable Air Force Security Police Squadron guarding the base to give the governor up.

The lead Defender vehicle pulled toward the main gate. It stopped short of it and crossed the road for traffic coming in the opposite direction. In turn, Defender vehicles followed suit. As they did, Air Force SPs deployed six M113 Armored Personnel Carriers and an equal number of Lenco Bearcats equipped with enhanced armor and weapons mounts that supported M2 .50 caliber machine guns. To their credit, the Defenders stood their ground. Not a single vehicle could pass in or out of the base. However, the Air Force SP commander had different plans.

"Main Gate, Command. We have a SITREP," radioed the SP detachment commander to Base Operations.

"Go ahead, Main Gate."

"Command, these locals are blocking the main entrance. A dozen vehicles, comprising roughly 50 uniformed men, have dismounted and are armed with AR-15s. I don't see heavy weapons. Only assault rifles," the detachment commander reported.

"Any demands?" Command inquired.

"Nothing," replied the detachment commander.

"Wait one, Main Gate. The base commander wants to get on the line."

The base commander, a full-bird colonel, picked up the microphone.

"Base Command, Main Gate. Send someone out there, establish contact with those morons, and see what they want. Do not fire on those nuggets unless they fire on you first. If they do, wear them slick!"

"Copy that," the detachment commander replied. "Main Gate, Out."

The detachment commander walked over to a senior master sergeant named Jefferson.

"What do you think? Base Command wants us to go out and talk," asked the younger detachment commander.

"Well, sir, whatever Base Command wants, Base Command gets," Jefferson replied. "Want me to go out there and see what's what?"

"Why not," the detachment commander allowed. "Leave your weapon here. Don't give those assholes a reason to shoot you. But if those fuckers so much as put a finger on a trigger, I will light their asses up."

"Easy, sir. Let me talk with these guys."

Jefferson sat his weapon next to a Humvee and approached the line of black Suburbans with his hands in the air.

Jefferson was an African American from Cherry Valley, Arkansas, who had enlisted in the Air Force nearly twenty years ago. This was his terminal assignment, and even though he was nearing retirement, he was still built like a brick shithouse from cover to boots. He cut an imposing figure as he held his hands above his head and walked toward the line of black Suburbans that were two deep, parked across both lanes of the otherwise busy road. The July heat in the Arkansas River valley was suffocating as he approached the Defenders, who trained their assault rifles on him.

The Defender captain was a 50-year-old man named Bobby who had served ten years in the U.S. Army right out of high school before spending the next twenty years working as a deputy sheriff of Cross County, Arkansas. His last day of service as a sheriff's deputy was his 48th birthday. He thought he had his fill of law enforcement until the Defenders recruited him. So here

334

he was, with the rank of a Captain of Defenders, enthusiastically serving the most recent extension of MAGA.

"Hold it right there, Boy," Bobby commanded.

Senior Master Sergeant Jefferson was about 50 yards away and kept walking.

"The only man who ever got away with calling me 'boy' was my old man, and he's been dead for 30 years," Jefferson said. "You can call me Jefferson. I'm from Cherry Valley. Ever heard of it?" Jefferson said as he continued striding toward the Defenders' position.

This guy deserves a beat down, Jefferson thought as he continued walking.

Bobby was also from Cross County, having grown up in Wynne, the county seat.

"No shit," Bobby the Defender yelled, "I'm from Wynne. What's your name?"

"Jefferson's my name. What's yours?"

"Bobby Wilcox. Wait, Jefferson. Jefferson. I knew some Jeffersons from Cherry Valley back when I was a kid," Wilcox said.

"First name is Tindell," Jefferson said. "I remember you, Bobby Wilcox. You were a couple of years ahead of me. Your dad and my dad worked together at the Copper Tubing Plant."

"Jesus Christ. Yep. That is you," Wilcox said. "Well, partner, we got us a problem here, I reckon. Come on over, then. Let's talk."

Jefferson turned to his commander, who was watching closely, shot him a thumbs-up, then walked over to Bobby Wilcox. The two shook hands.

Jefferson looked at Bobby and asked, "What do you all expect from this?"

"All I know is that the adjutant general ordered us to come here to get the governor back. Until I do, my orders are to hold this position—no one on or off the base. I expect to hear from the adjutant general soon."

"Look, Bobby," Jefferson explained, "The governor isn't on the base."

"What do you mean?" Bobby said incredulously, "I saw the helicopters fly across town toward the base after they raided the Governor's Mansion. Saw it with my own eyes, dude."

"You and I saw the same thing, but did you see that C-130 take off not long ago? The governor was on it."

"Well, shit. I'm going to have to call this in." Bobby said.

Jefferson volunteered, "I'd do that if I were you, and you might want to ask the people who sent you over here to order you to pack up. None of this is going to end well for you, Bobby. It won't end well for you, for your boys here, or for whatever MAGA idea you all are fighting for."

"Oh hell, Tindell, you're all right, but people like me, like us, my boys here, we've been shut out and ignored, and we're not having it anymore. Things aren't like when you and I were kids growing up."

"I don't think you'd say that if your skin was as black as mine," Jefferson said without guile.

"Maybe not," Bobby replied, "but just the same, things aren't going our way anymore."

Tindell Jefferson wasn't a progressive. He was like most people he knew who believed people should mind their own fuckin' business. He also thought these MAGA asshats were dangerous. Even though this guy might be from his childhood, if that motherfucker stepped out of line, Jefferson would be the first to pull the trigger.

"Bobby, I have to go back and report to my commander in a minute. What am I going to tell him?"

Bobby and his 200 lbs. frame stood in the July heat, sweating profusely under the black fatigues.

"Tindell, tell him not to get trigger-happy and to give us a few to sort this out," Bobby said.

"Bobby, let me suggest something. We have you outgunned. This shit could easily get out of hand the longer you drag this out. But our rules of engagement are that we won't fire on you if you don't fire on us. You're not on federal property. If you were, we probably wouldn't be catching up on our Cross County childhood. Hear me? I will walk back to my boss and give them a SITREP. I want it to say that you all are bugging out."

"Let me see what I can do. I need some time," Bobby said.

Jefferson shook Bobby's hand again and returned to the vehicles before the main gate.

As he walked away, he heard one of the Defenders say, "Hey Bobby, you're not going to let that nigger tell you what to do, are you?"

Jefferson stopped, turned around, and looked at the twenty-something scraggly-looking redheaded man talking at Bobby Wilcox with less than a full complement of teeth.

"Hey, care to repeat what you just said to my face, you snaggle-tooth motherfucker?" demanded Jefferson of Redhead.

Bobby stuck his arm across Redhead's chest and said, "Hold on a minute, Tindell, he didn't mean anything by it. Just slow your roll, man."

"No, there ain't no slowin' this roll! Let this little punk back up his shit." Jefferson kept walking toward Bobby and Redhead.

The detachment commander couldn't hear what was happening, but he saw it, and it didn't look like a de-escalating event to him.

What the fuck, Sergeant?

"Where's the bullhorn?" The commander barked.

"Right here, sir," said one of the airmen standing nearby, handing it to the commander.

The detachment commander grabbed the bull horn, "Senior Master Sergeant Jefferson. What's going on over there?"

Jefferson turned around and yelled his reply to the commander, "Oh, nothing, sir, I just need to finish a conversation."

He kept walking back toward Red.

"Say that again, mother fucker!"

The detachment commander noticed some Defenders pull the charging handles on their AR-15s.

Holy shit, that is not a good sign, the detachment commander thought.

He whispered an order to his detachment, "Get ready!"

When he said so, he heard the machine gunners pulling the retracting handles on their M2 .50 Caliber Machine Guns mounted on each of the Bear Cats. Then he stepped behind the chassis of one of the Bear Cats to get some cover.

Jefferson heard the .50 Cals charging, too. Just before he was within arms reach of Bobby and Red, he said, "You hear that sound? Try calling me a

337

nigger again, you piece of red-neck shit," and then Tindell glared at the indignant redhead and clenched his fists before pivoting on his left leg.

The roundhouse kick with his right foot happened too fast for Red. How many teeth Red once had, he lost in an explosion of grit, enamel, and blood as he fell backward against Bobby Wilcox, who yelled out, "Goddammit, settle the fuck down!"

It was too late. One of the other Defenders standing nearby shot Jefferson in the chest with his side-arm, knocking him down. It was a .45 ACP slug, but Jefferson's body armor caught it. Otherwise, Jefferson would have had a hole in his chest wide enough to nest a softball. The impact fractured his sternum, but that was a small price to pay for the satisfaction of kicking that piece of shit's remaining teeth out. It also had the benefit of putting him flat on the ground because the next thing that happened was a hail of gunfire from all six .50 caliber machine guns directly over his head. What a delightful sound the Ma Deuce produced when fired in anger toward bad guys.

Jefferson rolled to the side of the defender's formation as they tried to duck or run away. The first row of Defender vehicles suddenly featured a porous exterior.

"CEASE FIRE, CEASE FIRE, CEASE FIRE," the detachment commander ordered. "COVER THE SENIOR MASTER SERGEANT. ADVANCE AND FLANK TO THE RIGHT."

At his command, one of the M113s came to life, spewing out a cloud of black diesel exhaust as it rolled slowly along the right side of the boulevard leading from the base with six SPs running alongside, using the APC as cover. Several shots originated from the Defender side toward the advancing APC, with the bullets barely nicking the paint.

The response from the Air Force detachment was brief and violent. Another hailstorm of lead was served up courtesy of Ma Deuce times six.

Taking the bullhorn, the detachment commander addressed the Defenders.

"If you want to survive the day, withdraw. On a count of ten, if you do not withdraw, we will finish you off, down to the last man. Ten. Nine. Eight.

Seven. Six. Five. Four. Three. Two. One. Jesus," he said under his breath, "these fuckers are hardcore."

There was no movement from the Defenders, who were ducking behind what was left of their Suburbans. Bobby Wilcox had taken a .50 caliber bullet to the chest, so only half of him was left, with the other half resting peacefully on the hot pavement.

"Collect the Senior Master Sergeant," the commander ordered, and by the time he said it, Jefferson was close enough to roll over and get behind the approaching APC, which was about 10 yards away from the Defenders. The covering fire had done what it was supposed to but with the added benefit of paralyzing the Defenders. It was a miracle that one of them had not gotten off another shot to take out Jefferson.

The commander continued with the bullhorn. "Arkansas Defenders. I am a man of my word. Good luck. DETACHMENT, ADVANCE! GO! GO! GO!"

The APCs and Bear Cats began a slow roll toward the Defender position across Marshall Boulevard as they opened fire again with the mounted .50s. Then, in a rapid flanking move from both sides, the dismounted base security contingent fanned out in leapfrog maneuvers, with one group advancing while the other group provided covering fire. After the first barrage of .50 caliber fire, the SPs tossed in stun grenades and resumed the .50 caliber fire until the soldiers performing a double envelopment, or pincer movement, were directly positioned to engage the dazed, confused, and utterly ill-equipped defenders. It was a slaughter.

"CEASE FIRE! CEASE FIRE! CEASE FIRE! A-TEAM LEADER, SITREP!" the detachment commander ordered.

Smoke from the red-hot machine guns, small arms, and grenades wafted gently in the still summer air, and the A-Team Leader made his report.

"Wait one, Command," said the Team Leader over his headset as he surveyed the situation.

He gave a hand single to the point man for his team, who advanced in a crouched position, stepping over dead bodies through the lingering smoke. He stopped after looking around and along the line of vehicles reduced to metal shells, shards, and pellets of broken tempered glass. He looked back at his Team Leader and made another motion with his right hand, flat, swiveling it back and forth at his neck as if to say, "They are all dead." And they were. There were 48 dead Defender bodies. Some were cut up so badly by the .50 caliber fire that one would not know they were human but for shreds of their black uniforms clinging to severed body parts.

"A-Team Leader, Command. The hostiles are neutralized. The area is secure."

The detachment commander radioed in to report the situation to the base commander.

"Main Gate, Base Command. Request a team to clean up the mess and account for the dead. The hostiles engaged, and we neutralized them. We have one casualty but no fatalities on our side."

At about that time, news trucks, ambulances, fire trucks, and local police from all over the area were pulling up Marshall Boulevard. Even though the Defenders' standoff scene was technically off the base, the detachment commander's decision to return fire and secure the off-base scene was legal since the passage of the Security Restoration Act. He summoned more security police to join the detail's job to document and clean up the gruesome scene.

When the operation ended, Jon and President Aidun rose from their seats in the White House bunker and walked toward the blast doors to go topside. Jon muttered a quote under his breath from Herman Melville's *Moby-Dick*:

> *He piled upon the whale's white hump the sum of all the general rage and hate felt by his whole race from Adam down; and then, as if his chest had been a mortar, he burst his hot heart's shell upon it.*

As the scene at Little Rock Air Force Base was cleared, the Governor of Arkansas, an associate justice of the Supreme Court, and his wife were destined to be new residents at the Guantanamo Bay Naval Base detention camp.

Jon's rage was unabated. The fact that Buckshot and her MAGA backers had brought the country to such a low point was unforgivable, and there could be only one answer: to bring them all to justice.

31

The Pantex Incident

Jon and President Aidun received after-action reviews several days after Little Rock and examined the scene. The secretary of defense spared them no detail.

Jon was angry.

"Jesus Christ, the butcher's bill for Operation Red Boots was as steep as it was necessary," Jon said to Secretary Ironwood. "All of that to arrest that woman. What were those Defenders thinking? They didn't stand a chance. Why wouldn't the governor or any of them sit down and talk with us? Mr. Secretary, it is a goddamn shame."

After the briefing, Jon felt an otherworldly welling up of wrath, fury, and rage. He couldn't shake it, and even an hour after Jon left the White House Situation Room, he was preoccupied, desperately trying to refocus as his security detail ferried him to the Pentagon. That was when Secretary Ironwood called him.

"Mr. Vice President, we need you back at the White House. Texas National Guard cavalry and infantry converged on the Pantex Plant in Amarillo and seized it. The force leader threatens to detonate a nuclear device. We have a team of experts from the National Nuclear Security Administration and other nuclear weapons experts preparing a briefing for you and the president."

Once at the White House, the Under Secretary of Energy for Nuclear

Security, with a team of experts, briefed the president and vice president from various locations through video links to the Situation Room.

"Mr. President, Mr. Vice President, the Pantex Security Forces failed to repel an armed incursion by elements of the Texas National Guard. Light infantry, mechanized infantry, and armored cavalry staged an assault on the Pantex Plant. There is a report that MQ-9 Reapers provided air support."

The president interrupted angrily. "I thought I ordered all the air assets to relocate outside the compact states to secure bases?"

Secretary Ironwood replied, "You did, but our inventories did not reveal that the Texas Air Guard held back some of their aircraft. We are still assessing what they may have retained. We know about two-thirds of the Texas National Guard refused the federalization order, so our information out of Texas is deeply flawed."

"Go on, Mister Undersecretary," Aidun said.

"Mr. President, Mr. Vice President," the undersecretary continued, "the Pentagon received a message from a burner phone that the occupying force leader demands to speak with the vice president. The transmission was cut off, but we captured the number."

"Who is this person?" Jon asked.

"He did not identify himself. We are trying to set up a direct and secure communications line because he is not picking up when we call back. Unfortunately, communication equipment at Pantex was destroyed during the assault, so the cell phone is the only way we can reach him."

"What do we know," President Aidun asked.

"The message the Pentagon received was the caller's claim that they secured an operational M-83 Gravity Bomb on-site for maintenance."

"And you mean to tell me that they not only have a bomb but the means to set it off?" Jon interrupted.

"Yes, we believe the equipment is there to detonate the device, especially because in the older model gravity bombs, the triggering device is integrated into the design of the overall warhead. Anyway, much, if not all, of our nuclear arsenal is assembled, tested, maintained, or decommissioned at Pantex, so all of the components could theoretically be there simultaneously.

We still know very little, but what we do know is the information suggests that the occupants intend to detonate the M-83 if their demands are unmet."

"Have you assessed what might happen if they detonate the M-83?" Jon inquired.

"Yes, Mr. Vice President," the undersecretary answered. "We have made an initial assessment about the impact of a detonation should they light one-off."

"Wait a goddamned minute," Jon injected. "How in the hell could anyone detonate one of those devices? I'm new here, but surely some codes keep those things secure. Right?"

"The codes on your biscuit, Mr. Vice President, and the codes pro-grammed into the nuclear football are only there to authenticate the release of nuclear weapons. Mechanisms and equipment are required to detonate one that sometimes must be manually initiated by hitting a switch."

"And you're telling me all that equipment is there and joined with the device? That is insanity!"

"Believe me, Mr. Vice President, we are working on this problem, and we have a team at Los Alamos on it as we speak. For now, we need to assume the device can be detonated with help from the inside."

"This is an unbelievable lapse in security," President Aidun added.

"Yes, it is, Mr. President. And I'm afraid there is more bad news on the security side."

"How much worse could it be?" Jon asked.

"According to intelligence," the undersecretary continued patiently, "the North Texas Militias have been at work for a long time trying to infiltrate the plant and succeeded, but our counterintelligence has not revealed any real information about that—only speculation. If they infiltrated the plant, we have no idea how they did it or who they managed to get to assist them. But there is one thing I can guarantee. With the right help, I am confident they can light off one of those devices."

"What happens if they do? You said you had assessed that," Jon asked.

"Mr. Vice President, if the information is true and they have acquired access to a B-83 nuclear gravity bomb, the detonation would be a ground burst. It is a variable yield device. If someone assists them from the inside, they could deliver an explosion of up to 1.2 megatons."

"Better put that in terms I understand," Jon said, "and assume the worst. How big an explosion, damage, fallout, and how many deaths do you reckon?"

"Assuming a 1.2-megaton detonation at ground level, the explosion would result in a roughly 100 yards-deep crater, with the outside lip extending to a radius of about 450 yards. The inside radius of the crater would be about 220 yards, give or take. The fireball from a ground burst explosion would vaporize everything within about a mile radius of ground zero. It would send an immense amount of material from the ground up into the atmosphere that will fall back to Earth as fallout. The cloud itself would be nearly 13 miles high with the mushroom head spanning a diameter of at least 18 miles."

"Jesus. How many dead?" Jon inquired.

"Pantex employs about 3,000 people, of which about 1,500 are at the facility at any time. Anyone at the facility will be instantly killed, so at least 1,500 people. That would be ground zero. The surrounding area, which is not highly populated, would add another 500 deaths, with an additional 500 severely injured. These figures from the blast itself do not include what might result from radioactive fallout. We estimate that about 2,200 to 2,500 people are in the blast range within any 24-hour period derived from that assumption."

The undersecretary continued his explanation.

"The ground burst's fallout is much more significant than if the device were detonated above the ground. By comparison, an air burst would result in about the same number of deaths, but the number of those seriously injured skyrockets. An air burst would injure thousands more persons because of thermal radiation and an increased blast radius, but an air burst results in much less fallout. We cannot predict where the fallout will go until the detonation happens because fallout will depend on wind speed and direction. So, if there is a detonation, the best we could hope for is the wind blowing in a northerly direction, either northwest, due north or northeast. East or west would cover the I-40 corridor and shut down interstate traffic. If a radioactive cloud floated south or southwest, you are talking about Amarillo and areas beyond being dusted with radioactive fallout. Southeast would have a minimal impact, but still more severe than if there is a northerly wind."

The president looked upon the proceedings with a blank stare. Never in any vision or nightmare had he imagined such a scenario. Looking over to Jon and the secretary of defense, he asked, "Recommendations, gentlemen?"

Jon looked up from his notes and was first to speak.

"I presume we must evacuate as many people as possible from the area, including Amarillo, but there is always the risk of this being a false alarm. Jesus!"

"It's a risk, Jon, no matter what we do," Aidun observed.

"True. I don't know, Mr. President. But if you're asking me, I think we need to get this on national television as soon as possible and remind the people of Texas that some of their own are poised to light off a nuke. Let's turn this on them. I'm no propaganda expert, but surely it would play in the federal government's favor to show the everyday people of this country what these extremists are capable of doing. Beyond that, we need the military planners to devise a plan to neuter what is left of the Texas National Guard that ignored the federal call-up. As to our other facilities where nuclear material is stored, we must relocate the material and harden our defenses."

"I agree with Vice President Freeman about the risk of a false alarm," Secretary Ironwood said, "but I think it is important to spring the trap. Plus, to get the people of Amarillo ready for what will essentially be a military occupation. You will need the military to help maintain order, evacuate people, decontaminate, and provide basic services."

"Right," said Aidun. "I agree. Hopefully, we can get that guy to answer our call and talk with us."

Jon and President Aidun were in the White House Briefing Room packed with the press an hour later.

President Aidun walked to the podium.

"While the nation is still in a state of emergency, I have declared an additional state of emergency to exist in Amarillo, Texas, and the surrounding counties of the Texas Panhandle. Because of new developments, I must report a group of heavily armed Texans claiming to be part of the Texas National Guard seized control of the Pantex Plant located northeast of Amarillo. The Pantex plant is a facility that develops, tests, maintains, and decommissions our nation's nuclear stockpile. The group leader who took control over the plant gave the federal government an ultimatum: either the federal government agrees to allow the State of Texas to secede, or he will detonate a nuclear weapon at that facility. We have been given until 5:00 pm Eastern Time to respond. I'd like to now hand this over to the vice president, who will brief you on the details of our response."

* * *

While Jon began his remarks, Judith Wells, who had just celebrated her 50th birthday, was driving her new F-150 pickup east on I-40 from her home outside Vega, Texas. She proceeded across the pancake flat plains along the interstate toward Amarillo to bargain hunt at second-hand stores she fancied. Judith tuned her radio to a country gospel station when the president's announcement interrupted her favorite rendition of "I'll Fly Away."

She thought, *what in the hell is wrong with those people in Washington? Do they expect anyone to believe this stuff? It is all of the Devil!*

Judith reached toward the console to change the channel. As she reached forward, there was a loud buzz, then the radio cut out, and her motor died. In less than a second, she felt her eyes burning as she glanced toward the searing light that filled the horizon over Amarillo.

Her F-150 rolled to a stop in the outside lane just by the Cadillac Ranch when the shock wave hit, blowing dirt and sand against her windshield. A vehicle behind her crashed into the rear of her brand-new truck. She was shocked and started praying, not knowing what else to do.

While Jon was continuing his report to the public, an aide approached

347

the president and whispered the news in his ear. The president leaned over to Jon and said, "They did it. We need to get to the Situation Room right now."

The president walked to the podium. "Ladies and gentlemen, a nuclear device was detonated near Amarillo. We will keep you informed of further developments. Emergency Management will transmit instructions on what to do for those in the Amarillo area and update you with fallout forecasts. If you are in Amarillo and hear this message, shelter in place, wherever you are, and wait for instructions."

Jon and President Aidun rushed from the press briefing room.

When they arrived at the bunker, Aidun summoned the secretary of defense, all the military chiefs of staff, the national security advisor, and the administrator of Emergency Management. Once the staff assembled, he spoke up. "Can any of you tell us anything?"

Secretary Ironwood replied to the question. "Mr. President, reports come from several sources that saw the blast. Observations estimate the yield at one megaton based on the size of the mushroom cloud. The wind direction is southwest at about 20 knots. The most intense fallout radiation will nearly completely cover Amarillo. Those people need to shelter in place. There won't be enough time for them to escape the fallout path. The radioactive plume will extend as far as Roswell, New Mexico, at the current wind speed and direction. FEMA is engaged and will advise the public through all channels, including the Emergency Broadcast System."

"Thank you," President Aidun said. "Please put the word out for all people in the fallout path to shelter in place. Make that happen immediately. If you haven't already done it, FEMA, engage the Emergency Alert System and immediately broadcast instructions."

Speaking directly to the FEMA administrator, Aidun said, "Ma'am, you have all my confidence. Keep the vice president and me updated. Whatever resources you need, you will have."

"Our people have trained for a domestic nuclear incident, Mr. President. FEMA is on it," she replied.

Turning to Jon, he said, "Jon, do you have any thoughts about a response?"

"Our priority should be assuring the public that the federal government will do everything possible to ensure their safety, but that cannot be with words. It must be with action - swift action. We need to get resources there as soon as possible."

Then Jon turned to Secretary Ironwood.

"Mr. Secretary, you're about to earn your pay."

"The military awaits its orders," Ironwood replied.

"Assuming the president agrees, besides sending military resources to assist the people there, we must apprehend the Governor of Texas and annihilate the Texas National Guard armories where the equipment used in the Pantex Plant assault came from. We must also remove or destroy all the military and aviation assets that the State of Texas could use. Perhaps if the apprehension of the Governor of Arkansas weren't enough, this would be a message that this government will not sit idly by and allow the compact states to wage war unanswered. But I digress because we have American citizens to protect. So, our forces must try to lend aid as soon as possible in cooperation with FEMA. What do you think, Mr. President?"

"A swift response is essential," Aidun said. "I presume we can walk and chew gum at the same time. Right, Secretary Ironwood?"

"Indeed we can. With advice from the Joint Chiefs, I'll put the wheels in motion to get troops on the ground there to assist the populace, and we'll devise an operation to respond militarily as the vice president suggested."

* * *

Two days following the Pantex incident, an extensive federal investigation identified which Texas armories deployed the armored vehicles and infantry that attacked Pantex. The Reapers the Texans used at Pantex were found in an empty hangar on an abandoned airfield near Ellington Air Force Base. Using precision laser-guided munitions, the Air Force leveled three National Guard armories and the hangers where the Texas Air National Guard hid its Reapers. The attack on the facilities happened simultaneously courtesy of four B-2 Spirit Stealth Bombers dispatched from Nellis Air

Force Base.

* * *

Several weeks passed after the federally sponsored reprisals for the Pantex Incident, and a weary vice president once more went before the American Public in a nationally televised address.

"My fellow Americans, I wanted to update you on the situation since the nuclear incident in Amarillo, Texas. We sent B-2s to remind the State of Texas and its sponsored right-wing militias that we won't permit them to hurt US Citizens and ignore the rights of Americans without consequence, so we destroyed the military facilities Texas insurgents used to attack the Pantex Plant. The Pantex Incident cost the lives of over 7,500 Texans from the effects of the blast and exposure to radioactive fallout. We have evidence that the Texas governor was behind it, but he is hiding, so we have been unable to apprehend him. We have declared him a war criminal because of his complicity in the Pantex incident."

"Nevertheless," Jon continued, "the least we could do was remove the facilities that supplied the equipment, troops, and air assets. The Texas governor was a tough talker until he went into hiding. Once we find him, he can join his cohort, the former Governor of Arkansas, in military prison. Like her, he will be charged with genocide, sedition, and treason."

"Ladies and gentlemen, the most important thing I want to tell you is that we have deployed all the resources to help Amarillo, Texas. Not only has FEMA appeared to set up temporary shelters for people, but we have dispatched specialized military teams equipped and trained to deal with radiological incidents and contamination. Their mission responsibilities include detecting, assessing, and decontaminating all the areas impacted by radiation from the detonation. So, if you see them, they are there to help you. Please cooperate with them."

"On another note, I want you to know that as long as I hold this office, I will do everything I can to ensure the governors of Arkansas and Texas, along with anyone in league with them, receive the most severe justice our

350

government can deliver under the law. I am here to say unequivocally that we will not hold back to protect every American from domestic terrorism at the hands of any compact state government. And I promise you, compact state leadership, we will use all our force and military capacity to dismember every state administration that continues implementing the New Law or continues to hurt, harm, jail, or kill innocent American citizens. If the compact states wish to avoid the full force of justice, they should end the rebellion now."

Jon's wrath, a constant companion over the last many months, was welling up again.

"The white nationalist, right-wing agenda? It's over," he exclaimed. "You will pay with your lives if you do not end it. We have asked you to come here to join the president and me to discuss how we can resolve the differences that divide our nation and bring you back into the fold, and you have collectively ignored our invitations. You will come to regret ignoring our invitations to talk. So, in the event my speech is too nuanced for you, let me put this in terms that you governors can understand: I will see that we take ten of you and your supporters for each innocent American life you have taken unless you can come to the table unconditionally, and surrender. If you do that, perhaps there is a chance we can begin finding a way back to being a nation again. Therefore, I am giving each compact state governor one more chance to accept the president's invitation to sit down to find a way to end this madness. You will have seven days from today to do so. We will arrange a meeting time and place if you accept his invitation. If you do not accept this invitation, we will, at a time and place of our choosing, apprehend and arrest every compact state governor who signed the Declaration of July 4th. After that, we will systematically destroy your military, political, and economic assets."

* * *

After the presser, Jon walked down to the Oval Office and let himself in. He knew President Aidun was waiting.

"Hey, Jon," Aidun said. "I watched you just now. If there wasn't a line in the sand, there is now."

"I hope it achieves the desired effect," Jon offered. "I prepared an executive order for you to sign to transmit the terms of the invitation to each compact state governor. It can go out to each state capitol within the hour."

"Sure, Jon, send it over. I'll sign it and get it out," he said.

"One other thing, Mr. President," Jon added. "I want to return to the Valle Grande for a few days. I need some time to cool off and get my head together before the deadline for the governors to respond to your invitation."

"Do that, Jon. You've been going non-stop since you got here. And you know, while you are out there, why not use some time to think about something else."

"What's on your mind, Mr. President?" Jon asked.

"The former president was going to run for a second term," President Aidun said, "and he was unopposed. The Republicans haven't been pushing a candidate since their convention because they can't get far enough away from the crazy wing of their party. So, I want you to consider running. November is just around the corner."

"The hell you say, Mr. President. With respect, no fuckin' way!" Jon expressed.

"Hear me out on this, Jon. The Democrats have a convention coming up, and I have already told the chairman I am not interested in running. It's not me. I never wanted this job," the president explained.

"Well, Mr. President, that makes two of us. Hell, I never wanted this job, either, but I answered the call," voiced Jon.

"And you need to answer the call once again, Jon. I cannot think of a better person to see this through. And there is another thing. You're a Southerner, well, a displaced Southerner at this point. If anyone can get through the chatter of the compact states, it is you. I mean, look at me. I'm an East Coast liberal and a Muslim. There's no way I could pull it off."

"'President' is the last title I would ever want to have. Truly. But thank you for your words."

"Think about it, Jon. The fact that you don't want to be president is precisely what would make you a good one. We have an opportunity, and we could do something unprecedented. The word is that both parties are considering backing you. On top of that, the parties are considering legislation that will remove money from politics and federally fund all federal elections. It would be historic. But for now, get home and get some rest. Call me in a couple of days, why don't you?"

"I will, Mr. President. I will," Jon said. "We've got some breathing room before the compact governors respond. I hope they do, Mr. President. I truly do. In the meantime, I also thought I might visit the Amarillo FEMA Camps to assess the recovery since Pantex. One must get there and see it all from the ground."

Jon left the Oval Office and met Sims in the hallway.

"Sims, would you arrange for my return to the ranch later today or tomorrow? I want to be back in Washington the day before the deadline for those governors to respond to our invitation. I also want you to work out a day that I can go to visit the FEMA facilities in the Amarillo area, perhaps on the back end of my trip to New Mexico. They tell me the radiation from the fallout has subsided significantly. Put a place on the manifest for yourself, too. You'll be coming along. I hope you know how to ride horses."

Jon walked out of the West Wing exit across the lane toward the Executive Office Building. He stood momentarily in the sunshine, looking up at the sky, and took a deep breath.

I cannot wait to get home to the Jemez, to the scent of ponderosa and sage on the mountain air, soak in Hidden Spring, and sleep in my bed with Martin by my side. Home.

As he stood there, Jon's heart started to thud painfully against his ribcage as the horrors he had seen since the New Law invaded his consciousness. It was an unwelcome and dark visitor, threatening to drown him.

The unimaginable savagery of Americans turning on their own, driven by poisonous ideologies, clashed brutally with the ideals of a nation he once thought he knew. Every face and every cry painted a visceral picture of human suffering — innocent souls rounded up like livestock,

353

imprisoned, some brutally stoned or left hanging lifeless from gallows. And the unfathomable devastation in Texas by thousands snuffed out instantly by the monstrous detonation of a nuclear weapon. The haunting question echoed endlessly in his mind: *Why? To what end? Why me?* The suffocating weight of grief rested upon him like a leaden blanket threatening to pull him under.

What has become of us? Have we descended to such base instincts that we are governed by anger and rage? And this grief, will it ever be diminished? It walks hand-in-hand with the rage today. Will I ever be free from this yolk?

Melville interrupted his thoughts again as he walked out of the West Wing with Sims.

Heaven have mercy on us all - Presbyterians and Pagans alike - for we are all somehow dreadfully cracked about the head, and sadly need mending.

"Mr. Vice President, are you alright?" Sim asked as Jon stood motionless in the sunshine.

Jon shook his head. "Sorry, Sims. I just had to take a moment. Let's get me home to New Mexico, shall we?"

We all needed mending, he thought as he walked toward the Executive Office Building with Major Sims, *but am I the one to help with the mending when all I want to do is burn these fuckers to the ground?*

Epilogue

A view of the Valle Grande from New Mexico Highway 4

The sun was setting over the Valle Grande, casting long, dramatic shadows across the terrain. Jon Freeman was weary as he gazed out at the beauty surrounding him. In those moments, he reflected on his friends who were still missing or dead. At least Paul Joseph had escaped Arkansas as Tiny did, but many others didn't make it out in time. Jon was home on a much-needed vacation from Washington, and Martin was safe once again in the embrace of the Valles. This temporary comfort would have to suffice for now.

He won the presidency in a landslide victory, proving a testament to the nation's faith in unity and democracy. Yet, beneath his victory remained an unrelenting and seething feeling of hostility because the compact states refused to bow down. Whispers of a convention of states grew louder, while Martin's sacrifice in a counter-insurgency operation fueled Jon's pre-verbal rage. Even if unity could be achieved, Jon would never forgive the horrible things done to his husband at the hands of the Arkansas Defenders.

The arrest and trial of the governors of Arkansas and Texas might have brought justice, but the process laid bare the depth of division and discontent. Buckshot's deal to disclose the location of the former Attorney General of Arkansas in exchange for her life only added another layer of complexity, revealing the extensive networks supporting the secessionist cause.

But nothing could prepare Jon for the next shock when a courier approached carrying a sealed envelope. "Mr. President, a message from Brian Kuroda," the courier said. Jon's heart sank. The Pacific states. Were they the final piece in the constitutional puzzle? He opened the letter, and as he read, the weight of his presidency, and the future of the United States, pressed ever more heavily. The states of Hawaii, Oregon, Washington, and Alaska were poised to turn the tide in favor of a proposed secession amendment that could irrevocably change the landscape of North America by splitting it into separate nations. The United States, while still vast, could soon be vulnerable, surrounded by new neighbors with unknown intentions.

Jon faced the most challenging decision of his life: to settle the secessionist movement with military forces or let the Constitutional process play out, no matter how uncertain. Could he still lead this fractured nation? Or was it time to leave the world of politics and return to the solace of his ranch once and for all? The United States he knew was fading, but his unwavering sense of duty to its people remained. Would the nation find unity, or would it forever remain fragmented?

He mounted his horse as dusk drew nigh and rode back into the heart of the turmoil. Valle Grande, his sanctuary, would have to wait a little longer. There was work to be done because the next chapter in America's history was about to be written with Jon at its epicenter.

The fight for unity was far from over, and the echoes of The Last Independence Day would reverberate for years to come.

To be continued...

Afterword

This novel is a call to responsibility. It's an encouragement to be informed, to understand the roots of our democracy, and to recognize the crucial role each citizen plays in preserving it. The story is fictional, but the themes are real. In the end, I hope you, the reader, will reflect on the what-ifs and consider that it could happen here if enough of us remain silent in the face of extremism.

Notes

RED WAVE

1   Donald Trump's 2016 campaign popularized the slogan "Make America Great Again" (MAGA).

2   The 34 states that went "red" consisted of Alabama, Alaska, Arizona, Arkansas, Florida, Georgia, Idaho, Indiana, Iowa, Kansas, Kentucky, Louisiana, Michigan, Minnesota, Mississippi, Missouri, Montana, Nebraska, Nevada, North Carolina, North Dakota, Ohio, Oklahoma, Oregon, Pennsylvania, South Carolina, South Dakota, Tennessee, Texas, Utah, Virginia, West Virginia, Wisconsin, and Wyoming.

VALLE GRANDE

3   Towa is a Tanoan language spoken by the Jemez Pueblo people in New Mexico. It lacks a standard written form because tribal rules prohibit its transcription. Linguists use the Americanist phonetic notation to describe the language.

BUCKSHOT BRANDY

4   The original Confederate States were Alabama, Arkansas, Florida, Georgia, Louisiana, Mississippi, North Carolina, South Carolina, Tennessee, Texas, and Virginia.

5   Article 5 of the United States Constitution requires Congress to convene a constitutional convention or "convention of states" if requested by 34 states which make up two thirds of the states in the union. Article 5 of the Constitution reads: "The Congress, whenever two thirds of both houses shall deem it necessary, shall propose amendments to this Constitution, or, on the application of the legislatures of two thirds of the several states, shall call a convention for proposing amendments, which, in either case, shall be valid to all intents and purposes, as part of this Constitution, when ratified by the legislatures of three fourths of the several states, or by conventions in three fourths thereof, as the one or the other mode of ratification may be proposed by the Congress; provided that no amendment which may be made prior to the year one thousand eight hundred and eight shall in any manner affect the first and fourth clauses in the ninth section of the first article; and that no state, without its consent, shall be deprived of its equal suffrage in the Senate."

RANCH BUSINESS

6   The Checkerboard area of the Navajo Nation, located in parts of McKinley, San Juan,

and Cibola counties in New Mexico, has a patchwork of mixed land ownership between Navajo and non-Native ownership. This mixed ownership complicates the Navajo Nation's land use, leading to economic challenges and jurisdictional disputes.

7   *Hosteen* is a term of respectful address in Navajo.

8   *Llano* is a Spanish word used in the Southwest to describe a treeless grassy plain. In central and northern New Mexico, it specifically refers to the grasslands on the eastern side of the Continental Divide.

THE ARKANSAS GENERAL ASSEMBLY

9   "FBO" is a reference to "Fixed Base Operator." An airport-authorized FBO provides aeronautical services like fueling, hangaring, parking, aircraft rental, maintenance, and flight instruction. FBOs support general aviation operators at public-use airports and are located on leased airport land or adjacent property. The town may handle fuel services in some small airports and operate a basic FBO. Most FBOs in high to moderate-traffic airports are non-governmental companies.

10   In the United States, thirteen states, Arkansas, Idaho, Kentucky, Louisiana, Mississippi, Missouri, North Dakota, Oklahoma, South Dakota, Tennessee, Texas, Utah, and Wyoming, enacted trigger laws that automatically banned abortion in the first and second trimesters when the landmark case *Roe v. Wade* were overturned. The case that overturned *Roe v. Wade* was *Dobbs v. Jackson Women's Health Organization*. The Supreme Court decided *Dobbs* in 2021.

11   *Korematsu v. United States*, 323 U.S. 214 (1944), upheld the exclusion of Japanese Americans from the West Coast Military Area during WWII.

12   Originalism is a legal interpretation theory that advocates for giving the constitutional text its original public meaning as intended at the time of its enactment. In U.S. law, it emphasizes the original understanding of the Constitution, viewing its meaning as fixed unless changed by an amendment. Contrasting with this is the "living Constitution" approach, which interprets the Constitution in light of current contexts, differing from its original intent. While originalism was dominant until the New Deal era, critics suggest its modern appeal stems from conservative pushback against landmark civil rights rulings. Originalism encompasses various theories, differentiating between the intent of the Constitution's authors or ratifiers, the text's original meaning, or a blend of both.

JUSTICE DELAYED

13   An *ex post facto* law changes the consequences of past actions or relationships retroactively from when it was passed.

14   *Loving v. Virginia*, a 1967 Supreme Court case, declared laws against interracial marriage unconstitutional under the Fourteenth Amendment's Equal Protection and Due Process Clauses.

JUSTICE DENIED

15   A dismissal "with prejudice" means the case was dismissed as a final judgment and may not be brought again.

SMITH V. SMITH

16   When a party to a lawsuit is dissatisfied with the decision of a lower court, they may file a petition for a *writ of certiorari* with the higher court. The higher court then has the discretion to decide whether to grant or deny the writ. If the writ is granted, it means the higher court has agreed to review the case.

17   *Dobbs v. Jackson Women's Health Organization* is a landmark U.S. Supreme Court decision handed down in 2022. It overruled *Roe v. Wade* (1973) and *Planned Parenthood v. Casey* (1992), stating that the Constitution does not grant a right to abortion. This decision restores state authority to regulate aspects of abortion not protected by federal law. The case involved a 2018 Mississippi state law banning most abortion operations after 15 weeks of pregnancy.

COUNTER MOVES

18   The Insurrection Act of 1807, a law still in effect, authorizes the president to deploy military forces inside the United States to suppress rebellion or domestic violence or to enforce the law in certain situations.

MISTY'S JOURNEY

19   A "body attachment" is similar to a criminal warrant issued by a judge but used to bring a person before the court or to a place in a civil case.

CONTINUITY OF GOVERNMENT

20   The 21 states that joined the Red State Compact were Alabama, Arkansas, Florida, Georgia, Idaho, Indiana, Kansas, Kentucky, Louisiana, Mississippi, Missouri, Nebraska, North Carolina, North Dakota, Oklahoma, South Carolina, South Dakota, Tennessee, Texas, West Virginia, and Wyoming. This represents 42 Senate seats and 188 House seats in Congress who are from those states.

21   Article Two, Section Three of the U.S. Constitution says that the president shall, "from time to time give to the Congress Information of the State of the Union, and recommend to their Consideration such Measures as he shall judge necessary and expedient; he may, on extraordinary Occasions, convene both Houses, or either of them, and in Case of Disagreement between them, with Respect to the Time of Adjournment, he may adjourn them to such Time as he shall think proper; he shall receive Ambassadors and other public Ministers; he shall take Care that the Laws be faithfully executed, and shall Commission all the Officers of the United States.

22   Section Three of the Fourteenth Amendment to the Constitution says: "No person shall be a Senator or Representative in Congress, or elector of President and Vice-President,

or hold any office, civil or military, under the United States, or under any State, who, having previously taken an oath, as a member of Congress, or as an officer of the United States, or as a member of any State legislature, or as an executive or judicial officer of any State, to support the Constitution of the United States, shall have engaged in insurrection or rebellion against the same, or given aid or comfort to the enemies thereof. But Congress may by a vote of two-thirds of each House, remove such disability."

23 FLOTUS is an acronym that stands for "First Lady of the United States."

24 The FBI National Command Information Center (NCIC) is the FBI's primary 24/7 operations hub, responsible for monitoring global events, coordinating the FBI's crisis responses, sharing information with federal agencies, and supporting field operations. It is distinct from the similarly abbreviated National Crime Information Center.

25 The nuclear football, officially named the President's Emergency Satchel, is a briefcase enabling the U.S. President to authorize a nuclear attack when away from established command centers. It contains no launch 'button' but has authentication codes and secure communication devices to facilitate a potential nuclear launch. Always nearby, a military aide carries it, ensuring the president can validate their identity and communicate with the National Military Command Center during emergencies, adhering to a process vetted for legal compliance.

26 For these purposes, "Snap Count" was a code to indicate the government must begin a series of coordinated actions. The phrase comes from American and Canadian football, where a "snap count" is the sequence of signals given by the quarterback before the ball's release. It helps organize the offense and aims to catch the defense off-guard, potentially leading to a penalty.

27 The U.S. Continuity of Government (COG) plan outlines measures to ensure federal government operations continue during catastrophic events, such as nuclear war or major terrorist attacks. Key elements include relocating officials to predetermined sites like the Raven Rock Mountain Complex, a clear presidential succession plan, preserving leadership by keeping critical leaders dispersed, upholding a functioning federal authority across all government branches, and maintaining open communication lines. Initially designed during the Cold War for nuclear threats, it was updated post-9/11 to address modern challenges. Although many specifics are classified, the COG underscores the U.S. commitment to government stability.

28 The DEFCON system denotes the U.S. Armed Forces' state of readiness, with five levels. DEFCON 1 is the highest alert, indicating imminent nuclear war, while DEFCON 5 is normal peacetime operations. The levels assess readiness, from heightened intelligence watch to full combat preparedness, and change based on global situations and threats.

29 The Boeing E-4 Advanced Airborne Command Post (AACP), known as "Nightwatch," is a modified Boeing 747-200B used by the USAF as a mobile command post for the U.S. President, secretary of defense, and successors during national emergencies. Operated by the 1st Airborne Command and Control Squadron at Offutt Air Force Base in Nebraska,

it's referred to as a "National Airborne Operations Center" when active.

30   Air Force One is the official air traffic control call sign for a United States Air Force aircraft carrying the President of the United States. In popular culture and among the general public, "Air Force One" is often used as a metonym for the President's aircraft, although in reality, the call sign can refer to any Air Force aircraft with the President on board.

THE LONG CALICHE ROAD

31   Like POTUS is an abbreviation for "President of the United States," SECDEF is an abbreviation for "Secretary of Defense."

OATHS

32   The United States National Command Authority (NCA) refers to the ultimate source of lawful military orders, primarily consisting of the president and the secretary of defense or their duly deputized successors. It is the entity responsible for the final decision and authorization of military actions, including the use of nuclear weapons. The NCA is supported by various command and control centers. One of the most well-known is the National Military Command Center (NMCC) located at the Pentagon. The NMCC serves as the primary source of command and operational control for the U.S. military and is equipped to support the NCA in times of national emergency.

33   The National Security Agency (NSA) is a U.S. agency founded in 1952 that intercepts foreign electronic communications, protects U.S. government data, and ensures cybersecurity. It operates under the Department of Defense.

THE EASY WAY, OR THE HARD WAY

34   Section 12406 - National Guard in Federal service: call
     Whenever-
     (1) the United States, or any of the Commonwealths or possessions, is invaded or is in danger of invasion by a foreign nation;
     (2) there is a rebellion or danger of a rebellion against the authority of the Government of the United States; or
     (3) the President is unable with the regular forces to execute the laws of the United States;
     the President may call into Federal service members and units of the National Guard of any State in such numbers as he considers necessary to repel the invasion, suppress the rebellion, or execute those laws. Orders for these purposes shall be issued through the governors of the States or, in the case of the District of Columbia, through the commanding general of the National Guard of the District of Columbia.

35   "ACU" stands for "Army Combat Uniform."

36   AWOL is an acronym that stands for "absent without leave."

THE LAST INDEPENDENCE DAY

WASHINGTON, DC

37   The Eisenhower Executive Office Building, or EEOB, sometimes referred to as the "Old Executive Office Building," was once called the State, War, and Navy Building. It is part of the White House complex in Washington, DC. It's managed by the General Services Administration and houses the Executive Office, including the vice president's Office. It was renamed in 1999 after President Dwight D. Eisenhower, a five-star general in World War II. The Naval Observatory has served as the residence of the vice president off and on since the mid-1970s.

38   The Pantex Plant is a U.S. facility located in Texas that assembles, disassembles, and maintains nuclear weapons components. The Savannah River Site is a U.S. Department of Energy complex in South Carolina, primarily dedicated to processing nuclear materials and environmental cleanup.

CONSTITUTIONAL LAW

39   *Habeas corpus* is a legal principle that protects individuals from unlawful detention. It allows a person who believes they are being held without legal justification to petition a court for a determination on whether their detention is lawful. If the court finds the detention to be unlawful, the individual must be released. The term "habeas corpus" is Latin for "you shall have the body," emphasizing the physical presence of the detainee before the court.

40   The Insurrection Act and the *Posse Comitatus* Act are related but distinct laws in the United States that pertain to military use within the country. The *Posse Comitatus* Act restricts the use of federal military personnel in domestic law enforcement, whereas the Insurrection Act provides conditions under which such use can be authorized.

41   The Enforcement Acts, enacted by the United States Congress from 1870 to 1871, comprised a trio of legislative measures. These laws constituted a set of criminal statutes aimed at safeguarding voting rights, eligibility for public office, participation in juries, and equal legal protection for African Americans.

SECURITY RESTORATION ACT

42   The U.S. vice president is the constitutional president of the Senate, but he can only vote in the event of a tie. While he may have the authority to oversee Senate sessions, a vice president often attends only for tie-breaking votes or ceremonies. In his absence, the "president pro *tempore*," a senior majority party member, or another designated senator oversees daily Senate activities.

43   The Security Restoration Act was a comprehensive act that enabled the federal government to move forward without the constraints of *habeas corpus, posse comitatus,* and other prior acts that prohibited the use of federal troops domestically.

44   A filibuster in the United States Senate is a tactic used by senators to delay or block legislative action by speaking for extended periods or using other procedural maneuvers.

45 Anarcho-syndicalism blends anarchism and syndicalism, promoting a stateless, classless society where workers organize into decentralized unions to manage production. It relies on direct action, like strikes, to achieve this goal by eliminating the state and capitalism for greater equality and self-governance.

46 Cloture is a procedure in the United States Senate used to end a filibuster and bring a debate to a vote.

About the Author

Raymond L. Niblock brings a wealth of life experience to his debut novel, delving into a future where political and legal institutions teeter on the brink of collapse.

Educated at the New Mexico Military Institute for high school and junior college between 1981 and 1986, Raymond adopted a disciplined approach to life that permeates his writing. After military school, he accepted a commission in the United States Army Reserves and further honed his leadership capabilities. These ingredients richly color the intricate power plays and tactical maneuverings evident in his political thriller.

He completed his college education at the University of New Mexico, immersing himself in philosophy and political theory—themes that resound throughout his novel as he grapples with ideologies, moral questions, and the dark possibilities of unchecked political power.

In 1994, he transitioned into a legal career after obtaining a Juris Doctor from the University of Arkansas School of Law in Fayetteville, Arkansas, where he has practiced trial law ever since. His legal expertise brings a raw authenticity to his work, navigating through the corridors of political and legal schemes with a masterful grip.

An attentive observer of the political climate, Raymond infuses his novel with the fears, hopes, and complexities of contemporary socio-political discourse, engaging readers in exploring "what ifs." He intends to continue crafting stories to entertain and provoke thought, inviting readers to navigate the tempestuous and thrilling seas of political and legal dystopia alongside him.

Raymond resides with his husband, Jesse, in Northwest Arkansas. They enjoy flying, traveling, and adventures with their two dogs, Tuesday and Mazzy Mae.

You can connect with me on:

🌐 http://www.raymondlniblock.com

f https://www.facebook.com/profile.php?id=61553124673938

Subscribe to my newsletter:

✉ https://www.raymondlniblock.com/blog